DARK WIZARD'S CASE

Book one

By Kirill Klevanski

Introduced by Valeria Kornosenko.
Translated by Ingrid Wolf
Edited by Jared Firth
Cover designed by Valeria Vlasova
Illustrations by Natalia Breeva

Preface

The year was 2031. And while it would have been not unlike any other year, what made it remarkable was the Magic Lens market release.

Although to be fair, it wasn't your normal release. The blueprints, documentation, and everything else for the breakthrough device appeared out of nowhere on Reddit on September 1, 2031, instantly spreading across the internet like wildfire.

Who posted the dump? Who created the device, one that hid smartphone-esque computing power and microLED image quality in what looked like plain contact lenses? Half a century later, that remains a mystery.

All we have is a screen name: Prophet.

Growth shot through the roof for the company manufacturing Magic Lenses. Software was supplied by a variety of developers, including some industry giants.

In just one year, the Magic Lens became as ubiquitous as smartphones. Many people got rid of their smartphones, in fact.

But it was then, on September 1, 2032, one year to the day after Prophet posted the lens blueprints to Reddit, that he struck again with a new piece of software for the Magic Lens.

It was open-source, available to everyone absolutely free of charge.

We all remember how quickly the entire world downloaded it.

But when they installed it…

At first, everyone thought it was a game.

It took two or three days of people having a blast destroying monsters, using magic, and beating dungeons to realize that it actually wasn't. It was reality.

It was reality revealed by the Magic Lens.

Some governments tried to ban the lenses and their software, but Prophet had taken care of that by making everything open-source and available online. It would have been easier to shut down the internet than to keep humanity from their magic.

That's when the research began.

Magic had always been around, it turned out. The problem was that with each generation, fewer and fewer humans were capable of seeing, feeling, and sensing it.

As a result, the magic that had once been an inherent part of everyday life was confined to legends and fairy tales. The mortal world and the magic world co-existed as two sides of the same coin, never interacting with each other. Humans, with very rare exceptions, were unable to spot the magic creatures. The latter kept their distance.

To be fair, the exceptions on the magic side were far more common. That explained why about ten million people around the world went missing every year, never to be heard from again.

The magic creatures, vampires and all the rest, needed food. Vampires require an absurd amount of blood just to stay alive, while werewolves… Well, they're in a category all to themselves.

The Magic Lens restored the gift of magic to humanity. Research showed that its ability to transform mysterious magic into ordinary numbers and figures was based on quantum uncertainty, hyperposition, string theory, ray gravity, and the distortion of time-space by speed, or the gravitational difference between two points. There's more, but the list gets even more incomprehensible from there.

In 2032, regardless, magic once again became a normal part of life on Earth again.

Humans suddenly discovered that the Ural, Himalayan, and Andean Mountains are inhabited by dwarves, the forests of Canada and Siberia by elves. Fish swim side by side with mermaids, nagas, kappas, and other magic creatures. And it isn't just birds soaring through the skies; there are also dragons, phoenixes, griffins, and even creatures whose names had long since disappeared from legends and fairy tales.

Ogres. Trolls. Wargs. Goblins. Orcs. Fairies. Giants. Cyclopes. Medusas. Centaurs. Cyclopes…did I mention them already? Regular old humans were suddenly in contact with all of them.

Remember Tony Stark's speech in one of those superhero movies? (How quaint they look today.) You know, the guy in the iron suit who started by fighting normal people before moving on to superhumans, aliens, and even gods? That trajectory, it turns out, extends much further than previously thought.

But magic advanced by leaps and bounds after 2032. Humans worked on it. Studied it. Believed in it. (At least, if the clerics and other zealots of the Word are right about everything on Earth being moved by Faith.)

In other words, magic didn't become just another part of life on New Earth. It worked its way deeply into every aspect of life, developing and transforming as it went. The age of digital technology was followed by the age of magic and technology integration.

They even found Atlantis.

Sure, it wasn't that hard. For thousands of years, the state of Atlantis had been thriving on a continent hidden from the mortal world under the water, with just its tip protruding above the waves for everyone as New Zealand.

It also turned out that the old non-magical technology we used to use had failed to grasp Earth's full size. The planet is almost half again as large as people used to think.

Scientists went back to the drawing board, poring over what they thought they knew to combine physical laws with the laws of magic and sorcery.

Just to take one example, no one yet knows why the larger Earth discovery didn't change the number of days in the year, the number of hours in the solar day, or even gravitational acceleration.

Fifty years later, in 2081, our stack of unsolved riddles still dwarfs the ones we've figured out the answers to.

But humans went on living.

They learned magic at schools of witchcraft and wizardry. They visited the lands of sapient magic creatures. They hunted non-sapient magic creatures. They explored dungeons. They loved. They betrayed. They gave birth. They died.

They fought wars, too.

Back in 2040, the First Magic War changed the global map and all but destroyed the planet. More on that later.

Reddit was successful in its mission to change the world. (For better or worse? Hard to say.)

Some are still adamantly set against the usage of Magic Lenses, rejecting all forms of magic. But they're few and capable of nothing more than scattered terrorist attacks.

We've already gone through two generations—and there's a third maturing—for whom magic is just as commonplace as the internet once was. (Of course, the internet is still around.)

Just don't be surprised if you come across an elf wearing sneakers and a baseball cap, drinking a Starbucks, and tapping away at a Mac laptop. Of course, you're still unlikely to come across one like that, be it in New York, Tokyo, London, or Moscow, unless you can get your hands on a pass for the city sector occupied by the magic races. That's your best shot.

The only place where you're sure to bump into someone from one of the magic races is Myers City, the capital of Atlantis deep in the Pacific Ocean. The birthplace of magic.

But how did magic come to be?

Who was the Prophet?
Why was the Magic Lens created?
Alex Doom, also known as Alexander Dumsky, had no idea.
And who is Alex Doom?
Good question.

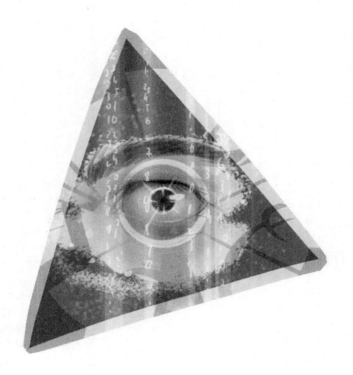

Chapter 1

Straightening his shabby leather jacket, Alex waited for the gate to rattle off to the side, revealing a time-worn asphalt road.

"Get out of here, Doom," boomed a voice from behind him.

Alex turned toward the steel tower and the fat guard behind the reinforced glass. He couldn't remember the tubby man's name, though that didn't keep him from flashing a middle finger tattooed with the word *DOOM*.

The guard shouted something back, but Alex was already too far away to hear what it was.

Flipping his jacket collar up, he left the grounds of the Special Correctional Institution for Uniquely Gifted Humans. It was a prison for wizards, in other words, and it was where Alex had spent the past few years. The past *four* years, to be precise.

His hands shivered from the cold as he fished a crumpled pack of unfiltered cigarettes out of his pocket. Catching a glimpse of it, he smiled, tossed a cancer stick out, and caught it deftly out of the air with his lips.

Odd as this may sound, he'd actually hadn't learned that trick outside prison. It had been back in those barracks buried several miles underground, the ones where everyone wore magic-inhibiting collars.

Alex rubbed his neck. He could still feel the weight of the *adamantius*, the accursed metal used by the government to inhibit wizards when they broke the law. Of course, that wasn't all they used. There were also the bullying guards who were only too happy to overstep what they were allowed to do, not to mention plenty of other unpleasantries.

"Damn it," Alex muttered. By force of habit, he'd held a thumb to his cigarette only for it to not light up.

Glancing at the heavy manacle around his left ankle, Alex cursed again. He was going to be without his magic for a while longer.

And he didn't have a lighter. How were you supposed to get one onto an island forgotten by gods, humans, spirits, demons, fairies, and all the other beings, one connected to Myers City by just a single bridge?

Leading to the bridge was a broken road traversed once a day by a bus. Given that the sun was already sinking toward the ocean in the west, Alex had been released shortly after the solitary steel lifeboat had left.

Alex picked up the gray bag he'd had with him when he was arrested by the Department of Law and Order, walked to the bus stop, and sat down on the wooden bench.

There was a piercing northern wind blowing. Myers City had a short summer, and the weather had already gone downhill with August still up on the calendar. Alex wrapped his thin jacket tighter around himself, anxious for some warmth. Chewing on his cigarette, his mind wandered to what was left of his life. He didn't have many choices, not fresh out of prison with a serious black-magic conviction on his record.

And, to be honest, magic was all he was good at.

"Life is such a blast," he drawled, peering out over the endless stone ridge battered by the cold sea waves. The prison was rumored to be a replica of once-famous Alcatraz. It was the first prison for wizards modeled after a regular one.

His reflection on that particular historical irony was interrupted by the squeal of brakes as a long, imposing limo came to a sudden stop next to the rusty bus station. The plentiful chrome accents accentuated its black, all-business look. And the classic gas exhaust spoke volumes about the car owner—in an age of magic modules, few people could afford the ownership tax on a classic gas car, let alone buy one.

A man got out of the driver's seat. Tall, broad-shouldered, and wearing an insanely expensive suit and dazzling shoes, his face was crisscrossed by scars.

Alex shuddered. He'd see people like that before, just not as drivers. They'd been the best fighters the High Garden gangs had to offer.

Analyze, Alex commanded the neurochip in his lens.

A reddish message flashed in front of his eyes.

[Name: ??? Race: Human. Mana level: 4561.]

Alex almost choked on his cigarette. Four and a half thousand conventional mana points made for an awfully strong Adept.

What kind of monster could afford to hire a full-fledged Adept as his *driver*? Alex didn't know, and he didn't want to find out, either. But he had a feeling he wasn't going to be given much of a choice.

The introduction was about to be made.

The driver pushed his cap over steel eyes that could have belonged to a soldier or a hitman before opening the passenger door.

"Thanks, Duncan," a sleek, melodious voice said. "Get in, Mr. Dumsky. We have some things to discuss."

Alex glanced up at the gray, overhanging sky. Shrouded in dark clouds, it weighed on his shoulders like a granite coffin lid.

Any normal person in his shoes would have refused, only to get tucked into the limo anyway, just less presentably.

When a clearly official car stops in front of you, declining an invitation isn't stupid. It's suicide.

Shouldering his bag, Alex walked over to the limo and smiled insolently at the driver.

"Hi, Dunk," he said with a wave before ducking into the car without waiting for a response.

He had to admit, even in his good days, his buttocks had never felt such comfort. Far from a regular car seat, it was an actual armchair. The upholstery was beige leather, and it had wooden armrests, a footrest, ventilation, massage rollers, and presumably a whole litany of other absurdly expensive and incredibly luxurious features.

Sitting in an identical armchair facing his was a middle-aged man. In the outside world, one of racist and sexist mortals, he wouldn't have escaped being labelled as Asian. But there, in the land of magic, he was just a state official with yellowish skin and narrow eyes.

His well-groomed hands, shiny with fresh body lotion and nail polish, held a plain file folder. That's right—not a tablet or even a smartphone. It was a *hard copy*. Alex didn't think anyone used them anymore, at least not outside the mafia.

Analyze.

[Name: ??? Race: ??? Mana level: ???]

Just as Alex suspected, the suit worked for some government agency. No one but high-ranking officials were permitted by Myers City law to hide their race or mana level.

Shit.

Alex didn't even feel the limo start moving. His only clue was the scenery outside starting to coast by.

"Alex Dumsky. Raised at St. Frederick Orphanage. Escaped at age seven. First brought to the police station at eight. For stealing…" The suit stopped turning the pages lazily and raised his eyebrows. "A cat?"

"Troubled childhood," Alex replied, specifying that he'd been robbing an apartment when the cat had swallowed its owner's earring. *Crazy animal.*

"Joined the Tkils gang at ten, according to the police. The youngest gang member ever?"

"I have a gift," Alex said with a smile.

"No argument here." The suit nodded. "Two hundred mana points at age twelve indicates incredibly rare potential. By twelve, you'd already hit five hundred mana points and the Practitioner level. If you'd been studying at a public school, they'd have labeled you a genius."

"No, they wouldn't have."

"You're right," the suit agreed. "Most likely, they'd have done mental body surgery right away to keep you from practicing dark magic."

"…which isn't prohibited." An evil note crept into Alex's voice as the suit's words stirred up an old grudge. "But you use it as a reason to maim children."

"We spare them a hard and unnecessary fate. But that's not what we're here to discuss. So, a young boy of twelve with Practitioner power…no, a Practitioner dark wizard decides that the Tkils gang isn't quite right for him." The suit turned a page, and Alex spotted a few pictures. What he saw there was even less to his liking than the dreary view out the window.

"When he saw that, Duncan noted that you deserved a bunk in a mental hospital, not a prison."

"And the gangsters thought I deserved a bunk in the next world." Alex kept looking out the window. "I disagreed."

"I see," the suit said, nodding again. "So, for a long time, our unattested Practitioner dark wizard fall off the radar. And two years later, the city's black market was booming."

Alex couldn't help chuckling smugly. He'd had so much fun working with the old dwarf back in those days.

"Dozens of top-level spells, all the way up to Mystic, and a gang war triggered in the High Garden district." The suit turned another page. "Then you made a mistake, Mr. Dumsky: you underestimated law enforcement. However skilled you were at averting eyes, buying a sports car with a magic drive at fourteen is ridiculous. That's more than *I* can afford with my government salary."

Alex coughed. If his guess about the suit's position was true, he could afford a *dozen* of them.

"And that was how they got you," the man posing as a simple civil servant went on.

"You don't happen to have a lighter on you, do you?"

"No smoking in here," the suit snapped. "Two years spent chasing down a mouse like you, and the whole time you were living a street over from the High Garden police department. The nerve."

Alex had a different opinion. As the two-bit scammers said in the streets that were his alma mater, the best hiding places are in plain sight.

"Then two attempts at detention. A sixteen-year-old at the Mystic level, twelve hundred mana points strong. I'll admit, I've never seen anyone like that before." There were more pictures, and that set filled Alex with pride. "You sent three operatives, all seasoned Practitioners, into intensive care. Four more spent months at the hospital recovering from a variety of injuries."

Alex hadn't been looking for a fight that day. But they smashed his car! And even though he could have easily afforded a new one back then, it was a matter of principle. He'd invested so much energy in the fraudulent scheme it had taken to buy the thing that it had sentimental value.

Or maybe he was just the sick bastard the media portrayed him as. He tried to remember if he'd kept that article.

"For a whole month, no one hears a peep from you until you pop up in a meaningless bar brawl. Ridiculous."

Alex winced. That memory wasn't a pleasant one.

"You were in custody a week later." The suit glanced over another page from the file and whistled. "Detained by an Adept and forty Mystic-level operatives. They really came at you."

Alex would have escaped that time as well if it hadn't been for the bloody Adept. The trained Mystics had been stupid and clumsy. *If it hadn't been for the bloody Adept.*

"Then the court hearings. Your case had seventeen volumes, almost as many as you were years old, no? And what did they throw at you? Fifteen counts of theft. A hundred and ninety-nine counts of illegal dark spell crafting with intent to sell. Five counts of aggravated assault. Thirty-six counts of assault on an officer of the law. Seven counts of murder by dark magic." The suit coughed and pressed a button. Wooden cabinet doors opened, revealing their gilded interior and a china set that a complex mechanism instantly filled with water. It even dropped some ice in. "None of the seven counts held up. Otherwise, I'll be frank, we wouldn't be having this talk."

It didn't escape Alex that the suit stole a glance at his ankle cuff. *Damn. Damn!*

The whole thing was heading somewhere very bad.

"And the cherry on top: demonology and demonic magic. Both of those are prohibited by law."

Alex chewed the cigarette silently, oblivious to the fact that he'd already eaten just about the entire thing.

"Given that you weren't a first-time offender, you were sentenced to…three hundred and fourteen years in prison."

"That's nothing," Alex replied with a nervous snort. He had a sudden urge to throw open the door and hurl himself onto the sharp rocks. He liked that ending better than what was coming.

"Released on parole four year later, on the condition that you keep that cuff on for the rest of your life." He glanced back at the ankle adorned by the artifact blocking Alex's magic.

The suit slammed the file shut and leaned back in his armchair. With his little finger waving in the air, he took a noisy gulp of water from a faceted glass.

"So, what do we have here? An incredibly talented—even brilliant—self-taught wizard choosing dark magic and reaching levels of power most can only dream of at the age of sixteen."

If it hadn't been for that bloody prison and the four years I lost, Alex thought, *I'd have your Duncan on his knees.*

"The state can't—well, can't and shouldn't—waste a gift like yours. So—"

"Let me interrupt," Alex said, raising a hand like a student at one of the schools he never attended. "Why did you get me out of prison?"

"You're quick. We wanted to make it a surp—"

"Why?"

They stared at each other for a few seconds.

"As you've no doubt guessed, we'd like to offer collaboration that, if you prove your worth, will let you forget your past and find a place in the upper echelons of society."

"Just tell me what you want."

"Okay, I'll put it simply." The suit intertwined his fingers and flashed a predatory gaze, his good-natured mask gone. "On either side of you are sharp rocks and limo doors badly in need of repair. Behind you is a prison where, as far as I can tell, you don't have many fans. And in front of you is me, promising you a job and the chance to get that cuff off your ankle."

"Sounds delightful."

"A better offer than what most get." The suit held up his hands. "So, what will it be?"

Alex glanced into the suit's eyes. They were made of cold steel. *Shit. Which department is he from exactly?*

"Four years getting myself off in my bed," Alex sighed. "I never thought I'd be screwed by government officials the minute I walked out the door."

"Is that a yes?"

"I don't think I have much choice," Doom replied with a nod and a sad smile. He'd long since gotten used to the nickname, almost forgetting his actual last name. "What's the job?"

"In a nutshell, you'll be entering First Magic University," the suit replied, smiling disarmingly. "You're going to be its Professor of Dark Magic."

Pausing, Alex waited for the suit to say that he was joking. He didn't.

"Wha-a..."

Alex's stunned cry dissolved into coughing as he swallowed the remains of his cigarette.

Chapter 2

Turning up his jacket collar, Alex made a fist and flicked his thumb up. A small tongue of flame flashed over its tip.

[Elementary magic action. Mana used: 0.5 points/sec.]

Anyone even at the lower end of the Apprentice level (0-250 mana points) was used to messages like that popping up in their peripheral vision thanks to the lenses they wore.

That was particularly true there, in Myers City, the heart of New Earth's magical world.

But not for Alex.

Four years. The four goddamn years he'd spent in the underground prison kept him from taking the little things for granted.

Lens messages. The freedom to use magic. Unlocked doors. The joy of taking a shit any time he wanted to without having to wait for the moment when none of his roommates were eating.

"Your belongings are at the safe house already, Mr. Dunsky."

"Dumsky," Alex replied.

"Whatever," Duncan responded blithely before pressing the button that controlled the limo's windows, closing them in Alex's face. "I hope you fuck it up."

Any old-school dark wizard worth their salt would have cursed Duncan for his lip. And at the very least, it would have been a curse that covered his penis in boils the next time he tried to get it on with a woman.

But Doom was cut from a different cloth.

He adjusted his glasses with his middle finger, the one that had *DOOM* tattooed on it in the runic script of the fae people.

He hated those bloody fairies.

Sidelights flashing, the limo vanished around a corner. Alex followed it with his eyes, bowed low and mockingly in its direction, and wheeled around, only to immediately bump into the breasts of a very tall lady. In her cashmere coat, the collar of which had been made from a two-tailed fox, she looked like just any other working girl.

"You lost, boy?" she snarled.

And it wasn't a figurative snarl. No, she *actually* snarled. Her skin was green, and she smelled something like an animal, or maybe like a dried raisin. Her claw-like nails and fangs were yellow, all pierced with golden rings.

[Name: ??? Race: Troll. Mana level: 129.]

"Ma'am," Alex said, reaching to tip his hat to her but suddenly remembering that he hadn't gotten it back when he'd been discharged from the city's best all-inclusive resort. *Bastards.*

"I'm a miss," the troll hummed. "Want a look at the goods?"

Alex just turned the pockets of his pants inside out to show that they were empty.

"Fuck off then, beggar." The troll gave him a shove so forceful that he almost stumbled out onto the street. "You aren't the only one here."

Doom glanced over at the dark alleyway behind her. There, in the glaring light of a cheap hotel's neon sign, stood a bunch of half-naked women, all from several races. Alex could have sworn he even spotted some with the white pointed ears of elves, but he told himself he had to be imagining that. Even the poorest elven families were wealthier than the desert sheiks.

"Why you stickin' 'round 'ere?" Someone shouldered Alex.

"What you gapin' for?" When Alex turned around, another shoulder drove itself into him, knocking him off balance.

Tipping over the edge of the sidewalk and almost falling onto the asphalt road, Alex just missed a speeding bike that shot by a second before he'd have been run over.

"Got a spare head, moron?" The wind carried the shout over to him despite the roar of the gasoline engine. The rider had to have been a gangster—in High Garden, Myers City's main cesspit, only gangsters could afford the gasoline tax.

Well, that's not quite accurate. They just didn't pay it.

Shaking his head and popping his jacket collar again, Alex turned around and looked up at the dark sky. The clouds were dense and illuminated by searchlights flashing regularly through the darkness, not to mention the occasional magic airship or glider.

High Garden was the only place in the city where the sky didn't look like a Christmas tree. Not far away, the night never really had the chance to take over, what with how brightly lit the sky was.

Alex was in one of the central districts in Myers City. Despite being twenty subway stations away (and that was actually including a shortcut), they were visible even from High Garden.

Think Manhattan in the 2010s. Make the island six times larger, merge it with Hong Kong, and you'll have downtown Myers City.

No one could count all the skyscrapers, as there were more of them popping up every year. It was a jungle of chromium and steel, metal and glass.

And there were thirty-six million sapient creatures living there, from humans to fairies.

It was an anthill that never slept, was always active and lively, and was soaked through with magic, from the sewer system where the troglodytes dwelled (Alex had personally killed three of them and would've killed the fourth if he hadn't escaped, almost chopping Alex's leg off in the process) to the spires of the highest towers the ever-wandering thunderbirds sometimes alighted on.

Alex breathed in deeply.

The fragrance of perfumes mixed oddly with the stench of mud and trash-quality dope. It stank of money and misery. Even the gleaming shop windows of the best boutiques were overshadowed by the darkness of the alleys and dens, and the roar of luxury sports cars was sometimes drowned out by the noise of diesel-powered self-propelled guns.

A city of contrasts.

A city where all the races dwelled.

The capital of Atlantis.

The city of magic.

"There's no place like home," Alex said with a smile. Reaching out, he snatched a black hat right off some random guy's head.

"Hey," came the protest, though his victim slipped into the maze of alleyways when he saw the misty lilac flash of a magic seal on Alex's palm.

"And there's certainly no place like High Garden." Alex adjusted the brim of the felt hat, his favorite kind, and ripped the stripe off the crown for a more predatory look. "Well, Mr. Bromwoord, I'm coming to take what's mine."

Shoving his hands into his pockets, Alex started toward the lower park. Not far from the orphanage where he'd been raised, next to Seven Corner Square where he'd fought in many a gang war, and some two blocks away from the house of the crazy old man who'd taught him dark magic, there was an inconspicuous shop. The sign read *Hunting & Fishing*. No one but a few (that is, everyone in High Garden, including the policemen who were in it for the cash rather than the honor of the badge) knew it was one of the biggest smuggling fronts in the district.

But Alex had something more important than smuggling in mind.

He had to find out what the hell the government needed from him. Whatever it was, they needed him badly enough to yank him out of the wizard prison, knocking several centuries off his sentence in the process.

And he had to find out why the hell they wanted him to attend First Magic University. As a professor!

Professor of Black Magic, huh? Anyone who actually had that title would've sold their soul—and their ass, to boot—for the knowledge Alex had in his head.

As a side project, he wanted to figure out who Duncan and the narrow-eyed man really were.

And finally, while a trifle barely worth mentioning, he needed to repay his debt to one of the biggest crime syndicates in the city. They'd kept Alex from ending up a spinner around someone's genitals while he'd been in jail. It was a debt of one hundred thousand credits, which converted to dollars at a rate of one to ten.

Neat, huh?

The clock on his debt was already ticking.

But Alex's most pressing concern was finding some grub. He blew his nose into a dumpster and inhaled deeply before adding out loud, "and someone to fuck."

"Oh, you made up your mind?" the female troll called out from behind him.

Alex did the exact same thing he always did when he wasn't sure what to do.

He breathed in deeply, blew out a ring of smoke, flashed his *DOOM* tattoo, and trudged off down the street.

One bearded dwarf in particular, one who owed him buckets of money and a good dinner, was probably tired of waiting for him.

Chapter 3

"It's like I didn't even spend the last four years on vacation," Alex drawled, flicking his cigar butt into the trashcan at the bus stop.

High Garden was the only area in the city that still had electric buses instead of the usual magic-powered ones. For magic buses, you needed a special kind of pavement that had been recently (if four years prior counts as recently) laid on most downtown streets. But High Garden still had regular asphalt, albeit the good, durable kind.

Doom was standing by a small, two-story building. The crooked *Hunting & Fishing* sign swayed in the wind. Some of the neon letters on the sign were burnt out—if it hadn't been for the light cast by a nearby streetlamp, it would have been difficult to make sense of the whole thing.

The shop was flanked by taller, five-story apartment blocks. Made of red brick and peppered with wooden shutters covering plain glass windows, they looked more like anthills than homes for self-respecting Atlanteans. They were where the city's blue-collar workers lived.

Head to the factory in the morning. Work all day. Back to the doghouse at night.

"Doghouse" was the only word that really fit the tiny apartments, especially since there were always six to eight family members cooped up in each one.

After seeing the inside of one of them back when he was little, Alex had realized that he'd rather live on the streets than in one of those cramped hellholes.

Walking up to the stone porch leading to the shop entrance, Doom wiped the soles of the sneakers he'd been arrested in on the familiar, almost comforting stone path.

He pushed the door open and shuddered the way he always did at the banshee-like howl of the magic doorbell. A curse later, it struck him that nothing had changed.

"How many times do I need to tell you to get a new doorbell?" he snarled, holding the door open behind him.

Four years may have passed, but everything was the same inside the old dwarf's shop. The same shabby green carpet was still on the wooden floor, making the spacious room appear even larger.

The wooden tables by the walls featured glass display cases housing a variety of tools. Fishing tools on the left; hunting tools on the right.

Driven by curiosity, Alex approached the table on the right. A long, jagged knife instantly caught his eye. It had a carved, wooden hilt and several runes along the broad, gray blade.

[Item: Hunting Knife. Item rank: F. Maximum mana level: 12. Price: 145 credits.]

"The old man lost his last scrap of conscience." Alex whistled. "A hundred and fifty credits for an F-class item? I'd rather rip a Dark Rat's throat out with my bare hands than pay that much."

F was the lowest class of magical items, meaning that a knife like that could only have been used to hunt Dark Rats or other random mutants.

Of course, for beginner monster hunters, that was possibly enough. For non-magic hunters, anyway. An artifact with 12 mana points was a blessing from heaven to them.

Hanging on the walls above the tables were items of clothing. Pants and jackets were on racks, while the boots were on shelves.

"Columbia Jacket," Alex read on the price tag of a dark green double-buckle jacket made from apparently very durable fabric.

[Item: Jacket. Item rank: F. Maximum mana absorption: 7.5. Ice resistance: 0.5%. Price: 210 credits.]

Alex was so astonished, he almost started muttering a prayer, just about forgetting that prayers were worse for dark wizards than holy water was for vampires. Once, back when he'd been young and stupid, Doom had walked over to the entrance to a church. The gang had to spend an entire week nursing him back to health.

And the burns he'd gotten while being tortured with a cross back in prison would probably never heal.

"Are you looking for something specific or just browsing? Mr...?"

Alex turned toward the voice. Behind the counter, leaning on a retro-style cash register and looking bored out of his mind, stood a pimply student listening to a single wireless earbud.

His pimples had nothing to do with his age—he wasn't much younger than Alex. It looked like he'd just never washed his face with soap.

Getting ready for a life in jail.

But Alex wasn't going to spend much time joking on that topic. He'd already graduated, or left it, and he had no intention of ever going back. Not in the near future, nor any time after that—never again.

"Where's Jeremy?" Alex asked, stepping closer to the student. He reeked of cheap cologne, and his sweaty armpits cut a sharp contrast to the soft, sweet smell of the baby cream on his wet palms. The perspiration on his forehead and the tablet that was turned over face down told him exactly what the old dwarf's shop assistant had been up to.

Does this Probationer—let's call him that—know there are cameras everywhere?

"There's no Jeremy here anymore," the Probationer answered unpleasantly.

"May his memory stay with us forever," Alex replied, lifting his hat slightly.

"No, it's not that!"

"What then?"

"He was fired." The Probationer shrugged and, probably thinking he was being smooth about it, slipped the tablet off the countertop and onto the bottom shelf. What he didn't realize was that there was a reflection of the screen in the cabinet glass. *Kids really watch stuff like that?* "About four months ago."

"Why was he fired?" Alex was surprised. "I really liked him. He always offered me a cookie, and it doesn't look like you have anything for me."

"Well, I'd say you're asking too many questions," the Probationer said as he squinted at Alex. "If you're not here to buy something, fuck off, beggar."

Alex sighed, easing his glasses upward to massage the bridge of his nose.

"You're the second person to call me a beggar tonight. And that's not helping my rotten mood."

"Oh, no? I apologize for ruining your evening." The Probationer moved subtly, bringing a non-magic but still deadly Colt 45 up to point at Doom's face. "Might *this* improve your mood?"

"Do you know how to…"

The Probationer clicked the safety off deftly.

"…use it?" Alex finished calmly. "You do. But why the big hole?"

"What?"

"I'm just saying, your hole's caliber is too big."

The Probationer blinked, looking confused.

"Damn it," Alex spat. "I'm trying to say you're a bottom boy. A knob jockey. Been dropping any soap in jail? Hey, stop it, I'm not kiddi—"

"Oh, I got that!" the Probationer yelled. "Are you crazy? I could shoot you right in the—"

Before he could finish, Alex latched his right hand around the student's wrist, locking it down firmly, and rested his thumb against the trigger. His left hand shoved the muzzle away. Then, using both hands, he jerked it toward himself.

Everything happened faster than the Probationer could blink. Suddenly, there he was, clutching a sprained wrist and staring down the barrel of his gun.

"I *told* you," Alex said firmly, no longer clowning around, "I'm in a bad mood. Where's Bromwoord?"

"H-he t-told m-me n-not t-to l-let a-anyone i-in," the Probationer stammered.

"Would you be so kind as to make an exception for me?" Alex smiled.

He probably shouldn't have done that. The smell of cologne and baby cream was instantly complemented by the sharp, sour stench of ammonia. Spreading over the floor between the boy's feet was a pool of unpleasant-looking liquid.

Oh, wow. Jeremy was much tougher.

"S-s-sure."

The student pressed something beneath the counter. A part of the wall with a griffin's head mounted on it (a fake one, of course; just one real griffin's head would've bought half the old man's shop) slid aside, revealing a passage that led to a staircase spiraling down into a dark cellar.

Dwarves sure do love their caves.

"Good," Alex nodded.

Letting some magic seep into his hands, he used a bit of mental force to draw a simple pentagram on his palm and then cast a rotting curse.

"These kinds of toys aren't for kids... They're not kids' toys at all. Hell, what am I saying? I sound like an idiot."

Lamenting the fact that he'd apparently lost his gift for eloquence, Alex headed toward the staircase as the Probationer, still trembling, watched his gun dissolve. It spread over the counter like an odd discoloration in the wood.

Chapter 4

After descending the staircase, Alex found himself in a spacious room that was dimly lit, making it appear much larger than it actually was.

"Dwarves and their caves," Doom drawled in amusement.

The sloping brick walls were styled to look like natural stone. No baseboards; just gutters with gurgling water.

But that was a necessity, and not merely a designer's weird flight of fancy. Apart from the small office hidden behind the frosted, bulletproof glass, the room had lots of incomplete and illegal artifacts scattered across oaken tables and bound in metal.

Alex approached one of the artifacts, a knife apparently identical to the one he'd seen in the smuggling shop's storefront. Considering that the knife he was looking at was made of a rare alloy containing a bit of magic-blocking *adamantius*, it could easily penetrate protective magic up to the capacity of 100 or even 150 mana points.

The item wasn't registered, of course, so Alex couldn't scan it using his lenses.

It was still incomplete, but it was already emitting magic that could actually be sensed, if not from a mile away. And it was right there, in front of Alex.

"Ah," he drawled, bathing his fingertips in the air above the blade.

They tingled slightly. And he was a Mystic! That made him a relatively strong, mid-tier magic user there in Atlantis and someone like Gandalf the White to the rest of the New Earth world.

Or at least someone like Harry Potter, although that was a series Alex didn't particularly enjoy. The dark wizards were always *defeated*.

For long ages, a tingling sensation like the one he was enjoying or an unexplainable feeling of uneasiness had been the only way humans could detect magic.

Small wonder human magic all but died out.

"Alood?" a surprised and very deep voice called out from the depths of the cave.

Alex turned toward the sound. At the anvil, next to the bellows (everything was automated, of course, but it still looked ancient), stood a dwarf, short even by the standards of his race, and shaped like a square: almost as broad in the shoulders as he was tall. He was absolutely bald and even beardless. A fight with the clan he'd been born into had resulted in him being exiled, shaved, and enchanted.

That incident had also set Bromwoord on the crooked path of a smuggler and, ultimately, ended with him residing in High Garden.

"Hi, old man," Alex waved.

Bromwoord took his gauntlets off and put aside the metal tongs he'd been using to dip another illegally crafted item into a smelly solution.

The tub, which was full of a volatile alchemical compound, was what all the gutters were for. The devil only knew what substances were sloshing around in there, apart from water.

Alex had seen with his own eyes one of the dwarf's debtors losing his right hand to one of the "decorative" gutters, his manhood very nearly following suit.

"Stones and rocks, Alood! Am I seeing a ghost? What did I do for Black-Bearded Budut to punish me with a visit from your phantom? You were nasty in life, and now that you're dead... Damnation. I need to call the Inquisition!"

Tossing his leather apron onto the anvil, the dwarf rummaged around in the pockets of his oily track pants, looking for his phone.

"Calm down, Bromie." Walking over to the dwarf, whose head barely reached his waist, Alex clapped him on the shoulder. It was like slapping a boulder. "It's me. Good, old Alex Doom, wiser and slightly unshaven."

Bromwoord recoiled at first. Shifting his gaze back and forth between his shoulder and the visitor, he muttered a curse in the language of the Himalayan dwarves before heading silently into his office.

Pushing open the glass door and climbing up a ladder onto the leather armchair he used when doing business, he opened the upper drawer of his desk and retrieved a dark bottle.

Once he uncorked it, Alex could smell the stunning aroma of dwarven mushroom liqueur, which was priced at 5 credits per ounce.

But he preferred whiskey, and he definitely wasn't about to drink with a dwarf. Their ability to hold their alcohol was rivaled only by trolls. The strongest trolls.

"Bloody stones and rocks." After staring at the glass bottle for a bit, Bromwoord took two large gulps straight from it. Alex winced. "The only way anyone's going to call you *good* is if they're comparing you to the Supreme Priest of the Bloody Skull cult. That's pure orc shit. And old... Spare me, mortal. You haven't even hit a *century* yet!"

Alex hummed. If his math was right, Bromwoord had turned 227 the previous month. A dwarf in his prime.

"But I still..." Alex ran his fingers over his stubble. "...have a better beard than you."

The dwarf squinted at him. To dwarves, the size of their beards mattered just as much as the size of the body part the debtor had almost lost mattered to male humans.

"You bastard, Alood," he said through gritted teeth. Taking two more swigs of the liqueur, he pointed at a chair. "Sit down."

The dwarf's office wasn't much different from any middle manager's. A powerful computer sported the bitten apple logo. There was a convenient, multi-functional table, some trinkets were scattered around the screen, and piles of papers, a landline phone, and other miscellaneous office rubbish completed the picture.

And one of the walls featured the portrait of someone who was obviously his tribe's chieftain.

Darts were buried in both his eyes.

Bromwoord hated that gray-haired dwarf.

"It's good to see you, Bromie." Alex held out his hand.

"I beg to differ, Alood," the dwarf replied, though he took Alex's hand in a firm handshake.

Alood. It was the name Bromwoord had given Alex when he was young, altering his original human name the way the dwarves did. He'd started calling him that the moment Alex had tried to steal his boots. Alex's own boots back then hadn't just been gaping; they tried to devour everything that crossed their path.

"How long did they put you away for? A lifetime?"

Alex held up three fingers.

"Even more." The dwarf brought his hand down on the table. "*Three* lifetimes! What are you doing here then? If you escaped, don't even think about asking me to hide you. I violated the New Convention once, and now even a glorified baby's ass like your face has more hair than me. Stones and rocks! Why did you have to come here, Alood? I downed five bottles when they sent you to that island."

"Because you were happy or sad?"

"Three."

"Three what?"

"Three because I was happy, two because I was sad," the dwarf said. "So, did you escape or what?"

"No one has ever escaped from that island, Bromie."

"*You* could've done it," he replied with a snort. "You're crazy, Alood. Only a crazy kid like you would've stolen a cat. *A cat*, stones and rocks!"

Alex rubbed the bridge of his nose beneath his glasses and muttered a barely audible curse.

"Would you stop that? Is everyone going to keep bringing that bloody cat up until I kick the bucket?"

They fell silent and then laughed aloud. The very next moment, both of them straightened up, staring at each other seriously.

"Why are you here, Doom?"

"You know why, Bromwoord. Before they got me, I left a small notebook at your place. If memory serves, it had three brand-new, top-of-the-line dark magic combat spells, all Mystic level. Inflation has been killer since I've behind bars, though I'll give you a discount since we're friends—you owe me ninety thousand credits. Thirty per spell."

Bromwoord tugged at his nonexistent beard thoughtfully and then opened another drawer. Slowly and purposefully, he pulled out a small magic staff covered in so many radiant runes you could barely see the metal surface. He placed it in front of Alex.

[*Item: Cold Fire Staff. Item rank: C. Maximum mana generation: 750. Elements: Ice, Fire.*]

Wow. He even got a license for it. Alex's lenses wouldn't have shown him anything if that hadn't been the case.

"So, human," Bromwoord started in a cold, hostile voice. "You came to my home to demand money? I think you forgot your place, Alood. Get out now, or I'll deflower your ass with this staff. That is, if you didn't lose your anal virginity on the island."

Chapter 5

I f Alex had been the same person he'd been four years before, he would've responded with a full-fledged attack. His Decaying Fire spell would have forced Bromwoord to defend himself, and he would have followed it up with Hellish Lightning, his fastest and most powerful spell.

Seizing the initiative would have bought him enough time to figure out what to do about the damn staff. As his teacher used to say, magic wasn't like fighting with clubs, where the larger club won. It was a duel with rapiers, the kind of encounter where victory went to the person who was smartest and most skilled.

But he wasn't the same person. Four long years had gone by.

They may not have been good for his health, physical or mental, but they'd still taught Alex a few things, restraint and prudence chief among them.

The last time he'd checked his magic capacity, the doctor had clocked it at 1132 mana points. That was above the minimum threshold of the Mystic level, which ranged from 1000 to 3000 points.

In other words, Alex was a level eleven Mystic. Not bad at all, even regardless of the fact that he'd reached that level at age 16.

Over the time he'd spent in prison, he couldn't possibly have lost more than 30 mana points.

But Bromwoord was holding a magic battle staff capable of releasing 750 mana points *instantly*, unlike Alex's spells, and it would be using two elements at once. That meant Alex would have to shield himself against both if he wanted to avoid taking damage.

He might have been able to do so if he cast his spells quickly enough, but that was highly unlikely.

He was powerful, not omnipotent.

"What's the matter, Bromwoord?" Alex sighed. "We used to work together so well. I pulled a few things over on you, you pulled a few things over on me. It may not have been honest from beginning to end, but it was great. *Mutually beneficial*, too."

"I'm not going to repeat myself," the dwarf said through clenched, square teeth. "Get out, Alood. Don't make me do something I'd hate to do."

Again, the man Alex had been four years ago would've flared up instantly, but the Alex of that day just caught the dwarf's turn of phrase.

"You'd hate to do it? Why?"

As far as Alex could remember, the dwarf had never been tenderhearted or good-natured. He wouldn't have been able to keep his business running for so many years in Atlantis' most crime-ridden district otherwise.

"Try to put yourself in my shoes, Alood. I want my beard back. Stones and rocks, at my age, I should be thinking about a wife! *Two* wives, even!"

Alex squinted at him. Then he had a flash of insight.

"Was it the Syndicate? Did they get to you?"

"Those human gangsters?" Bromwoord snorted. "If it was them, I'd happily give you your money back, and then I'd also buy that thing poking out of your pocket so seductively. And none of your homophobic jokes, please."

Alex pulled a small notebook out of his pants pocket. Using ink he'd made from the rubber soles of his prison sneakers, he'd written down about a dozen different spells over the four years.

"Think about it, Bromwoord. This is pretty good stuff right here." Alex waved the notebook back and forth slowly, then put it down on the table next to Bromwoord. It was close enough for him to see the greedy flash in the dwarf's square-pupiled eyes. (Dwarves seemed to only have square body parts.) "Dark battle magic. Several curses. Two of them with a bit of demonic magic mixed in. The maximum mana generation goes up to four hundred, enough to pierce any cop's magic-proof vest."

"And they'll get through it?"

"They will," Doom replied with a nod. "I'd stake my reputation on it, not to mention—"

"Enough!" The dwarf, his staff still aimed at Alex's face, shook his head like a dog trying to get dry. "Stop trying to change my mind with your tall tales. You *had* a reputation, Alood, but that was four years ago. There's new talent on the market now, and law enforcement is really tightening the screws on dark magic and dark magic practitioners. If something like that found its way onto the streets, I'd be arrested in a flash."

"Why..." Alex didn't finish his sentence. He looked into the dwarf's eyes and cursed, loudly and emotionally. A sudden pain stabbed at his heart. It wasn't a strong one, but it was still unpleasant. "I should have guessed how the prosecutor knew about all my cash flows."

"You'd have done the same, Alood," Bromwoord replied with a dismissive wave. "What else could I do? The uniforms leaned on me hard. I'm already bald, and if I were broke, too, I'd spend the rest of my days in some circus gnawing on stones to make humans laugh."

"So, you *sold* me, Bromie. You sold me out to avoid inconveniencing yourself."

"You'd have done the same, *dark wizard*," the dwarf said again.

No, I wouldn't have.

"If you need e-cash that badly, I'll discount the stuff and—"

"I don't need it discounted. Not for free. Not even if *you* pay *me!*" the dwarf barked. His breathing became ragged, gray vapor burst out of his mouth, and his chest rose and fell like a bellows. Outside his glass-enclosed office, the many magic items and artifacts started to quiver. The staff wasn't the only argument the dwarf had to back him up there in his workshop. "Don't you get it, Alood? A little while ago, I got a visit by some men so powerful that…that… Damn you, Alood! Don't make me do it. I'm asking you in the name of Black-Bearded Budut, don't force my hand! Please, just leave."

Alex finally realized what was behind the dwarf's outburst.

In all their years of illegal activity, all the dozens of deals they'd made with the worst bastards of High Garden, he'd never seen Bromwoord show fear.

Not even once. Until that day.

The most unnerving part was that he wasn't afraid of Alex. It was the people he'd just mentioned that terrified him.

"Who could have you this scared, Bromie? Who was it?"

"I'm saying this for the third and final time, Doom. *Leave.*"

For a few moments, they played a silent staring game. As Alex peered at the man—dwarf, rather—his heartbeat gradually slowed.

He should have been used to it by then. He should have accepted that simple truth a long time before.

Dark wizards don't have friends.

They only have temporary allies and eternal enemies.

"This is the last time we'll be meeting, Bromwoord, son of Baburd." Alex stood and went to button up his suit only to realize he wasn't wearing one. There was no vest or even dress shirt, either. He'd been arrested while jogging in track pants and a T-shirt, and an attorney had brought him the leather jacket he was wearing. It was the only help he'd dared offer. "Because the next time we come face to face, I'm going to kill you."

His piece said, Alex turned and left the workshop of his old—no, not friend—former business partner, one who was now on the other side of a barricade along with the rest of the world.

He ascended the staircase and found himself back in the storefront, where he stole a glance at the Probationer. The latter backed away into the farthest and darkest corner of his fenced-off workplace, whining pitifully as he went.

The bulletproof glass was no longer hissing and spitting up red-hot sparks. The melted gun had stuck to its surface like a steel crust.

Alex took out a pack of cigarettes.

"N-n-no smoking in here," the pimpled boy mumbled.

Alex froze and stared at him in astonishment.

"The world is off its rocker," he whispered as he walked out without lighting his cigarette.

There was one more thing he had to do before heading to the apartment the state had provided him with.

lex hated buses. Of course, as a dark wizard, there were lots of things he hated. It would have been easier to list the things he liked, in fact. Number one on that list would have been magic, number two would have been beautiful women, and the third spot would have been split between fast transportation, adrenaline, alcohol (only in the form of whiskey with lemon), cigarettes, and good food.

But buses were the mode of transportation he hated the most. Even taking the subway didn't crush Alex's spirit the way those bulky, clumsy, public four-wheelers did.

High Garden only had one night bus. Honestly, Alex would have rather gotten where he was going by taking the number eleven, but the feds had only given him four hours to settle his personal affairs in his home district. After that, Alex wasn't supposed to visit unless he absolutely had to.

"Are they trying to cover up my release?" Alex grumbled. "Why visit baldy then?"

He had no doubt the person Bromwoord had talked to was the same guy who'd shown up to meet him when he was released. But what was the point of the whole spectacle with the dwarf?

"Damnation." Alex clenched his fists. An even, dark violet glow flashed around them.

The bus swerved, distracting Alex from his thoughts once again.

"What the hell is going on?" Doom growled. The vehicle swerved from side to side again.

He was sitting at the back. Twenty other human, troll, and even orc passengers crowded together at the opposite end, pressing up against the grate separating them from the driver's seat. The driver, a fat, middle-aged male human, was sweating profusely as he muttered under his breath.

Judging by the annoying itch spreading over Alex's body, the driver was praying.

"Ger... t... r... d... st... et." The lisping, mechanical voice of the announcer was barely discernible.

Tossing his cigar butt under his seat, Alex stepped out onto the street. The graffitied, iron-bound night bus with doors and windows covered in steel mesh started off so quickly that the tires spun and smoked before gripping the pavement and screeching away.

Doom stood alone on a small street cloaked in predawn mist that ran parallel to the railroad bridge. The penetrating darkness was dispersed somewhat by several streetlamps.

Occasional howls broke the silence—wolves, not dogs.

Herbert Road was at the very edge of the city. Beyond it were the wild lands of Atlantis. And regardless of the effort the hunters put into clearing the approaches to the capital, some monsters still managed to slip in.

The story went that even with everything the wizards used to do (they had guarded the borders between the mortal and magical worlds in keeping with the First Convention before the invention of the Magic Lens), the monsters would still sneak in and have fun in the mortal cities.

Even in the age of internet and video surveillance, the wizards had managed to pass the incidents off as natural gas explosions, house fires, or even terrorist acts where there were too many victims.

Alex lit another cigarette. It must have been his seventh since he'd left prison.

Seven cigarettes in three hours was still way below the number he'd smoked before. As a rule, he went through two or three packs a day.

It was a habit he'd indulged since he was little.

Smoking was a great way to dull hunger pangs.

"Well." Cracking his neck, Alex trudged toward the underside of the bridge.

There, sheltered from the biting wind and rain, lived the lowest classes of Myers City. Alex walked between the trash cans where the homeless were burning all the useless junk they could find. Never newspapers, though. They used newspapers as padding for their old vests, coats, and jackets to keep themselves warm.

Alex had used to do the same once.

They fried whatever food they could over those trash cans. Sometimes, they'd buy it with money they'd earned any way they could find. Others, they'd scrounge up something to eat at the dumps, or maybe even catch something running around.

"Spare a cigarette, young man?" An old man in a torn, heavy overcoat, ragged knitted hat, and fingerless gloves stepped out from a group of homeless people.

Alex handed him a cigarette.

"Thank you, thank you so much." The homeless man almost bowed. He returned to the "campfire" with the air of a primitive hunter who'd bagged a mammoth alone and was hauling meat back to the tribe.

The six homeless people in his group, old and young alike, passed the cigarette from mouth to mouth. Nearby groups gazed at them enviously.

It was a part of the magic city's life that tourists never got to see.

Passing by where the homeless spent their nights, Alex stopped in front of one of the pillars supporting the railroad bridge. It was separated from the next one by impassable heavy debris—a veritable wall. There would have been no point trying to clamber over it.

"I hope my subscription didn't run out this month."

Alex held out his palm and, using mental force, created a glowing, dark red pentagram that contained a code with his name and last payment date.

At first, nothing happened. Doom was already starting to worry that his subscription had expired when, two seconds later, a magic symbol flashed on the pillar.

With an unpleasant, metallic screech, part of the debris transformed into a conventional-looking metal door that opened to let Alex in.

Once he crossed the threshold, the door closed behind him. He was in a fairly spacious hangar with stacks of shipping containers towering on either side.

The containers were organized into three levels. The first was the most expensive, with the next two successively cheaper. The third level, which was accessed via a wobbly ladder, was used to store smaller items. The bottom level was for vehicles and other means of transportation.

"Love it," Alex drawled. "I wonder how much they pay the cops to protect this place."

The warehouse, unmarked on any map you could find, wasn't cheap. The annual rent on a first-level container cost twenty thousand credits.

Alex had made a mistake back then.

He'd paid for four years in advance, using up almost all the cash he'd had. And his bank accounts, thanks to a particular bald dwarf's betrayal, had been emptied out by the government, benefitting the corrupt official who had arranged for the absolutely illegal seizure.

And as a dark wizard, Alex wasn't in a position to report illegal activity.

"B7," Alex repeated to himself as he examined the writing on the containers. "You have to be around here somewhere."

Its complete automation meant that the warehouse was always empty. In all the years Alex had been using it, he'd never bumped into another client, although he'd heard that big shots like Felix Bertoni, from the Bertoni family, used it to keep their trinkets safe.

"There you are." Smiling broadly, Alex stopped at the container with *B7* inscribed on it in white paint.

Placing his palm on the lock, he sent a thin ray of energy through it—the authentic signature that served as his key.

Noiselessly, the iron door of the container opened to let its owner in.

"Untouched," Alex said with a sigh of relief. "Hi, baby. You got tired of waiting for me, didn't you?"

Chapter 7

In the middle of the almost empty container stood Alex's pride and joy. Spokes made of chrome-plated steel. A leather seat. A shiny glass windshield. Saddle bags decorated with leather in the back. A V8 engine. Individually adjusted front and rear suspension. The motorcycle had been custom-made for Alex.

It was a classic Road King by Harley-Davidson. Assembled manually from all-natural components, with no faux leather or magic metal, the old girl was 100% authentic.

There was no magic drive or crystals in place of the cylinders. Only gas.

In the age of high-magic technology, the rarity in front of Alex had cost him a fortune. The price he'd paid was the entire Tkils gang.

Doom had actually ordered the chopper custom made, but he'd used the crew's shared funds and claimed he'd be giving the bike to the Tkils boss as a gift.

But after terminating his membership in the gang, Alex had taken both the lives of its higher-ups and the bike.

The exact price was so high that it wasn't polite to say it out loud in decent company. Just the annual tax charged for a bike like that was higher than a middle manager's salary.

Alex patted the accelerator handle. Then he checked to see if the saddle bags were firmly affixed, the suspension was still tight, and the spokes were straight.

The bike was in perfect condition.

That's a custom-made Harley for you.

"Your wait is over," Alex whispered almost lovingly.

As though in response, the chrome stand reflected the light cast by the bulb swinging above them on the ceiling. Alex clapped his old metal friend on the seat and stepped over to get the second item he'd stored in his half-empty container.

Hanging on a wardrobe rack was his suit, encased to keep anything from happening to it. It was a simple, fitted, two-piece suit with two buttons and sleeves that barely reached his wrists. The shoulders were raised a bit, the white stitches visible.

The creased pants looked more like chinos than proper dress pants. They were perfect, making for exactly the kind of suit Alex loved.

Back in the day, he'd had a different suit for every day of the week, but right then...

[*Item: ArmaniMagico Suit*

Item rank: B

Maximum mana absorption: 1025.7

Physical resistance: 24.5%

Magic resistance (general): 7.8%

Magic resistance (specific): Fire 12.5%, Water 3%, Energy 15%, Nature 1%

Additional powers: Self-cleaning, Ventilation, Nonwrinkle]

"Nonwrinkle," Alex snorted. "There should be a dash there."

Changing into the suit and white shirt (plain silk, without any enchantments), he finally felt like a man again.

He also slipped a pair of patent leather shoes onto his bare feet, black and cinnamon brogues by the same brand.

ArmaniMagico was one of the best magic clothing makers out there. They offered fantastic pieces with unusual attributes.

After all, fire and energy were the magic elements most commonly used by the cops.

"It doesn't hold a candle to bespoke suits," Alex said as he adjusted the jacket's collar, "but it's good enough for a rainy day."

[*Item: ArmaniMagico Shoes*

Item rank: C

Maximum mana absorption: 84

Special powers: Levitation (4 sec), Leap (20 m)]

Alex had no idea when he would possibly need the built-in levitation spell or 20-meter leap. He just liked the way they looked.

Even dark wizards have their quirks.

Alexander Dumsky, an orphaned kid who'd never had any personal belongings, compensated for his childhood complexes with stylish and expensive clothes.

He looked good in them, after all.

"Move over, buddy." Grabbing the handlebar, Alex shoved the heavy bike aside.

Then he squatted to run his palm, now with a different sort of pentagram flashing on it, over the container floor. The steel hissed, boiling and melting to reveal a small hollow in the hangar's cement floor.

Groping around in the hollow, Alex found a small item wrapped in a rag. It was about the size and shape of the flash drives so prevalent a century before.

It was his digital wallet.

Quite the convenient little thing to keep e-cash in.

After pulling it out, Alex unwrapped and inspected it.

"Cash in," he said. "Code: 17B72221."

The transaction was soon complete. Alex saw his wallet balance in the lower left corner of his vision: 17,147 credits. It was a tidy little sum, if nothing compared to what he owed the Syndicate. The suit hadn't mentioned anything about his salary, either. *Damnation.*

But all his thoughts and worries disappeared the moment he placed the second item from his cache onto his finger: a simple black ring engraved with magical runes.

There was nothing special about it, only…

"Let's go." Alex jumped onto the bike, kicked the stand up, turned the key, and yanked back on the throttle.

The engine roared to life like a rearing mustang. Without a single spin of the tires, the steel horse burst out of the container and hurtled through the hangar. Alex ducked beneath the rising gate, which also looked like a pile of trash, and raced off down the street.

The wind tousled his curly, overgrown black hair. The slim black tie flapped around behind him like the end of a rope.

Alex had no idea what lay in store for him, though there was one thing he did know for sure: anyone trying to pull one over on a dark wizard might just as well have pulled the same stunt with the devil himself.

And while Satan wasn't someone Alex knew personally, rumors have a way of spreading.

"This is going to be interesting." He almost laughed, pressing down on the gas and skidding around a turn that took him toward downtown Myers City.

* * *

Much as he may have denied it, Alex still had a bit of sentimentality to him. He attributed it to the same thing responsible for his taste in clothes: his early years spent on the streets and at the orphanage.

Before leaving High Garden for the foreseeable future, he decided to pay back the last debt he owed to his small but unforgettable homeland.

Stopping by a 24/7 shop, Doom parked his bike and calmly walked in. He wasn't at all worried that someone might try to hijack or scratch his steel horse.

Life in High Garden had a way of quickly teaching one to understand the limits of their power.

A small bell tinkled over Alex's head, the sound melodious and entirely unlike the one at Bromwoord's. Behind a counter stacked high with chocolate bars and cookies, a nice-looking girl appeared.

"Good evening," she said.

She was about sixteen, with long red hair flowing down behind her slim neck. Her firm breasts and protruding collarbones were conspicuous even in her baggy uniform. And her long, slender legs and sexy buttocks, reflected in the glass door of the drink fridge, were accentuated by the short skirt she was wearing.

"A pack of Kents, please."

The girl slid back the aluminum lid of the cigarette case and, after finding what he was looking for, placed it on the counter.

"That'll be two credits and five cents."

"Sure." Alex nodded and ran his fingers through the air. Perceiving his command, his lenses transferred the exact amount to the store account.

"Thank you for your purchase, and—"

Before the girl could finish her spiel, Alex flashed her his most disarming smile, one he'd practiced over years spent as a panhandler. It had filled his "pan" with money when he was little; it had started landing girls in his bed when he got a little older.

"The tip of your nose is insanely beautiful," he said. "I've honestly never seen one like it."

"That's a very strange compliment," the girl said with a smile.

"Trivial, you mean?"

"Maybe," she replied evasively.

"Maybe you'll agree to…"

Alex hadn't yet decided what he was going to ask the red-haired girl to agree to, but he knew she was going to say yes.

Unfortunately, he didn't get to finish his question.

The reflection in the same fridge he'd noticed before told him that three youngsters were pawing at his bike, wriggling around on it like strippers on a pole and taking pictures on their cheap smartphones.

"Damn," he spat. "What a shitty day this has been."

"What?"

"Sorry, dear. Maybe next time."

Leaving ten credits as a tip, Alex walked out of the shop, slamming the door shut behind him.

Chapter 8

It was your typical trio of little bitches looking for the kind of street cred that would get them into a gang, even a small one. First, there was the big alpha male, wearing a leather jacket and steel-toed boots. He was a meathead whose face showed off his miserable IQ.

Next was the skinny ringleader with the cruel, beady eyes and thinning hair.

To round it off, they had the ever-hesitant wimp who was just there to tell the morons they should've quit when they were ahead.

Revoltingly stereotypical.

Alex had seen more "gangsters" like them than he had rats, and that was despite the fact that there were more rats in each square foot of High Garden than there were doves in a pigeon coop.

"Get *on* it, Miles." The ringleader was hovering around the bike with his phone in hand. "Don't be a jackass."

"Hurry, Miles," the big guy echoed from his spot off to the side. He'd presumably taken his picture already. "The subway opens soon, and I want to take the first train home."

He wants to take the first train, does he?

Standing behind Rat and Muscle (Alex had a weird penchant for giving everyone nicknames based on their most conspicuous traits, even when they sounded odd), he crossed his arms and frowned.

Alex was no scrawny nerd. Almost six feet tall and weighing 176 pounds, he just looked like a regular guy. Not athletic, not sinewy, and far from having the impressive physique Muscle sported.

But there was something about him that made whole busloads of trolls and orcs back away.

Whatever that something was, it was spotted by Weakling, who was sitting on Alex's bike.

"Gu-u-uys," he whined.

"What?" Rat blurted out impatiently.

Instead of answering, he pointed a shaky finger behind his compadres.

Rat was the first to turn around. Muscle followed suit a moment later, and they both took a step back when they saw Alex.

Cocking his head, Alex called over to Weakling.

"Get off my bike."

The boy was starting to obey when Muscle's deep voice interjected with a curt, "Stay where you are."

Had Weakling been smarter, he would have realized that Alex was the one to be afraid of, and not the bruiser he was with. Unfortunately, he wasn't. He wouldn't have gotten mixed up with the other two in the first place if he were.

"You really mind us taking a few pictures?" His confidence boosted by the enforcer at his side, Rat stepped over to Alex. "We didn't scratch it or anything. Just took some pictures."

"Didn't your parents teach you that taking pictures with another man's bike without his permission is the same as fucking his wife?" Alex's response was calm.

"Without his permission, huh?" Rat's voice was nasally. "But you *are* giving us permission, aren't you? You don't mind us taking pictures and riding…your wife."

It takes just three months to develop a new habit. And after spending *years* in a place where conflict resolution happened with fists instead of magic, Alex had turned his habit into a conditioned response.

A knee to the groin (not the most honorable way of doing things, but Alex had learned how to fight on the streets and polished his skills in jail) bent Rat over, leaving him vulnerable to an elbow buried in the back of his head.

The kid collapsed onto the pavement, his eyes rolling back and his mouth foaming. He started to twitch unpleasantly and moan in pain.

"The fuck was that?!"

After asking his rhetorical question, Muscle cocked his club-like arm to deliver a clean, direct blow, his elbow far behind his back.

If the shot had landed on Alex's face, even the built-in defense his suit provided wouldn't have saved him from a broken nose and getting knocked out. But he wasn't about to get hit.

After all, he finally had someone to take his foul mood out on.

Taking a half-step toward his opponent, he angled his torso and caught Muscle's right arm in midair. Then he wheeled around, the arm clenched between his chest and forearm.

The elbow crunched as it turned inside out. Muscle shrieked in pain, and Alex's heel slammed into his kneecap before he could recover.

There was another crunch, that time duller and meatier. Muscle's shriek turned into a squeal. Blood splattered across the pavement, and Muscle collapsed, joining Rat on the ground. His right arm was bent backward, his leg looked grasshopper-like, and there was a bleeding, open fracture right below his knee.

"Esma'otor'shurag."

Gripping his right wrist with his left hand and advancing on Alex, a bluish light glowing at the tip of his index finger, Weakling was painstakingly drawing magic symbols in the air.

"Are you kidding me?" Alex arched his right eyebrow.

He knew without even needing to see it that Weakling was tracing the contours of signs projected by his lenses.

That's what an education in Myers City will get you these days. Why exercise your will and mind learning all those complicated magic patterns when you can just run a finger along a projected picture?

The kid was apparently trying to cast some sort of combat spell from the Earth Magic School. He must have passed an entrance exam and gotten a low-level grimoire downloaded to his lenses.

Alex could've let Weakling finish his spell just out of curiosity. Instead, he used pure magic energy to create a dark violet ball in his palm.

[Elementary magic action. Mana used: 25 points/use.]

Winding up like a baseball pitcher, Alex hurled the ball of energy right at Weakling's chest, interrupting his reading. Weakling shrieked. Before he could dodge, the ball knocked him out of the bike's seat and sent him flying, dropping him three feet away on the pavement.

"That h-hurts," he moaned.

"Call an ambulance," Alex shot back.

Stepping over the bleeding, groaning Muscle, he was on his way to his bike when his instincts started screaming at him.

Alex moved a palm in front of himself. Through willpower alone, he envisioned the spell pattern in his mind and then filled it with energy to create the seal.

A gust of emerald wind with sharp daggers whirling inside it hit the open maw of the black wolf that emerged from the seal, eyes red and gleaming.

The wolf's head grew larger as it consumed the enemy spell. Long claws flashed out of the seal, followed by fangs. Finally, jumping out of the seal and landing on the ground with an odd sort of flair, the wolf gave a low growl. Magic signs flashed around it as a blue fire flared up.

[Attention! You're using an unregistered Black Magic School spell. Mana volume: 490+770.]

Pushing off the melting pavement, the wolf leaped at the enemy. Consuming a spell almost 800 points strong meant the wolf created from black fire had brought its total power to over 1000. That was enough to force any Mystic back onto the defensive.

"Not bad, Mr. Dumsky. Not bad at all."

However, when it hit the stranger standing near the small shop, the wolf just burst into sparks of energy that soon disappeared, accompanied by flashes that looked like fireworks.

"A fast defensive spell that attacks immediately after consuming the incoming projectile? You know, I was offered that exact same thing for a price of 50,000 credits a few years ago."

"Damn dwarf," Alex hissed. "That's way too low. Who are you?"

Dusting his sleeves off, the stranger stepped into the light to reveal the back of his right hand, which had been magically tattooed with a shimmering *S*.

The Syndicate!

Chapter 9

Alex didn't need his lenses to identify the stranger as a high-level wizard. He was at least an Adept if not stronger.

[Name: ??? Race: Human. Mana level: 5372.]

Shit. Shit. Shit. The wizard wasn't just out of Alex's league; his power was incredible. A level 53 Adept. No wonder Alex's spell hadn't even ruffled him.

The clothes worn by the Syndicate's fixer (that was the only position a powerful wizard like him could have held) didn't register in Alex's lenses, something he expected. Personal belongings could be hidden by their owner, keeping all but their most general attributes private. But Alex could still see that the fixer's suit and coat were tailor-made.

Given that the fixer was an Adept, he could afford the best. Alex couldn't even begin to imagine what attributes his clothes gave him.

He was wearing a dark blue cashmere coat that came down to below his knees, a black three-piece suit, leather gloves, and a scarlet scarf tied around his neck. Every single article of clothing made Alex feel like there was an army of needles marching around on his fingertips.

And they were all top-shelf artifacts.

"My name is Pyotr, Mr. Dumsky," the fixer said. His name explained why he had such a strong Russian accent. "Nice to meet you."

Alex glanced around quickly. The blaring sirens on the cop cars reacting to the unregistered black magic spell were still several blocks away, and it was highly unlikely they would get there any time soon as it was. The High Garden cops preferred to let the trash take out the trash.

Doom covered the black ring he was wearing on a finger with his other hand. It was enough to buy him several seconds, though the main thing was jumping on his bike and—

"Easy, Mr. Dumsky." Pyotr held up his hands. "I was just saying hi."

"A combat spell from the Wind Magic School clocking in at nearly 800 points? You have a…peculiar way of greeting people, Pyotr."

"Noblesse oblige," the fixer replied, shrugging and keeping his palms up and open. "Negotiating from a position of strength tends to work when you're collecting debts. And you, Mr. Dumsky, owe us an indecent amount of money."

"I'm aware, Pyotr. I know who and how much I owe."

"Can I put my hands down?"

"What?"

"This coat is too stiff, and it's making it uncomfortable to hold them up. Can I put them down, Mr. Dumsky? As a gentleman, I'm not going to ruin this morning any more than it already has been." Pyotr nodded at the gangsters nursing their wounds on the asphalt.

"Sure, go for it."

"Thank you," the fixer said seriously, without a trace of sarcasm. Then he smoothed back his long, black hair. His hairstyle accentuated his pale face and the dark circles under his green eyes. "So, Mr. Dumsky, I'm here to remind you that you owe the organization 100,000 credits. You have three months to repay us, starting tomorrow. If you don't pay on time, then…"

"I get it," Alex interrupted dryly.

Pyotr frowned, then nodded as though listening to something.

"No, Mr. Dumsky. You won't be killed. We prefer not to waste assets, particularly when they're as valuable as your gift."

"Really? And what does the Syndicate have in mind for me?"

"You'll find out in due time," Pyotr answered, pausing before continuing. "Although…you'd probably rather not find out."

With a gust of wind, Pyotr disappeared, there one moment and gone the next. Running a scan with his lenses turned up no messages about magical activity, nor did they show the Adept's position. Alex couldn't tell if he'd cast a spell to avoid detection, used one to turn invisible, or—worst of all by far—had actually used a teleport.

"Show-off," he said through gritted teeth as he got on his bike.

He rode slowly toward 11th Avenue, which led to Myers City's Western District. That was where First Magic University and the apartment the state had provided Alex were.

"Don't forget to call that ambulance," he reminded the shocked Weakling, who had witnessed the entire conversation between the two wizards.

Without a backward glance, Alex sped off down the street. The locals were already waking up, getting out of their beds, and trudging along to work. More and more cars appeared on the road. By the time he'd stopped at his tenth traffic light, Doom was maneuvering his way carefully through a traffic jam. It wasn't that he cared about the rust buckets around him. No, his bike was his only concern. *Damn that Pyotr.*

***

Entering downtown Myers City was such a drastic change that it was almost like stepping into another world.

The first noticeable difference was how clean it was. The

sidewalks were so polished you could see your reflection in them, there were no piles of shit left by stray animals, and there weren't any of the stray animals themselves, either.

Beggars never came up to you asking for money or a cigarette. Instead, any of them who did venture downtown were immediately detained by the cops, who patrolled that area far more diligently than the outskirts, and brought to the station.

Even the cops there—the ones Alex had seen, at least—looked like they could have played the main characters in some old movie. They were physically fit, athletic, and, most surprisingly, not all human.

On his way, Doom even saw *bunnies* among the cops. Or elves, to be politically correct. That was going to take some getting used to. He was no longer in High Garden, where a man could get his limbs broken just for venturing into the orc district. Humans did the same to orcs when the reverse happened.

Meeting an elf, a fairy, or any another highborn was considered to be rare good fortune in the outskirts of the city (often turning into bad luck), but downtown... After no more than an hour spent working his way through numerous traffic jams, Alex had seen at least fifty very expensive sports and luxury magic vehicles.

Only the highborn had the means to afford them. Ever since the world of magic became reality, the highborn had had more money than the founders of Amazon and Facebook could have ever dreamed of.

But the greatest difference was in the architecture.

The old brick buildings, often dilapidated and looking like death traps, gave way to fine skyscrapers made of glass, chromium, and magic metals. Like a true concrete jungle, they rose dozens, even hundreds of stories into the sky.

Some buildings were made of stone, elegant creations designed by the best architects of past and present.

After getting used to the new styles, Alex was surprised when he stopped at a small bar that looked completely out of place and old-fashioned in the heart of the city. It was a three-story cube that sat between two skyscrapers both seventy stories tall, it had cracked red brick walls, and the crooked sign hanging above the entrance in the shape of a steering wheel read *Schooner Belis*. There was even a concrete porch and a bin overflowing with cigarette butts.

The spot was like a misplaced drop of black paint on the fair canvas of downtown Myers City.

Once again, Alex checked the map in the periphery of his vision.

"What's going on?" He frowned when he realized that his directions had taken him to the right place. He was standing at the threshold of his new apartment.

"Well, then…" Alex started toward the door of the bar modeled after a Texas saloon in the Wild West era, but he quickly stopped and looked back at his steel horse.

He wasn't in High Garden anymore. Where he was, the law of the street was something only the characters in gangster movies followed.

Alex raised his hand to cast a protection spell but stopped.

Again, he wasn't in High Garden anymore. Using an unregistered spell there, particularly a black magic one, would have instantly attracted the attention not only of the cops, but also of some even more unpleasant organizations.

"Damnation." Racking his brain, he finally remembered a simple alarm spell.

[Spell used: BANSHEE HOWL of the Black Magic School. Mana used: 25 points/use + 0.5 points/min.]

After glancing skeptically at the shimmering, semi-transparent female face hovering above his bike, Alex stepped into the Schooner.

"I hope you sneeze so hard you die, Bromie."

Chapter 10

"Hey, did you hear?" A guy with reddish hair, sharp facial features, and warm, green eyes put his burger aside. "They say we're going to be able to take an optional black magic course this year!"

"Black magic?" Another guy, this one with platinum blonde hair and so thin he almost looked like a girl, fluttered his long, apparently colored eyelashes. "Is that some politically correct term for magic?"

"Get lost, Leo," the redhead replied with a wave. "What do you think, Jing?"

A rather short but athletic, lean, and muscular young Asian man with hair tied back in a bun was using a knife and fork to cut into a juicy steak. On either side of him was a girl eating sushi with chopsticks.

"Maybe it's true," Jing shrugged and continued eating.

"So informative." The redhead sighed.

"What did you expect from our quiet friend?" a fair-haired girl with big blue eyes laughed. But it wasn't just her eyes that caught your attention—she had an hourglass figure, a short skirt revealing long, slender legs, and stilettos that were almost six inches tall. Clearly, a heartbreaker. Her hair was long; her clothes were far too revealing for the weather. She sat with her legs crossed, rocking a foot back and forth, and several men at the bar were rocking their heads in time with it. The sight was funny and scary at the same time.

"More than I'd expect from you, Ellie," the redhead snapped. "What are *you* doing here, anyway? Did your doofus have to run away for work again?"

"Darryl," the beauty corrected. "Yes, he's away on business—his dad's business in Scotland. Daryl went with him to get some experience."

"Experience, huh? He went there to drink and fuck Scottish girls on his dad's dime. And here you are, just so happy to twitter at his tall tales and spread your—"

Ellie squinted at him. The chopsticks in her hands suddenly looked menacing.

"Don't you dare finish that sentence, Travis. Or my mouth will be the least of your concerns."

"Oh, I couldn't care less," the redheaded guy, whose name was apparently Travis, replied with a snort.

"Then stop being jealous."

"Jealous? *What?*" The guy leaned forward again, abandoning his previous casual posture. "If there's anyone I'm jealous of, it's his *dad.* He has the money to buy half this district. Your doofus—"

"Darryl!" the blonde interrupted.

"I don't give a fuck what his name is! And—"

"Stop. Enough," a muffled but calm and confident voice interjected. It belonged to a very short, pretty girl with brown hair, a clean, oval face, a turned-up nose, and…no, she wasn't overweight. There was some fluff to her though. She might have even been beautiful, just definitely not as sexy as the blonde.

"Mara's right." Travis waved the argument aside. "None of this matters. What really worries me is that optional course on black magic. Did they go completely insane? They're actually going to bring in a dark wizard to teach us?"

"A *professor*," Jing added neutrally before once again tucking into his steak.

"All the more reason to worry!" Travis slapped a hand down on the table. "Instead of calling that…that piece of shit in, they should teach us how to protect ourselves against dark magic."

"You can pass the access tests for battle magic and get a couple good grimoires downloaded to your lenses," Ellie said, shrugging. "Or pick up something on sale if you want to save money. Although that would hardly be enough to help *you*."

Travis turned to Mara and pointed at Ellie with a potato.

"Hey, is she starting something again?"

"*You* started it," the miniature girl replied with a smile. "And you're wrong, Travis. You have to know dark magic before you can protect yourself against it. If you didn't sleep through history class, you'd know there aren't any spells from any of the battle magic schools that compare to black magic at the same level when it comes to how lethal they are."

"Travis staying awake through a class that isn't P.E. or practical magic?" Ellie asked venomously. "That's asking way too much, Mara. I have no idea how this blockhead even passed the entrance exams to get into First Magic with us. Before him, I thought they only accepted gifted students."

"Stop it already!" Travis pounded the table with both hands and stood up. "Enou—"

"Do you need something?" Jing asked suddenly, though he wasn't addressing any of the people at his table.

They all lapsed into silence.

Travis and the others turned toward the bar. Not far from them, a colorful character was cleaning up. He was a tall, lean young man with sharp but attractive facial features, black hair, and bright, emerald green eyes. Some work clothes made up his outfit, and he was leaning on a broom.

"How old *are* you kids?" His voice was arrogance and annoyed. "This is a bar, you know. Not a café. If you're not going to order any alcohol, go hang out at Mickey D's. They have a discounted Happy Meal today."

The five sat stupefied and silent, blinking at him owlishly.

"You… you…" Travis struggled to even form a coherent sentence, choking with indignation.

"How *dare* you talk to customers like that?" Ellie stood, immediately attracting the hungry gazes of most of the men—and not just the men—at the bar. "Get your manager. I demand—"

"Oh, I beg your pardon." A rather large character in his mid-forties seemed to appear out of nowhere next to the kitchen door. He had a protruding beer belly and a very obvious bald spot, and he was wearing an apron similar to his rude employee's, just not white. It was black and sported the Jolly Roger. The look was completed by a wooden crutch (just about in the 22nd century!), a patch over his right eye, and several gold teeth that marred an otherwise snow-white smile.

"He's a new hire, an immigrant from Old Earth. We're still training him. Could I give you something to make up for the inconvenience? How about a loyalty card?" The innkeeper (who else could such a colorful man be in a bar that looked like a ship's quarters?) produced a plastic card out of thin air. There was no magic to the trick, just sleight of hand. "Every fifth visit, you'll get a free glass of the best craft beer in the district."

Storming over to the pirate, Travis grabbed the card and made a gesture, apparently transferring a payment to the bar's account.

"I lost my appetite," he said through gritted teeth as he started toward the door.

"Sure," the cleaner mumbled. "You already inhaled three double burgers. Who could eat more after that?"

Travis stopped, turned around slowly, and opened his mouth, only to have Mara take him by the hand and silently walk him out. The carefree, platinum blonde guy followed them out, humming some tune as he went.

"I don't think we'll be needing your card," the beauty said arrogantly. After paying for her order, she left as well. "Shit. I was so happy to find a place with good food so close to the university, too. What a cruel world."

The Asian was the last to leave. Finishing his meal, which only took a couple more seconds, he stood up calmly and wiped his lips with a napkin before turning to the cleaner, bowing slightly.

"Please forgive my friend's insult. He didn't mean to offend you."

Then he exited the bar and joined his friends, who were already crossing the street. Directly opposite the bar was First Magic University.

***

"What the hell was that about?" Deaglan asked.

Shaking his head, Alex continued cleaning the floor.

"Hey, doesn't it seem strange to you," he drawled with exaggerated thoughtfulness, "that your name is Deaglan, which means 'absolutely good' in Irish? And yet, here you are, an ex-con."

Deaglan buried his face in his hands, wheeled around, and rushed back to the kitchen.

"Bloody officials," he whispered. "Damn them. Damn them. Damn. Damn."

Alex completely agreed with him. He would've never imagined that the deal he'd made with the mysterious suit would include an apartment over a *bar*, if not a cheap one, and that he'd have to work for his keep.

By doing honest work!

Cleaning floors at the bar!

Damnation. What other terrors did those officials have in store for an unfortunate and honest dark wizard?

"How did *you* notice it, boy?" Doom squinted in thought. "Eh... Maybe things are going to go better than I was expecting at the university."

As he pondered, Alex continued mopping away diligently. Faced with the choice of cleaning the damn floor to keep his magic or going back to jail, he obviously preferred the former.

The whole thing was just temporary, after all.

Chapter 11

Alex pulled his apron off and tossed it right onto the hooked aluminum needle protruding from the wall. In his small room, it served as both his clothes rack and his wardrobe.

Removing his oily, dusty work pants on the go, he flung them across the only armchair, which doubled as study and seating area in the cramped, dark space located right over the bar. It had just one window overlooking the fire escape and a ceiling so low he could reach up and touch it.

Even Doom's room at the orphanage had been bigger. The suite, as they'd called it jokingly, had accommodated two dozen growing boys, so it had been twice as large as this closet.

Alex tripping over the creaking floorboards of the once-durable floor, got tangled up in a sweater that smelled like mold, and managed to plop down onto the bed. It creaked plaintively, and his weight kicked up a small cloud of dust, but it nonetheless withstood the sudden onslaught.

At least the bed was normal-sized, wide enough to accommodate three people or so. The red velvet blanket, probably forgotten by a renter long ago, was a joy to behold.

Dropping his sweater on the floor, Alex looked over at the windowsill. His suit hung there, safe in its plastic bag, the only expensive possession he still had. At least, apart from his bike and the ring on his finger. Things were looking up, even if they were still pretty bad.

"Give me one good reason not to turn your blood into hippogriff urine," Alex said into the silent semi-darkness of his new home.

At first, the only answer he received was crows cawing somewhere outside the window. They mixed with the horns, engines, and everything else making up the symphony wafting in from the street. Myers City wasn't a quiet place at all.

"You wouldn't be able to if you tried," a soft, pleasant voice finally replied.

Hell's bells.

Had Alex been unaware of who the voice belonged to, he'd have thought a goddess had come to visit him. That melodious, honeyed voice was enough to force any man to hide the sudden tension in his pants.

But Alex knew well—too well, even—who stood behind the alluring voice.

A tall, slender girl stepped out from the dark corner. To call her *beautiful* would have been to cheapen every other time the compliment had been given to a woman.

To describe her as *wonderful* would have stretched the word beyond recognition.

Divine? That was a question best left to theologians.

To put it simply, she combined the sex appeal of the blonde from the bar (Ellie was her name, right?), the grace of a swan, and the stately bearing of a queen.

Her yellow hair, the color of wet gold, cascaded down to her knees, and her business suit accentuated all her curves.

She was a fairy woman.

And Alex didn't need his lenses to tell him that his visitor belonged to Goddess Danu's tribe.

He hated fairies.

"I wouldn't," Doom agreed. "But I would thoroughly enjoy the attempt."

The fairy, who sported a badge on her absurdly beautiful, high, and firm breast, came over to the armchair and sat down gracefully on the armrest, her seductive legs and hips a hormonal teenager's wet dream.

"Mr. Dumsky, my name is Lieutenant O'Hara." Alex noted instantly how unusual a last name that was for a fairy. Generally speaking, you could only pronounce their family names after slurring your speech with a few liters of unfiltered beer. "I was sent to—"

"Get on my nerves," Alex interrupted. Leaning back on his bed, he stared up at the ceiling and made a vague gesture with his hand. "But go on, beau—"

At first, he didn't realize what had happened, not expecting the excruciating pain that seized him the very next second. It felt like a superpower's entire nuclear reserve was being brought to bear on him.

He clutched at his wrist in an attempt to endure the waves of molten lava radiating from it. His entire body throbbed, every nerve ending on fire. Finally, he rolled off the bed to collapse face down on the floorboards.

The moments he spent in unspeakable agony felt like the eternal hell he'd read about in those old religious books.

At last, the pain subsided. Dark circles stopped dancing in front of him, and he could breathe again. He pulled in air with the greed of someone who had nearly drowned coming to grips with the simple fact that they were still alive.

"What...the..." Alex croaked, the words barely forced out of his numb and smarting throat. Had he been screaming? "What...t-the...f-fuck?"

He glanced at the bracelet on his right wrist. Made of steel and looking even kind of stylish, it was decorated with engraved runes. Very familiar runes. The smooth curls, sharp lines, and continuous ligature of symbols flowed into each other.

The language of the fae people.

Bloody fairies.

"That was setting seven out of ten, Mr. Dumsky." The lieutenant waved a small remote control for him to see.

The room was still spinning for Alex, making it unsurprising that he hit his head on the central radiator when he dove forward to grab the bloody thing from out of her hand.

What was somewhat more surprising was that the radiator was at the opposite end of the room from the damn fairy.

"Now that's an odd noise," she said with a laugh a poet might have compared to wind chimes or a bird singing. All Alex could hear was a snake hissing. "Mr. Dumsky, don't think you can escape from us as easily as committing suicide. Okay, maybe not so easy. But smashing your head against a radiator? The major was right—you're psycho. I should've realized that when I heard about the cat."

"Shut up." Alex rolled over onto his back and wiped the blood away from the cut on his forehead. "I'm going to kill you. I swear. And that's not just an empty threat to maintain my reputation; I really am going to kill you."

"Aren't you going to rape me first?"

A vivid image of him raping the fairy appeared in Alex's imagination …and he almost vomited. It was a good thing he hadn't eaten anything that day. That made it easier to rein in his disgust.

"What a weird imagination you—"

"Stop!" Alex interrupted. "You can go ahead and activate that bloody bracelet if it means leaving my imagination alone! Me fucking you? I'd rather do it with a meat grinder."

The girl was silent for a bit.

"Most *humans*," she said finally, pronouncing the word the way only non-humans did, "have responded to that very differently."

"Who *are* you?!" Bracing himself against the windowsill, Alex staggered to his feet. He looked at the bracelet and squinted, issuing a command to his lenses.

[Item: ERROR. No information in the database.]

"No point, Alexander. The design is unique. R&D worked overtime for a month to put that sexy little piece together for you."

"Have I told you that I'm going to kill you?"

"Twice."

"Make it three times." Alex waved her away and returned to the bed. His head ached as though…well, as though he'd just tried to head-butt a cast-iron radiator.

"Killing someone *three* times would be complicated."

"I screwed a necromancer girl once…or twice… That after-sex glow makes for the best little talks about working with magic."

"There's no accounting for taste," Lieutenant O'Hara replied with a shrug. "Anyway, let's get down to business. I have a message from Major Chon Sook."

"What spook?" Alex asked. "I haven't met any spooks since I served my time. Well, except for you. You're a world-class bitch, and I'm going to kill you last even though I don't like you."

She said nothing.

"Bloody hell! That's a meme from Commando! How old are you? Five?"

"Ninety-six," O'Hara replied in an icy voice, hiding the remote control in the inside pocket of her jacket. "Major Chon Sook. You enjoyed a limo ride with him after leaving prison."

"Ah, that son of a bitch. Well, let's hear what you—"

His wrist was pierced by another flash of acute pain. And while it wasn't half as strong as the first attack had been, it was still unpleasant. Alex had apparently traded his adamantius collar in for that damn bracelet, and the cramped cell of the underground prison for a more spacious one in Myers City.

"Be respectful, human. I'm enjoying your company less and less, so why don't I just get this over with? As you already heard from Deaglan, you either pay your rent yourself or do whatever work he asks you to do. As far as your job at the university goes, the whole of your salary will be paid to the city as compensation for the damage you caused during your arrest. As of right now, your total debt is…" O'Hara twitched her eyelids, which meant she was using her magic lenses. The magic races had gotten addicted to the puny humans' technology, too. "…1,440,000 credits."

Alex silently shifted his gaze from the bracelet to the lieutenant, then back to the bracelet, and finally to the radiator.

They won't get away with it that easily.

"How much is a professor of dark magic paid?"

"Ask that tomorrow when you visit the accounting department." The girl stood up with the practiced grace of a leaping cat and walked toward the door. "For now, that's all you need to know. Your partner will help you settle in."

She gripped the door handle and…

Alex felt another surge of acute pain.

Attacking her from behind was apparently also a punishable offense.

"Nice try, Alexander. Could you try to do that more often? I'm starting to like this bracelet." Her piece said, she walked down the corridor with a clatter of high heels.

Alex stayed where he was, lying on the floor next to the threshold. In only his underwear. Drenched in sweat and exhausted.

Unsurprisingly, Deaglan reached the obvious conclusion when he came upstairs to investigate the noise.

"You're no fool, boy," he said, flashing a thumbs up. "I heard you going at it hard with that chick and—"

Alex vomited.

His imagination was just too vivid.

Chapter 12

The first day at a new job means different things to different people depending on what kind of person they are. Some see it as a mandatory initiation into adulthood; others think nothing of it. Some people celebrate; others couldn't care less.

Alex belonged to that rare class of people who once believed they'd never have to work a day in their lives.

And so, as he kicked his bike's footrest back (he'd had to visit a vet earlier in the morning) and puffed away at the cigarette he held in his left hand, Doom was utterly confused. How had it come to that? *Is this really how miserable my life is going to be now?*

"Shit," he said when he had to move his right hand awkwardly as he dismounted the bike.

He'd spent the whole night trying to remove the bracelet. Every spell he knew had been pressed into service, registered and illegal alike. He couldn't remember the last time he'd been that exhausted. Perhaps after practicing with the Old Man back in his beardless youth. Those days were long behind him judging by all the facial hair he had going on.

But none of the magic had worked.

Finally, Alex had broken a leg off his decrepit armchair and…very nearly ended up breaking his arm along with it. That explained his trip to the vet.

The horse doctor had been surprised to see someone coming in without an animal at first, but a couple black magic pentagrams had convinced him to get to work regardless.

Old habits die hard. Alex had been halfway back to the university when he realized that he was probably not wanted by the cops anymore and could therefore have just gone to a human doctor.

That realization had soured his mood even further.

"Hey," someone said as they clapped him on the shoulder. "You left your bike in the wrong…"

Slowly, his lip twitching from the stress, Doom turned toward the voice.

The gaggle of freshmen stepped away from him. He could tell they were freshmen by the appliques they had on the right side of their blue blazers: the number one surrounded by intricate patterns and resting on a golden shield. Overall, their uniforms were pleasant enough to look at. Gray pants and navy-blue blazers for the guys, gray skirts and navy-blue blazers for the girls. The skirts went down to a bit above the knee, long enough to be decent.

"I'll shove your hand up your own ass," Alex said through clenched teeth, holding his cigarette so tightly he almost crushed it. "Then I'll pull it out your throat and beat you to death with it. If your carcass isn't too disgusting at that point, I'll take it to the nearest pub and feed it to some senile bum. Why a senile one, you ask? No idea. Just because."

There were seven freshmen around him. They weren't as strong as the ones he'd met in the Schooner the day before, but they each still boasted a respectable 400-500 mana points.

Without waiting for a response, Alex went up to the front gate.

First Magic University took up quite a bit of space, enough to cover four large city blocks. Surrounded by a tall wrought-iron fence with stone pillars, it was one of the city's landmarks and tourist attractions.

Every September 1st, large crowds flooded the place. But right then, two days before classes were set to start, the only people around were the occasional tourist and groups of freshmen hurrying to take care of what had to be urgent and extremely important problems.

Of course, there was also a sullen dark wizard wearing a very expensive suit. A cigarette was clutched in his teeth, and there was a cast on his right arm.

Alex clomped down the cobbled path that cut through the local park all the way to the central building. The colossal palace complex had been built in very ancient times by a very ancient wizard.

It had once been named Avalon, though that had sounded too pompous for the modern era. The name had therefore been changed to First Magic University.

Major repairs were the norm every century or so.

Needless to say, that was unsurprising, particularly after the invention of the Magic Lens. The university was where the brightest and most powerful members of the new magic generation studied, so the buildings took a lot of punishment.

The small towers and galleries, the great clock tower over the entrance, the oriels, the bas-reliefs, the statues on the rooftops, the stained-glass windows, and everything else were destroyed far too often.

But the restorations cost the city's budget nothing. The expenses were covered by the tuition fees, which were exorbitant.

Alex stopped at the entrance, which was essentially a giant porch: twelve marble stairs ascending to a broad platform with a roof supported by statues of the great wizards of the past in place of columns. Merlin. Morgana. Baba Yaga. Faust. Flamel. Crowley. And so on.

"All they're missing is Harry Potter," Alex said through gritted teeth before trudging up the stairs.

As he walked across the marble, he felt somewhat uneasy, almost out of place.

The last time he'd felt like that was when, as a kid, he'd decided to rob a museum exhibit. He'd been a barefoot ragamuffin surrounded by fine art.

The feeling Alex was experiencing right then was awfully similar. He wasn't a fan.

"Did you hear the news?"

"About the optional black magic course?"

"Yeah."

"The freshmen are lucky. I'd have opted for it, too, if it weren't for transmutation. I need it to pass my exams."

"You do? I'm taking mathematical analysis."

"*Why?* Tired of having a life?"

"No, I just want to study magic engineering and invent new spells."

"Um…well, good luck."

"And the freshman girls this year…"

Seniors chatted with each other as they walked up and down the wide halls with carpeted floors, plasma screens on the walls, and rippling protective spells over the windows. Ignoring their conversations, Alex made his way to the map that stood in the hall close to the entrance. It was right below the pointing finger of a giant statue of Prometheus, the main symbol of magic.

Prometheus actually *hadn't* brought fire to humanity from Mount Olympus. He'd brought something very different.

"Amusing," Alex said, commenting on the idea of putting a smart table with a map right beneath the ancient Titan's finger. "So, where's account—"

"Alexander Dumsky?"

The voice was strident. Strict. Arrogant.

Alex had never attended a school, though all the teachers he'd ever imagined had had voices like that one.

Turning around, he saw a classic erudite. Straight-backed, she was wearing an ankle-length skirt and a jacket with a white blouse, her graying hair tied tightly in a bun. The look was completed by her sharp, predatory face and the oversized glasses perched on her straight nose.

"Ma'am?" The word escaped Alex's lips without his permission.

"Professor Theresa Bloom," she replied, holding out a hand.

Alex may have been a dark wizard, but he wasn't a total psycho, so he shook her hand calmly and was taken aback at the strength of her elderly, wrinkled palm. Some High Garden thugs didn't shake hands as firmly as the old woman.

"We've been expecting you since early this morning." Alex had an angry retort ready to go for when she reprimanded him for being late, but there was no reprimand forthcoming. "Honestly, it's a good thing you were late. You missed the council."

"Missed *what*?"

Alex looked around nervously. Atlantis as a whole was an enlightened place, but High Garden… "Councils" were gatherings of homosexuals, and homosexuals were treated horribly. It was common to drag them through the streets with their male parts tied to a car's exhaust pipe.

A red-light tour it was called.

A terrifying, creepy sight indeed.

Anyway, Alex had little desire to attend a meeting of the kind of people he'd been taught to despise since he was very young. He was doing his best to overcome the attitude, knowing it was wrong, but the battle was still far from won.

The man who'd saved his life in prison slept with other men, and not because he had to. He just genuinely enjoyed it.

"The education council," the old woman explained, sighing before continuing. "They're important and entirely pointless meetings. Do you not have them back on Old Earth?"

Old Earth? The Asian major had mentioned something about that in the limo, but Alex hadn't been paying attention.

According to his new backstory, Doom had come from somewhere in Eastern Europe.

"Yes," he said. "Of course. But we call them something else."

"Really? That's interesting. What are they called?"

Lowering his voice to a conspiratorial whisper, Alex replied, "Conferences."

Professor Bloom nodded with the air of a person fully aware of the danger of divulging a secret like that.

Am I a dark wizard or what? Alex asked himself. He had a reputation to uphold, after all.

"I made a cheat sheet for you." The old woman handed him an A4 sheet of paper.

Alex accepted it and read it over.

Point one: lecture program. The assessment sheet. List of learning outcomes in line with the latest state standards. Consultation schedule.

Complete Reporting Journal No. 1 by September 30th, Reporting Journal No. 2 due by November 17th. Parent meetings. Attend courses No. 1-7 as you see fit. Have programs certified by the dean. Submit the certificate to the Rectorate to get...

The more Alex read, the less he understood what was going on. He stopped at point 32, which wasn't even halfway down the list.

The list was entitled: *First Semester Checklist.*

"It's so stuffy in here, Professor Bloom," Alex said, his index finger tugging at his tie knot.

"It is?" The old woman seemed surprised. "The air conditioners are all on full blast. Ever since that incident with the fire magic department last week, we've been keeping them at sixteen degrees Celsius."

"Really? Actually, I'm here to visit the accounting department." As he wiped sweat off his brow, Alex realized he'd been following the old woman through the maze of a university as they talked. "I have a question about my salary. You know us Old Earthers..."

"Do you have a family back home?"

Alex nodded. "Cats."

"Cats?"

"I support a shelter for homeless cats, so I'd like to know how much I'll be able to send them."

"What a strange hobby for a man of...your interests," Bloom said tactfully, avoiding any mention of black magic.

"Professor, we're not all scoundrels, villains, psychos, and dark overlords." *That may be true, but it doesn't apply in this case*, Alex added to himself.

"I see," Bloom nodded. "Well, let's figure it out... You have a strong resume, but no lecturing experience whatsoever. Considering you're at level 11 Adept...well, the reduction coefficients for inexperience are going to apply... Sorry, Professor Dumsky, but the university will only be able to offer you a minimal salary this year."

Alex barely held back a curse. He'd already established a rather friendly relationship with the old woman, and he preferred to keep it that way. At least for the time being.

"12,000 credits per month, another 6,000 for research."

Alex tripped, clutching at the windowsill as his eyes bugged out. The Professor, oblivious to his reaction, took a few more steps forward before looking back.

"Were you smoking a cigarette?" she squinted. "Professors are allowed to smoke in the hallways—our air-purifying spells can handle it. But you can't smoke in the lecture halls."

"Y-yeah, s-sure," Alex coughed, exhaling smoke from the cancer stick he'd swallowed.

"What's wrong, Professor? Are you feeling okay?"

"It's just stuffy in here," Alex replied, waved a hand vaguely and straightening up. "So, 18,000 is the minimum salary?"

"It's 12,000, actually. Earning the 6,000 for research is challenging—you'll have to prepare a report on how you spent each credit. It's explained in point 49 of your cheat sheet."

"Point 49? Ah, okay."

Alex wiped more sweat off his forehead. During his wild youth, one spent risking his ass in every sense of the word until landing himself in jail, Alex had made 50,000 credits a month at most.

But there he was, about to get paid half that just to spend a few hours in a lecture hall full of youngsters.

"Here we are." Professor Bloom stopped at a door marked B-52.

Thrilling. Do they have a minibar in there?

"Where is here?"

"Didn't I tell you, Mr. Dumsky? As a young professional, you're going to have to be a group supervisor. It isn't much, but you do get paid extra for the work—250 credits. You need the experience."

Bloom turned the gilded handle, opening the door.

"A group supervisor?" Alex replied. "What's that?"

"Managing a group of students. You'll be fully responsible for their academic performance and extracurricular activities."

Alex entered the lecture hall and froze on the spot.

A moment of deathly silence ensued until a scream escaped the blonde bombshell's lips.

"You??"

Oh, hell's bells. Can I go back to jail now?

Chapter 13

Alex slammed the lecture hall door shut. Pushing his glasses up the way he always did, he massaged the bridge of his nose before turning to Professor Bloom.

The old woman looked rather shocked, adjusting her own glasses with a long, gnarled finger.

"Do you know them, Professor Dumsky?" she asked in confusion.

"Sort of," Alex replied evasively. "Where's the dean's office again?"

"Straight down the hall, then take a right, and it's the third door on your left," Bloom blurted out automatically, still shocked. Not until Alex vanished around the corner did she remember to shout at his retreating back, "Wait, Professor!"

But Doom wasn't about to wait. He followed her directions, his brisk walk almost a run. Fortunately, the university halls were almost empty. The semester hadn't started yet, so he only knocked over a few dawdling freshmen before stopping at the dean's office door. It looked just like any other lecture hall door save for the name plate being made out of marble instead of plastic.

Alex had no idea what etiquette was for walking into the office of your boss-to-be. When you never had a teacher, you take whatever learning you can get.

The Old Man, his actual teacher (*may the demons of hell devour that bastard's flesh*), was rumored to have kicked open closed doors that got in his way back in his younger years.

Well, if it worked for him...

Bending his knee and swinging his leg in a broad arc, Alex slammed the sole of his shoe right against the lock. The door gave a plaintive groan; the thin wood cracked. The steel lock dropped to the floor as the door swung open.

Doom found himself stepping into the middle of an oval room with a stained-glass bay window facing a table covered with papers. Beneath the mountain of paperwork, a computer with a bitten apple logo on it was barely visible. A file cabinet made its home next to the table.

A short, slim, and dark-haired girl with clean, satiny skin froze on the chair she was standing on, her whole body stretched upward. Inexpensive shoes sat on the floor next to the chair. Her blouse was unbuttoned slightly to keep it from tearing, and the girl herself was trying to shove a book twice as wide as her torso onto the top shelf of the cabinet.

She had a pretty face, dimpled cheeks, and warm, brown eyes.

Basically, she looked like the kind of girl next door every male teenager is bound to fall in love with only to quickly forget her name once he gets older.

"*You're* the dean?"

"N-n-no, I'm his secretary. Wait, what do you think you're doing?" Suddenly, she came to her senses after the initial stammered shock. "Office hours for students start at noon! How did you open the door? I could have sworn I locked it."

"What are you doing tonight?"

The secretary blinked her long eyelashes twice.

"Excuse me?"

Flashing one of his best smiles, Alex stepped closer.

"The tip of your nose is insanely beautiful. I've honestly never seen one like it." The trick had never failed him. "So, let me ask you again: what are you doing tonight? I know a great place that serves—"

"I have a boyfriend."

"And I don't," Doom replied instantly, his smile unwavering. "We have so much in common."

The girl squinted at him. Then, suddenly, the enormous book barely missed Alex's head. Growing up in the High Garden ghetto, he'd learned to be as fast as a mongoose, so he dodged it easily. The girl gripped the corner of the cabinet, doing her best not to topple over onto the ground, though she dropped a stack of files in the process. Dozens of papers covered in all kinds of graphs and tables flew out like startled birds.

"Am I just rusty or did I lose my touch?" Alex whispered to himself in surprise before continuing more loudly, the same smile on his face. "Well, have fun, miss."

"*Ms,*" the secretary corrected him angrily. "Hey, young man, where are you going?"

Yes, he'd lost his touch. In the past, Alex had been particularly good at dealing with married women. That had been his preferred way of earning his dinner, in fact, back when he was fifteen. Some people didn't approve, but it was something he'd had to learn. He hadn't been born with it. And it beat dealing with a beef baton the way other homeless boys in High Garden lived.

Stepping past her, Alex entered the dean's actual office. It also had a marble name plate, though it read: *Dean Travis Lebenstein.*

Alex entered a far more spacious room, closed the door behind him, and cast a simple smell on it. Nothing harmful, it just meant that anyone who tried to open the door would feel the sudden urge to release their bowels.

[Spell used: SHIT of the Black Magic School. Mana used: 18 points/cast + 2 points/min.]

It was hard to judge Alex for the name and the mana cost not being rounded—he'd written the spell when he was eight. In fact, it was one of the first he'd created after becoming the Old Man's apprentice.

The dean's office was large enough to accommodate a bit of open space. It had lots of bookshelves, the floors were carpeted, and a picture window made up the entire eastern wall.

The wall opposite the window was covered in portraits, all of them featuring the same man wearing a crown and holding an orb. Dressed in a scholar's mantle and bent over a parchment. With some women. Surrounded by animals. Even—*hell's bells!*—wearing a Roman toga and holding a plate of fruit.

He was short and balding with a protruding belly.

The belly wasn't featured in any of the portraits; it took glancing at the marble statue standing almost in the middle of the room next to a T-shaped table for Alex to notice it.

The dean himself was seated at the head of the table. A short man, no taller than 5'4", he wasn't really obese. Just a bit plump. He had a high sweaty forehead that gradually transitioned into the bald patch he was wiping with a handkerchief, shifty eyes, and fat fingers studded with rings.

"Who are you?" he asked in a low, velvety bass voice that contrasted sharply with his appearance. He pressed a button on the phone standing by his computer. "Judy, what's—"

"Professor Alexander Dumsky," Alex jumped in. "You asked to see me."

"Really? I don't remember that." Still, he pulled his chubby finger off the button. A sound, something like a scream of indignation, had been coming from the speaker, but it ceased instantly. "Although, well, maybe I did. You're the Professor of Black Magic from eastern Europe, aren't you? Here to teach the optional course."

"Exactly." Without asking permission, Alex sat down at the opposite end of the table and put his feet up on another chair. They were aching after his brief run down the hall—he hadn't gotten much exercise in prison. "I'd like to know if I can turn down whatever this 'group supervisor' thing is."

"For starters, get your feet off that chair. What do you think you're doing, Professor Dumsky? You're in the holy of holies—"

"If this place were *actually* the holy of holies," Doom said, "I'd be twitching on the floor. Which department is this, anyway?"

Lebenstein's piggish eyes widened in shock.

"Wha-a-at?" he bellowed like a wounded bison. "You don't even know what department this is? You don't know where you were accepted thanks only to the rector's personal patronage? I was right—you shouldn't even be a lab assistant here!"

"Oh, I'm in complete agreement," Alex replied with a nod. "I couldn't be more out of place. Still, it was written in the stars that I'd come here, so here I am."

"This is the holy land!" The plump man jerked an index finger upward as he started into a stilted, pompous speech. "Here, and only here, is where real magic happens. This is the only place where real science is used! We don't have time for slight of hand and parlor tricks like everyone else."

"Where, the ceiling?" Alex asked curiously.

"Excuse me?" The sound coming out of the dean's mouth sounded like a deflating balloon.

"You're pointing at the ceiling," Alex replied, "when you should be pointing outside the window. But whatever, doesn't really matter. Can we get to the point?"

The short, plump dean with an outsized ego even for his substantial body turned pink. "The Department of Theory and Magic Calculation."

"Theory and Magic Calculation?" Alex was surprised. "So, bookworms? Not researchers, not engineers, but magic mathematicians?"

"Magic mathematics is the queen of all the sciences!" the enraged Lebenstein shot back, turning a deep shade of red. "If it weren't for our department, no one would ever be able to determine the marginal boundaries of conventional mana point coefficients! No one would've been able to compute the minimum absorption reduction threshold! And—"

"Wow," Alex drawled in surprise.

"There you go, young man. Rejoice at your good-for—"

"You actually used the whole 'conventional mana point' term," Doom continued. "I haven't heard the full name in forever. But what were you saying about those coefficients? I just Google them when I need them."

The dean's red face turned violet.

"I'll report you to the rector!" he squealed. *Where did that deep voice go?* "I'll die if that's what it takes to get you expelled from the department!"

Why is he being so rude?

And his defenses? Standard artifacts and flat, single-element shields.

"A fraud in my department!"

Nothing complicated.

"A *dark magician* from some forsaken Old Earth hole! I will not tolerate this. I won't stand for it!"

Alex snapped a finger, summoning a small lilac fire to light his cigarette with.

"Get out of my office *right now*, young man! And pray to all the gods or demons or whatever people like you worship that the rector continues to patronize…his patronage…to give you his support!"

Alex had learned the trick of concealing one spell by using another right about when he'd picked up carjacking.

"So, you won't let me quit being a supervisor?"

"Get o-o-out!" Lebenstein bellowed, jumping up and almost falling over as he did so.

Alex stood, wiped his feet on the expensive Persian rug, and left the office. Opening the door, he winked at the secretary, whose name was apparently Judy, and walked out into the corridor past the front door. It was hanging on a single hinge.

But he wasn't about to leave entirely.

Stepping around the corner so as not to be seen, he stopped by the window and continued smoking.

Magic math really is an important science, but he could have been less…obnoxious. He should take some lessons from Professor Bloom, for example. A true wonder woman.

"Professor Dumsky!"

Alex turned around. Standing next to him was a short, pretty girl with brown hair and squarish ears. Their shape attracted attention, but not in a way that put you off—they were captivating. *Mara*, Alex recalled.

"Please forgive Ellie," the girl said. "She didn't really mean it. We just weren't expecting the man we saw cleaning the bar to turn out to be our professor...and our supervisor, too! Now it makes sense why you reacted to Travis the way you did. Our Travis, not the dean. It was so brave of you to go see Lebenstein! The whole university is afraid of him! They say no one passes his exam on the first try, and everyone, even the guys from the battle department, comes out of there crying. But you...you kicked his door down! And you spoke to Prorector Bloom without batting an eye. She's second only to the rector, and...and... Are you listening to me, Professor?"

"No," Doom answered honestly. "Three."

"Three?"

"Two."

"Two?"

"One."

"One?"

"Here it comes!"

Alex seized the girl, pressed her against himself and covered her neck and mouth to keep her from giving away that they were there. If she had tried to break free, she would have just strangled herself. Mara, if that actually was her name, made a confused noise, but then froze quietly.

"What's going on here?" a familiar squeaky bass yelled. Is there such a thing as a squeaky bass? Apparently, there is. "Clean that up *this instant*, Judy! And call the repairman to fix the door."

Lebenstein stomped out into the corridor. A small group of freshmen was passing by, and they giggled and pulled out their smartphones as soon as they saw him.

"Your skirt is an inch shorter than the dress code standard," the dean bellowed. "Who's your supervisor? Why are you laughing? What's wrong? Is it my hair?"

"Bingo," Alex smiled gleefully.

Just then, the dean turned to look at a mirror.

"Ah-h-h!" A horrified shriek almost broke the stained-glass windows. "RECTOR! I need to see the rector!"

The dean dashed off toward the stairs like a rocket, his attempts to cover up his new hairstyle mixing equal parts awkwardness and disgust.

Right on the dean's bald spot, swaying as he ran (if one could even call what he was doing running), was a pair of hairy…male canine genitals.

[Spell used: BALLS of the Black Magic School. Mana used: 41 points/cast + 16 points/min.]

That was the second spell Alex had invented as a kid, and it was just as rough and clumsy as the first. Of course, in all fairness, he'd been a cold and starving wolf pup snatched up by the Old Man from the streets of High Garden. His imagination had been rather poor back then.

Besides, Alex had a feeling that *balls* were exactly what the plump dean was missing.

"Don't worry, my dear." Alex released his grip on Mara and clapped her on the shoulder. "You'll get a new, normal supervisor soon enough and be able to remember me as…a very pleasant interlude."

He wheeled around and headed toward the exit. The shocked and dumbfounded student remained where she was, standing in the dark niche by the dean's half-destroyed office.

Chapter 14

"**N**o. No."

Alex was lying on the bed in his tiny apartment over the pirate bar and scrolling through the ads on the Hunter Guild's board. Before going to jail, he'd paid for a ten-year guild membership he needed for a con he was running. Who could have imagined back then that Doom would one day actually try his hand at hunting monsters?

Although, in all honesty, he hadn't found any good opportunities so far.

The day before, after completing his shift at the bar, Alex had found out through experimentation that his leash, which was tethered to the bracelet on his right wrist (what was the point of moving it from his ankle to his wrist?), reached exactly to the city perimeter. When he tried to cross the invisible line denoting the border, he nearly sent his spirit down to hell.

The pain that had racked his body had proven without a doubt that Lieutenant O'Hara really had used just 70% of the bracelet's total power on him.

How had Doom managed to make his way back to the city without even crashing his bike on the way? He had no idea.

Ten miles down the western highway was the edge of the zone where he was relatively free, one that circled around the city center at that distance.

"Another nope."

Hiring: The Alchemist Guild

Job: Capture morlocks in the Gudon Swamps

Goal: 15 paws

Pay: 100 crd/paw

Morlocks were C-level creatures. Not that weak, but a piece of cake for a group of hunters. Alex could have even done it alone if the Gudon Swamps hadn't been six hours north of the city by car. Definitely too far for him.

Hiring: The Alchemist Guild

Job: Catch the Fiery Pard

Goal: 1

Location: Somewhere in the Ferd'Khan Mountains. The exact coordinates of where the target was last sighted will be provided after the contract is signed.

Pay:

Body – 16,000 crd

Magic core – 25,000 crd

The Fiery Pard was what people called the Bakeneko, a fiery cat from Japanese folktales that could transform into a seductive woman. No one had ever survived a night with her.

The creature was B-level, too strong for Alex to fight on his own. Assembling a group was also out—nobody would have wanted to sign a joint Hunter Guild contract with a dark wizard.

It was just too dangerous.

Hiring: Myers City Police

Task: Help us capture T. B. Cooper

Charged with: Grand theft

Pay: 10% of the stolen amount

Enticing, but against Alex's principles.

He continued browsing through the ads popping up one after the other. The lenses kept him connected to the web and provided the information he needed, the whole thing so unobtrusive it was easy to forget he was even wearing them.

Alex waved his hand, discarding the quests he couldn't accept or that didn't pay well enough.

The best gigs were always offered by alchemists or archeologists (read: ancient tomb and dungeon raiders), followed by the ones from the police. The simplest and most common were put up by the municipality and traditionally considered side jobs for school kids. In order to go looking for a lost dog and earn your 25 credits, you didn't have to be a member of the Hunter Guild. It was enough to have valid official identification and not be listed on the police's blacklist.

But that put the whole thing out of reach for the vast majority of High Gardeners.

The practice of hiring hunters originated in the distant past, a time when Atlantis was in chaos and ruin after the Great Disaster. There was no centralized authority or government—might made right.

The nation had long since risen from the ashes, but some old traditions had survived.

Doom swept the last notice aside and tried to tell if he'd been imagining the sudden noise he heard.

"Damn."

When the door opened, his unexpected visitor found himself facing the business end of a long spear made of black fire. Smoking and hissing in midair, it was aimed right between the man's eyes.

[Spell used: DARK SPEAR of the Black Magic School. Level:

Practitioner. Mana used: 890 points/use + 15 points/sec.]

Alex could only use it once as it drained almost all his mana reserves. With that said, it was one of the most powerful spells he had. It could punch through most two-element shields up to the 20th Mystic level.

"Not bad," a calm, somewhat grumpy voice said. "My name is Lieutenant Gribovsky."

"Care to show me your documents?"

"Only after I shoot you in the head."

That was when Alex saw that the stranger was aiming a silver handgun at him from his thigh, and that it was covered in shiny runes and symbols.

Hell's bells…

An enchanted firearm!

The lenses definitely weren't going to show him anything.

Enchanted firearms were an urban legend. A myth. A tall tale. No one actually believed they existed.

Long before, people had invented a way to enchant weapons such that they cast magic during fights. Alex's Dark Spear, for instance, could be housed in a sword. A skilled fighter could then use the enchantment in the sword five or six times during the course of a battle.

Enchanted blades were prohibitively expensive for all but the wealthiest.

And enchanted firearms…

"Is it true that every bullet in the magazine carries a different spell?" Alex asked with juvenile curiosity and even a measure of exhilaration.

"You'll find out if you don't cancel your spear."

"Damn you. That's tempting."

For a moment, they just stared at each other. That gave Doom enough time to see exactly what his nighttime visitor looked like.

He was tall, much taller than Alex. No less than seven feet, perhaps even seven and a half. Athletic, with impressive muscles, definitely not thin or wiry.

His left ear was pierced from top to bottom. (At least, it wasn't his *right* ear.)

Red hair. Sharp facial features. An aquiline nose. A pointy chin and piercing green eyes. He had a conspicuous scar on his temple, above his right eye, and it was apparent that it hadn't been caused by a bullet, spell, or blade. Rather, a claw had made that scar…several of them, perhaps.

"Did they pick you because of your last name?" Alex dismissed the spell with a wave of his hand. Only half the mana was restored to his reserves. "So I could say it without spraining my tongue?"

"No," Gribovsky replied shortly. Spinning his gun, he slipped it deftly back into its holster and closed his trench coat. "What kind of spear was that? Or were you just happy to see me?"

Doom squinted at the lieutenant.

"I'm still not sure if I like you or if I'd rather try to take that gun from you."

"I'm not sure either, inmate. I don't know if I like you or if I'd rather shove that spear of yours up your ass."

Doom stood and walked over to the lieutenant. He barely came up to the red-haired man's chin. *Where did they find a giant like this guy?*

"So, you're my partner," Doom guessed.

"You're quick on the uptake. Is your skull too tight for your brain, pumpkin? I can loosen things up a bit."

Alex gave him a wry smirk.

"What do you have for me?"

"Some lead."

"It's not true about the spells, then? All you have in the gun are bullets?"

"Sure, I have spells, but lead sounds tougher."

"Tougher, yeah..." Alex knew better than to argue. "So, what's up? I'm supposed to be getting ready for my first lecture tomorrow."

Gribovsky squinted and leaned his back against the doorframe. It creaked plaintively.

"I envy you, pumpkin. First Magic has delicious babes... mm-mm!"

Alex choked on air.

"Are you crazy, Lieutenant? They're *kids*! The freshmen aren't even eighteen yet."

Gribovsky waved his protests away.

"The age of consent is sixteen. Damn it. I was so looking forward to having a fun partner for once, and you're just as boring as the rest of them. You and your suit. It isn't too tight, is it? Is there enough space for your balls?"

"You don't have to worry about my balls, pervert."

Alex had already forgotten his own attempt to pick up the high school-aged shop girl. It had happened right after he'd gotten out of prison, anyway—he'd just been too high on testosterone.

"Well, let's go." Motioning for Alex to follow, Gribovsky headed toward the stairs.

"Go where?"

"Oh, relax. I'll tell you on the way."

Chapter 15

In the fifteen minutes Alex spent with Lieutenant Gribovsky in his car, he learned several things about his partner.

First of all, despite his outlandish height, he drove a coupé sports car, and he did so like he was playing a racing simulator rather than driving down city streets that were busy even at night.

The next thing he learned was that, despite being straight, Gribovsky addressed everyone as pumpkin. That really started getting to Alex over the course of those fifteen minutes.

The third thing was that Gribovsky apparently didn't belong in the late 21st century—a better fit would have been the Wild West. He would've looked great sitting sullenly in the smoky corner of a saloon only to suddenly erupt in a torrent of bawdy boasting while shooting anything that moved.

"Watch where the hell you're going, pumpkin!" he shouted through the half-opened window at an elf driving a brand-new and very expensive Mercedes.

Without lowering his window, the elf replied with what looked like some choice language.

"You ran a red light," Alex pointed out.

He liked driving fast, too, but High Garden had taught him respect for other people. If you became an annoying neighbor there, they could get rid of you by feeding your body to the fish in the Alneez, Myers City's main river that emptied into the ocean.

"They're all animals." Gribovsky threw the wheel over so hard the tires squealed. Alex heard a distinct rattle coming from the magic engine. "Buying their driver's licenses and charging out onto the streets right away!"

He went on and on about how corrupt the city authorities were for allowing such negligence. Alex listened to the speech while huddled in his seat, gripping the handle above him.

Was he really going to end up getting out of prison just to die in some officer's car?

"Can you tell me where we're go—"

"We're here."

Gribovsky hit the brakes. After another semicircle, the car skidded to a stop on the opposite side of the street, right between two big, blue buses with *M.C.P.D* written on their side in white paint. Myers City Police Department.

"Be a man, pumpkin." Gribovsky shut off the engine and began the lengthy process of extricating his body from the fetters of his sports car, squeezing his considerable bulk through the rather narrow hole of the door. "If…they…even…recognize you…then… Oh, shit! My leg! …then they'll think it's just some other guy who looks like you. Ooh."

Getting out, Gribovsky straightened up and stretched, vertebrae popping. That was when Alex noticed that the lieutenant had *two* handguns, one for each hand.

"Home sweet home, yeah, pumpkin?"

Alex looked around. They were in the northern quarter of High Garden. It was the area closest to what the rest of the world called the *City of Wizards*—the countless skyscrapers of downtown—and hence looked the most decent. The people who lived there were a bit better off than most High Gardeners: small business owners, middle managers, the children of big gang bosses, and the like.

Houses there had less graffiti on the walls. There was almost no trash scattered around. The dumpsters were where they were supposed to be. There were even some *trees* growing in special beds by the road. The apartment blocks had five, seven, even nine stories, central heating, and water tanks on the rooftops.

By High Garden standards, it was a very good neighborhood to live in.

"Let's go." Gribovsky motioned to him before tramping off loudly toward a group of cops. After lingering for a moment to cover his ring with his left hand, Alex followed.

"Barney...seriously...I've never seen anything like this before."

"Oh please, things were way worse during the gang war six years ago."

"No, Barney, you don't get it. Nothing like *this* happened back then."

Two cops who were presumably standing guard were smoking by the entrance. One of them wasn't actually standing; he was sitting on the stairs and smoking rather nervously. Apparently, he was the one not named Barney.

Alex looked around once again.

Weird. The only cops on the street were the pair in front of them, even despite the two buses parked nearby. From what he remembered, buses like those always carried at least a score of blue uniforms.

"Hi guys," Gribovsky said with a smile and a wave.

"Who are you?"

Instead of answering, the lieutenant pulled his ID out and showed it to the cops. They straightened up so quickly they almost choked on their cigarettes.

"Sir!" they replied with an instant salute.

"At ease, soldiers. He's with me."

Walking past the two cops standing at attention, Alex had mixed feelings. There was a perverse sense of glee, on the one hand, though it was accompanied by a sense of foreboding.

His gut instinct said the whole thing meant trouble.

They went up the stairs and into the building.

The hall looked absolutely normal. Two elevators. A set of stairs zigzagging upward. Long rows of mailboxes across the opposite wall. The plaster was somewhat shabby, and the floor had apparently not been washed since the day before, but that was it.

Traces of drunken mishaps that hadn't yet been cleaned up clued the pair in to the building's cleaning schedule.

Alex followed Gribovsky onto the elevator.

Hell. Was it school kids throwing a party?

The elevator was smelly and dirty, too, though the lieutenant was unphased. Pressing the button for the ninth floor, he tapped a painfully familiar rhythm on the door.

"Nirvana?" Alex asked.

"Bingo," Gribovsky nodded. "You love Kurt, too?"

"Oh, no," Doom replied, shaking his head. "I'm more a Metallica guy."

"That's seriously ancient."

"Well, shit, it's not like Nirvana is any newer. They're both almost a century old. Pretty ancient stuff."

"Ancient stuff? I'll bash your teeth in, Dumsky."

As they talked about the sublime, they rattled (literally—the elevator was horribly shaky) up to the ninth floor.

The door slid open after the third attempt, letting cigarette smoke pour into the elevator.

"Ugh." Pinching his nose with one hand, Gribovsky waved the smoke away from his face with the other.

As he stepped out into the corridor, Alex saw why the smoke was so dense. Two scores of cops were standing along the walls, all of them smoking. Many of them were doing so for the first time, judging by all the coughing.

Along with the blue uniforms of all ages, Doom spotted specialists in their white smocks and detectives in their civilian suits.

They were all trying to get as far away as possible from apartment 172.

"Who are—"

Apparently expecting that question, Gribovsky flashed his ID on the go. The cops' leader, a menacing man in a shabby, cheap suit with a plain trench coat over his shoulders, just nodded.

"The specialists are done," he said. "We questioned the neighbors."

"And?" Gribovsky's bravado and frivolity, apparently feigned, were gone in a flash. He was once again the grumpy character who first entered Alex's apartment.

"Same as always, sir. No one saw anything. No one knows anything. Judging by their descriptions, the people who used to live in the apartment were saints... They're terrified. All of them."

"With good reason."

They fell silent for a moment.

"Can we go?" the detective asked.

"Yes." The lieutenant nodded and headed for the apartment door. "We'll take it from here."

Noticing the plural pronoun, Alex followed Gribovsky as he opened the door and entered the apartment.

He felt a tingling sensation in his fingertips as he stepped over the threshold.

That's a bad sign.

There was nothing special about the apartment. It had been remodeled a long time before, with subsequent generations doing nothing but repaint the walls and change the furniture.

First was a narrow hall cluttered with shoes and a cumbersome wardrobe with the standard built-in handles. Whoever had been living there probably thought it was fancy.

There was nothing special except the strong smell of copper and sulfur mixed with something like ammonia.

It was a creepy smell. One that tended to lodge itself in your skull and instantly ruin your appetite no matter how hungry you were a second before.

Following Gribovsky, Alex stepped into the first bedroom and froze on the threshold.

"Fucking hell's bells."

"You're probably right about that, pumpkin." Gribovsky pulled a pack of Skittles out of his inside pocket and tossed several of them into his mouth. "Or something even worse."

Smeared all over the white sheet covering the double bed was thick, dark blood. It had been used to paint circles around symbols pulled from various alphabets, not to mention lots of other geometric shapes.

There was also a huge magic seal that a non-magic person would've most likely called a pentagram. It was drawn in blood, too.

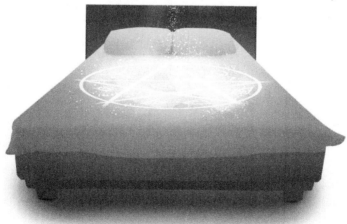

Alex already knew what he was going to see when he looked up.

Nailed to the ceiling, right over the seal, were two bodies...or rather, what remained of them. The carved up and shriveled remnants had their bellies slashed open, their entrails dangling out of them, their limbs broken, and some bones removed. The bones had probably been used to disembowel them.

It was only circumstantial evidence that told the pair that the two chunks of bloody flesh had once been a man and a woman.

Their eyeballs lay on the bedside table, from where they stared at the entrance.

Their hearts were impaled on the bed posts.

The blood and entrails soaked into the carpet squelched, and there was more strung across the window.

"So, *this* is why you actually got me out of jail," Alex said through gritted teeth.

"You're not the only dark wizard in this city," Gribovsky replied calmly, without an ounce of mirth. "But you're the only demonologist we know."

Holy shit.

Chapter 16

A s Alex gazed at the blood seal, he had the distinct impression that it was looking back at him. In those bold, scarlet lines and the glimmering lamplight reflected in the blood, Doom saw something he wished he could have forgotten for all eternity.

He saw one of his memories.

***

"Alex," a tall girl called, distracting him from the porn magazine he was paging through.

It was probably a surprising sight for passers-by: a boy no older than seven hiding beneath a dog rose shrub to read a fairly hefty porn magazine. It actually had *too* many pages to just be a glossy periodical.

However, upon seeing the tall and decrepit building of St. Frederick Orphanage behind the boy, not to mention the ramshackle fence with five gaps in each board, they would have hurried on, having reached a very definite conclusion.

And they wouldn't have noticed the dog-eared Practical Magic Math handbook hidden between the busty women of different races depicted on the cover of the magazine.

Had they seen it, those random passers-by would have wondered how a seven-year-old orphan was able to understand graphs and charts that were a mystery to most people with a bachelor's degree. But that would have been a completely different story.

"Alex!" the girl called again, this time a bit louder.

"Coming!" the boy shouted back. After placing a bookmark and hiding the book in his homemade stash under the shrub, he ran over to her.

She was wearing a sandy-colored dress, a wide-brimmed white hat, and blue shoes. A first-year student at the community college for domestic magic.

She was studying to become a florist.

Fortunately for Alex, she'd happened to draw the short straw and get an internship at St. Frederick Orphanage, where she was helping restore the garden.

The garden had supposedly once been used to teach kids how to take care of magic plants. But right then, overgrown with weeds almost as tall as Alex, it was a spot for…lots of things, none of which were academic.

"Miss Elisa," the boy said with a smile.

"Reading the handbook again, you naughty boy?" Frowning and putting her tiny (although they seemed huge to Alex back then) hands on her hips, she loomed over him like a giant shadow. "You should be playing with the other kids."

"They're boring," Alex lied. The real reason he avoided everyone was completely different. "The book's interesting."

For a while, Elisa stared at him, her warm, soft brown eyes shining as brightly as the midday sun on that fine spring day.

"You little devil," she laughed at last. "You know I can't be mad at you for long."

She reached out a hand to flick his nose.

"The tip of your nose is insanely beautiful," Elisa smiled.

Alex grabbed at the aforementioned part of his face and backed away.

"That's what my mom always told me to make me smile," Elisa explained. "So, will you help me today?"

"Sure," Alex replied. "And will you show me how to grow a peony?"

"That's advanced magic, but…sure! Okay, go get a spade and a trowel. No amount of magic will help if you don't know how to work with your hands."

Alex rushed over to the shed where the gardening tools were stored.

I should've just kept reading the handbook.

"What do you think, Doom?" Gribovsky's voice had taken on a gray, bleak tone once again. It was distant and absolutely devoid of emotion, no trace left of his recent joviality.

The giant, red-haired descendant of Eastern European immigrants chewed his candy, looking so natural among all the bloody chaos that he might have lived his whole life surrounded by it.

"Cheap props. All of it." Alex sighed, straightened up, and stepped away from the blood seal.

"Props? What do you mean?"

Wow. As he continued, the officer's voice suddenly flashed an emotion: surprise.

"These entrails look pretty real to me. And the hearts, too. Why did they place the eyes there? To see everyone who enters, something like a surveillance camera?"

As bleak as Gribovsky's voice might have been, his manner of speaking was largely unchanged.

"Not they. *He,*" Alex replied softly as he continued to examine the scene.

The farce was definitely not a proper crime scene. The officer smoking at the entrance had been right about that. When gangs waged wars, lots of violence was inevitable—Alex had been in many a fight back in his day. But when people got killed in them, it was civilized. They would be stabbed in the stomach. Shot in the chest. Killed with a spell.

Nothing like the scene in front of them.

Gribovsky froze, his hand just a few inches short of popping a tiny red Skittle into his mouth.

"One man, Doom? Are you sure?"

"If you know any other demonologists in Myers City, you're welcome to check with them."

"Explain," Gribovsky ordered before tossing the candy into his mouth. There was a loud crunch. "Pumpkin."

Somehow, it didn't sound as affected as all the other times he'd said it over the previous hour. It was more like a cocked gun.

Had he actually been a clowning fool, he definitely wouldn't have been assigned as a partner to the convicted dark wizard who'd been leashed and told to play nice.

"Gribovsky, everything here is designed to play a trick on the eye." Alex was standing close to the bedside table when he said that, and the unintended pun was not a good one.

"It wasn't done by a demon?"

"A demon couldn't have done this," Alex replied, shaking his head. "Only one powerful enough to command a legion, anyway. But if a beast like that had been summoned to Myers City, there would've been no way to conceal it."

"Are you sure about that?"

"Again, unless you want to…" Seeing the piercing glare of the man's green eyes, Alex sighed and made a vague gesture. It was a stupid habit he had. "It would be like trying to hide a nuclear explosion. Or a dragon attack."

"Well, as far as that last one goes, we've been concealing dragon attacks for over 1,500 years. We only failed once, in the 6th century AC."

Alex did his best to contain the surge of interest triggered by the words *we've been concealing*. Which department did the major, the fairy, and the redhead work for, exactly?

"Imagine you were drugged, yanked out of your warm bed, stripped naked, and thrown into the Arctic wilderness. How much time would you need to regain your senses and defeat a battle-ready polar bear?"

Gribovsky looked thoughtful.

"About…twenty minutes," he replied, not at all the *I'd be as good as dead* Alex was expecting—that was his point.

The scariest thing was that Gribovsky's words weren't an empty boast. They were a clear statement of fact.

Alex looked over at his partner once again.

[Name: Gribovsky. Race: Human. Mana level: 615.]

He was at the sixth Practitioner level. Sure, the information could have been a cover, but…Alex didn't think it was.

"Well, a demon would need more time." Alex ran his palm in front of his eyes. No tingling. Not that he'd expected any; the old-fashioned practice was just sometimes more useful than cutting-edge technology. "Like angels, they aren't just a different race. They're from another plane of existence entirely, and—"

"Did you say angels?" Finally, Gribovsky flashed a strong emotion. His candy fell to the floor. "Shit! Dropped them. That was my last pack, too."

"Yes. Angels," Alex replied with a shrug.

"But they don't exist. That's just a myth."

Doom knew better than to argue. But the scar running from his left shoulder to his right hip was a reminder that some myths were real.

"Demons are classified in a variety of ways, Gribovsky." Taking off his shoes, Alex stepped right onto the dried seal.

"What are you doing?! That's—"

"Also fake," Alex interrupted, stomping on the scarlet seal. "A strong demon, one of their ruling elite, can't be summoned by a human unless they have the power of a coven. Mid-level demons capable of teaching you something for the right price...hm...you need special equipment for that. The whole summoning process is very complicated and very dangerous. As far as I know, the last attempt was made in Mexico, where someone tried to summon an officer from a second-century legion. The whole thing ended up a horrific failure."

"A second-century legion?"

"Dante was only slightly off," Alex continued while examining the sacrifices nailed to the ceiling. "Did you know that the Divine Comedy was the first actual classification of the creatures living in hell?"

Gribovsky mumbled something unintelligible. His fingers twitched nervously as he periodically lifted them to his mouth.

He's giving up smoking—that's why he was eating those Skittles. I wonder why.

"The nine circles...don't really exist. Hell is a different plane of existence. It doesn't have a spiral shape, but it does have a structure: 900 legions, each of which has 6,666,666,666 soldiers. And the ruling elite— all the demonic barons, dukes, and so on—are at the top."

"Thanks for letting me know...and for the hours of peaceful sleep I'm sure I'll be getting now. But why are you telling me all of this? *You're* the expert here when it comes to demons and black magic. Not me."

"I just want you to understand what I'm talking about when I say that someone was trying to summon a bottom-legion soldier demon here."

Alex ran his palm through the air beneath the dead bodies. No tingling again. Just as expected. Then, he jumped off the bed and stepped over to Gribovsky. Standing next to the officer, he cracked his neck and shook his wrists.

So long.

It had been forever since the last time he'd done that.

"But you said it's all fake," the lieutenant frowned. "The summoning failed?"

Alex retrieved a pack of cigarettes, tapped the bottom to knock a cancer stick out, and caught it deftly out of the air with his lips. Lighting it with his finger, he inhaled deeply, drawing the air in forcefully while the fire was still burning. That way, he could smoke the whole cigarette up to its filter in a single breath.

It was a cheap trick he'd once used to win ten cents in a bet.

"If it had failed, you wouldn't have brought me here." Cupping his hand, Alex shook the still-hot ashes into it. He spat into his hand and started to mix them in with his saliva. "The demon *was* summoned. After that, the summoner left a message."

"A message? For who?"

Alex shrugged again.

"You're the detective here. I have no idea—*you* find out. I'm just going to show you what really happened. Hold out your hand."

"Why? So you can get it all dirty with your spit?"

"These ashes are from a plant grown in our reality. It absorbed the sun—that's fire. It was nourished by the rain—that's water. It dug its roots into the soil—earth. It breathed—wind. And since it lived, that's—"

"Life," Gribovsky cut in. "All five of the magic elements."

"Yes," Alex nodded. "Plants are some of the most easily available ingredients with a connection to all the elements at once. Sure, it would've been better to use a virgin's blood, but—"

"Where would you even find a virgin these days?" Gribovsky snorted, allowing his alter ego to slip out for a second.

"And the saliva is just used to smear the ashes better."

Gribovsky stood still for a moment, then stretched out his palm.

"I'll shoot you if it stinks."

Alex dipped his finger into the mixture and started to draw magic symbols.

"This is ancient magic, Gribovsky." Alex was very careful to draw the sigils precisely. Making even a minor error as he was creating the channels that conducted the magic might have resulted in the redhead ending up dead. And Alex had a feeling he wouldn't survive much longer after that, so he was doing his utmost to keep the officer alive. "Far more ancient than you can even imagine. It existed before the First Races came to be. Before the First Light started its struggle against the Dark, giving birth to the Nameless Mist and the Gate."

"Are you quoting Lovecraft?"

"Lovecraft. Mysteries of the Worm. The Key of Solomon," Alex listed as he completed the protective seal. "Those books, along with many others, describe the same thing, just in different ways. Okay, now stand there and, no matter what happens, stay still. And be quiet. Don't listen to anything. Try not to even *think* if you're able to. Actually, that shouldn't be a problem for you."

"I *will* shoot you." Despite his threat, Gribovsky stood in the bedroom corner, his large frame stiller than a Rodin statue.

Alex was right next to him. Bringing his heels and toes together, he held his left arm down at his side and lifted his right arm up straight ahead and a bit above his shoulder.

"Are you a Nazi?"

"From the heart to the sun. Using the Light, I'm going to breach the illusion left here to deceive us and show you the truth."

"Fancy," Gribovsky snorted. "But you're a *dark* wizard. How are you going to use the Light?"

"That's just a figure of speech," Alex explained. He put his right hand to his shoulder before suddenly jerking it back to its original position.

The bedroom and everything in it, even the air, was enveloped in a black, darkly shimmering fire. The whole space burned with a flame darker than a moonless night.

Chapter 17

The cops that hadn't yet left the ninth floor recoiled from the tongues of black fire slithering out from beneath the door.

"What the hell?" The closest one, dropping his cigarette in surprise and fright, shrunk away. A message appeared in front of his eyes.

[Object: ERROR. ERROR. That object should not exist. It is impossible.]

"What the fuck do you mean? It's *right there!*"

The guy definitely had no idea what was going on inside the apartment where, biting his lower lip from the strain, Alex was controlling the Black Fire of Truth. It was a magic so ancient and dangerous that any knowledge of it should've been consigned to the dustbin of history long before. Unfortunately (or fortunately?), the world still had a few people skilled at using it.

One of those was the Old Man, *may his rotten entrails be ripped out by demons.*

The magic was fighting like a crazed mustang, desperate to break free from Doom's control. Nothing but his willpower and mental fortitude kept the black fire from consuming every single thing within a five-block radius, stopping only at the running water of the High Garden waste channel.

Out of the corner of his eye, Alex saw Gribovsky's pale face. There was no doubt he enjoyed the sight, not to mention the stoic officer's trembling hand. It featured a violet protective seal made of saliva and ashes.

Closing his eyes, Alex started to immerse himself in his magic. He wasn't going to be able to hold it in check any longer than twenty seconds, so the spell had to be dismissed before that. He could only hope that would prove long enough to reveal the secrets the room held.

Doom could feel the fire resisting him as he mentally pushed deeper and deeper into it. The fire-life element perverted by the darkness had no desire to be approached even by a practitioner of the dark arts—it was an element capable of nothing but destruction and consuming all things. The truth was alien to it.

But extremes can meet and even produce excellent results.

"Show me," Alex said imperiously and coldly, with unwavering confidence. "Show me what happened here."

Had he allowed himself even a shred of weakness, a grain of hesitation, he'd have been instantly consumed by one of the darkest spells in existence.

Alex opened his eyes. The fire gradually ordered itself, converging from all corners of the apartment into the middle of the room until it was so dense it looked more like stone.

And from that stone, a silhouette appeared. Almost shapeless, it stood over a barely discernible seal. The seal wasn't painted in blood on the bed; it hung in the air.

Not far from it, trembling in fear by the window, were two more figures.

"Not enough," Alex whispered. Exerting all the willpower he could muster, he condensed the fire still further.

Blood spurted from his eyes, nostrils, mouth, and ears, running down his face to mix with the bitter, pungent sweat already there. But Alex had achieved his goal: for a few moments, the fire was so dense that he could even see the lips of the tall figure moving as they uttered several words.

Then everything vanished.

Alex and Gribovsky were standing in the middle of a burned-out apartment, the destruction having reached all the way to the outer walls. The window glazing had burst. The radiators had warped, almost melted by the heat. Ashes drifted in the breeze.

Doom stumbled, the lieutenant grabbing him to keep him from falling.

Realizing that he'd just been helped by a public servant, Doom shrank back, almost hitting the wall...or what was once a wall. Now it was just some brickwork demarcating the boundaries of the empty stone shell of an apartment. Everything that had once been inside the shell had been devoured by the fire.

Doom staggered toward the window and the chilled wind that was blowing in, retrieving a cigarette with a shaking hand.

He was cold.

Not because of the wind, but because, after exhausting his mana reserves, he'd been fueling his magic with his own life energy. From an apparently unimportant but rather vital source.

His body heat.

"What was that?" Gribovsky asked after a moment's pause.

He wandered around the ashes, examining what had so recently been a decent-looking apartment with disbelieving eyes. It looked like it had burned down several years before.

"Black magic," Doom answered. "Not dark, but *black*, like the void itself. Though you wouldn't feel the difference."

"That fire...I've heard about it. Is it true that it keeps burning until it completely destroys its target?"

"That's an understatement."

"How so?"

"Have you heard about Pompeii? As far as I can remember, they summoned the fire just to burn an unfaithful wife...after finding out who her lover was. You probably know what ended up happening."

"Pompeii," Gribovsky repeated. His face showed the urge to kick something, but the floor, burned down to its cement base, gave him nothing to vent his anger on. There wasn't even a single bit of burnt flooring left.

He settled for just cursing.

In fact, his language was so foul that Alex grimaced in respect mixed with revulsion.

"His face." Gribovsky stopped abruptly. "His face was..."

"Masked," Doom confirmed.

Gribovsky shuffled over to the window to stand by Doom's side. Together, they looked out across the street. The windows in the apartment blocks still had lights on inside. People were gathering for family dinner or watching TV, surfing the internet, or whatever else dulled the existential pain in their lives.

Occasionally, people strolled by on the sidewalk below. However safe and affluent the neighborhood was, three cop cars sitting in the street were, just like in the rest of High Garden, a sure sign of something going down around the corner.

Not the worst possible thing, though.

If it had been really bad, there would have been special forces vehicles parked nearby.

"Damn you. Why do you have to make smoking look so good, pumpkin? I just gave it up a month ago."

Alex's guess had been right on the money.

Just to rub salt in the wound, Doom inhaled deeply and blew out a fine ring of smoke.

"You scumbag," Gribovsky said.

"I even have an official document to confirm it." Alex shrugged. "No, wait, dark wizards don't get IDs. We're not supposed to exist, although we definitely do."

"Oh, feeling a touch discriminated against, are you?"

"Yeah. You know, where's my justice? All of that."

"Poor baby. Want me to get you a bottle of milk?"

Doom turned to Gribovsky, eyes flashing behind his glasses.

"I would break your nose, but I feel too crummy to bother." Alex sighed with regret and kept smoking.

They stood silently for a while.

"He said something, didn't he?" Gribovsky looked thoughtful. The wind was ruffling his red hair, making it look like there was an actual fire raging atop the officer's head. "Hell, if only I could've read his—"

"Forbear to judge."

Gribovsky turned toward Doom abruptly.

"Can *you* read lips, pumpkin?"

"It's a useful skill in jail," Doom replied calmly. "The guards talk to each other while they're carrying food around, and you can pick up the latest news and other useful stuff."

Gribovsky nodded and resumed his contemplation of the calm street, unaware as it was of what was happening on that block.

It must be nice to just be an ordinary person living a simple, normal life. Doom was determined to try that lifestyle out when he reached old age. But not before.

Although…they did say that no dark wizard had ever died of old age.

So poetic.

"Was that a spell or…"

"It was Shakespeare," Alex explained. "Henry VI, Part II. *Forbear to judge, for we are sinners all.*"

Alex blew another ring of smoke, put the cigarette out on the bit of windowsill that remained, and tossed the butt down onto the street. Its graceful arc ended inside the collar of a cop trudging toward the bus.

At first, nothing happened. Then the cop started squealing like a little girl as he tried to get the smoking cigarette butt out of his shirt.

Hilarious.

"Did you read a lot of Shakespeare in jail?" Gribovsky asked as he smirked coldly.

Alex didn't reply.

"Whatever," the redhead said with a dismissive wave. "A villain who loves old English poetry—so cliché. So, our culprit didn't give away any details of his plan to take over the world?"

"Sadly, no." Doom shrugged sadly. He was gradually recovering, no longer trembling, and reality had stopped dancing a drunken jig in front of him. As for magic, he was going to have to forget doing any of it except for his thumb lighter for the next few days. "With the creature he summoned, he'd barely be able to take over even a couple blocks in High Garden, let alone the world. But that's fine. No judgment here. Being supportive of other evil overlords is rule one from *Dark Wizards for Dummies.*"

"Very funny, pumpkin. How do *you* know what he summoned? I didn't see anything."

"Of course you didn't. The mirrors had all burned up already."

That time, it was Gribovsky's turn to have his eyes flash menacingly.

"You didn't break my nose because you felt sick, but I'm a healthy young man in his prime. You'd better behave."

Alex said nothing.

"Hey, pumpkin, I get that you don't like me. I'm not a big fan of yours, either. But the sooner we finish this, the sooner we'll get rid of each other, so fire away."

Doom clicked his tongue and spat out the window. To his regret, he didn't hit any of the cops. He would have loved that.

"The seal he used," Alex finally said. "It was designed to summon a weak soldier demon from a bottom legion."

"How weak, exactly?"

Doom thought it over for a moment. Things like that were tricky to explain to people without the right background.

"Strong enough to defeat three or four average combat wizards at the level of a Practitioner."

"So…is that where you'd place yourself?" Gribovsky asked, squinting.

Again, Alex said nothing. He was allergic to stupid questions and, for the sake of his own sanity, avoided answering them whenever possible.

"Okay then." The officer slapped the windowsill and turned toward the door. "Let's go."

Before he could take a single step, a scream of pain rang out from below. A piece of brick, first loosened by the fire and then dislodged by Gribovsky's slap, had broken off and fallen on the head of a helpful cop who'd come to the aid of the officer struggling with the cigar butt in his shirt.

Surreal.

"We're going home now, I hope?" Putting his hands in the pockets of his expensive pants, Alex followed the lieutenant.

"You could say that," Gribovsky replied evasively. "Headquarters is definitely home sweet home for some people."

"Headquarters? What do you mean, headquarters? I have my first lecture tomorrow, and I haven't even started working on it!"

Chapter 18

They reached the port rather quickly thanks to Gribovsky's unique style behind the wheel. On the way from High Garden in the south of the city to the docks on the western bay, they ran thirteen red lights, almost slammed into other vehicles four times, and nearly knocked down several scores of pedestrians.

After the first dozen, Alex stopped counting the poor Myers City residents screaming and jumping out of the way of the car. There were just too many of them.

But the sight of a giant ogre nearly ten feet tall wearing name brand sweat pants jumping back onto the sidewalk and shouting something at them as they sped away... He'd never seen anything like that in High Garden.

"What... the... hell." Puffing and groaning, Gribovsky barely got himself out of the car. In the process, he kept dragging his cowboy boots across the expensive leather upholstery. Doom was disgusted—he knew the value of the finer things in life.

"Where *are* we?" Retrieving another cigarette, Alex lit it. How many had he smoked that evening? Just like with the pedestrians, he'd long since stopped counting.

"At the port," the redhead replied briefly.

Adjusting his glasses, Doom flashed the lieutenant his tattoo, a testimony to just how much he disliked fairies. Truth be told, the animosity was often mutual.

The Myers City port probably looked like every other big city port. Rows of berths with round platforms and loading cranes towering above them. Endless piles of containers bearing the logos of a dozen different companies. A few office buildings covered in corrugated aluminum sheets.

But despite what the books of old might have said, the port didn't smell like fish, oil, or diesel. No, in this age of magic engines and crystal energy storage, the place smelled like *money*.

"You said we were going to headquarters." Alex squinted and made a subtle gesture.

[Mana reserve: 178 points. Recovery rate: 15points/30min.]

Not enough mana for a serious fight. But…

Alex stole a quick glance at the black ring on his finger.

"Calm down, pumpkin." Gribovsky clapped Alex on the shoulder. Leaving the car in the parking lot at the port entrance, he walked boldly toward the fifth berth. "Gangsters aren't the only ones who hide their warehouses."

Trudging after him and gazing up at the bright, star-studded sky, Alex didn't get what he meant at first.

Then he almost did something very stupid.

Only the wisdom he'd picked up in prison kept him from inflicting a rather vile dark magic curse on the officer.

"Of course, we knew about your small rainy-day reserve," Gribovsky continued. That was when Alex spotted the officer's hand on his gun. "Depriving a dark wizard of all his wealth… We needed a temporary ally, pumpkin. Not a nutjob villain just quoting Shakespeare."

Doom cursed.

It had been stupid to assume that an organization like the one that employed Gribovsky and others like him would miss the secret warehouse frequented by High Garden's gangsters.

That meant that he, however ugly and insulting it may have sounded, had been *permitted* to keep a relatively small amount of money, his bike, and…

Alex rolled the black ring around his finger again.

"That's a funny little thingy you're wearing," Gribovsky said, stopping at a glass vending machine full of snacks. After moving his fingers in front of the scanner, he waited a while before kicking the old machine forcefully with the tip of his boot. The dispenser yielded several packs of Skittles. "Bingo! Three for the price of one. I love this place."

He immediately used his teeth to open a red pack. Tossing several pieces of candy into his mouth, he closed his eyes and mumbled something unintelligible in apparent bliss.

"Our nerds tried to scan it, but none of their equipment worked. And our black magic researchers couldn't figure out a single symbol on it.

Maybe you can tell me what it is?"

"Ask your impotent techies," Doom said through gritted teeth, hiding his right hand in his pocket.

"Impotent? I think some of them have kids, but yeah, they're definitely jackasses. Any time I ruin something, they make sure I get fined on the spot. But your ring... We *can* see that it's some kind of mana storage. But it's really unusual."

Alex cursed again. Nothing was sacr—...nothing was *damned* to those people. They might as well have rummaged through his dirty laundry.

"You brought me here to discuss my ring? Or are we actually visiting some headquarters or other?"

"Not *some* headquarters. *The* headquarters!" Gribovsky corrected him with the air of a religious fanatic who'd just been told there wasn't a god. Actually, there was a god. Many gods, in fact. Or one god with many faces, a topic of ongoing debate among magic theologians. "And as for your ring... No, I'm not *that* kind of guy."

"How homophobic of you. Are we going somewhere, or can I finally head home?"

"We're already here." Tossing another candy into his mouth, Gribovsky held his military watch up to the scanner on the food dispenser.

At first, nothing happened. Then a small door opened, revealing a rather spacious elevator cabin instead of the machine's innards.

Given that the vending machine was right next to a shipping container, it was a safe bet that the container was fake as well.

"After you, pumpkin." Flashing him a silly grin, Gribovsky leaned his back against the door and waved his hand toward the cabin. He'd put his fool's mask back on again and was apparently not planning on removing it for a while. "Move your ass. I'd rather get some sleep at home today and not get stuck at the office."

Doom adjusted his glasses again before stepping onto the elevator.

It wasn't any different from the kind of elevator you'd find in a present-day office building. Double doors on both sides. A long, vertical sensor panel in place of the more common buttons. A TV set and a gilded logo on the floor.

Stepping onto the logo with both feet, Doom leaned against the other door so he could see what Gribovsky entered into the panel. Unfortunately, the latter just waved his watch in front of it.

The door closed. The elevator seemed to reach escape velocity right away.

"Aren't you afraid of earth dragons?" Alex asked. "Fucking men in black. You could've made your headquarters inside *a dam*, and no one would've ever suspected it was there."

"We could have. But this place has the same protective spells they use for subway stations."

"Oh, yes?"

"Yup."

Alex smirked. He knew a lot about history, New Earth and Old Earth alike. They said each metro station in the human world had to be enchanted by a whole squad of wizards to conceal it from mortals, and there were still leaks.

Right then, the age of magic blossoming once more, the leaks were becoming more frequent. More members of the magic races, not to mention more magic creatures, were being born every ten years, and the topic of overpopulation was starting to regain steam.

Alex glanced down at the logo once again.

He shifted his gaze to Gribovsky, then back to the logo.

It was a golden shield covered in ivy, with three red flowers set above it. But that wasn't the most remarkable feature. The shield bore the ancient symbol of wisdom and magic, one the ancient Egyptians had called

Wadjet—the Eye of Horus. His left eye, to be precise, and the symbol of the moon.

Doom had seen it before.

On T-shirts, mugs, baseball caps, and lots of other merchandise. In comic books and movies. Everyone, bloody hell, *every single person* that had ever had the most passing interest in pop culture or conspiracy theories couldn't help seeing it.

But Doom didn't think it was there as a joke.

No.

It was impossible.

With a ding, the elevator stopped, and the door behind Doom slid open.

If it hadn't been for Gribovsky catching his partner by the tie, he would've fallen backward, right into the headquarters of a mythical—but apparently real—organization with a very simple name.

The Guards.

Chapter 19

From a small dais that actually did resemble the one from *Men in Black*, Alex looked out over the expansive open-plan office filled with identical workstations and expensive iMacs. The chromed steel tables, with drawers on the left-hand side, were attached (Alex wondered why) to a floor so polished you could see the same symbol of the shield with the eye on the ceiling reflected in it.

There were dozens of people, all talking on their phones and running around with tablets or stacks of papers. The workday was in full swing.

It was 3 o'clock in the morning.

At the opposite end of the vast space was a wide monitor (Alex had already encountered one suit) showing a map of the world with points occasionally flashing on it. Most were green, but two were blue.

"Oh, two blue incidents." Gribovsky tossed another Skittle into his mouth. "Someone's doing unregistered magic above the Adept level."

Doom nearly choked on nothing but air.

Above the Adept level?

That meant they were at least at the Master level, level 60+ wizards. Sure, Alex had heard of wizards like that. They often featured in fairytales and travel booklets about Myers City, with ten Masters residing in the capital at that time, at least if Alex's memory served.

And now Gribovsky was telling him that there were *two* of those…monsters, one in the middle of Siberia, and another in the Amazonian jungle, both conducting their experiments right then.

"Shit. Ernie and his rapid response teams get all the fun." Gribovsky stashed the Skittles in the inside pocket of his trench coat and started down the stairs.

Doom followed him silently and zombie-like. He still found it hard to believe he was working for *the Guards* and not some secret government agency.

Although, when he thought about it, legend had it that the Guards protected the first king of Atlantis, the capital destroyed in the distant past.

After Atlantis fell and the world started to lose its magic, the Guards became a global organization tasked with concealing the magic world from the eyes of mortals. Border security, basically. It was their job to make sure mortals never knew that particular terrorist acts, earthquakes, and other disasters had *absolutely* been caused by something other than what the media told them.

That explained Gribovsky's dragon remark.

They were still law enforcement officers, at the end of the day. Just a somewhat different sort.

"So, you..."

"We were repurposed," Gribovsky replied, shaking someone's hand as they walked by and asking how their kids were. "Now we don't just protect mortals from the magic world, as well as the other way around sometimes; we also safeguard the magic world from itself."

"From itself?"

"Yep."

That time, Gribovsky didn't shake a hand, instead giving a young girl wearing a formal business suit a quick spank. She responded by slapping him and accusing him of never calling her back. Then, with a wave of her thick hair, she clacked away across the office on her high heels.

"I had to leave for a mission!" Gribovsky yelled after her. Then, more quietly, he added, "Though whatever, she isn't that great in bed. Not nearly as good as Linda from the spirit settlement department. She's just...mm."

Leaving the vast open space behind, the partners reached another door with a sensor panel reading *Level B* in fluorescent letters.

Alex assumed that only people with special clearance were allowed inside. And Gribovsky was apparently one of them: he waved his watch in front of the panel and held open the door, ushering Doom into a long, branching corridor.

Daylight lamps flickered. The wall on his right had five elevator doors, and Gribovsky walked over to the farthest.

"Down there," he said, pointing past the many doors in the corridor to the other side, "is the archive. You'll get access to it if you behave. There are plenty of books in there about why magic started to disappear."

"Because of the civil war in Atlantis? The war where the wizards nearly destroyed each other and the whole planet?"

"There's a reason behind every war, pumpkin."

"Yeah. Power, money, and women."

"That may be true for mortal wars." Gribovsky stepped onto the elevator first. It was much simpler than the central one, though it still conveyed a sense of the considerable technical prowess and financial resources the Guards had at their disposal. And Doom was genuinely surprised when the elevator started to move not vertically, but *horizontally*. "But magic wars are fought for different reasons. You should read more about them yourself when you have time—our accounts are far more detailed than the ones at the Museum of Natural History."

Alex said nothing. Gribovsky turned toward him slowly, opening his mouth slightly in surprise.

"Have you never been to the Museum of Natural History?"

"Nope."

"Get out! Are you kidding me? Everyone goes on a tour there every year, from their first year in elementary school all the way to their last year of university! Oh, right. You're an ignoramus."

Doom once again chose to hold his tongue. The very fact that he'd been called an ignoramus by a man who'd apparently only heard Shakespeare's name for the third time in his life just that day was already hilarious enough.

The person Alex had been four years before would've certainly tried to force-feed Gribovsky his own teeth, but his time in prison had taught him two things: keep a cool head and disregard the whims of the impetuous organ below his waist.

"Here we are." The elevator stopped, and the doors opened, dumping Doom into another corridor. Unlike the last one, it was dimly lit and as big as a hangar.

The first thing that caught Alex's eye wasn't even its size. No, it was the walls, which were made from enchanted, magic-proof glass instead of stone.

Stepping out of the elevator, Doom peered through the glass and froze.

"Welcome to Department 6, which is all about—"

"Demons!"

"Yes. Demons."

Alex could see many of the vile creatures, most of which he'd only encountered previously in the Old Man's (*may his thighs rot after being shoved up his own ass*) grimoires.

They weren't all demons from the bottom legions, almost indistinguishable from Earth's animals. Of course, that "almost" meant that the panther had horns, while its tail and upper body were half-covered in bony plates. The gorilla was clad in frightening armor and had a spark of intelligence in its yellow eyes. The crocodile had *eight* legs and a pair of creepy leather wings.

In addition to those low-ranking soldiers, there were two senior demons as well. They were fairly humanoid, only so disgusting that Alex couldn't look at them without shuddering despite all the shit he'd seen in his life.

"You're fucking kiddi—"

"Not at all, pumpkin." Gribovsky held up his hands to placate his partner. "I got transferred here a month ago, right after I gave up smoking, actually. And I still don't know much about all that demonic stuff. Your lecture came in really handy—you should give your students the same one tomorrow!"

The redhead gave him a thumbs-up and, flashing a Hollywood smile, winked.

"Come on, Alex. Chon Sook, the old scrooge, is tired of waiting for us."

"The Asian?"

"The Asian?" Gribovsky asked, thought it over for a moment, and nodded. "Good nickname. I like it. I'll call him that until he gets me a new car from the warehouse. You've seen the monstrosity I drive now—what a piece of crap! The only thing it's good for is doing the weekly grocery shopping at the mall."

Alex clapped his forehead.

He was starting to understand why Gribovsky had been transferred from…whatever department he'd been part of before. And it was probably the same reason why Doom was no longer terrified by the prospect of being devoured by one of the demons on the other side of the glass.

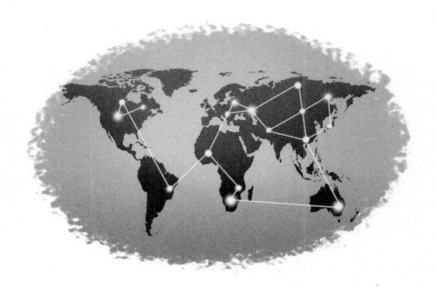

Chapter 20

A lex stood facing a wide picture window that covered the whole wall from floor to ceiling. He struggled to fathom what kind of magic was letting him see Myers City at night so easily as it shimmered in a light drizzle.

They were deep underground, but there it was—a magic window. With a view of the city. And it wasn't digital at all; it was pure magic.

Just an everyday, totally normal window.

A couple miles below ground.

Showing a bird's-eye view of the city.

"Please sit down, Mr. Dumsky." Major Chon Sook, the very same Asian man who'd picked him up outside the prison, pointed at the chairs set up around a T-shaped table.

The major's office looked rather...impressive. The bookcases didn't just feature a variety of manuscripts and grimoires; there were also statuettes from different nations and ages. Hanging on the walls, there were masks from African, South American, Australian, and Oceanic tribes. A few weapons used by those same tribes kept them company.

The solid oak table occupied most of the space in the office, which wasn't particularly large. The major's armchair looked especially comfortable, as did the chairs there for visitors.

A smaller copy of the monitor back in the office above them hung behind Chon Sook, while the indispensable steel vault with magical protection was to his right.

His table only had a display, a keyboard, a mouse, and a couple paper files on it.

The major was dressed that time in a very expensive three-piece suit that was a sort of...a salad-green color. But however gaudy it might have been, the color somehow suited him.

"So." The major steepled his fingers and stared at Gribovsky with sharp, piercing eyes, forcing him to abandon his clownish persona immediately. "What do you think?"

"Just like the police said," the red-haired man replied in a cold, emotionless voice. He even straightened up and somehow looked a bit older. "A double homicide intended to hide the traces of magic from the Demonology School. A summoning spell."

"What level summoning?"

"According to Alexander Dumsky, my consultant, the spell summoned a soldier demon of a bottom legion. I beg your pardon, Major, for not yet memorizing all of Department 6's classification."

"You'll take the test tomorrow. And you'll get 10% docked from your salary if you get even one question wrong."

"Sir. Yes, Sir."

Alex wasn't surprised that Gribovsky made no attempt to argue with the Asian. Despite his rather diminutive height, his lean stature, and the fact that Alex's fingertips weren't tingling (which meant that Chon Sook wasn't a particularly powerful wizard), the major emanated force.

It was a sort of unyielding force from deep within.

Then the major turned to Doom, bringing that force down on him like an avalanche. Alex immediately realized that Chon Sook didn't actually need Duncan to make Alex toe any line he wanted him to.

"What do *you* think, Mr. Dumsky?"

Alex looked at Gribovsky, then back at Chon Sook.

"The summoning was done three days ago," he replied. "It was a success. The bodies were hidden by a shroud of magic to keep them from being discovered earlier, and the man who did it—"

"Human? Are you sure?" the major interrupted, lifting a hand.

"Yes," Alex nodded. "The magic he used is exclusive to human demonology."

"That's good," Chon Sook replied with a nod of relief. The most suspicious thing was that he actually looked very happy to hear it, almost as though he'd been relieved of a heavy burden. "What can you tell me about the summoner?"

"He's experienced," Doom replied instantly. "Very experienced. Not someone who's just read a thing or two. Not self-taught, either. Well-trained. *Really* well-trained. His teacher might have even been as good as—"

Alex stopped.

"As good as *yours*," the major finished. "But that's hardly possible."

"I think so, too. Or rather, I *thought* so. Until tonight."

"Your teacher is dead, Mr. Dumsky. As are all his students, you being the sole exception."

All around Doom, shadows rose up. They crept over the oaken table like greedy, hungry jackals, leaving rot and decay in their wake. It was as if the table was aging thousands of years with each passing second, gradually vanishing into the dust of ages past.

The air grew heavy and acrid.

The light was dying away.

Suddenly, the sound of a gun cocking brought Alex back to his senses.

The glittering muzzle of the enchanted pistol did more to pull him back than any bucket of ice water would have.

Doom reigned in his powers.

The shadows vanished, the light brightened once again, and the air was fresh and even pleasant.

Slowly, Gribovsky holstered his gun.

"Have you heard of anyone else practicing demonology?" the major asked as if nothing had happened.

"No," Alex snapped. "After that incident…which, I see, you are well aware of…all my fri—… I became the only demonologist in the city. All the rest are either frauds who've read too much pulp shit or talentless beginners who wouldn't survive their first summoning rite. Given the number of demons you've caged, there must be a lot of them."

"Knowledge is spreading faster than we'd like it to." Chon Sook stood up, walked over to the window, and clasped his hands behind his back. He was just a small man against the backdrop of the endless city, but he still conveyed a sense of indomitable willpower and force of character. "Anything else?"

Doom sighed and massaged the bridge of his nose.

He would've preferred to keep some aces up his sleeve, only…he didn't want to share the fate of the creatures who had watched him with hungry eyes as he walked over to the major.

He'd been caged once. And he was prepared to do quite a bit to make sure that didn't happen again.

"He's an Adept."

"Are you sure?"

"Absolutely."

"How?"

"Because he knew I'd be using the Black Fire of Truth. And not only did he know that, he made sure to conceal himself from the spell. *And* he set a trap. If I hadn't spotted it, what remained of Gribovsky and me would've been brought here inside a vacuum cleaner."

"Hey, pumpkin, why am I hearing about this for the first time just n—"

"Agent Gribovsky," the major said calmly, and the lieutenant stopped talking at once and just squinted at Alex. The latter ignored him.

The two were on opposite sides of the barricades. Doom didn't have to inform the officer of every little thing going on right under his nose.

"In just a few hours, Mr. Dumsky, you've given me more information than our analysts have been able to in three months."

"Three months? Has that masked guy been roaming the city for *three months*?"

"Masked?" Chon Sook stopped contemplating the view and stared at Alex. "He was wearing a mask?"

"Yeah," Doom replied with a shrug.

"Why didn't you mention that right away?"

"Because, unlike everyone else here, I'm still not used to sitting in the headquarters of a non-existent organization, discussing a problem that, according to everything there is to read in Atlantis, also doesn't exist."

Chon Sook just nodded. Then he went over to the vault, opened it with an ordinary-looking steel key, retrieved two very thick paper files, and slid them across the table to Alex.

"What are they?" Doom asked.

"The first is our set of statutes. The second is all the information we have on the Mask's case."

"The Mask, sir?" Gribovsky looked depressed. "We already nicknamed him! He's the Elusive Demonologist."

"If I hear that name again, you'll get a *jeep* as your new car."

"Okay, okay, I'll shut up."

"You may go, Mr. Dumsky. Agent Gribovsky will drive you back to your apartment. Until you're called on again…try to keep your job."

"And what happens if I get fired?"

"Then you'll be flying business class to one of two destinations: the island or…"

The major didn't finish his sentence. He didn't need to.

Taking both files, Alex stood and, without saying goodbye, left the office.

Wizard levels:
1. Apprentice (0-250)
2. Practitioner (250-1000)
3. Mystic (1000-3000)
4. Adept (3000-6000)
5. Master (6000-13000)
6. Grandmaster (???)
7. Archmaster (???)
8. Archmage (???)

Chapter 21

T he first day of school at First Magic University began the same way it did every other year. At the central gate, a crowd of freshmen gathered to pretend they were really entering the holy of holies in New Earth's magic education system for the first time.

They were accompanied by proud parents.

Proud-looking parents, at least.

Some of them had actually raised a child who'd secured a scholarship at an institution where the cheapest major cost 50,000 credits per semester. Few families could afford that much. After all, you had to multiply that by eight to calculate the total cost of an undergraduate degree.

Then there was a master's degree, four times as expensive as a bachelor's. The doctoral was...well, only those with grants and scholarships were accepted. Not even the city mayor's children could take doctoral courses just by paying the tuition.

And that was even though the mayor of Myers City was a sort of king for all of Atlantis, which was a sovereign state...or maybe it wasn't. That was an affair too complicated for any Sphynx to ever tell heads or tails of it. Although one Sphynx did actually try.

So, the happy parents celebrating with their children represented a variety of backgrounds, from happy middle-class professionals and small-time entrepreneurs to the heads of aristocratic clans.

Yes, Atlantis still had an archaic institution like the aristocracy. It was just modernized, with boatloads of money and power concentrated in their hands.

Each clan had a skyscraper of its own, and they vied with each other to see who could make theirs the tallest and most luxurious. Currently leading the charge was the Liebeflamm clan, fire wizards rumored to be descended from the Ifrits, or Arabic fire spirits (if spirits can have a nationality, of course).

Luckily, the pompous ceremony, complete with speeches delivered by the rector, the prorector, the deans, the best students, the alumni, and the benefactor money bags didn't last long.

Shortly afterward, the uniformed crowds of students (both males and females) rushed through the gate and onto the campus. Most of them flocked into the central building where, after checking the schedules handed out by their course leaders, they hurried off for their first lectures.

The B-52 lecture hall was packed to capacity just fifteen minutes later. The twenty-three tiered rows buzzed with anticipation like a panicking anthill.

"Have you heard?" a voice came from a bunch of girls wearing make-up too ostentatious to stay unnoticed. "The professor's only twenty-one!"

"That's impossible," a guy one row higher shot back. "It takes dozens of years of practice to become a professor in any area of magic, not to mention lots of research articles published in peer-reviewed journals and a good impact factor."

"How do *you* know?"

"My grandpa is a professor."

"Fuck your grandpa then, kid."

The girls laughed. The young boy flushed, hunching up to hide his head like a tortoise in its shell. While he was apparently one of those lucky enough to be born with a head on their shoulders, the girls mocking him were just lucky to be born. At least, if they had brains, they weren't in any hurry to show them off.

Everyone was excited about their introduction to legendary black magic. The thrill had as much to do with the fact that it was prohibited as it did the mysteries that enshrouded it.

There was just one group of three guys and two girls huddled up in the farthest corner of the hall that wasn't inspired in the least. In fact, they were withdrawn and looking kind of even doomed.

Like a man going on a date despite being diagnosed with incurable impotence earlier that morning.

Yes, it was that kind of doom, one worse than what a prisoner sentenced to death feels on their way to the place of execution.

The prisoner knows that their pain is about to be over.

But for those five, the real pain was about to start.

"They have no idea *what* they're waiting for," the red-haired guy named Travis sighed.

"Who's waiting?" A young man with A-list celebrity good looks took his eyes off his reflection in a small mirror. "I'm totally booked for today. Two fittings, four photo shoots. Sorry, guys, I can't just—"

"Shut up, Leo," Travis, Elie (the blonde), and Mara (the small pretty girl) barked in unison.

Jing, the Asian, stayed impassive, peering off somewhere into the distance. Not into the lecture hall, but into himself.

"What exactly did he tell you, bestie?" Elie whispered…or rather hissed. Beautiful as she was, she was far from Leo's level. "That he wasn't listening to you?"

"I think he just wanted me to think so," the gray-haired girl smiled naively. "Maybe he's not that bad, after all."

"*Not that bad?*" Travis flared up instantly. "I asked my brother to dig up some info on Alexander Dumsky, and you know what?"

"You told us already," Elie replied, rolling her eyes. "A good twenty times. But whatever, go ahead. For the twenty-first time."

"I'll say it a twenty-second time if that's what it takes to get it through your thick skull. No. One. Has. Ever. Heard. Anything about an Alexander Dumsky in any of the Old Earth countries. Eastern or western Europe, the Americas, Asia, the Gulf, none of them. No. One. Ever. Anything! *And* when he tried to find out more about the so-called 'professor' here in Myers City, he was told to let it drop. And he's a Central Office detective!"

"All the personal info you could need about our supervisor," Elie said, stressing the last word, "is available for everyone to check out on the site. You can read his work, check out his articles, look through pictures from conferences. Do you really think he could have faked all that by himself?"

"I don't know, Elie. I don't know." The boy sighed. "But next month, my brother is going to a conference in China. He's going to visit a friend who lives there—I spotted him in one of the pictures you say are such good evidence. We'll expose the bastard and—"

Whatever else Travis was going to do with the black wizard would forever remain a mystery shrouded in darkness and terror. A young man kicked the door open and stepped into the lecture hall.

Paying no heed to the students who fell suddenly silent, he took a deep pull of his cigarette, let the smoke join the cloud already around his head, and sat down at his desk, hands in pockets.

He cursed happily as he rummaged through the drawers, his cigarette tucked in his mouth. But only the first few rows heard how nasty his language was.

The lecture hall became even quieter.

The professor of black magic, a genius who'd earned this rank by the age of twenty-one, a handsome man with short haircut styled the way it was done in the 2010s, a character dressed in a very expensive suit, put his feet up on the table and, still smoking his cigarette, opened in front of him...

Not a grimoire. Not a book on dark magic. Not some other book or even a course syllabus, but a very fat porn magazine complete with a lurid cover.

The lecture hall got *very* quiet.

A small feather fell from the ceiling, easing its way through the air. Every little rustle it made echoed like raging thunder in the spring.

"Ah, right." Checking himself, Professor Alexander Dumsky carelessly opened the laptop and pressed several buttons. On the large graphitic board (so backward) behind his back, projected by a previous-century apparatus, appeared a giant magic seal.

The very sight of it left many of the students there giddy, a group that used to think of themselves as some of the best and brightest young minds in the city.

Never before had they seen such a complicated, involved, and intricate tangle of magic symbols, signs, figures, and other shapes.

"Whoever doesn't solve this by the end of the semester will fail my exam and be expelled," the professor declared in the distant voice of a person engrossed in whatever they're reading. "The clock starts now."

Travis was about to say something when his gaze was met by the bright green stare of the black wizard.

Hiccupping, he got to work copying the seal onto his tablet.

"Did he hear me?" he muttered. His whole figure seemed to shrink.

A couple of moments later, everyone in the lecture hall was sliding their styluses across their tablets.

***

Alex dove into the dossier on the Mask, using the Asian's preferred term for the guy in his head. And he wasn't reading because he had to. Not because it was his job. Just because…

Well, because he hadn't told the Guards everything he knew. He'd actually revealed just a tiny bit of what he'd learned about the demonologist in that apartment. And if even half of Alex's guesses were true, hard times were about to come crashing down on him.

They were going to be much, much harder than those four years in the wizard prison. Much harder than playing guard dog for humanity's defenders.

"Professor?" Out of the corner of his eye, Doom saw a girl timidly raise her hand.

Slamming the dossier shut, he peered at the young prodigy.

[Name: Tasha. Race: Forest Elf. Mana level: 650. Open the extended dossier?]

The extended dossier? Ah, sure. He was a professor, and the bunny girl was his student. That's why the lenses offered him more info.

Damnation. All demons of hell.

An 18-year-old elf at the sixth level? Were all the other young prodigies there going to waste his precious time, too?

"What?"

The elven girl (rather good-looking, which was why Alex responded to her) seemed to shrink as she squeaked.

"What are we supposed to do with the seal?"

Alex shifted his gaze from the elven girl, the magic Pandora still ringing on the wrist of her raised hand, to the seal, then back, then to the seal again.

He'd already memorized all the demons of hell.

What morons.

"You're supposed to distribute the energy flows so that the spell consumes a max of 1,200 points instead of 1,900. So, you're in it up to your neck. Funny, yeah, up to your neck. Start working! The sun is high, and I haven't gotten any solutions yet."

After that, Alex donned his headphones demonstratively and got back to reading the dossier. He'd had more important things to take care of the previous night.

If he was going to meet the demonologist face to…well, face to mask, he wanted to be 147% ready.

***

Once the professor put his headphones on, no one in the lecture hall dared whisper or even look up from their tablets. No one but the redhead.

"Reduce 1,900 to 1,200? Cut mana consumption by *seven levels*?! I can't even figure out the *outline*! That's impossible! And—"

Once again, Travis's words would remain shrouded in secret and mystery forever. The shroud that time, however, was made up of the excessively strong smell of perfume coming from the short, plump, and balding dean entering the hall.

B-52 was visited by Travis Lebenstein in person, rather colorful as he was. And what he saw was more than he could take in.

So, he decided to go with his usual tack, distracting the professor and asking, "What's going on here?" in a voice so thunderingly loud that it almost shattered the windows.

The way Alexander Dumsky pulled a single headphone out of his ear was enough for many of the students to grip their protective charms.

They sensed that blood was about to be shed.

Chapter 22

lex turned to see what the sound was.

Standing by *his* lecturing desk was a puny, disgusting-looking man. Although, he wouldn't have been that bad if he had merely walked around with the looks he'd gotten from Mother Nature. But no, he had to top all his flaws by interrupting *Alex's* lecture.

Hell. Doom had spent half the night searching his notes for the spell he'd been working on for the past five years.

Tired of doing it alone, he'd decided to let the hundred students rack their brains over it.

"I'm sorry, but who are *you*?" Alex asked.

He should have just kicked the creature out, but he wasn't a street gangster anymore. He wore a suit for a reason. Alex Doom was now a professor, and he needed to behave accordingly to stay in the Guards' good graces.

The last thing he wanted was to fall out of those good graces.

Anything but that.

"Who...who...who am I?!" the man squealed. "I'm the department dean! I'm Travis Lebenstein! I'm—"

"The terror that flaps in the night, I get it," Alex interrupted. "I feel like we've met before. Hm...are you a regular at the Merry Sailor? They hired me to put up a magic defense to keep the ladies out once. It's a men-only bar, and they have a reputation to uphold."

"I've never been there." Alex quickly learned that the guy's fat, balding face was capable of taking on any color of the rainbow. "What flapping terror are you talking about?!"

"Darkwing Duck, sir," Doom replied indignantly. "You don't know that?"

"What bloody duck, Dumsky?! Are you crazy?"

Alex turned to the students. They seemed to have departed from that reality, staring blankly ahead. There was no way they were going to get the joke and recognize the phrase about the terror that flaps.

Shit. Where is *this world going?*

"Now that you ask, I guess I am," Doom sighed in dismay. "The very fact that I got myself stuck in this hole makes me wonder about my sanity."

"This hole?!" The dean drew more air into his already large chest. "Hole??! How dare you...you...you..."

"If you can't think of a swear word bad enough, I'll be happy to help. Just not until I finish my lecture. Dear Mr. Dean, would you be so kind as to turn around and close the door behind you? Considering your numerous academic degrees, I think you'll be able to figure out which side you should be standing on when you're done."

The small fat man choked in the middle of a word, then took a step forward as he slipped his right hand beneath his jacket.

The bookworm, who Alex definitely knew from somewhere, was not that dumb.

But it was even better that way.

Doom needed to test his theory about his place in the institution, and he was happy to get that out of the wa—

As ill luck would have it, the glass screen of a smartphone in the first row flashed.

The dean wheeled around instantly, venting his righteous indignation on his new victim.

"You? Recording? Me?!" In a few surprisingly long strides for such a vertically challenged body, Lebenstein appeared in front of the girl recording the incident. "Stop it! Now!"

He grabbed the phone from her and was about to smash it on the floor when he froze. It wasn't that he was shocked; he'd suddenly lost the ability to move.

The audience gasped.

Running down Alex's palm was a small drop of blood. Glowing over his fingers, emitting steady red light that seemed to penetrate the depths of every soul in the room, was a magic seal.

"Blood magic, my dear students." Alex stood up, walked over to the dean, and waved slightly with his hand.

The tubby man straightened up to attention and saluted with the hand holding the phone. The first, very soft giggles came. Measuring his pace out, the dean, whose eyes were popping out of their sockets, turned around and came up to the girl. Bowing low, he returned the phone to her and started a walk back to the lecturing desk.

The whole thing was accompanied by moves of Alex's hand.

"Very tricky to use. Prohibited since 2073 to everyone but those naturally predisposed towards black magic. But you are free to study its theoretical foundations. And you *must* study the practical techniques of defense. Or…"

Doom retrieved from his pocket an old, shabby penknife with several symbols carved into its handle. He made a few more passes.

Lebenstein's face dripped with sweat, the reflection of reality in his eyes drowning slowly in a cold quagmire of sticky fear. But he kept walking, tin soldier-like, puppet-like, toward the penknife's blade.

He didn't stop until his pupil was so close to the blade that a hair's breadth seemed a relative marathon.

Alex bent over the dean and hissed softly for no one but him to hear.

"Don't ever think you can enter *my* hall and interrupt *my* lecture like that."

Doom gestured a couple more times, and Lebenstein pursued the same broken pace out lecture hall B-52. Not until then did Alex dispel his magic and, doing his best to conceal the effort, sink back into his chair.

Damn that dean. With the number of amulets he had on, it was like he was a military investigator dealing with inter-racial crime, and not just employed in academia.

The Frozen Tear amulet alone was something—it could withstand pressure of up to 140 points, and it was worth a fortune. Fortunately, Alex was skilled and knowledgeable enough to get around all that mass-market stuff.

You need bespoke charms to avoid getting your ass kicked by a real black wizard. To be fair, Alex was not about to physically touch any part of Lebenstein's body. The very idea disgusted him.

"Any questions?"

Silence. Then, suddenly, a storm of voices.

"How did you bypass his defense, Professor?"

"The spell you used, was it Warlock's Doll? My lenses didn't recognize the structure."

"Are you really not afraid of Lebenstein?"

"How old are you?"

"Do you have a girlfriend?"

"Did you neutralize the energetic load in the reversive field using—"

"No questions. That's good," Alex interrupted, opening his 'porn magazine' again. "Get to work, juvie—…mm…kiddies. The sun is high and blah, blah, blah."

The lecture hall fell dead silent (that always sounded like a pun to Alex, what with his knowledge of necromancy) again. Cutting the stillness, a thin voice called out.

"Thank you so much, Professor. It was a gift from my mom."

Doom looked over at the girl who'd almost gotten her phone destroyed by the dean. He didn't need Detective Gribovsky's prompts to tell him that she was there on a scholarship she'd earned with wits instead of wealthy parents.

Alex looked away.

He just didn't care.

Not a damn.

He had to find out how badly the Guards needed him at the university. Dealing with the Mask and paying off his debt to the Syndicate was next, followed by catching the first tailwind out of Atlantis and leaving for good.

He didn't give a damn about those youngsters and their problems.

"My pleasure," Doom replied, showing with his whole demeanor how little he cared.

The girl smiled and went back to scribbling on her tablet.

****

Alex stretched and looked around. The sun was high and shining brightly, while the lecture hall was empty…almost.

He looked at his watch, a poor match for his expensive suit and shoes. It was plain. Childish. Shaped like the head of a baby lion from the beautiful old Disney cartoon that was later remade into a movie, a franchise, a series, and even a video game.

"Two o'clock. How many lectures did I sleep through?"

"Four," called a voice from the top row. Sitting there were five students: a stern-looking Asian guy, a flirty blonde, a youngster who looked like a fashion model, and two more atypical characters—a gray-haired girl and her ginger friend.

Why are they here…?

He remembered—he was supposed to supervise them.

"Do I owe you something?"

"A tour, Professor," the blonde replied instantly.

Doom was perplexed. The last person who'd told him he owed them something had found himself excreting a very unpleasant substance from his anus. That was when the negotiations stalled and the shooting began. Anyway, that was in past.

He'd meant for the question to be rhetorical.

"What tour?"

"You don't know? The Natural Museum! All the freshmen are going there today, and we're already late for the bus."

Alex glanced out of the window. *Damn you, Gribovsky.*

Chapter 23

As Alex discovered right then, the university had at least one other gate besides the central one, and it was right across the outdoor sports complex that included a football pitch, running tracks, bleachers, and several magic ranges.

Alex had never used the latter. As a rule, he, just like all the other prohibited black wizards, tested and practiced his new spells at the city dump.

That made his magic dirty in addition to being dark.

Three yellow buses, looking almost exactly like their counterparts for school children, stood by the road. Not all the groups riding them were as small as just five people—if that had been the case, the freshmen would have been accompanied by at least twenty-five adults.

But there were just three there.

Excluding Doom.

Two middle-aged women and one elderly man.

"Are you—"

"Yeah," Alex interrupted with a brusque wave as he got onto the bus ahead of his group. Greeting the driver by lifting his hat slightly, he glanced over at the young prodigies who instantly fell silent.

The faces were all ones he'd already seen at the first lecture. At least, he seemed to remember them. That blood magic trick had drained so much of his strength that the meditation he'd started to restore it gradually turned into a sound and healthy sleep.

Stepping past the students sitting there, Alex stopped in front of a group of youngsters occupying the wide seat at the back.

"Our apologies, Professor."

"Please, Professor, sit down."

"We'll find somewhere else."

The seven students looked stunned out of the merry hubbub they'd been making a moment before. Sitting down in the corner, Alex put his feet on top of the seat in front of him, opened the window, and pulled out a cigarette.

That brought instant relief.

"Can we go now?" The disgruntled driver, who was dressed very plainly, looked as if he'd just woken up from a quick nap grabbed after a night shift at some factory. In fact, it was quite possible that that was what had happened.

"Just a moment," one of the ladies replied a bit nervously. "We're waiting for one more colleague."

Alex almost choked on his smoke and cast a reproachful glance at the five padawans taking their seats at the opposite end of the back row. They kept pretending, rather realistically, that they hadn't woken him up a long time before they'd actually needed to.

"Excuse me, sir." The old man in a tweed suit was holding a brown leather briefcase with the demeanor of someone long married to his books, his gaze shifting back and forth between Alex and the driver. "Didn't you tell us smoking is prohibited inside the bus?"

"I did," the driver replied with a nod.

"Then why is Professor... er... What's your last name, young man?"

Purple fire flashed around Doom's fingers, but he subdued it.

Old habits die hard.

The scholar couldn't be expected to know the ways of High Garden.

But, hell, old habits die so hard.

"He didn't ask," the driver snickered.

Keeping his seat, Alex lifted his arms into the air and clapped. That time, it was the driver who tipped his hat to him.

"Oh, please forgive me," a thin, melodious voice came from outside. "I beg your pardon, everyone. So much to do... I lost track of time and—"

"We would be amazed, Miss Perriot," the older woman said in a tone more appropriate for reprimanding a subordinate than talking to a colleague, "if you managed to keep even a single appointment. Your group will have to ride *this* bus. With the new black magic teacher's group."

"Oh, that's fantastic! Thank you so much for your help."

Alex couldn't see the other woman, but her voice was pleasant. Too pleasant, even. Nice and bell-like.

Judging by the clatter of high heels, Miss Perriot, if that was her name, was already climbing onto the bus when she was stopped by the old man. Alex could see dry fingers holding a thin, slightly tanned wrist. Good skin she had. Smooth, apparently young, and well-groomed.

"Miss Perriot, may I ride with you?" The old man was speaking softly, but Alex put his lip-reading skills to good use. "That dark wizard... I don't like him. Dean Lebenstein had some very negative things to say about him."

"Dean Lebenstein has negative things to say about everyone lower than him," the girl replied in a suddenly loud, even abrupt voice. That did it—Alex was sure she *was* a young girl, and not just someone else born before 2050. "It looks like they're waiting for you in *your* bus, Professor Camil."

That said, Perriot deftly (which betrayed her skill) released her wrist from his grasp and flew onto the bus, bringing with her the aroma of young spring. Like a breeze coming from a well-kept garden, it scattered the stiff smells of old leather, textile, and rubber that filled the inside of the bus.

"Good afternoon, Miss Perriot!"

"Thanks for your lecture, Miss Perriot!"

"Please sit here."

"Could I ask you for some coaching?"

"*You*, idiot? Why? You don't need Magic History for your exams."

"As if *you* need it."

"Miss Perriot!" The pretty blonde suddenly jumped up. What was her name?

[Name: Eleonora Wessex. Race: Human. Mana level: 691. Open the extended dossier?]

The worldwide web. Incredibly useful at times...

That was when Alex actually did choke on his smoke.

Somehow, a girl from the Wessex family was part of his group!

The house whose emblem was a leprecone.

In ancient times, those white whales were lucky enough to become trade mediators between the mortal world and magic races. The fortune they acquired put them on par with the elven families and human mega-corporations.

"Elie, guys, great to see you all." Smiling at everyone, Miss Perriot floated through the air to the back row.

Her hair was the color of a ripe peach, wavy and falling down a bit below her shoulders to her white leather jacket. A light blouse and a wide, ankle-long skirt made up the rest of her outfit. The plain clothes did little to hide her fit body or long, strong legs and curvy, springy hips worthy of the front cover of the magazine Alex habitually used to disguise everything he was reading.

And he read a lot.

A graceful waistline eased into high, firm breasts.

A round face. Dimples on rosy cheeks. A chiseled nose, slightly upturned. Narrow cheekbones. Bushy, but well-groomed and spreading eyebrows.

She could have been anywhere between 18 and 25.

And to Alex's great surprise, her hair wasn't dyed.

The peach color of her hair *and* eyes was *natural*.

Hell's bells. She's an esper. An esper working at the very heart of the magic world. Who *let her in here? And why?*

Of course, that fact lessened in shock value when compared to Alexander Dumsky becoming a professor.

[Name: Leia Perriot. Race: Human Esper. Rank: D.]

Her eyes met Alex's. Knocking the ashes off, he pulled his feet off the seat back in front of him just to put them on the armrest of the empty seat next to him.

The girl with the princess name sat down and held out a hand.

"Leia Perriot, Magic History and Magic Law. Nice to meet you."

Alex looked down at her outstretched hand before glancing up at her. Smiling broadly, he puffed smoke right into her face.

"Professor Dumsky! What are you doing?"

"Professor!"

"Miss Perriot!"

The bus doors closed. The clamor inside not dying down, it followed the other buses in the direction of the next district over for the traditional museum tour.

Putting on his headphones demonstratively, Doom turned his

music up.

He liked the girl.

Too much, in fact.

And that was why he needed her ready to call the cops every time he got close.

Chapter 24

A little and somewhat plump boy watched Miss Elisa meandering around the magic flowers. Smeared in earth, with black traces on her hands and cheeks, her dress was a mess, though her white hat was immaculate.

"Hand me the small rake, please." She was tired, but still smiling openly and happily.

Alex, clutching his practical magic handbook (disguised as a porn magazine) to his chest, handed her the tool she'd asked for. It was old and shabby like everything else at St. Frederick Orphanage, including its employees and wards.

Miss Elisa pottered around for a while longer, the rake moving precisely and gracefully around the sprouts like a painter's brush.

They were tulips.

But not regular tulips.

They were the kind that only blossomed in the light of the full moon to soak up its silvery glow and turn into beautiful crystals.

The crystals were then used by wizards to decorate their homes, also helping them restore mana.

"That's all for today." She wiped her forehead with a forearm. Still smiling, she stood up heavily and plodded over to a small cherry tree.

As she sat down beneath the tree and half-closed her eyes, Elisa held her face up to the cool wind. Smelling of fuel oil and kerosene, it was blowing in from the industrial quarters. Everyone in High Garden was used to the smell and the factory smog.

Her hair swayed slightly.

Alex came over to stand in front of her. Even sitting, she was taller than him.

"You walk like a baby bear," she said, patting him on the cheek. "Waddling from side to side."

"So what?" Alex grumbled, dropping his gaze to the grass.

"Nothing." Elisa laughed. "I just feel bad for all the girls whose hearts you're going to break someday, you little devil."

Alex looked up at her with his bright green eyes.

"I'm not going to break any hearts at all! I—"

Before he could finish, Elisa gripped him tightly with her small but very strong arms. Laughing, he tried to break free from her as she squeezed him, tickled him, and whispered something in his ear.

Their game didn't last long, though it was enough to exhaust them both. They puffed, panted, and rested their backs against the tree.

"Miss Elisa?"

"Yes, little devil?"

"May I?"

"What?" she asked back with sly eyes.

She knew exactly what Alex wanted, but she wanted him to say it out loud.

"Sit on your lap," the plump boy said, blushing bright pink.

"Let me think." Elisa put her index finger to her chin in a funny way.

Alex was starting to get scared she'd refuse him when her strong arms lifted him off the ground and landed him on her soft legs. Then Elisa put her hands on his shoulders and clasped him tightly to her chest.

It felt so warm and soft. Cozy. Like curling up in bed and pulling the blanket over his head.

"So. Let's begin."

"Hurray!"

Alex opened the handbook at his special bookmark.

The Laughing Peony. That was the name of the spell graphically presented in the figures surrounded by paragraphs of terms and calculations.

"Look, Alexander. That's the central ley line. When you draw magic from a source, it mostly comes along this line. It's like a central highway or a tree trunk. The crown of the tree is what you see as a seal, and the root is you."

Elisa explained magic to him for several hours. They argued, they laughed, and then she fell silent so Alexander could concentrate on his calculations.

While he was busy doing them, she used her fingers to comb his curly, ever-tousled black hair. She used to say that his hair had been woven by fairies from the same silk they weave into the black veil of night to cover the sleeping universe.

Alex was too old to still believe in fairies. He knew very well that it was just the sun sinking beyond the horizon that caused the darkness of night.

And the stars weren't jewels strewn by fairies over their magic silk; they were distant balls of hot gas.

That was actually what they were arguing about.

"Look, you little devil." Elisa lifted a palm to the sky, bringing her big and index fingers together to "grab hold" of a star. "See me holding it?"

"That's just an optical illusion." Alex frowned.

"An optical illusion? Oh goodness. You *do* read too much, you little devil. But if it's just an illusion, how do you explain *this*?"

Twitching her wrist, Elisa showed him a small sparkling jewel lying on her palm.

"How…" Alex reached for the jewel, but it crumbled to dust as soon as he touched it.

He looked up and saw the same star Elisa had just plucked out of the sky.

"That was just a trick," the boy said, frowning again. That made his cheeks even bigger.

"You can think that." Elisa smiled and ruffled his hair. "Or you can believe I just plucked a star out of the sky for you. It's just a matter of faith."

"That's magic."

"Magic is faith, too. People believe in magic today more than ever, which is why it's growing stronger."

"Did you learn that at church?" Alex asked, still peering up at the starry sky. It was hard to see most of the stars thanks to the thick city fog. "Does god approve of magic?"

On a golden chain around her neck, Elisa wore a small cross with a crucified man on it. He was called god, though Alex had his doubts.

What kind of god would let ordinary people crucify him? The gods Alex had read about would crucify anyone who even thought about doing that to them.

"God approves of everything that makes this world even a little bit better."

"Then why did he create it this bad?"

Elisa smiled again, clasping Alex a bit tighter.

"Maybe for us to make it better?"

"That's sophistry."

"Sophistry? Jesus. You *do* read too much, you little devil. You should spend more time playing with the other kids."

Alex said nothing. They sat in silence for a while, listening to the crickets, the Klaxon horns, the tires hissing across the asphalt, the shouts of partiers, and the other sounds coming from the night streets.

"Your god will never love me," Alex whispered suddenly with a sniff. "Nobody will. They all hate me."

Elisa frowned. For the first time that evening, she looked serious and strict.

"Why do you think that, Alexander?"

Alex held out his hand, biting his lower lip hard enough that it bled.

Around his small fingers, a purple glow flashed just for a moment. But that was enough for the grass around him to fade.

"Because I can't make this world better," the boy whispered, panting and sniffing. "Because the other kids won't play with me. Alex Doom will become a madman. Alex Doom will be shot like a dog. Alex Doom, go back to your horror movies. Alex Doom is the new dark lord."

Elisa's stern face melted into a light, tired smile as she continued stroking the boy's hair.

"You're as stupid as you are smart, Alexander."

"But they *are* afraid of me! Just because that stupid doctor said I'm a black wizard. You know what people say about them: they…we all end up going insane. And doing evil things they execute us for. They even say kids like me are going to be given magic surgery to change their source soon."

"Nothing like that is ever going to happen. Don't worry."

"It is. It's *going* to happen. I'm positive. You should have seen that doctor shaking in fear when he saw the instrument readings."

"People are always afraid of what they don't understand," Elisa said, clasping Alex in her arms again. So warm. So cozy. So comforting. "If god created you like that, he did it for a reason."

"I don't think so."

Elisa turned Alex around suddenly, setting him down in front of her and crouching down so their eyes were on the same level. She placed a hand on top of his head.

"Remember this, you little devil, the day you believe your luck has turned against you. You haven't had anything to do with everything you're dealing with right now. It's the world forcing you to do it. But when that day comes, I want you to remember one thing."

Elisa shifted her hand from his head to his heart.

"In this life, there's only one thing you truly own. It's the only thing in the world that is completely in your hands, entirely up to you."

"What's that?"

"Your decisions, you little devil. They're the only thing that always comes from you. Not from those who say mean things about you. Not from your life, however complicated it gets. Not even from him." Elisa touched her cross. "Only from you. From *your* choice."

"That's complicated," Alex replied with a frown

"Well," Elisa said, smiling and standing up. "Don't you enjoy figuring complicated things out? You're the boy who reads too much."

"I like books more than games."

"You just haven't tried playing them."

"I don't need to." Alex stuck out his tongue, ending their argument. Or at least he thought that's what he was doing.

Elisa just laughed, loudly and deeply. She kept laughing until a girl's shriek came from the tall overgrown shrubs in the eastern part of the courtyard.

It wasn't a merry, playful scream; it was a desperate one, fearful and hopeless.

"Help…" The shout stopped abruptly, giving place to distant, muffled moaning.

Alex had heard those sounds before. When Elisa turned and took a step in that direction, he grabbed her wrist with both hands.

His handbook fell to the ground, its torn pages scattered by the wind.

"Please don't," Alex begged. "Please. Please. Please. Don't go over there."

Elisa looked stern, more so than he'd ever seen her. She bent over and pulled herself away before taking him by the shoulders and looking dead in the eye.

"Alexander, if someone's doing something wrong nearby, you can stop it, and you don't, you'll cause another wrong before you even know it."

With that, she left.

The boy remained there, standing alone among the scattered pages.

He should have followed her.

Run after her.

But he couldn't.

He couldn't take even one small step.

He was paralyzed by fear.

***

Alex emerged from his memories, which were hidden deeply and covered in dust and mold, to see that the bus was empty but for him and the driver.

Despite the heavy traffic, they'd already reached the Natural Museum. It was a sizeable building with a white stone façade that stood in stark contrast to the steel and chromium of the surrounding skyscrapers. Built in the Grecian style, it had pillars topped by a triangular porch roof that presumably had its own grandiloquent name. Alex didn't know what it was.

"Are you staying or going?" The driver was struggling to open his lunch box.

Alex gritted his teeth in pain. The cigarette had burned down devil knew when, and it had seared his fingers. He stood and walked toward the exit, dropping just one word on the way.

"Fool."

"Who?" the driver asked, a bit startled.

"The cat." Alex stepped out onto the street and lit another cancer stick.

"What cat?"

"The one I tried to steal."

"Why?"

"It swallowed an earring."

"Why?"

"Because it was a fool."

The driver fell silent for a moment before finally replying.

"That makes perfect sense."

"Exactly." Slipping his hands into his pockets, Alex trudged after the student procession, which was ascending the marble stairs to the museum door.

Nobody was yet aware that that particular museum tour would be the weirdest and most perilous in history.

Chapter 25

"**D**on't push! Take your time." The old man in tweed—Professor Camil seemed to be his name—was trying to get the apparently bored freshmen into line. "Please be respectful."

"Professor." At the front of the line was a big guy whose uniform bore the emblem of the battle faculty. *Those hunks always go first.* "With all due respect, we come here every year. Can we go in a bit faster? They're expecting us."

"Never mind, let them wait," the old man said with a dismissive wave of his dry, wrinkled hand. "You'll have plenty of time for your lust and devil's water."

"Lust and devil's water," came a whisper from the crowd. "Student parties haven't been described like that since Merlin's day."

"No, longer—since Ptolemais'!"

A wave of giggles washed over the rows of students. Professor Camil and his two female colleagues had finally been able to organize their young prodigies into some semblance of a column.

Standing apart from the procession and resting his shoulder against a pillar, Alex watched them in amusement. The recent high school graduates were apparently daydreaming about celebrating their first day of "adulthood" at some night club.

"Put your battle storages into the blue box." Two security guards in yellow uniforms stood at the entrance, flanking the archway magic detector. "Your consumer storages into the green box. Keep the tag. The fine for losing it is a hundred—"

"A hundred and fifty credits," a voice called from the crowd.

Of course, they'd been there plenty of times before. They knew the procedure for magic storage inside and out.

Calmly and without any arguing, the students removed all their magic storages and dropped them into the boxes.

Some wore their magic storages as bracelets, while others went for earrings, hair clips, or chains. Most, however, were shaped like rings, the most common form of consumer magic storage.

There weren't any students carrying battle storages. The blue box remained empty.

The only one who didn't hand in a special accessory was Miss Perriot. She just flashed her esper identity card to the guards and walked through the archway scanner.

Espers didn't need magic storages. It was wizards who had limited mana reserves that ran out quickly without an external supply.

Without his storage, even Alex could only use his best spell in a real battle…once. And that left him as powerless as a mere mortal for a good while.

Higher mana levels meant wizards could hold more magic in their body, though that benefit was outweighed by the fact that high-level spells consumed more mana. That was why all wizards used storages. Ninety percent went with consumer varieties; the other ten percent opted for battle storages.

"That goes for you, too, young man." The guard's outstretched baton barred the way for Doom.

He could already see the inside of the museum he'd never visited before, but the two yellow uniforms weren't letting him in. They were standing in front of a metal archway bracketed with sensors. At its side was a tall black box containing some equipment and topped by a monitor.

The magic detector.

Getting an artifact through without being spotted was impossible.

The baton the guard was holding looked like plain wood with a rubber handle, but it was actually a powerful battle magic staff.

[Item: ??? No access permit. Information unavailable.]

His lenses always failed him with things like that, but Alex felt the familiar tingling sensation in his fingertips.

"To begin with, that's Professor Dumsky to you, *young man*," Dumsky replied as he pushed the baton away. "Use that dildo on someone else."

"Forgive me, Professor." The guard stepped back instantly, hiding the baton behind him. "Rudeness won't get you in, however. Please remove your storage and head through."

"Professor Dumsky," old Camil said with a frown that made his face look even more like the wrinkled jacket he had on. "Stop being a clown. I don't know where you used to teach, but First Magic University is an old and respected institute where attitudes like that will not be tolerated."

"Old and respected?" Alex snorted, although too quietly for anyone but the two guards to hear. "Sounds like an ad for a brothel."

The yellow uniforms snorted back, losing their imperturbable calm for a split-second.

"I don't have any storages," Alex said.

"Then please walk through the archway detector."

"Hell's bells. I was going to walk through anyway!"

"Of course." The guard who'd been showing off his artifact

manhood flashed a predatory smile. "But now, if the magic detector shows that your ring *is* a storage, you will be fined 10,000 credits. If it's a *battle* storage, then multiple that by ten and add a criminal charge."

"A criminal charge?" Alex flicked his cigarette butt deftly into a trash can. "Oh, I'm so scared."

His piece said, he walked calmly through the archway. It didn't make a peep.

"I ap-pologize, Professor," the astonished guard said. He scratched the back of his head, pushing his cap over his eyes.

"*Who's* the clown, Professor Camil?" Doom asked as he walked by the old man.

Without waiting for his students or colleagues, he started through the first museum exhibit. He'd seen pictures online, but being there in person was completely different.

What Alex saw, if he was being honest, exceeded his wildest expectations. He had to wonder why the museum was only crammed with visitors a few days a year, in fact.

The exquisite wall mosaics didn't just portray historical scenes. They themselves were magic, with the figures they portrayed moving as you watched them. They fought, feasted, signed contracts, stormed fortresses, painted, and crossed seas and skies.

Up in the dome, the mosaics all came together to depict the starry universe. The sparkling constellations and nebulas drifted over visitors' heads, complete with various magic birds soaring around—from the Thunder Falcon to the giant Rukh and Phoenix.

Alex felt like he was once again the small boy climbing into the florist girl's lap so she could show him a magic trick and tell him about magic theory.

But all that was overshadowed by everything on the rows of shelves, on the velvet pillows under glass caps, and inside the giant glass cubes guarded by yellow uniforms.

The museum displays.

"Attention, please." A strict-looking girl in a business suit, her brown hair tied back tightly in a low bun, used her pointer to tap one of the posts holding the red cord separating an item on exhibit from the visitor space. "This is what we traditionally begin every tour with."

She was talking to a bunch of first-grade children, apparently from an elite school. The museum was too small for the crowds that wanted to get in on the first day of the school year, so it only allowed in a lucky few thousand.

Although it was too small for everyone to fit, the Natural Museum was no smaller than the Louvre or the Hermitage.

It was probably bigger, in fact.

The kids gasped, gripping the cord. Their guide had lost their attention. Instead, they were captivated by a large stone, smoothed and rounded by the glaciers that once formed it.

An absolutely ordinary stone.

...save for the sword protruding from it.

"One of the most powerful artifacts ever. It was created by Merlin, hardened by dragonfire, and forged from the light of a falling star."

A small hand poked up. It belonged to a little girl with braces and comical ponytails.

"Wasn't it forged from the star itself?"

"No, dear, from its light," the museum guide replied with a smile.

What an expressive smile. It spoke of weariness and impending doom but also resilience and resoluteness, and all at the same time.

That was when the tour began.

Darting a quick glance over at the freshmen, Alex followed the guide. It was his first visit there, after all, and he wanted a fresh look at the tourist mecca of Atlantis.

***

Two hours later, with most kids doing anything but listening, the museum guide at last got to the final part of her speech.

She looked just as bad as the kids' schoolteacher. Sweaty and panting the same way they were, she fanned her face with a tablet.

But Alex was happy.

In those two hours, he'd seen so many fragments of magic history that his memories were going to last him for the next few years. King Arthur's sword had given way to Merlin's staff and Morgana's wand. Then the real travel through the ages began.

Gilgamesh's club and Enkidu's belt. A small replica of the famous Hanging Gardens of Babylon. Scepters belonging to the pharaohs of ancient Egypt. The Book of the Living and the Book of the Dead. (That was surprising. Alex used to think those two were fakes, making it small wonder they were guarded so thoroughly.) The first totems. Ancient relics of magic races. The sword of Achilles. The lightning of Zeus. The Fountain of Youth. (It was completely dry, though, and featured a plate that read *Temporarily not working.* Alex had a feeling it was just a mold.) A jade sword from the Warring States period. The sword of Izanagi. The bow of...that Chinese guy who shot the sun with an arrow. The staff of Sun Wukong. And many, many more.

There were even skeletons and molds of all different species and varieties of incredible magic creatures.

In a word, the tour was packed. And it was nearing the end.

The bunch of first graders Alex was following stopped by a giant statue.

Apparently made by a Greek sculptor, it was a muscular man with his arms outstretched overhead to hold a black ball. An orb. Once whole, but now smashed.

"There's the crown jewel of our collection," the museum guide, panting a bit, told the children. "I'm sure you've all seen it in your history textbooks. It's called…"

"Poseidon's Pearl," came a whisper in Alex's ear. He turned to meet the peach-haired girl's eyes.

Leia Perriot was standing next to him.

"…Poseidon's Orb," the guide announced proudly.

"A common translation error," Leia said with a smile, flashing a row of even, snow-white teeth.

"Once upon a time, the god of the sea and storms, the patron of Atlantis, created this pearl to hide his island from the rest of the world. But as with the island of magic, he later had to conceal the magic itself from mortals. All of it. It was this artifact, this orb, that upheld the barrier between our worlds for thousands of years."

A small girl's hand popped up.

"Was that the thing they tried to destroy? I mean, those—"

"Those and many others." The museum guide interrupted the curious girl for the first time. She must have really been exhausted. "Everyone tried to destroy it. The total number of attempts is over a thousand."

"Seven hundred and forty-two, to be precise," Leia said, still in a whisper.

"What are you—"

Before Alex could finish, his colleague put a finger to her plump lips and hissed like a rattlesnake.

"But it all ended with the arrival of those little round things we all wear on our eyes today. The orb was no longer needed, so it was smashed during a special ceremony by the residents of Atlantis and representatives of the UN, a precursor to the United Races."

"So, if I take my lenses off, I'll be able to see all the places the orb used to hide?" the small girl asked, her forehead wrinkled.

"No, my dear. Those places belong to the magic races. They're their native homes, all known by different names. Olympus. Tir Na Nog.

Shambhala. Atlantis." The guide paused. "El Dorado. Etheria. Neverland. And many more. They're scattered around the world, and it was only recently that they changed the invitation-only policy."

"A fairy tale the magic races keep feeding to humanity." It was Leia's turn to frown. "She can't possibly be so incompetent she wouldn't know that."

"And now," the guide continued, "the Magic Lenses have made the lands concealed by the magic of other races visible to everyone. Entering them is still difficult though. What they told you at school about Earth expanding in size isn't exactly true—it's just that we're now able to see the third of our planet that used to be hidden from us."

"But what about researchers and scientists? Does that mean none of them ever—"

"No," the lady interrupted again. "But those scientists were all labelled as crazy or just misunderstood. Take Nikola Tesla, the best example. Read his biography, dear, and you'll see all the things he invented that we now use in our daily life."

The little girl was silent. With relief on her face, the guide clapped her hands and was about to open her mouth and wrap things up when the girl jumped in with yet another question.

"What about espers, ma'am? They're not human, but they aren't non-human either."

"*Non-human* is a rude word, miss. And the esper issue is too complicated to discuss today."

Alex glanced over at Leia. For a moment, her face was darker than a thundercloud, but then she relaxed and even smiled.

"Nothing complicated about it at all," she said loudly. The kids all looked at her and gasped. At the same time, the guide tensed up and reached for her tablet, probably in search of the SOS button she had on it. "The wizards looked down on espers as second-rate creatures. Mortals didn't believe in us. So, there we were, half-wizard, half-mortal, and never reckoned with."

"Is that why you made most of the attempts to break the orb?"

"Yes," Leia nodded with some pride. "Now let me walk you and your teacher to the exit to make sure you don't get lost."

A few moments later, Alex was alone with the museum guide.

"Was that your girlfriend?" she asked.

"Whose, mine?" It took Alex a second to realize she was talking to him. "No, she isn't. I was with you the whole time, and—"

"I saw you," the guide said with a tired smile as she tucked a stray lock of hair behind her ear.

"Well, I just wanted to say that the tip of your nose is insanely beaut—"

The last word was drowned out by a deafening alarm signal. All along the walls of the hall, which the first-graders hadn't yet left, steel grates slammed down.

Doom looked up. There were deep, winding cracks crisscrossing the ceiling with all its stars and nebulas.

He could smell sulfur and ashes.

"Demons of hell," Alex swore.

How right he was.

With a thundering roar, the ceiling shattered to send stone raining down. A giant, terrifying monster burst in through the hole.

Chapter 26

Tearing the clouds of dust and pulverizing stone into tiny pieces, a roar—not even a bestial roar, but one far more powerful and ancient—resounded through the hall.

Tongues of searing heat licked at Alex's face, and he staggered backward a few steps. Although his ArmaniMagico suit and brogues were made out of fire-proof materials and protective charms, they weren't going to be able to withstand the lava flow summoned by the monster for long.

Doom retrieved the pack of cigarettes from an inner pocket, his hand steady.

"No smoking in here," the guide whispered. She had apparently taken the magic P.E. lessons to heart, the ones where students were taught what to do if a magic beast appeared in the streets or, even worse, there was an underground magic breakout. She hid behind a fountain hanging in the air near Poseidon's Pearl or whatever the useless old piece of trash was called.

"Seriously?" Alex arched his right eyebrow. "My cigarette is the problem right now?"

"It's not allowed," the guide insisted.

"So that big gorilla with all its fucking armor is allowed to smash whatever it wants in here, and I'm not even allowed to smoke." Alex pointed his already lit cigarette at the source of the lava flooding the hall.

There, right in the middle and beneath the brand-new roof access hole, stood a giant gorilla. Some ten feet tall and probably as heavy as ten tons, it was clad head to paw in black, grotesque-looking armor.

Shoulder pads shaped like skulls and studded with sharp spikes. Steel gauntlets wound around with chains. A breastplate with another skull, this one belonging to a goat. And a terrifying horned helmet with two yellow eyes glowing on the other side of the slit.

[DANGER! Race: Demon. Level: Unknown. Mana level: Unknown. The neutralization authorities have been summoned.]

Unknown, sure. No, it's really just secret.

By the time the authorities arrived, there wasn't going to be anything left of the hall or the visitors hiding behind the ancient displays.

Sure, it was just a bottom-legion soldier demon. But even it was powerful enough to slaughter everyone there before the Guards could arrive.

Looking past the monster, Doom saw Miss Perriot shielding a bunch of kids with her own body. She didn't make for the best shield given how slender her body was, though she deserved a few brownie points for her bravery. The stupidity canceled them out, however.

A D-ranked esper was not about to stop a soldier demon.

As he smoked, Alex stepped calmly toward the monster breathing nervously and noisily, puffing out clouds of sulfur and ash. Alex was positive it had just been summoned. Probably in the apartment he'd visited with Gribovsky.

"I won't disturb your hunt," Doom said. He didn't think anyone there would understand him—the demonic language wasn't popular with anyone but a very few mortals. "You hunt. I'll leave."

The gorilla slowly turned to Alex, then covered the distance between them (no less than 30 feet) in a single giant leap.

"My hunt," the monster growled, "is you."

"Wha—"

A steel-gauntleted paw smashed into Alex's chest. Even with the protection provided by his suit, the impact was strong enough to reduce human flesh...not even to a bloody mess. It would have just swept his torso clean off, leaving two stumps of legs standing where they were.

But Alex was a black wizard. That meant smoking, drinking, and whoring, with the ability to defend himself a pleasant bonus on top.

His cigarette smoke turned violet and formed a thick veil that blocked the monster's paw a moment before it would have sent Alex to hell. Black wizards don't go to heaven, after all.

Soaring hundreds of feet up over the museum displays, Alex wheeled around in mid-flight and directed the magic energy from his source into his shoes. They each instantly grew a pair of smoky, raven-black wings. Gliding through the air like a hockey player across an icy field, Alex landed lightly on his feet just a few inches away from some insanely expensive painting. He could tell how expensive it was by the horrified look on the museum guide's face.

Spitting, Alex dispelled the magic, took a deep breath, and thrust his hands in his pockets.

"I may not have a banana, but..."

The demon reared up and pounded its chest with gauntleted hands. Each hit triggered a powerful sound wave that shook the glass cubes encasing the ancient artifacts.

"...I'm no stranger to dancing with gorillas. Obesity is a big problem in Myers City."

Alex used his right hand to crack his neck. His emerald eyes glittered with excitement and anticipation.

It had been far too long since he'd been able to put his gift through its paces.

The only proper use for a black wizard's gift was to destroy.

In front of his open palm, a seal formed instantly. It had so many different figures and symbols that the hostages in the room who dared look at it felt their head spin.

Magic energy obeyed Alex's will to rush from his source to the palm, soak the seal's ley lines, and gush out, forming a legally prohibited spell that blended blood magic with the darkest of magic arts: necromancy.

[ATTENTION! Prohibited spell used: THE LICH KING SCOURGE of the Blood and Darkness School. Mana consumption: N/A.]

The Guards could deal with the consequences of Alex using the prohibited art. He couldn't have cared less about what was going to happen afterwards, busy as he was making sure there was an afterwards for him to worry about. If there was ever a time for one of his most powerful spells, it was then.

The scourge shooting out of the seal seemed made of blood, only with a tinge of ash-gray. Unfolding through the air to become hundreds of feet long, it hit the gorilla right in the middle of its chest.

Doom waited for the demon's green blood to arc through the air. Instead, with a soft *clink*, the scourge crumbled. Alex lurched backward with the recoil of his destroyed spell. It had left just a tiny scratch on the monster's armor.

Having done no other damage, a spell strong enough to kill a battle Mystic was entirely destroyed.

Gripping a glass cube, Doom pointed his cigarette at the gorilla.

"Want a minute to catch your breath, buddy boy?"

The gorilla just roared again, clenched its mighty fists overhead, and took a running leap toward him.

"Oh, you're good to go."

He had enough mana left to cast another powerful spell, but Alex had a feeling it would share the fate of the scourge.

Hell's bells. Never before had he seen a soldier demon with armor like that. What kind of hellish creature was it?

The Vase of Ten Thousand Warriors, the writing on a jade vase dating back to the Three Kingdoms period read.

His spells may not have been enough to break through the monster's armor, but there was no reason they couldn't shatter a glass cube.

"No, not the vase!" the guide screamed. Too late.

Demolishing the glass cover with a bolt of black lightning, Alex grabbed the vase, leaped away from the mighty paws leaving two-foot craters in the floor, and hurled the artifact at the gorilla's head.

He looked around as he landed and rolled away from the potential line of fire.

Damn, I'm right in the middle of an incredible magic arsenal, he thought to himself suddenly.

"Well, my dear, shall we tango?"

While the demon was fighting off the dozens of fallen Chinese warrior spirits attacking it, Alex rushed over to the next item.

"Oh no," the guide whimpered.

Chapter 27

"**N**ot the Piercing Spear!" the museum guide shouted. She was hiding *inside* the fountain by that point, the water soaking her white blouse to reveal firm, springy breasts through the fabric.

Girl's got a little fire in her. She doesn't wear a bra.

It may have been those thoughts and his suddenly tight pants, or it may have been his prison experience (not so much a four-year period of sexual abstinence for a young black wizard's hormonal body as it was lots of physical exercise and an endless struggle to stay alive). Either way, Alex was able to slide nimbly past the stand that held a bronze spear topped with a very prominent bone head.

The ape roared again and...slid past it just as nimbly.

The water splashing out of the fountain had made the marble floor as slippery as ice. That created just enough of a miscalculation that a blow capable of shattering Alex's spine instead smashed the protective cap over the spear. It was a lucky break—Alex would have had a hard time with the same given how little mana he had left in his source.

Throwing his back against one of the pillars supporting the much lighter dome, Alex shifted his gaze from the guide's alluring curves to yet another cloud of dust and crushed stone left by the demonic ape. The monster had hit the very painting that had barely escaped a collision with Doom.

"I hope it—"

"Reinforced partitions filled with adamantius," the girl with the amazing curves whined.

"You've got to be kidding," Alex hissed.

Another bellow. Dusting itself off and shredding the huge painted canvas, the gorilla peeled itself off the reinforced partition and pulled itself out of the cave that had been created when its body hitting the wall.

"Hey, any other wizards here?" Alex shouted. Jumping to his feet, he activated the levitation spell in his shoes.

[LEVITATION recharging in 2s]

He glided through the air like Hermes, grabbed the spear, and rolled over the broken pedestal to find himself right in front of the giant demon.

"Apparently not," Doom said as the hundreds of visitors remained behind cover, trembling with fear. They probably knew that the monster would destroy everything in sight once it took out its target. The problem was that having a few drops of magic and knowing a couple spells didn't make you a wizard.

"Come on!"

The gorilla brought both fists down on its prey's head. But instead of reducing Alex to a bloody mess, the blow only carved out another crater in the floor.

Using the last split-second his levitation spell was active, Doom had jumped away, hurling the spear at the demon at the same time.

The ease with which Alex had dispatched the street gangsters in High Garden didn't mean he was a warrior wizard. Far from it—he was and always had been just a bookworm.

But missing an enormous beast that's eager to kill you and just a few feet away when you have a big sharpened stick was not something even Alex was about to do.

Expecting another *ding*, he was pleasantly surprised by how easily the spear broke through the dark armor to bury itself in the monster's flesh.

It screamed and spun on its hind legs, frantically waving its front paws like windmill blades.

Struggling to pull the spear out of the wound and oozing green blood, the demon smashed everything around it.

In the meantime, a strategy was forming in Alex's mind. What he cared about was rescuing the most valuable thing in the whole museum: himself. But he had to test out his theory.

Backing off to a very respectful distance, Alex, his cigarette still in his mouth, peered out of his cover and called over to the guide.

"Hey, mermaid!"

"What? Don't call me that! It's sex—"

"Agreed," Alex interrupted, inhaling and appreciating once again her wet blouse and the absence of a bra beneath it. "Do you have anything else like that spear?"

"Why do you ask—"

Her idiotic phrase was drowned out by the demon's roar. In addition to its bestial fury and might, it now had ancient magic on its side. And its magic was far more ancient than what fairies or any of the other magic races could wield.

That kind of magic came from the depths of history, reaching back to the beginning of time.

Out of the demon's jaws burst a horizontal tornado of red fire with black stars sparkling inside it, their dark glow so bright it outshone the bright afternoon sun.

No human-made thing could withstand that magic.

Nothing but *adamantius*.

No longer supported by the levitation spell in his shoes, Alex retrieved a cigarette and tossed it on the ground at his feet.

[ATTENTION! Prohibited spell used: RUPTURE of the Chaos School. Mana consumption: N/A.]

Two seals flashed in front of Alex's palms, one red and the other bloody. Overlapping, they flashed a multi-colored chaos, the glowing symbols and signs inside it completely foreign to ordinary wizards.

It was demonic magic.

One of the oldest of the world's arts.

The only ones who had more ancient (if not necessarily better, as much progress had been made in magic since then) knowledge were the angels. *May the Abyss devour them.*

The rupture spell would have easily destroyed a Mystic up to the 30th level. Alex targeted it at the smoldering cigarette butt and, when it flashed with bright black fire, waved a hand to re-direct it at the ape.

The strip of black fire looked pathetic against the backdrop of the raging fiery tornado. But at that very moment, shocking everyone who knew anything about magic, Alex raised his other hand.

His ability to create magic seals mentally rather than tracing a model projected by his lenses put him on par with military wizards.

But the ability to do so with *both* palms…

A second row of seals flashed over his left wrist.

Into the hall burst a dark-blue fog. It felt like wet autumn sweeping over a swampy graveyard.

Suddenly, the people in the room could see their breath hanging in the air. The graveyard wind fanned the black strip of fire until it was almost as high as the demon's.

The black and red flames collided in the middle of the hall with a powerful explosion, fire melting a hole in the floor that bared water pipes and electrical cables.

The demon was sent flying backward. Alex was almost killed by a collapsing pillar.

"Hurry, miss!" Alex yelled in a voice that didn't sound like him at all.

"The axe of Olaf the Northern!" The guide tapped something on her tablet, and the protective cover encasing one of the farther items in the museum was drawn into the pedestal.

Without waiting for the ape to regain its senses, Doom dashed over in that direction.

But it appeared that he had underestimated how resilient soldier demons were—even bottom-legion soldier demons.

The gorilla came to and, picking up a large chunk of the stone dome, hurled it at Doom. The latter called on his inner rock star, fell to his knees on the run, and slid across the wet floor.

The boulder hurtled past Doom's head, nicking his skin as it went.

On it flew, right at the huddled children.

"Shit!" Alex held out his palm, calling on his source. He only had mana for a single spell, and not a powerful one, but the bigger problem was that the boulder was flying much faster than anything he could have thrown at it.

Doom could already see blood splattering the wall in his head when the giant stone suddenly stopped. It hovered in place, hanging in the air.

But Alex had no time to wonder how that was even possible. The fact that it had happened was enough for the time being.

Sliding past the pedestal, he yanked the axe off it. Then he grabbed hold of a ledge to stop his momentum, wheeled around, and flung the weapon at the monster as he leaped to his feet.

The throw was a risk—axes aren't spears. But Alex's luck was good that day, and it was the axe's blade that hit the monster instead of its handle.

Sinking deep into the breastplate, right at the solar plexus, it crushed the ornamental goat skull and held the gorilla right where Alex wanted it.

Directly above the water pipe and electric cables.

How much money did they steal from the construction budget if that's the kind of contracting work they had done? The workers had run the electricity next to the water.

But right then, all Alex wanted to do was find a church to pray a blessing for them. If he could get in the front door.

He held out his right hand and snapped his fingers to create a small ball of purple fire that swished through the air, leaving a barely discernible smoky trace as it pierced the water pipe and electric cable in quick succession.

"Here we go!" Alex crossed his arms in front of himself, then spread them abruptly.

His will blended with his magic to gush out from his source. They intertwined with the water and electricity, becoming a single scourge.

The demon had just removed the axe from the gash in its armor when that same gash was pierced by the sparkling water scourge.

It began to bellow, but its roar stopped as suddenly as it began. The demon convulsed terribly and collapsed to the floor. The strong smell of burning flesh assaulted Alex's nostrils.

It wasn't until that moment that he heard the cavalry arriving. He was even pretty sure he heard a familiar "pumpkin."

"Timely as always," Doom groaned.

Limping and wiping blood from the cut on the top of his head, he went over to the twitching monster. He held a cigarette against the red-hot armor to light it, inhaled deeply, and ran his palm over the dead body. With a nasty smacking sound, a small red crystal flew out of the flesh.

[Magic Core. Race: Demon. Rank: E. Estimated value: Sale and personal use prohibited. The authorized agencies have been informed. Await their arrival.]

"Oh, really? I'm tired of waiting."

Alex dropped the crystal into his pocket before turning to the large stone with the kids crying behind it.

"Miss Perriot, you *are* full of surprises."

Chapter 28

Among the crowd of SWAT teams hurrying into the hall, Lieutenant Gribovsky was conspicuous thanks to his height, pierced ear, and scarred face. Alex was surprisingly happy to see his shabby leather coat in with all the clowns in their enchanted Kevlar garb marching behind full-height *adamantius* shields.

At least, he was as happy as a dark wizard who'd just had to fight for his life could be.

Thanks to the battle that had ended just a few seconds before (why is the cavalry always late?), the guard grates were stuck, blocking the soldiers' way. Techs armed with laser cutters set to work.

Where magic was of no help, Old World technology did the trick. The laser cutters sliced through *adamantius* as if it was plain steel. The magic of the enchanted metal gave in to the basic laws of physics, if that was what they were called.

Alex was never good at all that.

What he knew was how to judge people.

And he realized that the arrival of Gribovsky *and* the Asian boded poorly for him. Both were smart enough (Gribovsky was the key there, as Major Chon Sook's intelligence had been beyond doubt from the beginning) to not show they knew Alex.

"Help!" a guy called. Miss Perriot was bleeding in his arms, her peach hair a tangled mess smeared with the red liquid running from her eyes, nose, and ears. Her coral lips were chapped.

The girl had apparently gotten in over her head when she stopped the giant flying rock.

"She needs help! Hurry!" the guy screamed at the top of his lungs.

Rushing to her aid had been a good move—girls need knights in shining armor. Alex was nothing like that; he looked more like a weary giant bat than a hero of old.

Rescuing damsels in distress wasn't his cup of tea.

His flow of thought was interrupted by the sound of the grate falling to the floor followed by the tramping of steel-tipped boots. Dozens of pros rushed in, aiming their assault rifles at everything small enough to fit in their holographic sights, and formed a perimeter.

Doom knew the procedure all too well. He took the only right course of action: staying seated on the floor, leaning his back up against a piece of ruble, and quietly watching what was going around him.

"Don't touch me! I'm a victim!" the museum guide screamed when the soldiers pulled her out of the fountain. Their professionalism was praiseworthy—none of them stared at her enticing curves.

Doom was the only one doing that.

"Hey, get off!"

"What are you doing?"

"I'll go to the media! This is police brutality!"

The people in the hall were evacuated quickly, if somewhat roughly. Ten seconds later, no witnesses of the battle remained save for Alex, Miss Perriot, and Miss Perriot's cavalier.

The hall itself was empty and ravaged.

"Don't move her, young man!" Once the perimeter was established, the only civil servants Doom could tolerate burst into the room.

Emergency doctors and other first responders.

Dressed in red and white, they got to work on Miss Perriot. The medical trio consisted of a middle-aged man, a young girl, and a guy Doom's age, the middle-aged man a middling healer. Carefully, he drew a single pentagram in the air with his finger. The magic seal flashed green; the blood trickling down Miss Perriot's face slowed and then stopped.

"Get her on the stretcher!" the older doctor ordered. "Turn on the lights and rush her to the ward. Two cubes of adrenalin in her vein."

"Sir, yes, sir," the two youngsters replied in military fashion. They lifted the girl onto the stretcher and dashed for the exit.

"Hurry, young man! You need to go with her."

The cavalier looked like he was about to salute, though he thought better of it and just hustled after the stretcher.

Good call.

"Let's see what's going on here." The healer, who turned out to be much shorter than Doom and sporting a protruding beer belly and fat sausage fingers, came over to Alex. His palm had just started to move through the air over Doom's body when he winced in pain. The grimace was passing and barely perceptible—he deserved credit for trying to conceal the sensation.

From what Alex had been told, it felt like an open wound being sprinkled with salt, doused in tequila, and subjected to the administrations of a dog's rough tongue.

That was what all light wizards experienced when trying to apply magic to their dark counterparts.

Fortunately, it didn't work the same the other way around.

"You—"

"Metamizole and hydrogen peroxide would be great," Doom said, forcing a bleak smile. Running down his temple was a fairly thick stream of blood, and his hair a sticky mess.

"Maybe...?" The healer handed him a loaded syringe. "It's an anesthetic, and a strong one. It'll help restore your source."

"I don't do drugs," Alex said as he pushed the doctor's hand away and shook the ashes off onto the floor. "Only natural stuff."

"Oh, young man, if you only knew how many chemicals there are in your *natural stuff*. The pesticides, the fertilizers..."

For the next several minutes (the time it took the doctor to dress the wound on his head), Alex was lectured on the harmful substances contained in tobacco products. They were apparently more hazardous than chemical waste from factories.

When the doctor finished and gave Alex a firm handshake in parting, Gribovsky and Chon Sook started toward him.

A brief glance was all anyone needed to tell they worked for the same department. It wasn't even their tenacious eyes, a special gait, or the fact that they were obeyed by the seasoned operatives still holding the perimeter while they waited for the nerds to get there.

No.

Not at all.

It was as trivial as the fact that they were both wearing trench coats. Gribovsky preferred black leather; Chon Sook went with a brown reminiscent of sailcloth.

"What happened here?" roared a bass voice.

Alex looked over the shoulder of the major, who had yet to say a word. The appearance of the man in the doorway was in stark contrast to his voice. The deep, trumpeting bass belonged to a short, puny man with a head probably shaved to hide early balding. Or maybe he had just gotten tired of washing his hair.

The man started to run from one ruin to another, gasping and moaning.

"The vase of the dynasty... The spear of the... Oh goodness! *The axe*! The axe of Olaf the Northern! Do you even *know* how much it was worth?" The man, who was apparently the museum curator, picked the ancient artifact up with such affected tenderness the he looked like a mother taking her first baby in her arms.

The major coughed; the hall fell silent. It hadn't exactly been noisy before, but in that moment even the ghosts of sounds seemed to straighten up at attention and retreat into the corners.

"Mr. Svenstern, I think your axe is fine."

"Fine? *All right*?!" The rich voice really did sound odd coming from such a wimpy figure. "Just look at these dents! All these scratches!

I...I...you..."

"All museum displays are covered by insurance," Chon Sook interrupted, steel eyes flashing. "Plus, none of these items are truly valuable. If they were, they wouldn't be stored here. You know where they would be."

The curator fell silent. The transparent hint made the tiny wheels in his head spin at triple their usual speed.

"Excuse me, but which department are you—"

"Besides, Mr. Svenstern," the major interrupted again, "from what I remember, the most recent decree obligated you to reinforce not only the load-bearing internal walls, but also the *ceiling*. I don't see a single piece of adamantius here in the rubble, though the funds for the reinforcement project were allocated to the museum in full."

"Yes, Major, yes," Gribovsky chimed in. "Let him have it. That pumpkin is over there waving his axe at us, and look at the watch on his wrist—it's worth 18 months of my salary. Even 24 months, so long as I spent nothing on eating, drinking, and, worst of all, fucking. But I can't live without any of that. Especially not fucking."

Mr. Svenstern had apparently reached a decision. Without uttering a word, he swallowed and left to look over the rest of his devastated fiefdom.

The major coughed again as he turned to Alex.

"Mr. Dumsky?"

Alex threw up a hand vaguely.

"What happened? The short version."

"I brought the kids here for a tour only to have a giant gorilla, the kind we discussed recently, mistake me for a banana."

Gribovsky and Chon Sook exchanged glances.

Spies. Guard spies. They're not the only ones who know how to talk in code.

"It was after you?" Gribovsky asked.

Alex just pointed at his bandaged head.

"Mr. Dumsky," Chon Sook said, squinting, "are you sure the attempt was targe—"

"*Where's the orb?*" came a panicked scream. "Where the hell is Poseidon's Orb?!"

Alex, Gribovsky, and the mator slowly turned toward the demolished fountain. The ancient statue was holding...nothing. The shattered mashed artifact that had once cloven the world in two was missing, and Doom had a feeling the broken fragments weren't going to be found among the debris.

"Get me all the camera records," Chon Sook said in a flat voice that brooked no disobedience. "From the museum and everything in a three-block radius—ATMs, parking lots, shops, drones, phones. I need *all* video files recorded in this area over the past three hours. And I want them ten minutes ago."

Alex cursed under his breath.

Chapter 29

It was Alex's second visit to the major's office, and he found the wall-sized window just as incredible as it had been the first time. Although the office was underground, it looked out over rainy Myers City in the evening. And somehow, he didn't sense the least bit of magic. What else could it have been?

The group seated at the T-shaped table with Major Chon Sook, whose long, aristocratic fingers were intertwined in front of him, was almost as colorful.

Gribovsky, his feet on the table (the major didn't look bothered), was popping his Skittles. To his right hand sat a creature Doom avoided looking at.

Lieutenant O'Hara, the immensely beautiful fae. Their kind rarely wore a disguise, which made her different—yes, her appearance was an illusion. When they took their disguises off, the fae looked more like upright animals, though she was there looking like a beautiful girl with long, flowing golden hair. Her plain business suit had her looking sexier than a female escort.

A bit farther sat three humans in white smocks. All male, and of various ages, they each had a similar expression on their face: a mix of arrogance and utter confusion.

Doom adjusted his glasses, twiddling with his pack of cigarettes. Strange as it may seem, it wasn't that he felt the urge to smoke. Four years had turned his bad habit into a new way of breathing, one filtered by tobacco smoke.

"That's all you found?"

Chon Sook, for probably the tenth time already, rewound the recording pulled from the video surveillance camera on the roof of the shopping center next to the museum. The 12X zoom clearly showed a human figure stepping purposefully into a black cloud.

Like a portal or flying ship from Old Earth's fairy tales, the cloud was moored to the museum's devastated roof. And the tall figure, looking like it was the most normal thing in the world, entered the cloud. He was wearing a steel mask and a gray trench coat held closed with a wide belt. And in his hands was Poseidon's Orb, instantly recognizable and apparently heavy.

Several moments after engulfing the figure, the cloud accelerated to a scary speed, vanishing into the blue among the skyscrapers of downtown Myers City.

"All the other cameras are either damaged or don't have an angle," one of the white smocks reported.

"They're not the only source of video in the city," Chon Sook hinted.

"The Central Office hasn't yet signed the note permitting us to retrieve data from private smartphones and other civil video recorders," the same expert replied.

Alex slapped the table, pointing his cigarette pack at the group.

"I knew it! I *knew* you were watching us all! Fucking politicians. Soon you won't be able to take a shit without being spied on."

"You may rest assured that your defecation will remain confidential, young man." The oldest of the besmocked trio adjusted his glasses, exactly mirroring Doom's gesture.

"Look at Mr. Dictionary," Alex hissed, leaning back in his chair. He'd always been on the fence about getting a smartphone, but that was enough to make up his mind. *Never.*

It was essentially the same as slapping a label on his chest with all his personal info, letting anyone find him with a snap of their fingers once the Central Office signed whatever that new decree was.

Damn bureaucrats. They're going to save the world if they don't destroy it first.

"You know, boss—"

"Lieutenant Gribovsky, how many times have I told you not to call me that?"

The giant glanced over at Alex, who returned a pointedly blank stare.

"Major, sir," the lieutenant continued, "doesn't it seem weird to you that only one of the thousand cameras there survived the incident with its recording undamaged? And that it's the one with such a clear shot of the spot, the way the guy left, and the fact that he was holding the orb? And that thing can't be easy to carry. Our little pumpkin friend got to the spot awfully fast for what wasn't a short distance."

Despite Gribovsky's weird manner of speaking, Alex had to admit that he was right. Whoever the Mask was, he was...

"Baiting a trap to lure us in," the major said, finishing Alex's thought. Turning to the window, he watched the city through his intertwined fingers like a black falcon searching the stone, chromium, and steel jungle for its prey.

A dangerous man.

"A question, in that case," O'Hara drawled in the melodious way the bloody fairies talked. "What are we going to do with the bait? We've been chasing the Mask around the city for two full months, and this is the first time he's done something to really stand out. Stealing the cultural heritage of all the different civilizations is a big step up."

"Excellent question, O'Hara."

Everyone turned toward the door. There, leaning on a cane that looked both too long and too thick, and in a light-green shirt with a jacket thrown over his shoulders, stood a man Alex wouldn't have wanted to meet on a narrow road.

He looked as tough as a tanned leather vest after a full cycle in a concrete mixer packed with gravel. Like someone who'd fought in two world wars and one magic war, who was used to staying in hostels, eating instant noodles, and using newspapers to wipe his ass.

Average height. Average stature. Eyes that could hammer nails; a face that would have shattered a flying brick. A sharp, aquiline nose. A strong jaw. Narrow, protruding cheekbones. A prominent forehead.

His hands were gloved, his throat concealed by his shirt's tall collar.

But the wide, creepy scar winding up his neck so vividly that it was visible through the fabric hinted that his concrete mixer metaphor had been even more accurate than Alex meant it to be.

"Major Summerfall," Chon Sook said without turning. He remained looking out the window. But while his voice was as calm as ever, only someone with an atrophied sense of self-preservation wouldn't have felt the urge to run away and hide in the darkest and deepest hole they could find when they heard it. "I don't remember inviting you sit in on *my* department's internal meeting."

"Oh, Chon, I'm just here to pay all you incredible demon fighters a friendly visit." Summerfall's tone left no doubt about his actual opinion of Chon Sook's department. "Give this case to my department, where we have *real* operatives, and we'll have it closed in less than a week."

"The door is behind you, Summerfall. See you at the weekly department head meeting." Chon Sook pointed at the exit, still without turning.

"Up to you, old friend," Summerfall replied with a shrug. "But if you think this case will help you make up for your failure in the Czech Republic..."

For the first time, Alex saw emotion flash across the Asian's steel eyes. And, hell's bells, *that* was scary.

Summerfall abruptly turned to Alex.

"Oh, I see you brought the toy the little birds in payroll have been chirping so much about. *Professor* Dumsky. Who could have ever thought? Is headquarters now the kind of place that welcomes scum like arrested and convicted black wizards?"

"Yep," Alex said, adjusting his glasses with the finger tattooed with DOOM.

Major Summerfall was astonished.

"Do you *really* not know who I am?"

"Summerfall," Chon Sook said, a warning in his voice.

"Please, enlighten me, Sir Major," Alex snorted, "as to who you—
"

Before he could finish, the newly arrived major removed his gloves. Both hands were tattooed all over with tiny black skulls, so many and so close together that they could have easily been mistaken for scales.

Black Hands.

Alex stood up; Gribovsky aimed his enchanted gun at him.

"Murderer," Doom hissed.

"But you're still breathing, Professor," the major mocked as he slipped his gloves back on. "Though that's just because an old friend of mine needs you for some reason."

"Get out, Summerfall," Chon Sook pressed.

Black Hands. The most infamous black wizard hunter of all time. It wouldn't have been an overstatement to say that four out of every ten black wizards killed in the previous several decades had fallen victim to that very bastard.

Every skull tattooed on his hands stood for a life he'd taken.

Damn. Damn. Damn.

Alex had always thought of Black Hands as nothing but a bugaboo for those who were bugaboos to the rest of the world.

And imagining the psycho serving in the Guards, who were supposed to be judicial defenders protecting the whole world, was beyond him.

When the door closed behind the scumbag, Alex turned to Chon Sook.

"Major?"

"Permission to speak, Major," the Asian corrected him. "Go ahead."

"Next week, on Friday, send Gribovsky to the Schooner."

"Why?"

"Because there's only one place in the city where we can find a clue about why the Mask took the orb."

"Where's that, pumpkin?" Gribovsky tossed another brightly colored piece of candy into his mouth.

"The Abyss Club."

The lieutenant choked.

"That's…just…a…city myth."

"Bring your best weapons," Alex replied with a mysterious smile.

Gribovsky arched his brow as Alex's smile gradually faded.

"The club owner swore to kill me the next time we meet."

"Damn you, pumpkin. Is there anywhere in this city forgotten by gods and demons where no one wants to kill you?"

Alex pondered for a second.

He really did.

The question was a complicated one.

"What a shitty life." Taking a long windup, Gribovsky clapped his forehead.

Chapter 30

The following week was as calm as it could have been for a black wizard employed as a full-time professor in the holy of holies of Atlantis' magic education, one who also had a side job with the glorious Guards and a debt of 100,000 credits he needed to pay back to the Syndicate.

Surprisingly enough, neither the Guards nor the Syndicate reminded Doom of his obligations. His workdays all blended together into a single bleak gray mush.

His time from getting up until 4 or 5 p.m. belonged to the university. Lecturing turned out to be a piece of cake—all Doom had to do was turn on the projector.

The seal did the rest.

From first-year students to sixth-year students, no one had yet unraveled the mystery. But that was only to be expected. Alex had long since given up solving it himself.

If he couldn't do it, no one could. At least, no one on New Earth. As for Old Earth, particularly eastern Europe and Asia, where the dark arts hadn't been extinguished, there might have been some wizards skilled enough. It was just that hiring one of them as a consultant would have cost more than his debt to the Syndicate.

Alex rued the day he was tortured with that bloody cross and told he'd be needing some Vaseline. Luckily enough, he'd had the connections he needed to buy the Syndicate's protection and preserve his male honor and dignity.

Anyone who might have said he should have scattered the attackers Chuck Norris-style, going at it like a lone wolf, probably never found themselves in a cramped room face to face with several thugs for whom killing a man is just as easy as going to the bathroom.

Enough negativity. How about some ugliness?

After finishing his lectures and escaping the paperwork and his supervisor responsibilities (Doom had used the roof exit for that purpose the last time), he headed home.

He scrubbed the Schooner's floor. Washed the toilets. Did the dishes. Sometimes poured whiskey, but only when the Boatswain wasn't around. And only straight into his mouth.

Actually, Alex could have paid the rent without doing the menial work, but that would have burned through his money quickly. And every single credit he earned at the university went toward repaying his debt to the city.

Brutal.

Things were made even worse by the groups of B-52 students visiting the Schooner every evening. The mixed youngsters drank soft cocktails, gobbled down food, and tried to chat with Alex. He'd been successful in avoiding them to date.

"Professor!" The security guard, whose name was Ban, lifted his cap to Alex. He was a pleasant elderly man whose mana level was just a touch above a non-magical person's, barely enough for him to activate the magic barrier in the university gate. "You parked in the wrong spot again."

Alex looked back.

His chrome and steel horse stood by the curb, right on a yellow zigzag. The holographic sign above it said that a city bus was due to stop on that very zigzag in a few minutes.

Alex lit a cigarette and waved a hand.

[Spell used: UNDEAD of Black Magic and Necromancy School. Mana used: 75 points/one + 1.2 points/min.]

Clouds of black smoke gathered around the bike. One by one, seven-foot skeletons climbed out of them, stringy flesh hanging from white bones where their skin used to be. Most were clad in shabby old leather armor that looked to be the veteran of dozens of battles, while a few were wearing chainmail with broken rings. They held long, broken sabers and steel shields in their hands.

The spell wasn't particularly strong or cutting-edge, but Alex liked it. While effectively harmless, it was impressive and very cheap in terms of both its retail value and its mana consumption.

"Professor?" The guard closed the lattice of his hut. "Could you please find a... a more attractive way of protecting it next time?"

"This is just the second time I'm parking here," Alex replied, inhaling and puffing out a dense cloud of smoke. "How's your grandson, Ban? Did they stop bullying him?"

"Yes, they did, ever since then."

"Excellent."

"Why didn't you walk here the way you usually do, Professor?" Ban livened up—his thick, reddish-gray moustache bounced up and down like a cockroach. It looked more funny than disgusting. "You live across the street."

"I have a date today, Ban. Right after work."

"Oh. With Miss Perriot, right?"

Alex choked on the smoke and coughed, clutching at the wrought-iron fence.

"Oh, I'm sorry, Professor, I shouldn't have said that. Here, let me slap you on the back."

Alex eyed the hand poking out of the hut. It could have probably broken *nails* with a slap, not to mention a black wizard's back.

"What made you think of Miss Perriot, Ban?"

"Well, after the museum incident, the whole university's been talking…"

"Talking," Alex grumbled, squinting maliciously. "Looks like some people have too much free time during my lectures."

Thinking to himself how to fix that, Alex started toward the central building. Even then, surrounded by the bare trees of winter slowly giving place to spring, the main university building looked immaculate and airy.

Like a castle from an old fairy tale.

"Have a good day, Professor!" Ban shouted at his receding figure.

Alex replied with quick wave of his hand and, flying up the stairs like a bat, jerked the door open to see…an absolutely empty hall.

For once, luck showed him her *face*, and not her other side.

Alex's schedule was set up such that his lectures didn't begin until noon. Right then, half an hour before, everyone was in their other classes.

Walking down the halls, he only came across a few students on break, fellow professors, and secretaries.

Alex's luck ran out when he was almost to his lecture hall and bumped smack into Mrs. Hopps. Judy Hopps. She had the very same name as the rabbit from that movie about the animal city, and even her personality was somewhat similar.

Unfortunately, Alex had ruined their wonderful relationship before it ever got going.

It didn't matter that they hadn't started an actual relationship because Secretary Hopps turned him down; Alex kept right on believing.

Like Romeo and Juliet. Or a vampire and a school outsider.

In prison, he hadn't had much to do, so he'd amused himself by reading about a weird vampire who refused to devour his human dinner.

"Miss Hopps!" Alex tried to give her a hug, but the agile brunette sidestepped him. "It's so great to see you—your pretty face would salvage even my worst day. Hey, did you make me a cup of hot chocolate? Or a latte at least?"

"I'm Dean Lebenstein's secretary, not *yours*, Professor Dumsky," Hopps snapped. "And if you keep harassing me, I can—"

"Sure, sure." Alex, who'd already made it halfway to his lecture hall, waved vaguely as he left the secretary behind. "I think we make for the perfect couple, too, you and I. But, unfortunately, the path taken by two loving hearts is never an easy one. It's such a shame you can't break off your sinful affair with your husband."

Judy, complete with an armful of papers, just froze on the spot. Alex was a master at finding new ways to dumbfound her and avoid being buried under the papers she was holding.

He would have had to do an overwhelming amount of paperwork for free otherwise.

That was definitely not what he'd signed up for.

Signed up for? The pun wasn't just stupid; it was downright scary.

"Stop!" the usually calm secretary barked and, off like a shot, jumped around Alex to push the lecture hall door open with her shoulder. "You won't be getting away that easily, Professor."

"Get away? I *dream* of you every night, Mrs. Hopps. I can't even sleep, I need you so badly. My heart is broken." Alex all but shed an actor's tear. "And you—"

Suddenly, he heard a *click*.

Judy flashed a small recorder at him.

"I recorded everything you said, Professor," she crowed triumphantly. "That's harassment, and you could be sued for it. Although, I don't think you want that. Why don't you take this paper mountain off my hands, fill out all the forms by the end of the week, and I'll forget I have this recording."

Alex shifted his confused stare from the device to the secretary's triumphant face, then back to the device. "Are you...*blackmailing* me?"

"You leave me no other choice, Professor." Judy was offended, her pretty face taking on the look of a perplexed Fury. "I've been waiting a week for you to fill out all the forms, and I have neither the time nor the desire to do it for you."

"Why can't we just forget about them? That would be a simple enough way out for both of us."

"No, not for *me*. My boss won't leave me alone until I submit a full report to him. And I can't put it together without your papers."

Doom could have cracked a joke about the boss not leaving her alone, but he was a black wizard, not a complete jerk.

Although many women would have argued that he was both.

"You have my respect," Alex nodded, then moved his hand through the air. "That was a smart move."

Screaming, Judy dropped what had just a second before been her recorder. It quickly turned into a small hissing pool of melted plastic and metal spreading across the floor.

"But I put up my shields! I used a protection artifact!"

"So you did. I could see it from the stairs."

Hopps looked up at Alex with resolute, unwavering eyes. She was not about to give up.

"But still, I'll…" Doom took the pile of papers from her. "I hope you don't have a draft because of the broken door, Miss Hopps."

Closing his own door behind him and leaving the perplexed secretary outside, Alex, muttering the filthiest curses he knew, plodded toward his desk to dump the papers on it.

How did tiny Judy even lift the bloody pile? It felt like it weighed as much as the dumbbells Doom had spent so much time with in prison. And each of them weighed twenty pounds at least.

Well. He had to come up with a way to fill out all the forms. It wasn't anything he was about to himself.

"Professor Dumsky?" came a familiar voice from behind Alex.

Did I accidentally grab the lucky leprechaun coin from the museum when I was fighting that gorilla?

Looking over, Alex saw his whole group. All five were there, from the weird, affected Leo, the male model, to their true leader—gray-haired Mara Glomebood. A pretty half-blood girl, she mixed human and, oddly enough, dwarf.

"My darling students!" Doom rejoiced. "I could really use your help…"

As the wheels in Alex's head started turning at triple speed, it struck him that something was wrong.

"Why aren't you in class?" he asked, squinting at them.

"We're skipping," Travis, the red guy, told him defiantly.

"And we're going to keep it up," the Wessex blonde added. "Every class we miss will be another paper pain in your neck."

"Wow," Alex drawled, leaning back against his desk and crossing his arms over his chest. "Are you *threatening* me? Color me intrigued. What do you want?"

"We need your help," Mara said as she stepped forward. She may have been the bravest of the five or…well, the devil only knew what traits it took to be a leader in a human group. Alex was too anti-social to have a clue. "We need it so badly we'll keep causing problems for you if we don't get it."

Doom sighed and massaged the bridge of his nose.

"My dear students," he said in a whisper that was loud enough to be heard at the opposite end of the lecture hall. "This is the second time I'm being blackmailed in the past five minutes. Why don't you rephrase your request for help, preferably to include money as some sort of an offer to collaborate in a way that is mutually beneficial? Otherwise, you're going to share the first blackmailer's fate."

As he said that, he lit a purple fire around his hand.

His mentees exchanged glances.

"One sixth of the prize fund," the Asian, whose name was Jing, said coldly. He was the most dangerous-looking one in the group, at least as dangerous as an uneducated kid could be.

"Too little... Hey, wait. What prize fund?"

"You don't know?"

"Do I look like someone who would ask questions when he already knows the answer?"

For a moment or two, there was a weird silence. Then Mara took the lead again.

"There's an incoming student magic tournament in a month, this time with a much larger prize fund because of the jubilee. Half a million credits. We want...no, we *have to* get it. That's why we need your help, Professor. You defeated that demon, and... Professor? Professor Dumsky, are you listening to me? What are you looking for, Professor?"

"I think," Alex called from underneath his desk, "the coin must have rolled over here."

"What coin?"

"The lucky leprechaun one."

The students exchanged glances, suddenly doubting their brilliant plan.

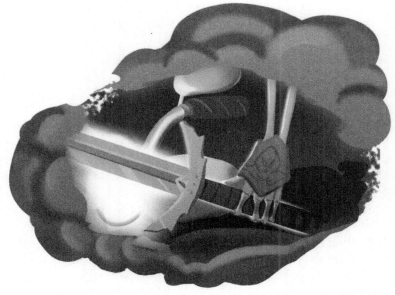

Chapter 31

Because of all the information Alex's students had dumped on him, his work day lasted well beyond what he'd initially planned. It had long been dark when he stepped out onto the street. The streetlamps were lit, bright yellow skirts of light rescuing parts of sidewalks and flower beds from the tender but cold embrace of darkness. There were lights on in the campus buildings and distant dorms, the voices of never-sleeping students drifting over on the breeze.

Doom turned up his jacket collar. Spring was slow to come to Myers City, the freezing winter still holding its own. An unpleasantly damp easterly wind was blowing, promising a heavy rain soon and perhaps the last thunderstorm as the year slipped away.

He needed a cigarette.

He always needed one.

It was an old habit.

Overcoming the urge, he walked over to the guard hut. Ban was fast asleep on the gate console the way he always was by the end of his shift. The gate closed and opened automatically all the same; the guard's post was just a tribute to the old days when the university was *actually* guarded.

That was back during the Magic War. It ended roughly the same time as Atlantis and the lands of the magic races separated from the rest of the world.

But in such a progressively conservative kind of society as Atlantis, old traditions were a thing to be reckoned with.

Passing the hut and stepping out onto Myers City's Central Boulevard, Alex winced—the lights were too bright. Thousands of them merged into a single multi-colored canvas that shone in the night like a never-fading lighthouse.

The light from the skyscrapers reached far past the clouds, up to the gliders of the sky patrols guarding the heavens.

Sky predators seldom approached big cities. The bright lights scared most of them away, though, to be fair, some were attracted to it. The sky patrols, recently introduced by the city government, were far from useless.

Out in the streets, the thousands of shop windows, the streetlamps, and the headlights of cars swishing by melted into rivers of cold, artificial light.

The nights in Myers City were sometimes brighter than the days. But the nights were also the time when the shadows cast by the bright lights seemed particularly vivid.

"I'm turning into a poet," Alex grumbled, adjusting his collar again.

The skeleton warriors were still on sentry duty by his steel horse. Judging by the number of parking tickets on the handlebars, they made for awfully lazy guards.

"You're fired." Alex waved a hand, reducing them to dust.

Humans and non-humans (however politically incorrect that sounded) scattered all around him. Paying no attention to the scared whispers behind his back and the hasty attempts to retrieve phones from bags and pockets, Doom jumped on the bike and opened the throttle.

Rearing up on the rear wheel, he sliced through the night traffic. Horns blared as cars screeched to a halt, trying not to run down the crazy biker. Shouts were hurled at his back from lowered windows.

They're fearless in the central district.

High Gardeners would have just crawled on to where they were going, aware that any careless move might attract the attention of shady characters.

"And you call *me* crazy, pumpkin." Gribovsky, wearing his usual hat and trench coat, stood leaning against his tiny sports car.

"The crossing was too far," Alex replied as he kicked the footpeg down and crossed his arms over the handlebar.

"You just came from right over there." The lieutenant pointed at the crossing some six hundred feet away.

"That's too far, I'm telling you. So, are we going? Or are we just going to stand here?"

Gribovsky whispered something under his breath. It sounded like a curse, albeit an admiring one.

"Get off that gasoline monster of yours, and we'll go."

Opening his car door, the guardsman realized that Alex was still mounted.

"Do you need an invitation, pumpkin?"

"We're taking my bike."

"Wait, what?" Gribovsky frowned.

Alex knew all too well why they were using a service car. The Guards didn't trust Doom (with good reason), and that was one of their precautions.

"They'll notice a strange car before we ever get close. There's no way we'll get into the Abyss."

Gribovsky squinted; his face looked even more predatory.

"You're lying," the cowboy more stated than asked.

"Maybe," Alex replied with a cunning smile. "But there's no way you can know for sure."

They stared each other down for a while until Gribovsky, muttering something like, *the Asian's going to kill me*, closed the car door, activated an alarm that made a funny quacking sound, and came over to the bike.

"Is that...?"

"My niece playing with the car computer. I'm already used to it," Gribovsky hissed through gritted teeth as he climbed into the passenger seat. He wrapped his arms tightly around Alex's belt.

With a quacking sound reminiscent of the alarm duck, Doom glanced down and then back at Gribovsky.

"Are you a homophobe, pumpkin?"

"I'm a High Gardener," Alex snapped. "You have a grip behind you. Use it."

"Touchy," the guardsman snorted, but he released his embrace and grabbed hold of the upright chrome stick that jutted up over the place for the bags.

"Try to keep your hat on," Alex said, kicking the footpeg up, rolling the throttle on, and slicing back through traffic onto the street.

The engine roared, cylinders rattling. The reinforced suspension maintained its sure grip of the road, letting Alex and his apparently non-sports bike make unimaginable turns without stopping at red lights. He accelerate to a scary speed, completely ignoring the magic car traffic.

Elves in their elegant and sporty coupes. Orcs and trolls in giant SUVs. Humans in all sorts of vehicles, and the Fae driving the brightest and newest cars they could find. All of them flashed by in Alex's peripheral vision.

The expensive boutique windows hurtled by, too. The plainest scarf in shops like those cost an uptown factory worker's annual salary.

So, too, did the gleaming signs of night clubs and cinemas sweep past. In and out walked young and old, humans and non-humans.

The nighttime glitter of downtown Myers City, with its broad avenues and crammed sidewalks, fell behind them. The district Alex was heading to was far less respectable than the center, though it still had its special kind of charm and chic.

Amalgam Street District, named after its central street, had once been a mecca for free minds. The anarchists gathered there to discuss the necessity of overthrowing the government and handing power to general assemblies of free wizards. Artists came to leave trendy graffiti on the walls or, sitting down at their easels, paint portraits or the cityscape. Writers and film directors came for inspiration.

Musicians, performers, drug addicts, vagrants, adventurers, sculptors, poets…all of them flocked (and continued to flock) to Amalgam Street.

And that made sense.

It was only there, in that district, that you could still find the remnants of past historical ages among the steel and chromium of the downtown skyscrapers. The asphalt sometimes gave place to cobblestones, the high-rise concrete jungle to the squat buildings in the old city. The style was pompous and somewhat grotesque pseudo-Gothic, with towers, gargoyles, houses looking like palaces, and palaces looking like castles.

Amalgam Street was the second (after the downtown) tourist mecca in Myers City.

It was the only place you could see a skyscraper with an actual garden and real medieval castles on the rooftop. It was the only place that still boasted rows of houses, each of which deserved its own mention in architectural guidebooks.

A beautiful and controversial place.

High Garden for the rich, it was called. Along with its luxurious architecture, the district had the greatest concentration of brothels, bars, cheap strip clubs, and night clubs where it was easier to buy drugs than a bottle of clean, fresh water.

But all of that was hidden in the shadow of the rich bohemian and cultural life. It wasn't as outright seedy as High Garden, though it was still better to avoid taking its far-too-attractive appearance at face value.

Alex stopped at a line of small, five-story houses from the eighteenth—or maybe seventeenth—century. They practically breathed France with their balconies, terraces, and stain-glass windows. The first floors were occupied by cafes, galleries, and boutiques.

"Follow me," Alex said without looking back. Not bothering to cast an alarm spell on his bike, he walked into the small alley between a boutique and a café.

Filled with sewage vapor and crammed with stinking trash bags, the alley was so narrow only one human and a half could walk shoulder to shoulder. And it was a perfect demonstration of Amalgam Street's seamy side, not to mention that of greater Myers City.

"I'm still not sure we *are* going to the Abyss." Gribovsky's voice had turned creepily serious again. Alex couldn't see what the cowboy was doing, but he assumed he had a hand at the ready on his enchanted gun.

"We're not," Doom replied with a shake of his head. "We're already here."

Having said that, he walked over to an inconspicuous steel door. It was the kind you wouldn't have even noticed as you walked by, and it looked like it led to the café's kitchen.

And it did.

It really was the café's back door.

Although it didn't lead to the kitchen.

Rummaging around in his pockets, Alex retrieved a gold coin big enough to cover two thirds of his palm. It was engraved with various symbols surrounding a face under a deep hood.

He stepped up to the door, moved one of the wall bricks aside, and tossed the coin into the hole behind it.

"Seriously?" Gribovsky was apparently surprised. "Pure gold?"

"A lot of *them* are allergic to silver."

"Good point. But still, so trivial and so...John Wickly."

Alex turned around to give Gribovsky an appraising once-over.

"The owner is a big fan of the John Wick movies. And Keanu Reeves. So, no Matrix jokes in there, got it?"

Gribovsky was about to reply when, with a metal clang, the door was unbolted and two dark, almost black eyes peered out.

Alex shuddered.

Damn.

He'd forgotten how uneasy Joe's eyes always made him.

Chapter 32

Farrokh, the head of the Dark Creatures' secret organization called the Abyss Club, looked very… ordinary. A classic black suit, straight pants, a gray pocket square peeking out of his chest pocket. His white shirt was washed so clean it shone like starlight in the stage lights.

A wide tie, its color exactly matching that of the pocket square, hung down to the bottom of his stomach.

His face was entirely nondescript. Coming across him somewhere downtown, you'd probably take him for the owner of a consulting firm or maybe a small-time banker.

His well-groomed goatee was reminiscent of Tony Stark. Sharp cheekbones. A wide nose. A thin line formed by ever-compressed lips. A hairstyle worth more than a factory worker's monthly salary.

The only thing out of step with the overall image of a typical financier was a strand of white—not gray, but actually *white*—hair starting right in the middle of his forehead and ending at the back of his head.

There was also Farrokh's constant companion: Silent Blake. A white skull carved with symbols and hieroglyphs hung in the air over Farrokh's left shoulder. The skull was always smiling, sometimes with an open mouth, but it never said a word.

It was rumored to have been extremely talkative until it annoyed some powerful wizard to the point that he cursed it with silence. That happened before the first steam engine was invented on Old Earth.

Farrokh was an ancient creature.

Perhaps the most ancient of the ones who remained in Myers City instead of moving, flying, or sailing off to another corner of Atlantis or Old Earth.

"So, Alex Doom. You come to the house from which you were banned, and on the day we all celebrate."

What a voice. He's had ages to practice the art of making opponents disable the defenses around their mind and soul with the very sound of his voice.

"Why? To make me keep my word and send you to the shadows and your partner to the light?"

Farrokh leaned on his long cane topped with a raven's metal skull. Not nearly life-sized, of course.

The ancient black wizard had an unhealthy passion for canes. Every time Doom saw him, he was walking around with a new one.

"Could we sit down at a table?" Alex asked.

Their conversation may have looked like small talk, but the club around them was strained to the breaking point. Doom could feel dozens and hundreds of eyes on him belonging to all sorts of wizards and magic creatures.

One gesture from Farrokh, and he and Gribovsky would have been torn to pieces in a moment.

"Why should I sit down with a traitor?" Farrokh arched his right brow in surprise.

"Because the Shadow Court acquitted me completely," Alex said with his regular defiant smirk, although inside he was trembling like an autumn leaf. He'd been taught never to show his fear to the abyss. Only his courage. *And if you have none, then your madness.* "I didn't betray anyone. I didn't *kill* anyone. What's dead can't be killed."

"And that is why you're still breathing and I rewrote the club rules so I could just ban you instead of declaring a hunt. So, we're even. But let me ask again and for the last time: why, Alexander Dumsky, *why* shouldn't I destroy your soul right now?"

There was a heavy pause. The music raged. The patrons pretended to be busy with their own business, but their eyes were drilling holes in the two visitors.

"In memory of Robin," Alex whispered as his heart was clutched by icy claws. "And the whole Follen School."

He felt short of breath.

Farrokh's spirits flagged. His shoulders drooped; he grasped his cane with both hands.

"Come over to the table, Alex." The owner of the establishment (and the whole organization) turned around and walked toward the table no one ever dared occupy. It was Farrokh's personal table.

Doom looked at Gribovsky.

"What, pumpkin?" Gribovsky asked with his usual bravado, but with eyes that were serious and piercing.

"I was exiled, lieutenant, but I'm still a black wizard."

"I know."

"You and whatever wizardry power you have stink of Light. So, for the locals, you're no better than a mere mortal."

"And?"

"Do you know what a group of dark, ever-starving creatures does when they see mortal meat in front of them?"

Gribovsky's face scrunched up in concentration. Then he lifted the flap of his trench coat to show the handles of his two enchanted guns.

"They're welcome to try."

To Alex's consternation, Gribovsky really meant what he said. If the club's clientele had attacked him right then, he wouldn't have retreated. He might have perished in the lopsided battle, but he apparently wasn't afraid of death. He preferred to take the lives (or afterlives) of those coming for his flesh.

Damn cowboy.

"They're going to push you, Gribovsky. Metaphorically and literally. You can defend yourself however you want, but don't kill anyone."

"Why not, pumpkin?"

"Because," Alex hissed, "if you do that, we'll both be murdered on spot. Or they'll have Joe kill us, which would be even worse. I'll try to finish the negotiations as fast as possible. And you…you just try to stay alive."

"Trust me, boy." Again, Gribovsky's eyes flashed in a way that was highly incongruent with the pumpkins he threw around so liberally. "These brutes have met their match."

Doom started at the word "brutes." But who was he, anyway, to try to change society's perception of Dark Creatures in general and black wizards in particular?

Alex turned around and followed Farrokh. With every step he

took, a tolling bell inside his mind awoke memories he'd been running from for over a decade.

***

The little boy with black, curly hair and funny glasses hiding his emerald eyes clutched the magic handbook disguised as a porn magazine as he watched the florist's sand-colored dress vanish into the overgrown weeds.

"No!" screamed a girl from the shrubs. "Help…"

Then the sound of blows. Lots of blows. Wailing. Men's shouts.

Alex had heard those sounds before at St. Frederick's Orphanage. Like all the locals, he knew you never *ever* went over to see what they were about.

There, in the dark…

Scary.

So scary.

He heard their voices again inside his head.

Look, it's Alex Doom! The dark wizard who's afraid of darkness!

What a terrifying dark lord—ha! Let's lock him up in the storeroom!

"No," Alex whispered. "No. Please don't."

Afraid of darkness, you villain? We light heroes will overcome you. Drag him down into the cellar.

Scary…

"Please don't. Please. We're friends, aren't we? We played together."

Friends with a black wizard?! Do I look like an idiot?

"Please don't." Alex curled up into a ball beneath the tree. "Don't go over there, Miss Elisa. Please."

He looked over at the tall weeds, waiting for the only human who hadn't teased, scared, or beat him over the previous few months, who had always been there for him, to come back.

The only warmth he knew.

The warmth doing battle for him with the encroaching darkness.

The darkness Alex feared so much.

He really *was* afraid of it.

Because he knew.

He could sense *what* was lurking there in the dark, waiting for him. It was a thousand times scarier than any monster under the bed or any creep from the horror movies the wards used to secretly watch at night.

"I'm scared."

Alex really was very, very scared. He had to follow Miss Elisa. Help her. Rescue her.

If only he had been able to move.

He knew all too well *what* was over there in the overgrown weeds.

"What are you…"

"A human wizard! Great, more flesh to go around!"

"No!" A woman's shriek pierced Alex's ears.

It was Miss Elisa.

Dropping his handbook, the boy rushed into the weeds.

Chapter 33

"**G**ood evening, Joe." Entering the small tambour sheathed with rusting tin, Alex tipped his hat.

Gribovsky swallowed noisily behind him.

It was hard to blame him. Sitting on the small stool beside the entrance was…a creature. It would have looked almost human if it weren't for the physique that would have been the envy of all the famous bodybuilders and powerlifters in Old Earth.

And not just human athletes. Even some small orcs and ogres would have envied Joe.

From head to toe, he was 7'4.3" tall. Doom knew his height so exactly because he'd once been suckered by local hustlers and lost a hefty sum betting on the club's eternal bouncer's height.

But lofty proportions didn't keep him from having an Apollo-like build. Muscular and absolutely symmetrical, he looked sculpted from bronze or stone, every fiber and tendon clearly visible.

He was some kind of living anatomic tutorial, always dressed in pants with suspenders. His white shirtsleeves were rolled up to expose tattooed forearms, there were black patent-leather shoes on his feet, and under them were…cartoon character socks.

"Who Framed Roger Rabbit," Doom said, recognizing the seductive, red-haired beauty on Joe's right sock.

"Here on business, Doom? Or just for fun?" Joe's voice matched his body. It didn't sound human—more like a nuclear-powered icebreaker cracking its way through the ever-frozen ocean. Alex couldn't bring himself to call it merely deep or husky.

"Business, actually."

Joe looked up from his book (judging by the cover, this time it was *The Old Man and the Sea*). His black eyes crossed Doom's emerald stare, sending shivers down the latter's spine.

Facing a whole pack of gorilla demons like the one in the museum wouldn't have been enough to make Doom shudder. At least, no more than any reasonable member of the black magical profession would have in that situation.

But Joe…

Still a callow youngster back then, Alexander had witnessed Joe, with his bare hands, break (literally, shedding lots of blood) a *Supreme Vampire* to the point of knuckling under. A nephew to the duke of Myers City.

Alex would have been damned if he, even were he as strong as

Peter from the Syndicate, could have even wriggled free of a Supreme Vampire in the middle of the night without losing his face. Not to mention wounding it.

But Joe had broken every single bone in its body. The only reason he hadn't killed it was because all killing was prohibited at the Abyss.

But only killing.

That was one of the club's few rules.

"You were expelled."

"Yeah, I heard Farrokh." Doom gave a wry smirk.

Putting a good face on a bad deal was something he'd learned from... Well, that didn't really matter.

"Then go ahead," Joe said, pointing up the spiral staircase with his big hand.

"Have a good evening, Joe." Alex doffed his hat and started up the familiar stairs. Too familiar.

Over the six years that Doom had been banned from the Abyss and its associated businesses, virtually nothing had changed. Even the stairs seemed to sway at his every step exactly the way they had in the past.

He had to hold onto the ever-damp steel railing. It must have accumulated the moisture from the brick walls of the tall well leading up into the main hall.

"Who...*what* was that sitting down there?" Gribovsky asked.

Alex heard the distinct click of the enchanted gun being cocked.

"Joe," Doom said with a shrug.

"Joe? What's that supposed to mean? That thing... My lenses couldn't scan it. They showed *nothing*."

Alex had been astonished by that fact as well when he met the club's bouncer for the first time. But over time, he'd gotten used to it. And he'd stopped asking questions he had no hope of getting a reasonable answer to.

"Mine can't either."

"Doom, fu—..." As Gribovsky stumbled on the stairs, his swear word turned into an unintelligible whisper. "You don't get it. *My* lenses are nothing like yours."

That confirmed Alex's guess. He'd heard the rumors that the lenses used by civil servants had different functionality than regular ones.

Gribovsky worked for the Guards, an organization so ancient that most Old Earth countries were too young to be its younger siblings.

"And they...they showed nothing. *Nothing*. So, let me ask you again: who—or what—was that sitting down there?"

"Joe," Doom repeated. "Just Joe. I hope that's the last time we're going to talk about him today."

Just then, they reached the well cover. And that wasn't a metaphor—it was an exact description of the entrance to the club's main hall.

The owner of the establishment (or rather a secret organization, a shadow government for those the world preferred to forget: the Dark Creatures), Farrokh, didn't just like Keanu Reeves. He was also a fan of horror movies.

And so, Alex and Gribovsky entered (or rather climbed into) the hall from a very real, authentic well. According to Farrokh, it had been the location where they'd filmed the original version of that same movie.

As soon as Doom stepped up into the Abyss, his ears were assaulted by deep, bass sounds. The rhythmical, knocking, and gliding music altered his heartbeat to match the local ambience.

And the place *did* have ambience.

The dim light created the illusion of a caustic semi-dark that was further amplified by smoke from cigarettes, cigars, pipes, hookahs, and even fog machines.

The red, pink, and crimson stage lights cut through the dark beneath the ceiling but didn't reach the floor. Instead, they stopped halfway in the air to turn into a variety of illusions floating over the heads of the crowds dancing next to the stages.

The illusions ranged from a sexy female vampire with a half-open mouth to a guitar-shaped bottle of expensive wine that wasn't actually wine at all.

Wriggling on the poles enclosed in columns of silvery-whitish light were naked and half-naked female dancers so sexy and beautiful they gave first-time visitors a hot sensation in their pants no matter their gender.

Alex had heard that Farrokh had been offered up to 500,000 credits for a night with one of them, but they were off-limits. Like museum paintings, they were there for everyone to feast their eyes on and keep their hands off of.

Beyond the fence, in the dense darkness, different kinds of creatures were eating and drinking at the round tables. They probably weren't there for fun. Instead, they'd come to discuss business or just feel at home.

It was a home where they weren't regarded as second-rate creatures ineligible for the presumption of innocence.

Although, to be honest, nobody innocent ever patronized the Abyss.

"What now?" Gribovsky yelled in Alex's ear.

Alex jumped aside and dug around in his ear with his little finger. Turning to the lieutenant, he looked into his eyes and replied softly.

"Don't shout. If you want to be heard, just look at the person and speak in a normal tone. The magic will do the rest."

"Magic?" Quick on the uptake, Gribovsky was already talking regularly. "Pumpkin, I'm in a place that's remained hidden for ages even from the Guards. *That's* real magic."

Alex ignored the compliment to the Dark Community. Over centuries of persecution and incessant wars with the constantly growing Light Community, the Darks had become unsurpassed masters of one art. The art of hiding.

Even then, with the actual wars and persecution long since turned into a cold war under the cloak of acceptance and tolerance, the Darks remained hidden in their communities. They avoided contact with an outer world that held far more danger for vampires and the rest of their ilk than there had been for mortals or champions of Light in the Dark Ages.

In other words, the Light had won.

And the Abyss remained the last fortress of the Dark. Or, as romantic youngsters put it, the last bastion of freedom.

Squeezing through a small crowd of werewolves, chimeras, and even a couple undead, Alex reached the bar counter. In the kingdom of hi-tech, chromium, steel, premium leather, and Persian carpets that the Abyss was, the counter was the single nod to the redneck spirit.

A shabby oak top. Tall chairs on wooden legs. Several beer vending machines. A couple poles. Hustling bartenders. An enormous mirror crisscrossed by shelves loaded with all kinds of bottles.

"Alexander," a slightly surprised and pleasant female voice called.

Valerie. She was a pretty blonde with long hair and shiny, cheerful eyes, her clothes just a bit revealing, yet still neat and stylish.

One of the Abyss' long-standing employees.

But Alex was probably the only one who saw her that way.

Valerie was a kind of human known as a *chameleon*. When speaking to someone, they became what the other person would be most comfortable dealing with. Doing it subconsciously rather than purposefully, Valerie still remained one of the most pleasant creatures at the Abyss.

Even though Alex realized it was all merely a game.

Just like the whole Abyss.

Damn. Stopping by the club always seemed to bring out the philosopher in him.

"But you're…"

"Pour me the usual, Valerie."

The girl flashed a calm, white-toothed smile. A smile Alex was sure to like. Alex and no one but him.

An exclusive sort of game.

"Russian tea?"

"Yep."

"And for your companion?"

"Orange soda, please," Gribovsky said, rebuffing Alex's suspicious glance with: "I'm at work. And what the hell is Russian tea?"

Alex was about to answer when another voice (a velvet baritone hiding a secret poisoned knife beneath unconditional hospitality) interrupted to explain.

"Two ounces of whiskey. One ice cube. Two teaspoons of lemon juice. One lime wedge. Mix until half the ice melts. The favorite drink of Robin and his little tail, one known as Alexander Dumsky."

Sighing to himself, Alex turned to the speaker.

"Hey there, Farrokh."

"Hi, Doom. Didn't I tell you I'd kill you the next time we met?"

Chapter 34

The tall, sharp grass cut his hands and face, big drops of blood falling onto the cold ground.

Stumbling, Alex fell, smashing his nose and breaking his teeth on the gravel, but jumping up and running on.

Not her. Please, not her.

Screaming. Blows. Bright flashes of all different colors illuminating figures in the dark.

Not her. Not Miss Elisa.

Alex ran out into a small clearing.

…and saw with his own eyes what the older boys had been talking about.

Four of them. Tall and creepily beautiful, straight and arrogant. Either humans looking like animals or animals doing their best to look human.

They were called *fairies*. The fae people. Worshippers of the Goddess Danu.

Half-naked, flashing their male parts and bodies as perfect as that of the Greek god of the sun, the fifth one was down, making weird twitching moves on top of an orphan girl from St. Frederick's. The girl was reduced to just weeping softly.

Her name was Ku Sin, if Alex remembered correctly. She had beautiful almond-shaped eyes and black hair.

But she and her silent tears weren't what he cared about right then.

"Look! A human boy."

Where is she?

"Any bum bandits here?"

Where's Miss Elisa?

"Are you insulting my honor, Viscount Porway?"

Where was his warmth in the endless dark?

"Just asking a rhetorical question, Baron Kelven. It's a joke."

"No more kidding like that."

A burst of laughter came from the beastly men or manly beasts.

Then Alex saw her. The torn pieces of the sand-color dress were scattered over ground soaked with blood.

Doom knelt next to her and touched her hand.

Cool. All warmth gone.

Red flowers had torn through her dress. Piercing her flesh with sharp thorns, breaking her bones, and slicing her tissue, they'd taken on the color of blood. Up and up they rose to the moon, growing right out of Elisa's body.

Her body no longer shivered or twitched.

It just disappeared beneath the flower roots, turning into a bloody, morbid flowerbed.

Her warm brown eyes disappeared, two creepy, thorny stems in their place.

What kind of magic is that?

"You..." Alex whispered.

Black wizard, the voice in his head said.

"Look! The human larva speaks!"

"You killed her?" Doom asked.

Black wizards don't have friends.

"Killed? Of course not, boy. We just primped her up a little."

"Oh yes. That mortal piece of flesh looks so much better as a flowerbed."

Another burst of laughter.

Alex turned toward them. Toward the beastly men.

They'd taken away the last bit of warmth protecting him from the darkness. And without it...

"I hate you," Alex hissed.

"What?" one of the monsters asked mockingly.

"I hate you all!" the boy yelled, jerking his right hand up. The lilac fire whirled around his fingers. Then...

...a sharp, sudden pain slashed across his right cheek, and a tremendous force picked him up, dragged him through the air, and flung him back onto the ground.

A shout of pain escaped the boy's lips to go along with a splash of blood.

"Kill him," a cold voice came.

The darkness was encroaching. Someone was coming for Alex.

He couldn't see that well, his vision blurred by blood and tears.

But that was nothing.

Come, come closer.

Alex reached for the darkness. A different sort of darkness. Not the outside one—he wasn't afraid of *that* darkness.

It was the creepy darkness living inside him. Somewhere next to his heart.

It would suffice.

Come closer.

It *must* suffice.

Come.

Suffice for…

"Hey!" called a merry, light-hearted voice. "You, furballs in the pasture!"

"What?"

A new figure stepped forward to shield Alex. He was a tall man, the hems of his stylish black jacket flapping in the wind, his narrow tie flowing too. His pants fluttered over brogue shoes polished to a shine, and his head was covered by a black, stripeless hat.

"Who the hell are you?"

"Me?" The stranger exhaled cigarette smoke. "I'm the terror that flaps in the night. I'm… Damn it, you monkeys. Judging by your faces, you haven't seen Duck Tales."

"What??"

"See how stupid they are, boy?" The stranger pointed his cigarette at the fae with a click of fingers. "That's what hormones do to animals. Creepy, isn't that?"

"Get out of here, whoever you are," one of the closest fae said through gritted teeth. "He's *our* prey."

"Prey?" the young man in black suit repeated. "What about playing with a different kind? Someone your own size?"

"Are you…?"

Before the fae could finish, the young man threw out a palm and cast a flash of lilac fire that was awfully familiar to Alex.

He was a black wizard.

Alex realized that a moment before losing consciousness.

***

"Hey!" Someone was slapping his cheeks. "Hey, young prodigy!"

The claps were strong but not painful.

"Yes, you, orphaned wonder kid. Hey! Earth to moon boy!"

Alex didn't want to wake up.

"Hey, come on little Rambo!"

"Rambo? Who's that?"

"Damn it. Another illiterate."

Alex opened his eyes.

He was seated on a bus stop bench. Squatting in front of him was that same young man, only with blood trickling down his face, his suit torn in several places, and his left arm bent unnaturally.

"You…"

"Oh, it's nothing," the stranger replied with a dismissive wave of his uninjured arm. "I'll be fine. You should have seen those other guys. Their own mothers aren't going to recognize them."

The young man sat down next to Alex. With a trembling hand, he retrieved a crumpled pack of cigarettes from his inner pocket. Taking one, he lit it with his thumb and puffed a cloud of smoke into the High Garden night sky.

"Where are we?" Alex asked.

The young man looked around and shrugged, instantly gritting his teeth. The movement was apparently painful.

"Somewhere between Rose Street and 17th Street."

"I can see that."

"Then why ask stupid questions, little one?"

"Why am I not back at the orphanage?"

"I got you out of there."

"Am I going back?"

"Do you want to?"

"No."

"Then why ask?" The young man smiled with a kind of defiance. "Remember, little one: *never* ask questions when you know the answer. Or when you don't want to know what it is."

Alex thought that over.

"Where are we going?"

"Now that's the right question, Mr. Spooner."

"My name's Alexander Dumsky. Not Mr. Spooner."

The young man cursed.

"You haven't seen *I, Robot* either. What a long way to go. That wasn't even a Matrix joke. Farrokh prefers Keanu, but I'm a big Will Smith guy. Maybe because he's *black*, too. Hey, that's a great racist joke!"

Alex had no idea what the strange man was saying.

"Well, boy," the young man stood as he held onto the lamp post with his bloody hand, stood up, and limped off down the street. "Let's go."

"Where?"

"Where?" The young man looked back and flashed a broad smile, merry and kind. Just like Miss Elisa's. "To Follen School."

"What's that?"

"A place for people like you and me," the young man explained. "For black wizards."

A place for black wizards? A place for them to live and…apparently study?

Alex jumped off the bench and followed him.

"I'm Robin, by the way. Robin Loxley."

"Like Robin Hood?"

"Oh abyss! The patient's more alive than dead. Not all is lost. I'll make a man of you yet, little one."

Chapter 35

Alex sank into a leather-and-velvet sofa that embraced his behind softer than a skilled siren of the first order at a five-star hotel in downtown Myers City. Although, honestly, Doom was no fan of the ladies of the night. His Semite spirit rebelled against a descendant of glorious lenders and jewellers paying for what he could get for free.

"So," Farrokh said, leaning back in his antiquarian armchair and intertwining his fingers. "For Robin's sake, your head will remain attached to your shoulders today, Alex."

"You have my gratitude," Doom nodded in absolute seriousness. If it hadn't been for Joe, he might have stood a chance of getting out of the Abyss alive, albeit by paying a heavy toll in blood (mostly his own). But…Joe *was* there to ruin whatever bloody chance he had.

Gribovsky, looking on high alert, sat down by his side and relaxed at once. The sofas of the Royal Boot where Farrokh entertained his personal guests were famous for their comfort.

But the lieutenant was right to tense up—Alex had to admit that. Every dark predator in the club was lying in wait. Literally.

Vampires, fangs bared, squinted at the smell of human blood as it hit their special olfactory receptors. Alex tried to recall exactly were those receptors were, but he couldn't. He'd spent dark creature anatomy at school (if Follen could be…could *have* been called a school) studying his favorite subject: spell construction. That's how he spent almost every class.

Following the vampires, the werewolves, their eternal enemies, started to rise from their seats. Both fractions were civilized inside the club. At least, as civilized as either of them could be with an eternal enemy in sight.

Some werewolves had hair stirring on their heads and arms, a sure sign of an urge to transform into their animal form and start hunting.

But neither the vampires nor the werewolves were close to being the *greatest* threat awaiting mortals in the dark. There were other creatures, far more sinister and powerful, if fewer in number, who also turned their eyes (and more) on Gribovsky.

The prey can always sense the hungry predator's stare.

But Gribovsky was apparently unused to being the prey.

"So, what brings you to our club this wonderful evening?" Farrokh thanked the waitress with a nod. She was a young girl with snow-white skin, night-black hair, sky-blue eyes, and a pretty doll's face, her uniform stylized to resemble that of a past century governess but with a distinct sex shop touch.

The fishnet stockings were tight around her springy hips and long, slender legs.

She looked almost as good as the strippers (if you can use the word "good" to describe female embodiments of sex appeal and sensual desire) if not for...

Another damn "if not for."

Her neck was wrapped with a white kerchief, two distinct red spots showing through it.

Some club visitors whose purses were full of (literal) gold needed a *fresh product*. That made the girl and her glassy eyes as repulsive as she was alluring.

"Shit," Gribovsky swore and reached for his gun. Alex grabbed his wrist.

"If you move, we're both dead," Alex hissed through gritted teeth.

"Damn you, Doom. She's a mortal. I swore to protect her with my life and—"

"But not mine," Alex interrupted. "Not with *my* life, Lieutenant. Plus, she isn't alive anymore. Several vampires have tasted her blood recently, so she'll become a ghoul at best soon. A mindless low-class undead creature."

Gribovsky ripped his hand free and swore filthily.

"I know what a ghoul is," he snapped before retreating into the labyrinth of his mind.

That was when the club music changed. The electronic strokes gave place to viscous blues that gradually transformed into a fast, rhythmic, but still smoky jazzy funk. A male voice and a female voice sang a duet.

Neon lights were replaced by archaic stage lights, cigarette smoke by cigar smoke. The elaborate illusionary clothing the dancers were wearing changed from gleaming mini dresses to flowing pieces in 1930s fashion.

"Still hate vampires, Alex?" Farrokh struck a plain match, lighting a fat cigar. "They hate you, too. If I remember correctly, you destroyed one of the Lord's family."

"The Shadow Court acquitted me," Alex said again. "On all counts."

"Oh yes. The only court that ever acquitted Alexander Dumsky." Farrokh's light smile was more predatory than anything the vampires, werewolves, and other night monsters could muster. "How did you get off the island, wonder kid?"

Hearing the last two words, Alex shuddered. His fingers clenched into tight fists, knuckles turning white.

I can't let him get to me with a simple provocation like that.

Flowing over their heads was a piano melody. A melody far too familiar to Alex.

It's impossible not to recognize a recording of your own performance.

"I have business to disc—"

"Mr. Farrokh," someone interrupted Alex, who instantly summoned the lilac fire around his fingers. To interrupt a full-fledged black wizard, you had to be either a madman or...

Standing behind Alex was a group that included vampires, werewolves, a few high-level undead creatures, and even a leech looking like a skeleton encased in skin. Out in the streets, they cloaked themselves in illusions so powerful that they could only be penetrated by the lenses law enforcement wore. Ordinary people were unaware of the kind of monsters that roamed the city at night.

"My hospitality only extends to members of our society," Farrokh answered the unasked question in a calm, flat voice. "Including exiles."

"Good evening, Alex," one of the vampires said, flashing the red-hot coals of his eyes.

"And a warm sun to you, bloodsucker." Doom turned his back on the vampire pointedly.

No predator can tolerate someone turning their back on them. A sapient predator, their sense of superiority fed generously by the media long before the Prophet and the Magic Lens, even less so.

Alex could only guess how many young and stupid girls had been dinner for the monster.

"You..."

Alex tasted copper on his lips, a sure sign that an aggressive vampire was close.

"Just give me a reason, bloodsucker, and you'll follow your brother."

Someone hissed. It wasn't like a cat or a snake; the sound was much higher pitched, casting a mental fog on anyone not used to hearing it.

"Enough," Farrokh said. "Viscount Jeremiah, wait to collect your blood debt until you're outside."

"Sure," the bloodsucker replied with a bow. "As the respected Ferryman wishes."

Farrokh paid no heed to the apparent offense, his welcoming smile remaining on his face.

"Hey, wha—" Gribovsky swallowed the remaining words as the

air was knocked out of his lungs and strong hands jerked him up by shoulders, sending him flying off behind the sofa. "You want to dance, you fanged pumpkin? I'm all your—"

The sound was cut off. Alex couldn't see what was going on behind his back, but he had a strong guess that Gribovsky was engaged in a sort of entertainment very uncommon at the Abyss: a brawl.

"Why did you have to destroy his *brother*, Klaus?" Farrokh sighed. "If you'd sent Jeremiah himself to dust, I probably would have even let you keep your club membership."

"Klaus was no better."

"He wasn't, no, but he owed the club two hundred coins."

Alex almost choked on air. *Two hundred coins.* The heritage of the entire Follen School that he'd managed to retrieve from ruins was just *one* hundred Abyss coins.

How was it even possible to spend that much of the club's internal currency?

"Did he exchange them for credits?"

"For the night's sake, Alex. The last person who tried that trick is still at the bottom of the Pit."

Doom shrugged.

The Pit was another tale from the crypt. The literal crypt.

"Here's…" Coming over to the table, Valerie froze before setting the tray of drinks down. Flying across the table at that very moment was Gribovsky, flashing a black eye and a bloody gap-toothed smile. Strangely, his left shoe was missing. And he had some broken fangs clutched in his fists. "…your Russian tea."

"Thanks," Alex said.

Placidly, Valerie went back to the bar.

"Your friend's doing well." Farrokh puffed out a dense cloud of smoke.

"I can't see from here."

"He just threw Clive O'Shaughnessy over his back."

"The Irish werewolf?"

"Exactly."

"He really is doing well then."

Doom took the glass, stuck out his little finger the way Robin had taught him, and took a sip of his tea. It was a bit sour and tart. Ever the perfect drink.

"So, Alex, what do you…" Farrokh tilted his head to the side just in time to avoid a broken chair leg that otherwise would have hit him in the ear. "What do you want?"

"You already know, Farrokh."

"Do I?" the club owner asked in surprise. Crossing his legs, he sat back in his armchair. "Maybe so, but your partner could die while we ask our rhetoric questions."

Alex shrugged.

"Oh, so you're not really that attached to him. Does Alex Doom ever get attached to anyone?"

"That has nothing to do with what I'm here to discuss."

"Maybe," Farrokh drawled. "But—"

It was Doom's turn to bend over in order to avoid getting hit in the back of the head by the shattered body of a young werewolf. Even without his guns, the guardsman was no fading lily.

"I'm still curious how the wonder kid came to be in the company of a guardsman."

Chapter 36

Alex pretended (as well as he could) to be surprised at Farrokh's insightfulness.

"Oh please, boy." The old wizard knocked his cigar against the ashtray. "Coming here on Follen School memorial day was stupid. But bringing a guardsman here…cunning, smart, defiant. You do understand that if I report that to the Shadow Court, you'll be hanged for treason and betraying the organization to its direct enemies?"

"But you'd show your own incompetence if you did that, Farrokh." Alex held up his hands. "You have too many enemies to risk your position as the Abyss' central division head."

Farrokh inhaled, then leaned forward. The darkness clouded behind his back. It wasn't some deceitful dark smoke used by charlatans to scare kids; no, this was *true*, primeval, original darkness. The immense space of *nothing*. A force eclipsing the stars.

"Are you calling me a coward, boy? Are you calling me unworthy of my power?"

"I'm calling you Farrokh ibn Amir Shaha," Alex replied with a seated bow. "The Lord of a Hundred Genies. The Desert Jackal obeyed by the Worms guarding the Gate Beyond. The Master of Depth. The Lord of Black Sands and Bloody Waters. I know who you are. And you know who *I* am."

Farrokh inhaled again and leaned back in his armchair. The Darkness behind his back vanished into the smoke from the cigars and fog machines.

"I heard what happened at the museum. A regrettable incident that brought too much attention to the organization."

"Do you know who's behind the mask?"

"You made too good a move, boy, to be as stupid as you're trying to pretend you are," Farrokh said, wincing slightly. "If I knew who that crafty bastard was, I'd be drinking my wine from his skull right now. No, I don't know who the demonologist is."

"So, he *is* a demonologist."

"And a very strong one," Farrokh nodded. "Much stronger than you or Robin… although you've already excelled our late friend in that art. I saw the recordings, Alex. That wizard-from-nowhere might be as strong as the Professor."

Alex shuddered again. Small trickles of blood ran down his palms, betraying how hard his nails were pressed into the skin.

A broken glass jug of wine swished past, splashing the hem of

Alex's suit jacket with red. Somebody with broken arms came flying after it, but that was nothing compared to the storm of memories arising inside.

Alex managed to drive it away.

"The Professor's dead," Alex said in a dry whisper.

"He is." Farrokh knocked his ashes off again, that time his move a bit more abrupt. "I was the first to make sure back then, Alex. The Professor *is* dead. But the one in the mask..."

"What?"

Farrokh said nothing, just tearing a piece off someone's pants as they flew by to wipe the wine and blood off the table.

"I don't know, wonder kid. I don't know. But his style is so similar to the Professor's."

"No one has ever come back from there."

"Name me a Shadow Judge who wouldn't laugh at that."

"The Professor wasn't an Apostle. He was just human."

"Maybe," Farrokh agreed. "Or maybe we didn't know enough about him. Not nearly enough."

"If you'd known a bit more, Follen School might still be around," Alex forced out bitterly. "And with it..."

He stopped short and sighed.

Doom knew his visit would reopen old wounds. He just hadn't known how bad it would be.

"You want to ask why he took Poseidon's Orb?"

"I've heard it has a different name."

"Half-educates," Farrokh shot back with a dismissive wave. "*That's* the artifact's real name."

Doom just shrugged. He didn't give a damn about the real name of the thing stolen by the unknown demonologist whose style smacked of the Professor's.

Neither did he care about the artifact itself or why it was stolen.

He just wanted to find that wizard. Not for the Guard or for his freedom, but... If the Professor's face was hiding beneath that mask, no force, demonic or angelic, was going to keep Doom from burning the old man's accursed soul.

In memory of everyone who'd been buried in that thrice-damned cellar as cold bodies sacrificed on the altars.

"I have no idea, Alex," Farrokh said with a helpless gesture. "But I kno—"

"Alex! Pumpkin!" Gribovsky fell over the back of the sofa. Bruised and blood-stained, he was strangling a green, scaly monster hanging over him. "You didn't tell me this place was so much fun!"

He was jerked out of Doom's sight.

"I know who can tell you more." An archaic type, Farrokh retrieved a pen from his inner pocket, scribbled something on a napkin, and handed it to Alex. *16 7ᵗʰ Street, Simon Shulman."*

"Who's that?"

"A good friend of mine," Farrokh replied. "A dealer in antiquities. A collector of rarities. Of the same descent as you, by the way. I think you two will hit it off."

Doom waved a hand. The napkin vanished in a flash of lilac fire.

"It was good seeing you, Farrokh." Doom stood and turned around to appraise the battlefield.

Scattered furniture. Some broken, bloody fragments apparently used as improvised weapons. Bodies sprawled on the floor, tucked into armchairs, and hanging from ceiling beams, unconscious but alive (or undead).

Standing in a boxing stance in the very middle of the room, reeling, bloody, and bashed in all over, was Gribovsky. Some teeth were stuck in his right cheek, his left fist had swelled to the size of a hammer head, and his clothes had been reduced to blood-stained rags.

But he was still on his feet.

"Let's go, pumpkins! Bring it!"

Surrounding him on all sides were opponents much stronger than the ones he'd already brought down.

Doom took a step forward. As soon as his right foot touched the floor, clouds of deep darkness billowed up from beneath it. It was just as creepy as the darkness spreading its wings behind Farrokh's back.

"This light one is mine," Alex said loud enough for everyone to hear. "Anyone willing to challenge me?"

One second ticked by. Then another. No one moved.

Doom grabbed Gribovsky and headed toward the exit.

"You said you know who I am and I know who you are," said a voice delivered to Alex's back by Farrokh's magic. Hardly anyone but Doom could hear it. "You're no fit for the dark, Alexander. No fit for the battles to come. You need to leave."

"I can't."

"If you swear to leave Atlantis and live a good and peaceful life, I'll remove your collar, Alexander."

"Why?"

Silence.

Alex had almost reached the stairs descending into the well from the old horror movie when the final words wafted over to him.

"In memory of Robin and Anastasia."

Doom stopped and looked back into Farrokh's eyes. They were black, so black that the night was nothing but a golden dawning sky against them.

"Goodbye, Farrokh," Alex said without moving his lips. The unconscious Gribovsky over his shoulder, he left the place he'd once thought of as home.

***

The darkness behind Farrokh congealed into a figure wrapped in a dark cloak. Its presence brought the taste of copper to the lips of those around him.

"Why didn't you let me appease my hunger with that renegade, Ferryman?"

"Baron Lucius." Farrokh smiled welcomingly but did not turn toward the second speaker. "Who am I to keep you from collecting your blood debt? Your son's murderer was right there in front of you. But you did nothing. *You* let him leave."

A clawed hand encased in gray skin reached for Farrokh's shoulder but stopped halfway. However strong the Vampire Baron was, the Lord of Worms and Desert Jackal was out of his league.

"You were blocking my path to him, Ferryman."

"You think so?" Farrokh put out his cigar in the ashtray and, dusting off his jacket, stood up. "I was just making sure my club didn't share the fate of Follen School."

"Are you afraid of that boy? You, the Desert Jackal?" The voice of the figure cloaked in shadow was mocking.

"I'm being called a coward *again*?" the ancient black wizard asked, his right eyebrow arched in surprise. The dark figure doubled up with a scream full of pain and humiliation, albeit just for a moment. "Begone, Baron. You're banned from the Abyss' premises for the next week. That time should be enough for you to figure out whether *you* should be afraid of Professor Raewsky's best student, the best student of the wizard who destroyed a Supreme Demon when you were still wetting your bed."

The figure disappeared. Farrokh was alone at his table.

He lifted a glass of whiskey with lemon, Robin's favorite drink.

"You raised a successor to be proud of. That boy…" Farrokh smiled sadly. "I'd rather not kill him, but… Damn it, Robin, he's crazy! He's totally crazy. Only someone that crazy would steal that bloody cat."

Chapter 37

Under Joe's intent and somewhat surprised stare, Alex dragged Gribovsky out into the street and lifted his hat in parting.

"Have a good night, Joe."

"See you, Alex," the club's eternal bouncer replied.

Amalgam Street welcomed the battered lieutenant from the super-secret organization and the skinny black wizard carrying him on his back with its usual busy indifference.

Humans and non-humans alike hurried in all directions on their personal business (to restaurants, artistic expositions, interracial swinger parties) or just strolled around. Just like the residents and visitors of Myers City's bohemian district always did.

No one cared about Alex or Gribovsky.

And so, leaning the guardsman against a green hydrant (for some unknown reason, all the hydrants on Amalgam Street were painted green), Alex wasn't worried that a well-intentioned passer-by would call the cops or an ambulance. The locals knew better than that.

"Are they coming from the gay club?"

"Probably had a fight."

"Is he a drug dealer?"

"Oh, I'm out of *amestris*! Can we go get some?"

"Yeah, once *he* wakes up."

"Haha!"

That was the size of the attention the two men garnered.

Alex rummaged through Gribovsky's pockets for his phone.

"Just...use...yours," the Polish guardsman groaned, spitting out blood and broken teeth.

"I wasn't a call bitch in prison. Why become one on the outside?" Alex meant it as a joke, but Gribovsky didn't seem that amused.

The bloody rags were slippery in Alex's hands. The pockets wouldn't open. And when they did, out poured some teeth, bits of glass, and other nastiness.

"Of...fensive?"

"I just hate being available all the ti—...oh, there it is!"

Alex pulled the brand new Apple iPhone out into the light of the neon signs and streetlamps.

"Such a hipster," he snorted. "What's your password?"

Gribovsky tried to put his thumb on the screen instead of

answering, but that didn't help—it was broken and covered in blood.

"Four ones."

"Quite the imagination," Alex smirked, giving Gribovsky a friendly clap on the shoulder that elicited a groan. "Oh, sorry."

"Get...lost...Doom." Gribovsky coughed up blood and rasped (it sounded like a punctured lung). "Dial 117-/-615."

Doom did just that. After three tones, a voice responded.

"24-hour laundry. Where's your pickup?"

"Amalgam Street District," Alex replied, totally unsurprised by the verbal coding. If even the Abyss had branches nicknamed *laundries, repair shops*, and *cleaning services*, why shouldn't the Guards? "214 Plave Street. It's urgent—the laundry is *very* messy."

"Urgent order, 214 Plave Street. Expect a car in three minutes."

"Say...unacc...ompanied," Gribovsky coughed.

"Unaccompanied," Alex repeated into the phone.

"Accepted. Wait there," the voice on the line said, followed instantly by the dial tone.

Switching off the smartphone screen, Doom dropped it back into Gribovsky's torn and bloody pocket. How had it not been smashed to pieces? Were all the ads about the new iPhone being shatter-proof true?

"Leave," Gribovsky spat more blood. "They'll...ask...questions."

Alex nodded and stood to leave but stopped to wave a hand and curse.

[ATTENTION! Prohibited spell used: DEAD NECROMANCER SEAL of the Blood, Darkness, and Death School. Mana consumption: N/A.]

The shadows around Gribovsky and the hydrant condensed, turning into a dark, barely transparent, and fanged giant skull. The humans and non-humans walking by recoiled and hastily retreated to the opposite side of the street.

Amalgam Street wasn't just a bohemian mecca. It was also the heart of Darkness in Myers City.

The Dark Creatures' organization is best hidden in the most obvious place.

Making sure the defense was strong enough to even hold off an Adept (at least, their first attempt), Doom lurched wearily over to his parked bike.

"Hey, pumpkin?"

Alex looked back.

Gribovsky winked at him with the eye that wasn't yet black while clumsily retrieving a Skittle with broken fingers and tossing it into his mouth.

"We're even…for O'Hara."

"Now we are," Alex nodded.

Having said that, he rolled on the throttle and galloped his steel horse down the street.

You had to have been an idiot not to guess that it was Gribovsky who'd sent the uniformed fairy to see Alex back then.

He'd wanted to see if Alex could handle it.

But Doom knew how to make people show what they were made of, too.

***

Turning up the collar of her cashmere coat, Mara stood at the entrance to the Schooner Belis.

Despite its close proximity to the university, it wasn't an especially popular establishment with students. There was a large selection of alcoholic drinks, but very few dining options. And drinking in front of tutors and professors was considered bad form.

(Then why did they still have drinking parties in the dorms? That was a different question.)

In the few weeks she'd spent at the university, Glomebood had only met someone in student uniform at the Schooner once or twice.

"Closed," she said, reading the sign out loud.

That was odd for a *night* establishment. Just as weird was the fact that it was empty at that hour.

Only the dim light of the lamps over the bar counter dispersing the caustic semi-darkness hinted that there *was* someone inside.

Mara pushed open the door. Sure, it was locked, but a plain mechanical lock with a bit of magic wasn't enough to stop someone from her famous dwarf blacksmith line. It was less about her physical strength and more about the magic she had in her blood. *Half* her blood, to be precise.

The hall styled to look like a ship's lower deck was almost empty and almost silent. The floor was washed clean, and the chairs were upturned on the tables. Barely perceptible cigarette smoke and piano music eased through the air.

Across the hall, by the stage with musical instruments covered with a tarp to protect them from dust, stood a grand piano.

It was old and shabby, long unplayed. Visitors put bags on it; waiters used it to hold trays with food and drinks. There were rumors that a couple at some party had fucked long and hard on it for the whole full house to see.

The piano was still there for just one reason: it was too big to be carried out through any of the bar's doors. (How did it come to be inside then? That was the question.)

An old instrument.

An idle instrument.

Almost forgotten.

But it was polished to a shine and freshly varnished. The lid stood up like a shark's fin once again, cleaving the cigarette smoke, a glass of whiskey with lemon on the music stand.

Long, elegant fingers fluttered over the keys, making music that was high-pitched and beautiful, fast and slow at times, reminiscent of long-forgotten animated movies from Mara's early childhood.

Movies about a fluffy magic neighbor, a girl flying a broomstick, a moving castle with a wizard and a fire spirit.

Mara loved those movies.

And she knew the tune.

"Is that Yiruma, If I Could See You Again?" she asked when the last note died away.

Professor Alexander Dumsky, looking neither sober nor fresh, lifted the glass, dropped his pinky, and dumped the whiskey down his throat.

"Are you that bad at reading, Glomebood?" he asked in his usual voice—a bit of mockery, a ton of pride, and a pinch of arrogance. "The sign plate on the door should say *closed*. Doesn't it?"

"I saw a light on inside and came in."

The professor stood, went over to the counter, and poured himself more whiskey from the bottle. It was less than a quarter full. He had to have been drinking several hours straight.

"You're going to find yourself in trouble if you keep walking into closed places just because there's a light on."

"But I knew you were here."

"And?" Going back over to the piano, the professor put his fingers on the keys. They looked surprisingly slender and at home there. It was like they were made to play.

"Where did you learn how to play so well?" Mara asked.

The professor froze, his eyes dimming for a moment as he was mentally transported back to some very distant memory.

"So, you broke into the bar to discuss my past with me, Glomebood? That's definitely not a good way to keep yourself well and healthy."

"Actually, I came to ask a question."

"And you asked it. You even got an answer."

"A different question, I mean."

"Alas," the professor said, lifting his glass to her. "Outside of class, I'm only charitable enough to give *one* answer for free. One per year. So, come back after January 1st. I just can't promise I won't have modified my student charity support program by then…"

"Do you always talk this much when you want to hide what you're actually thinking, Professor?"

Dumsky paused and looked at her.

"I'm really at a loss. Should I be surprised that you're brave enough to interrupt me or share a funeral agent's business card with you? With an approach like that, I'm not sure you'll live to see graduation."

"You said you'll help us with the tournament for half the prize money. We're in. So, I'm here to find out when we start practices."

With a respectful cough, the professor lifted his glass to her again.

"You asked a question without actually asking it. I see the patient's more alive than dead."

"Excuse me?"

"Damn. You're good at spoiling things—it's another question!"

"So, when's practice, Professor?"

Instead of answering, Alexander Dumsky placed his glass back on the music stand and continued playing.

Mara's words had pulled him back into the past. Just like everything else that evening. *Everything* reminded him of probably the best time of his life.

The time he'd spent at Follen School.

Chapter 38

The door creaked, unwilling to open. Massive and ponderous, the sunlight glinted on cracked varnish, broken ornaments, and some greasy spots.

The twisted, rusty hinges made opening the door quite the ordeal. Little Alexander used the old reading room as his personal asylum, one only penetrated by the few who dared enter the west wing of the castle.

Yes, the west wing. Just like in the cartoon with the living furniture pieces he'd watched with Robin a short time before.

"There you are, Sasha," a female voice with a thick eastern European accent said from next to his ear as he sat in a deep, giant armchair upholstered in chintz.

Just like the door, the west wing, and really the whole manor house, the armchair was old, smelling of dust, mold, and cat poop.

The Follen manor had *lots* of cats.

"Anastasia," Alexander smiled, closing his textbook and trying to hide it behind his back. That definitely wasn't enough to escape the Russian witch's warm, brown eyes.

She was tall, taller than Robin. And beautiful. If Alexander were older, he'd have called her *sexy*, but in those days he didn't know much about sex. Actually, all he knew was that it was one of things most frequently bought and sold in High Garden.

She almost never wore dresses, preferring a shabby Star Wars hoodie, threadbare Levi's jeans, and Converse sneakers. She had only one pair of Converse, but she put in different colored laces every three days.

And is it even worth mentioning that she was dating Robin?

Neither the height difference nor the age gap bothered them.

Robin had turned seventeen the previous week, Alexander's third at Follen, while Anastasia was coming up on her twenty-second birthday.

That provided an endless supply of jokes for the other students at Follen School of Dark Wizardry and the Forbidden Arts. (That was what Robin called it, a reference to some Hogwarts or other. Alexander had no idea what kind of place that was, though his older friend promised to show him a bunch of movies about a bespectacled wizard the next weekend.) Everyone agreed that Robin and Anastasia had probably come together as the only adults outside Professor Raewsky at the school.

"Why aren't you playing with the other kids?"

Alexander had laughed at Anastasia's accent at first. She sounded like a character straight out of an old spy movie. He'd teased her until she poured a bucket of cold water over him.

Unsurprisingly, that had cooled him off.

"Are they hurting cats again?" Dumsky squinted.

"Um…" Anastasia pretended to fall thoughtful. "Patrick and Jessie call it a game. Irma and Ganesh agree with them."

"Little bastards." Jumping to his feet, Alexander was about to dash for the door when he literally bumped into Robin.
As always, the latter was wearing a suit, a narrow tie, and a stripeless hat. There was a cigarette in his fingers.

Robin was a heavy smoker.

A very heavy smoker.

He said smoking used to take the edge off the hunger when he was begging for food in the High Garden streets. Alexander didn't believe that. How could smoke replace food? Robin was presumably just making up excuses for his bad habit.

"Looking like a bad boy again." Robin ruffled Alexander's hair. "If you stay like that, you won't lose your innocence until you turn as old as the main character from the movie we watched yesterday."

"Forty years is a pittance for a true wizard."

"*Pittance?* If you keep using words like that, you're going to *die* a virgin."

Dumsky pushed Robin's hands away and took another step toward the dark corridor flanked by suits of armor. Its walls were hung with tapestries and paintings, its floor covered with once-thick carpet long worn out.

"One against four, Alex?" Robin inhaled and blew smoke out of his nose. "Anastasia and I spent two days nursing you back to health last time."

"They're *hurting cats*!"

"Oh Loki, god of the dark arts," Robin said with an eyeroll. "Why did you endow this wonder kid with such a great love for those flea carriers?"

"They're soft and fluffy." Alex frowned. "And they don't have fleas. They don't run away when I come to pet them, either."

"They don't," Anastasia smiled, coming up from behind him. "Sometimes it's scary how this seven-year-old's—"

"I'm almost eight!"

"This almost-eight-year-old's," the Russian witch corrected herself with the same smile on her lips and deep in her eyes, "body is shared by a black magic genius and…a boy of eight."

"A boy in the shiny black armor of a dark knight," Robin added.

"Fear him! He's the terror that flaps in the night, the—"

"That's *not* from Duck Tales," Dumsky interrupted. "I Googled it. It's Darkwing Duck. A separate series."

"You don't know anything." Robin poked Alex's forehead with a finger. He always did that when he wanted to explain something but didn't have the words. "Well, do you remember what I taught you?"

"First, watch my feet. Second, don't let anyone get behind me. Third, use mana sparingly so I still have some in reserve after the fight. Fourth—"

Robin's hand flashed in front of Alex's eyes.

"What's *this*?"

"A notebook."

"I can see that. What are you using it for?"

"Writing down your lessons."

"Damn it! Damn it, you fucking..."

The rest of Robin's cursing was drowned out by Anastasia's ringing laughter.

"I'm going to start calling you Sheldon Cooper." Embracing him from behind, she started to squeeze slightly.

"Stop...cuddling...me," Doom said, barely getting the words out.

"Well, wifey, it's time to let our son go fight his battle."

"I'm not your wifey," Anastasia shot back, sticking her tongue out at him. "And I'm not letting my son go."

"If you're not my wifey, then was he born in sin?"

"No. He's just not yours."

"Oh Loki. Why? Why did you punish me with a non-wife who cheats on me?! The only good thing is that you had such a cute wonder kid. Here, let me hug him, too."

"You're *strangling* me!" Trapped between their bodies, Alexander got away. He dusted off the sweater that fell nearly to his heels and completely covered his sliced jeans and plain sneakers. "And I'm not your son!"

"How awful."

"You heard that, too, dear? Our son abandoned us!"

"Oh dear. I don't know where we went wrong as parents."

"A couple of idiots," Alexander said through gritted teeth before realizing that no one was blocking his way anymore and dashing off into the corridor.

"Come back with your shield or on it, my boy!" Robin shouted after him.

Putting one chair on the floor and sitting down on it, Mara listened to her professor and supervisor play. So absorbed. So obsessed. And so painful. His fingers fluttered easily over the keys, touching them briefly and lightly, but…

But still she had the impression that Professor Dumsky was playing more on broken glass than on a piano, each touch bringing with it unbearable pain.

Pain that was mental, not physical.

It was as if the broken shards of glass were cutting straight through to his heart.

All that dulled the pain were the cigarette in his mouth and the glass of whiskey.

"What happened to you, Professor?" Mara whispered, then clapped both hands over her mouth.

Fortunately for her, the black wizard was too engrossed in the music representing the broken shards of other people's hearts to hear what she said.

The music played on, Dumsky's stare growing darker and darker as he immersed himself deeper and deeper into his past.

Chapter 39

Making his way along the dark, half-flooded underground passage, Doom clutched the rubber boots he'd stolen at a flea market with both hands to keep them on.

"You couldn't care less about your appearance, but you still do your best to keep yourself clean," Robin said from a deep armchair.

Anastasia was warming a small teapot on a hot plate.

They used the small room, a former boiler closet Robin had transformed into a movie theater, as their hiding place. As it was somewhat elevated above the rest of the basement, it wasn't flooded, though the way there was blocked by intricate black-magic traps in addition to the water. When they went there the first time (prompted by Robin, who claimed there was an untold treasure of knowledge waiting at the finish line), Alexander had literally gotten in over his head destroying other people's spells.

"What are we watching today?" Robin clicked the remote control, scrolling down the virtually endless list of movies. "Titanic? Les Miserables? Hachiko?"

The hot plate Anastasia pottered around stood on a wood stub. The halved log served as a table. Meanwhile, the giant, almost 80-inch TV screen was connected to…a dozen potatoes and forty oranges pierced with wires.

Needless to say, the potatoes and oranges were enchanted. By Anastasia. That kind of magic was too fine for Robin, and Alex was just learning how to use it. Anastasia was teaching him.

If Professor Raewsky had known Anastasia (*Nastya*, as he called her) did that, he…

He'd probably have praised her first. And then he would have burned the whole basement down.

The main rule at Follen School was: *no technology.*

Coal heating. No electricity. A Faraday cage inside the walls to fully block off wireless signals coming in from outside.

No web access.

No magic lenses.

How did Robin get the TV and hot plate in here? That was a riddle Alexander struggled to solve.

"The Pianist, maybe?"

"*The Pianist?* Are you crazy, wifey? The basement's already flooded. When the wonder kid sees The Pianist, it'll be like drowning inside the Titanic. I'm not DiCaprio, and I'll be able to get on the raft, but…"

"You think Hachiko would be less emotional?"

"The kid is a total cat person. He'll just giggle at a great comedy like that."

"No. The Pianist."

To emphasize that it was her final word, Anastasia dropped a tray with three plain tin mugs on the log table. Delicious vapor came from the strong black tea with lemon and sugar. A weird but tasty drink.

***

Mara wondered how someone could drink that much without getting drunk. Professor Dumsky was already pouring a glass from his *third* bottle of whiskey, and his rhythm remained perfect. There was not a single false note as his fingers glided over the keys just as smoothly, shedding invisible blood.

***

"That's it. Just a bit slower," Anastasia said again. "Don't hurry. Feel the rhythm."

In the middle of the vast dark hall with curtained-off windows, a little boy and a tall, beautiful girl from the icy lands of northern Russia were playing a grand piano.

Anastasia was playing it, actually. Alexander was just learning.

For the second straight week.

But he could at least play a small, two-act piece.

"Oh, Sasha, I don't know. Honestly."

"Is there *anything* you don't know, Anastasia?"

"Sure. Why so surprised?"

"Um…" The boy was embarrassed. "I don't know. I always used to think you knew *everything*. Not like Robin."

"Hey!" came an indignant echo from the far corner. "I'm right here."

"I know," Dumsky teased.

Anastasia laughed and patted the boy's hair down. Unlike her boyfriend, she never ruffled it.

Alexander hated having his hair ruffled.

"No one in the world can know *everything*, Sasha."

"Even Professor Raewsky?"

A heavy silence fell on the room. It was so heavy that the black curtains covering the old stained-glass windows felt like spider silks or flying fluff in comparison.

"Not even him, wonder kid. Not even him. Okay, let's move on to the third part."

"Great!"

***

"May the Serpent guide you through the sands, Farrokh."

"Loki by your hearth, Robin. Who's that hiding behind your back?"

"I'm not hiding!"

"He isn't."

"Oh, I beg my pardon then, monsieur, for daring to disrespect you. Would you care to share your good name?"

"Alexander Dumsky."

"What a brave name. Like a general."

"Don't tell me you knew Alexander the Great."

"What if I do?"

"Then you're a liar."

"Why?"

"Because you're no more than four hundred years old. Sure, you're *really* old even though you pretend otherwise, but that's not old enough to have met Alexander the Great. He lived much earlier."

"Wow."

"You can call him *wonder kid*, Farrokh. When he grows up, he's going to beat every single member of the club."

"Even you, Robin?"

"Pffft, I'll be first. Actually, I'm here for a drink and to enlist Alexander in the organization. But I don't see you letting me get started with either."

"You're his guarantee?"

"Yes."

"It looks like this young genius is the only Follen student you brought here."

"The others—"

"...are hurting cats! And Robin won't let me curse them."

"Enough of your cursing. Jessie already spent six weeks in the hospital."

"That's because *you* stepped in. I'd have had him there for six*teen*."

"Oh Serpent. Who did you bring us, Robin Loxley?"

"Oh, Farrokh, if you only knew. If you only knew."

"The Robin Loxley & Alexander Dumsky spacecraft embarks on a long voyage across the ether ocean, sails filling out—"

"The Treasure Planet had ships," the boy interrupted. "Not spacecraft."

"It's descending from the stratosphere." Robin reached for the boy to pull him down off his shoulders, but Alexander clenched his legs tighter around Robin's neck. Robin snorted. "Then stop arguing."

Anastasia was putting out sandwiches on the tablecloth as her men peered up at the starry heavens.

Dumsky loved the night sky over the manor lost somewhere in the Myers City suburbs. It looked like the curtain in the piano hall, the one pierced by needles in multiple places and then illuminated from the other side with stage lights of all different colors.

The way they did it at the Abyss.

But Anastasia wasn't supposed to hear that.

Not the part about the sky, of course, but about the Abyss. About Robin taking him there.

Anastasia would have killed him.

"Dinner's ready," the witch called over.

"Let's go, wonder kid." Robin started for the tablecloth.

They were having a picnic that beautiful summer night while the other ten Follen students were snoring peacefully in their beds.

"Robin?"

"What, kid?"

"Why does no one want to make friends with me?"

Robin choked on air and almost stumbled.

"Hey, stop it. First of all, you *do* have two friends: me and Anastasia. And the rest…um… How should I put this?"

"Put it the way it is."

"Okay, I will. You're really weird, Alexander. Why insist on being called that, by the way? Alexander. So boring. Why not Alex? And you talk like you're as old as the Professor, not an eight-year-old kid. I won't call you a *kid*, though. A little nerd and Mr. Books, that's you. Nobody likes people like that. If you want to be liked, keep it simple, Alex. Comb your hair. Take a shower twice a day, not when you start smelling like your books or your cats. Wear decent clothes instead of that sack of yours. Basically, be an eight year old, not an old man trapped in a boy's body."

"So, you want me to be like you?"

"Like me?" Robin laughed. "You could hardly achieve that degree of perfection. But still, you can use my example as a reference point for your long and complicated journey from wonder kid to normal black wizard."

"So grandiose."

"Oh, and stop lecturing other people! Particularly when they're twice as old as you."

***

The music stopped abruptly. That seemed to wake Mara from a deep sleep.

Blood was dripping onto the keys.

That time it wasn't metaphorical blood. It was real.

And the professor was plucking the shards of his crushed glass out of his palm. Silently, without a trace of emotion on his poker face.

***

"Help…"

"Alex, help…"

"Sasha…"

"Alex…"

"Alex…"

"Doom…"

The little boy, chained by magic and unable to move, stood in the middle of a giant pentagram. Its twelve rays ended in stone altars, each with a human body on it.

They were all naked.

Cut up.

Disemboweled.

But still alive and able to speak.

And there was a man. The Professor in his white smock, a twisted ritual dagger carved with ancient runes and symbols in his hands.

He stepped slowly toward Alex.

"It ends. It all ends now."

But Alex wasn't looking at the Professor. He couldn't take his eyes off the hands reaching out to him.

Jessie. Patrick. Irma. Ganesh. Parfen. Idma. Hayasie. Olaf. Helen. Jessica. Barry.

Robin and Anastasia.

All Follen students.

All his friends.

They were begging for his help, and he couldn't move. He couldn't break the chains of Professor Raewsky's magic.

"It all ends *now*!"

Raewsky lifted his dagger over Alex's head.

"Help…"

"Save us…"

"Help…

***

"…help…"

Blinking, Doom woke up from his daydreams.

Alcohol, recently getting out of jail, the rush of adrenaline, and the memorable date made for a nasty cocktail.

"Can I do anything for you, Professor?"

Alex turned to see Mara Glomebood holding out a couple bandages.

"Tomorrow, 8 a. m., Magic Range One."

"Excuse me?"

"Anyone who's late will earn themselves a curse." Alex closed the piano lid, leaving a bloody handprint on it, and plodded toward the stairs.

He didn't look back.

Chapter 40

"Are you sure he's coming?" Travis was working on a Rubik's cube in the stands of Magic Range One, which looked much like a regular university stadium. "Ten minutes after the time he set."

"Hey, Travis, what do you want Mara to say?" Eleonora, a breathtaking beauty even in a sweat suit, came to loom the whole of her perfect figure over Travis. "*You* weren't the one who slipped out of the dorm late last night to talk to Werewolf at the Schooner!"

"I was too busy working on my term paper for Magic Principl—"

"That thing isn't due for two *months*! You were playing League of Legends 2 all night, so stop lying to me, you geek!"

"I won't say anything about what *you* were doing all night."

"You're just jealous."

"And you—"

"…had better all shut up if you don't want me to curse you."

The stands instantly fell silent. The students (four of the five, as Leo was too busy polishing his nails) turned toward the exit. Swaying slightly as he ascended the stairs and holding to his forehead a bottle filled (instead of the mineral water the label said was in it) with melting ice cubes, the crumpled-looking Black Magic Professor of First Magic University was walking toward them.

Alexander Dumsky in the flesh.

Unshaven, wearing a wrinkled shirt and half-loosened tie.

The friends had yet to see their supervisor looking like that in the four weeks they'd spent at the university.

"Did you drink all night?" Travis dropped his cube in surprise.

Bouncing across the concrete, the cube rolled up to the feet of the professor, whose face betrayed the pain every impact triggered in the space between his temples.

"I get your youthful curiosity about what other people do at night…"

"You're less than four years older than us!"

The professor cringed at Eleonora's indignant scream.

"…but no. I wasn't drinking."

The students were about to comment on that when the professor finished.

"I was bingeing. Bingeing like the dickens. I remember filling the Schooner's cash register to the brim… Hell's bells. But drinking… No, I only got started with that this morning." The professor shook his bottle of water, grimacing once again. "Stupid hangover. Who invented them?"

"Are you going to run our first practice session like that?" Jing Wai asked calmly with his usual poker face. He was wearing his favorite black-and-yellow gym suit.

"Ah, Bruce Li. Good morning to you, too. To answer your question, I could train you little kittens high on *amestris*."

"You're on drugs?!"

"Oh, stop yelling," the professor shouted back and groaned in pain. "No, I'm not. But enough talking. Head to the range."

The students exchanged glances and started down to the practice field, which was actually somewhat different from regular stadiums. The perfectly trimmed lawns, the running tracks, and plenty of other things were the same, but they came with tall concrete walls enclosing it all. The walls were literally stuffed with magic crystals to absorb all the magic and make sure none of it leaked outside the stadium.

Not only could the crystals accumulate mana, they could also release it. The energy they produced, while unusable for wizards, was enough to power part of the campus.

A sustainable cycle.

"Leo, wake up," Mara said as she clapped her friend on the shoulder.

The pink-haired (apparently in preparation for another photo shoot) idol in his gaudy suit gave a small start but went back to polishing his nails.

"Oh, Mara, you smell fantastic today. Dior? Chanel? Did you go see the stylist I recommended?"

"Leo. We're on the range."

"Range? Which diet is that, dear? I eat only healthy carbs."

Smiling, Mara patted her friend's hair and pulled him slightly by the hand. He followed obediently, still running the file over his nails.

Alex shook his head as he watched, though he stopped short in pain.

Sure, the pain was caused more by what he saw than by shaking his head. The buzzing in his skull made it feel like there were a dozen firemen at work trying to put out the fire in his... And all because he'd been unfortunate enough to bump into Lebenstein on his way to the range.

The dean had apparently misunderstood his request not to shout—he'd started squealing like a pig before Christmas.

Whatever. I'll straighten things out with the fat one right after I finish up with these students.

"Interesting." Alex bent over, regretting the move immediately, to pick up the Rubik's cube. It looked like the usual child's toy, but to assemble it, wizards had to use pure magic instead of their fingers. Excessive pressure could crack the cube. It was a great exercise for training fine magic motor skills.

Anastasia would have solved it in a flash. Robin would have ruined scores of them.

What surprised Doom as he straightened up, also regretting that move immediately, was that the Ibn Sina's cube he was holding didn't have a single crack, however tiny. That meant Travis What's-his-last-name wasn't just good at controlling his magic; he was *perfect*.

"Hey," Alex called to the students ahead of him. "Think fast."

He tossed the cube to Travis, who turned around to catch it. While in the air, the cube assembled itself, forming six perfect surfaces that were each a different color.

"How did you...?" The redhead turned the cube over in his hands, obviously struggling to come up with an explanation.

"Years of practice, boy," Doom smirked.

Assembling the cube was the very first thing he'd learned at Follen School. Anyone who failed to assemble it in ten minutes with zero damage to any side got lashed.

With a literal lash.

At Raewsky's (*may his soul be devoured by hell's demons*) own hand.

Robin had just gotten used to the lashes.

But Doom didn't want to.

Making his way down to the practice field behind his students, he leaned his back against a football goalpost. The European version of football was more popular in Atlantis than the American game.

"Professor, we'll go activate the practice stands." Eleonora headed toward the control panel, but Alex stopped her.

"Hey, blondie, don't bother."

"What did he call me?" she hissed to the other girl, apparently assuming that Alex couldn't hear her.

And he really couldn't. But he did know how to read lips.

"I think he said *blondie*." Mara appeared equally astonished.

Is she a half-dwarf or a Thumbelina? Pampered kids. All of them.

"How are you going to test our abilities, Professor?" Jing squinted. "You haven't visited any of our magic practice sessions, unlike the other supervisors. And I don't think you've read any of our reports."

"Relax, Jet Li," Doom waved aside. "I have a great idea."

"And please," the Asian guy continued, far exceeding his normal self-limit of talking, "stop trying to nickname us. We all have names. Please use *them*."

"What are you talking about, Jackie Chan?" Alex unscrewed the bottle to drop some ice into his mouth, rolling it around for a while before swallowing. His students winced. "Your nicknames have already been issued and assigned. So here you go. Donnie Yen. Rupert Green. Jared Leto. And..."

Alex looked at Mara and Elie. For some reason, he wasn't able to associate them with actresses from the golden era of film.

"...and you two. Your job is to try to make me stand up."

The students gaped at him. Then they slammed their mouths shut and exchanged glances.

Mara took a step forward, confirming Doom's initial guess that she was the informal leader of the good-looking bunch.

"Excuse me, Professor? What do you mean by that?"

"Exactly what I said. Magic tournaments are a rough contact sport, aren't they? So, work the rough contact. You can use any spells you know regardless of the grimoire and school. Knock yourselves out. See what you can do."

Silence again.

"But, Professor? There are *five* of us."

"Miss Glomebood. I already know you have potential as a burglar, but being so bad at counting... Don't make my disappointment, as they say in High Gar—" Alex bit his tongue just in time, although the students were too startled to notice his slip of the tongue anyway.

"But..."

"Here, let's get this going." Alex lifted a hand. A small ball of lilac fire formed on each of his fingertips, shooting off toward their targets trailing smoke behind them.

None of the five students evaded. Only Jackie was fast enough to put a defense up. The others found themselves down on the sand, struggling to catch their breath.

"I can do that again." Alex held his bottle against his head. "So, you'd better use the best defense: a good offense."

Chapter 41

Alex wasn't expecting anything special from the students he apparently had to win that bloody tournament with if he was going to finally get Pyotr and the Syndicate off his back.

To make things even worse, Mara Glomebood and company were Magic Theorists. In the tournament, they'd be confronted by the full force of the Practical Magic Department spearheaded by its Battle Magic School.

On closer inspection, only the fan of Asian martial arts was someone to be reckoned with.

[*Name: Jing Wai. Race: Human. Mana level: 802.*]

A Practitioner at the 8th level. Eleonora and all the rest were at level 6.

[*Name: Leo Stone. Race: Human. Mana level: 647.*]

The pretty boy struggling to regain his wind and stand back up wasn't just a great fashion magazine model. He also knew a thing or two about magic. At least, judging by his mana level.

Alex wasn't going to be able to draft a winning strategy until he saw the youngsters in actual combat.

[*Name: Travis Chavert. Race: Human. Mana level: 652.*]

The redhead who'd surprised Alex with his superior command of magic power appeared to be not much stronger than Leo. That was odd. And confusing.

Then there was the last team member. (Doom skipped blondie, as he'd scanned her before the ill-fated museum tour.) The informal leader. Mara Glomebood. Half-dwarf, half-human. Doom didn't want to know which of her parents was which.

Although, considering she was a member of the Glomebood clan, it had to have been a human woman bedded by a male dwarf.

She must have been really drunk, Alex thought, recalling Bromwoord, the bald traitor. *Blind drunk.*

[*Name: Mara Glomebood. Race: Human/Dwarf. Mana level: 610.*]

Just as one would expect of a half-blood, she was the weakest of the five. For some unknown reason, people with half magic race blood always progressed slower through the magic levels than purebloods. Regardless of which races they mixed.

Travis came to first, just as Alex expected. He looked the most vigorous of the five.

Lifting both hands, Travis started to move them, drawing signs and placing them inside a green hexagram. Simultaneously, dense flows of dust were sucked from the ground into his seal.

"Not bad," Doom said. His lenses didn't display the magic school or mana amount used by his opponent. That feature was rumored to only be enabled for the lenses used by special forces—neither the military nor the police had it. "An Earth Magic spell. To reduce mana usage, you added a physical element. That saves you twenty percent of the mana, but..."

With a loud *crack*, Travis's pentagram shot out a big hammer. At least, it was a big lump of earth shaped like a hammer.

Gaia's Hammer, Alex said to himself, recalling the spell's name. As it had been cast by a Practitioner at just the sixth level, it didn't look all that impressive. When that same spell (included in most of the grimoires available on the market) had been used against Doom by the Adept coming to arrest him, it looked like fantasy game art.

"There's just one problem." Alex held out a palm. He didn't actually need his hands to form a seal, but showing that to the students was a bit too much for their first day of practice. "By adding that element to your spell, you make it too physical. And physical objects can be stopped by other physical objects."

A gray seal flashed on Doom's palm. With a nasty bony screech, a skeleton pulled itself out of the ground. It was so weak and fragile it would have crumbled if someone had spit on it. Alex had only put ten mana points into it.

The hammer crashed into the half-transparent skeleton to send a dusty storm soaring into the sky. When it settled, Alex was sitting exactly where he had been, leaning against the gate. A startled Travis examined the site of the collision.

His hammer had been shattered and scattered around the whole practice yard, the skeleton gone without a trace. But, far more important, the spell collision hadn't affected the professor in the slightest.

The redhead's friends looked as startled as he was.

"And that does it," Doom said with a disappointed sigh. "None of you pampered kids has never been in a real battle."

"But—"

"School duels and street fights don't count," Alex interrupted. "How much magic did you put into that spell? A hundred and forty? A hundred and seventy? That used up almost a fifth of your reserve. And I spent exactly *ten points*."

"But that's impossible!"

"Physical objects can be blocked by other physical objects."

"But the hammer should've destroyed that skeleton!" blondie screamed with such ardor that the words came with a sway of her brea—

No.

No, no, no. Stop that.

Alex still hadn't had sex since getting out of prison, extending his abstinence past the four-year sentence, but they were *kids*. It didn't matter that they were just four years younger than him.

They're kids. Kids. They even haven't gotten their multi-purpose IDs yet.

"The skeleton had explosive magic," the karate kid said. "That's why the hammer exploded when it hit it."

"Damn!"

"Shit."

The students looked at their professor with different eyes.

Suddenly, they better understood how he'd bypassed the faculty dean's defensive artifacts and survived the battle with the demon.

Professor Dumsky was just out of everyone else's league.

In the meantime, Alex, still holding the bottle of ice to his head, was hit with more recollections of his lessons at Follen School.

"My turn!"

Eleonora Wessex, the aristocrat, had probably had plenty of excellent practice with strong wizard tutors ever since she was young, but…

Yes, she used both hands. Yes, the seal was formed quickly. Yes, the fire she summoned was pure magic, without a physical element.

It would have burned through a ten-meter-thick steel wall without meeting any resistance. Steel, after all, belongs to the physical world, and her fire was pure magic.

But still…

"Too slow," Alex said, waving a hand.

Flying toward him was a Practitioner-cast Pyromancer's Storm, a fire flow as thick as a Russian pyramid ball, but still too slow. *Two hundred mana points wasted.*

From the ground beneath blondie's feet, a bony hand appeared, gripping at her ankle and jerking her to the side.

"What the fu…" The end of the aristocrat girl's filthy curse was drowned out by a loud smacking sound. She had fallen face first into the long-jump landing pit, the sand cushioning the impact.

"That must taste nasty," Alex smirked. "You're strong and have excellent technique. But your speed… My granny could have done it faster. She'd have cast *ten* spells in the same amount of time."

"I…"

"You're already out."

Before Glomebood could lift her hands to form a seal, she was surrounded by three wolves burning with black fire.

[Spell used: HELL HOUNDS of the Black Magic School. Mana used: 75 points/one + 45 points/min.]

Half-bloods. Magically weak, but with their special skills. Almost like espers.

Underestimating either half-bloods or Espers was stupid. And a stupid black wizard was a dead black wizard.

"When did you...?"

"Before I blocked Travis. Kiddies, you keep forgetting that the tournament is a *team* event. I asked you to try to get me to stand up, but I didn't say you had to do it one at a time. So—"

Alex saw something flash before his eyes. Acting on pure instinct, he sent his will to his magic source, drained a healthy helping, and formed a lilac lightning bolt that snapped out of the seal instantly appearing in midair.

"You can cast hands-free?!"

"A lot of Adepts can't do that!"

While Elie and Travis admired (and somewhat resented) him, the karate kid suffered the impact. The tiger tattoos on his legs still glowed with blue magic energy, but he was already flying backward into the stands, a bloody trace behind him and a black burn mark on his chest.

"Damn," Alex cursed.

He'd instinctively used a battle spell on the kid. *Who would have expected one of the five to actually be good?*

He was a shaman. A real, hereditary shaman capable of summoning animal powers. Meeting him among that bunch of pampered kids was...unexpected.

"Jing?" Leo turned to his friend who, after smacking into the concrete wall loaded with crystals, collapsed motionless to the sand. "Jing, bro. Hey! You good?"

"He's all right," Alex called over. "Take him to the hospital when he wakes up."

"Jing, get up, you stupid dog!"

Saying that Alex was surprised to hear that would be a severe understatement. In a split second, Leo's voice and posture had changed completely. He hunched over slightly, becoming shorter.

The boy who didn't look dangerous at all held out a perfectly manicured hand.

"This motherfucking shit again?"

"What's go—"

"Professor, watch out!" Mara shouted. "That's not Leo."

"What? Not Leo? What do you mean?"

In the meantime, Travis started warily toward his friend.

"Hey, Leonard, let's not get worked up and—"

"Shut up, you red monkey." Leo…*Leonard* turned. And when he saw his face, Alex realized that it really *wasn't* Leo. It looked like his evil doppelganger, with completely different eyes and all of his wizardry aura gone—Doom could no longer feel a tingle in his fingertips. *How's that even possible?* "So, *you* were the one who knocked Jing down, you nerd? Pray, scumbag."

Leonard threw out his palm. For the first time in a long while, Alex was *truly* scared for his life.

"Run, Professor!"

Chapter 42

"**R**un, Professor!" called a young voice from next to Alex.

Still sitting by the gate, he was trying to figure out if his eyes were failing him. A moment before, he'd been looking at a kid no one would sell alcohol to at a club, but now…

Some kind of dangerous criminal had appeared in his place. Doom had seen plenty of his kind when he was a gang member and later in wizard prison.

But the transformation was more about Leo's abilities than his appearance.

Leo Stone the wizard was gone, replaced by an esper.

An esper who was close to the B rank. Enough power to hold his own against low-level Adepts (if one could describe any Adept as low-level), meaning that the prostrate Doom was on the verge of passing on to hell.

Leonard, or whatever his name was, shot a ray of bright white light from his palm. Instantly, the ray expanded to become a river of light a dozen feet wide and just as many tall. It carved a trench in the ground that was large enough to house a skating rink.

"Not bad," Alex said once he'd recovered from his initial shock. In front of him, four small seals formed, one after another. Each shot out a black bolt of lightning. Entwining together, they formed a dark glowing raven that flew screeching into the current of light.

Against the broad wave of snow-white light, the black bird was a miserable dot. However, it used the pure Darkness glowing from its beak to cleave through the flow of light.

Rushing by on either side of Alex, the two trains of brightness reduced the soccer goal and the referee stand to melted, shapeless lumps of red-hot metal.

The open ground and grass smoked when the raven grabbed Leonard by shoulder, piercing it through, to jerk him up into the air and fling him against the concrete wall next to where the Asian shaman had landed.

The impact knocked the air out of Leonard's lungs. The esper fell to the ground, unconscious.

The practice yard lapsed into silence.

Exhausted, Alex shook his head, opened his bottle, and took a gulp of delicious cold water.

Two of his students were out cold. One was suffering from open wounds and burns; another had at least a fractured clavicle.

The aristocrat girl had just gotten back to her feet, presenting the world with her smeared make-up. *Smashing your nose up isn't the best look.*

The redhead and the half-dwarf were in the best shape. (Not counting Alex, of course.)

"Would you care to explain what happened here?"

However odd this might sound, it took Alex a second to realize that he wasn't the one who said that.

It was Miss Perriot, the history teacher who'd been with Alex in that museum, complete with peach hair, bright eyes, a white blouse, and jeans.

"Oh goodness!" she screamed, darting down the stairs. Running up to the unconscious Leo and Jing, she checked their pulse, then pulled out her phone and started tapping nervously on the screen. "Is this the hospital? We have an emergency on Range One. Two people wounded, both with dark magic injuries. What? Ah, Professor Dumsky's group."

"Uh-oh," Alex sighed. "She ratted me out."

Miss Perriot finished and, paying no attention to Doom, called over to the students.

"Mara, hold Jing's head up so he doesn't choke on his tongue. Travis, hold Leo's wound closed with a handkerchief or your T-shirt. Elie, don't look up."

"Wow," Alex drawled, "looks like you know more than just history."

To Doom's surprise, the students jumped to follow Perriot's instructions. For her part, she finally spotted Alex and started over in his direction. The pebbles beneath her feet swirled faster and faster with each step until some of them flew into the air to form miniature asteroids orbiting around her.

Strange things were happening with Leia's hair too. It looked like Medusa's hissing snakes, alive and wriggling furiously.

"You," the esper literally growled. "How *dare* you attack—"

"No, you got it all wrong!"

That time, Alex wasn't surprised that it wasn't him talking. Making excuses wasn't his thing.

He wasn't about to get up, either.

The kerfuffle had joined forces with his hangover, and his head was throbbing. Doom wasn't sure he would have held onto the semblance of a breakfast he'd had that morning if he'd stood up.

"Travis is right, Miss Perriot," Mara joined in as Elie held her T-shirt to her nose. Stripping out of it, she was left in just a sports bra, making it even more challenging for Alex to convince himself that she was a child, and not a breathtaking young aristocrat beauty. He'd never bedded an aristocrat woman. "The professor didn't do anything wrong."

"Is that right?" Perriot screamed indignantly, though she stopped. Of course, the pebbles kept sizzling around her like the ammo belt of a machine gun in action.

"We asked him—"

"Asked him what?"

"To train us for the tournament," Mara blurted out. "But things got out of control, and Leonard came out."

Silence fell again, with no sound but Alex sipping water from his bottle. He wished he had some popcorn, too. Watching everything unfold was as good as a trip to a movie theater.

On the other hand, just thinking about popcorn (like any other food) almost made him vomit.

"Are you insane?!" Perriot raged on. "You asked a *black wizard* to train you for the tournament? You, magic theory majors? Knowing Leo's condition?"

So, Miss Perriot knew about Leo/Leonard, Alex said to himself. *She knew what he is. How can you be an esper and a wizard?*

"And what for?" the peach-haired woman went on. "For the prize money? Or just to show off? Putting your life at stake just for some—"

"We have a good reason," Elie interrupted, although she might as well have kept silent. Her words were barely audible anyway.

"Fucking bitch," Perriot spat out. The words sounded obscene coming from her, the woman's gentle appearance forming too stark a contrast. "We'll talk later."

The conversation stopped when a few male nurses wearing blue uniforms with a red cross on the back came running onto the practice field. They quickly loaded the two students onto flying mag-suspension stretchers and rushed them to the hospital.

First Magic University's hospital had all the necessary equipment and staff to treat a variety of emergencies. The university had a battle magic school, after all, and injuries sustained from battle spells weren't out of the ordinary if not an everyday occurrence.

At some point, Alex realized he'd been left alone with Miss Perriot, whose powers were still active. Stones were still flying around.

"Hi there, colleague," he said with a wave. The urge to smoke came over him, but that would have meant pulling the bottle of water away from his forehead. That wasn't about to happen.

Using his left hand was a no-go, as well. *Wizards should always have at least one hand free and at the ready.* That lesson had been knocked into him (literally) at Follen School.

"Do you have any idea how screwed you are, Professor?" Perriot squinted.

"I'm not a fan of getting screwed." His joke was on the bawdy side, but Alex's limp sense of humor made sense given what he'd just been through. "Can you tell me what's wrong with Leo Stone? And how *you* know about him while I'm completely in the dark?"

"That's none of your business," Perriot snapped.

"Really?" Alex pretended to be surprised. "Forgive me for being blunt, but the last time I checked, *I* was their supervisor. Not you."

"I'm surprised you remember that, Professor. For the past four weeks, *I've* been doing all the work as the B-52 group supervisor. Not you."

"Thank you for being so kind as to help a new colleague out." Alex gave her a thumbs-up.

Perriot's jaw muscles flexed, betraying her level of fitness. And *she* was by no means a kid, so...

Alex knew he had to kick those thoughts away.

He liked her too much.

"Stand up, Professor."

"You don't hit guys when they're down? I wouldn't mind being under a girl like you."

"Getting me mad is going to take more than your toilet humor, Professor. Stand up. We need to go."

"If that's your way of challenging me to a duel, we can get started the way we are." Alex's tone made his hint a transparent one.

Why?

It was just his shitty mood. And the need to maintain his reputation as a black wizard. Being a jerk and a brute came with the territory.

"The rector, Professor," Perriot said through gritted teeth. "He'll want to hear from you. And I don't have time for your childish games."

"Childish? Oh, the games I have in mind are anything but childish."

Perriot held out a palm. For a moment, Doom thought she really was going to attack, though...

"Why do you keep pushing me, Professor?" Perriot said with a sigh. As she brought her hand down, the pebbles landed at her feet and her hair fell back to her shoulders.

Damn. His plan had failed.

Alex stood and, barely containing his hangover vomit, wobbled toward the range exit. Passing by Perriot, he stopped and whispered in her ear.

"I've loved riddles ever since I was a kid. And now, I'm racking my brain over this one: how could a D-ranked esper stop a rock weighing not a few tons in midair?"

Leaving Miss Perriot taken aback in the middle of the demolished practice grounds, Alex drank some more water from his bottle.

First, the Syndicate. Then the Guards. Now the espers. What next? Are the ancient gods going to wake up and wage a war for the mortal world?

Chapter 43

By the time Alex, with a sulking Miss Perriot at his side, reached the rector's office, he had both polished off his bottle of melted ice and nearly burned the drink machine on the landing to the ground.

It had charged his account several credits while refusing to dispense the drink he'd purchased.

"You racist scum!" Alex screamed, which didn't help with his headache. He kicked the machine with the tip of his shoe and endured another flash of pain.

"You need to see a psychotherapist, Professor." The history teacher stepped over to the machine and pressed a button. A steel robot hand appeared out of the opening Alex expected his bottle to fall from, buzzed, and handed him his cold soda.

"Technology," Alex snorted. Taking his drink from the robot, he turned to thank Miss Perriot as the gentleman who sometimes woke up in him, but the esper was no longer there. "All the better."

He looked up at the heavy oak door.

Stretching from floor to ceiling, it was more reminiscent of a castle gate from some medieval movie than the entrance to a modern education manager's office.

Alex ignored the name plate, stepped in, and found himself in an administrative office similar to Lebenstein's. The only difference was that it was far more spacious and had *three* secretaries.

Two of them were men. Both were wearing very expensive suits. Their noses were buried in papers, they were clicking away at mice, tapping on keyboards, and ardently discussing something on the phone all at once. Since they were so busy, Alex was approached by the third secretary, a red-haired girl walking on such high heels that he wondered if she'd initially applied for a stilt-walker's job at the circus.

She definitely looked amazing. Given the salaries there, most of the staff could afford magic cosmetic surgery.

Her best asset was her booty.

Devil. As soon as Alex imagined that juicy behind naked and curving up against his thighs, he had to quickly open his soda and take a couple swallows to cool himself off.

He wasn't a sex addict. Years of abstinence, however, had taken their toll.

"Do you have an appointment?" the red-haired succubus asked in a strict tone that was all business.

"Probably not," Alex replied.

"In that case—"

"But my name's Dumsky. Professor Dumsky. I'm pretty sure the rector's expecting me."

The secretary checked her tablet, nodded, and went over to push open a much plainer frosted glass door.

"Go ahead in, Professor. The rector's waiting for you."

After giving the secretary one last look-over as she went back to her desk *(damn, that booty in a pencil skirt and suspender stockings)*, Alex followed her instructions.

"You look almost the same, Alex. Just a bit taller. And maybe leaner."

Alex's gut instinct reacted before his brain could process anything. By the time he turned to face the voice, he was already surrounded by two scores of glowing black magic seals.

They had completely drained his magic source. But even they weren't enough to make his interlocutor, a Master at level 62, even the slightest bit uncomfortable.

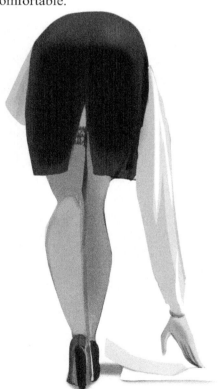

"Hey, wonder kid. Psst. Hey! Wake up!"

Alex was roused by Robin shaking his shoulder. Opening his eyes and finding himself slumped over on the piano bench, he stood up and stretched.

"Did I miss dinner?" the boy asked, rubbing his eyes sleepily.

"This isn't about dinner, sonny boy."

"I'm not your sonny boy."

"Whatever," Robin said with a wave.

That was when Dumsky finally noticed that his big friend was apparently anxious about something.

There were very few things in the world besides Anastasia and movies that could make Robin emotional.

"What's up?" Dumsky asked, immediately tense.

"The professor has a visitor." Robin literally jerked Alex to his feet and dragged him off down the corridor. Mumbling and floundering, he tried to explain everything to the boy as they went. "I had just gotten everyone into bed when Anastasia asked for some juice. She's not feeling well. So, I went to the kitchen, and—"

"Just tell me, Robin."

"Yeah, sorry. So…when I was in the kitchen, I saw Raewsky's shadows getting wine from the cellar."

Shadows were Professor Raewsky's fleshless and shapeless servants, the creatures he summoned from the deepest dark. Alex once tried to summon one of them, but all he'd managed was a tiny black puff of smoke. And even that was a major accomplishment for his magic level.

"You know how the professor only drinks on special occasions even though he's Russian."

"So, what's the occasion, Robin? At two in the morning?"

"I asked myself the same question, and—"

The two of them had almost reached the living room. At that late hour, it was usually dark and silent, but right then the sounds of two male voices reached them from inside. Light fell from the slit between the two wings of the door.

"Be quiet," Robin whispered.

Treading as softly as cats, they approached the door to peep through the slit like a two-headed Native American totem. The upper head belonging to Robin, the bottom one to Alex.

They couldn't make out what either speaker was saying, but the sight was captivating.

One of the men was Professor Raewsky. He was sharp-nosed, narrow-cheeked, balding, and shifty-eyed, lean to the point of being scrawny, covered in scars and burns, and wearing an old, worn-out suit and gloves that he never took off.

Despite his grotesque appearance, he looked like an aristocrat with a long line of noble ancestors. Actually, he came from a small Russian village somewhere near the city of Murmansk, which had been destroyed in the last Magic War.

That was when Raewsky moved there.

Seated in the armchair facing his was a very tall, broad-shouldered man with fists the size of hammers, a strong chin, a red face, thick golden hair, and insanely clear blue eyes.

He breathed life and vigor while looking simple and relatable.

"Can you feel that?" Robin asked.

Neither of them was wearing magic lenses, so they weren't able to scan the visitor.

"Yeah," Alex replied.

His fingertips weren't tingling. They felt like...

***

...like they'd been dipped in boiling water.

Sitting at the carved oak desk, in the great oval office with rows of shelves and a designated lounge area with its Italian sofa and giant plasma TV screen, was Julio Lupen. The light wizard from the Mediterranean.

He looked just like he had during those few visits to Follen School. Strong and mighty as a *bogatyr*, a Russian hero of enormous strength from Anastasia's tales.

He never wore a business suit. Just a track suit, and always Nike.

A golden chain hung from his neck, which was as thick and mighty as a bull's. Shiny alligator shoes adorned his feet. The description sounds ridiculous, but somehow the outfit looked good on Lupen.

[Name: Julio Lupen. Race: Human. Mana level: 6298.]
Damn. Damn. Damn.

Chapter 44

*A*ll the demons of hell. He was just two mana points short of the next level.

The 63rd Master level.

Alex was a kitten to his tiger.

No, more like a kitten to his intercontinental ballistic missile.

"You actually look like a professor."

The seals around Alex flashed with magic power.

"Sorry," the rector of First Magic University said, waving a hand. A wave of pure, uncut Light passed through Doom tenderly, all his seals vanishing into thin air and a puny hundred mana points finding its way back to his magic source. "Forgive me for being rude, but I see you're rather surprised, and this place is stuffed with sensors. I don't want to ruin some police officer's day with a false alarm."

The Master-level Light wizard watched Alex with radiant blue eyes that promising all-overcoming sympathy and all-embracing care.

Alex had never trusted them.

"No," Alex shot back, dropping into a visitor's armchair.

Oh Abyss. The chair was just as comfortable as the one in the major's limo.

"No what?" Lupen was somewhat taken aback. The whole wall behind him was taken up by a map of the capital city, all its districts and streets marked.

"I *was* surprised, but I'm not anymore. May I?" Without waiting for permission, Alex reached for a bowl of candy and helped himself to a few.

The rector's brows flew up.

"I thought you hated candy."

"You need to update your file, Mr. Lupen."

The truth was that Alex still hated them. He just desperately needed a way to calm down while saving face, and the chocolate candy with the famous Oreo taste was perfect.

"You can call me Julio." The wizard, whose power was beyond Alex's imagination, settled back in his armchair. "We know each other well. I was the only friend of your adoptive fa—"

Lilac fire flashed around Alex's fingers.

Damn, I'm behaving like a kid. Can't keep a grip on myself.

But that's just the alcohol. And the stupid date. Nothing more.

"Forgive me," Julio said again. That time it sounded less formal and more like genuine regret. "We all fight our inner demons. It's such a shame Pavel lost to his."

"...and tried to summon another," Doom said with a wry smirk, "killing all my friends. He almost killed me, too, only I escaped. Do you remember *when* that was, *Mr. Lupen*? I can tell you—yesterday was the tenth anniversary of that day. It's been ten years and one day since you visited and had your falling out with the Professor."

A silence fell over the expansive office.

The Rector's brows flew upward, almost reaching the ceiling.

"So, you...all these years..." he whispered breathily before holding out his palm. "Let the Magic be my witness: I never wanted Follen School to be destroyed. I never wanted my best friend to die. I never wanted innocent people to get hurt. And I didn't want you, Alex, to spend your childhood in the streets and your adolescence in prison."

A bright white ball of light flashed on Julio's palm.

The Magic heard him.

The Magic accepted his words.

Not every wizard could summon Pure Magic, and those who could only did it for matters of life and death.

The words Julio Lupen uttered were as strong as *adamantius* and as true as those given to Moses on stone tablets.

Otherwise, they wouldn't have been accepted by the Magic.

Alex cursed in disappointment.

"I knew that," he drawled, tossing another piece of candy into his mouth.

"You surprise me again. Why are you upset that I didn't have a hand in the tragedy?"

Alex shrugged.

"It was easier to label you an accomplice and hate you for that."

Julio nodded understandingly

"Hating is always easy. *Forgiving* is hard. But hating kills you, while forgiving cures."

Alex clenched his fist with such force that a red trickle ran down his palm. *I need to cut my fingernails.*

"Are you asking me to forgive Raewsky?" Alex whispered, making no attempt to hide the threat in his voice.

"May god forgive him," Julio said and crossed himself.

Doom felt uncomfortable. Physically uncomfortable. It was as if a bonfire had been lit in the room, its heat searing the wizard's face.

Lupen wasn't just making the sacred gesture for its own sake. He truly *believed.*

It wasn't uncommon for light wizards to address the one in the heavens, but very few of them actually believed. The rector of First Magic University was apparently one of those few.

If Alex ever came into physical contact with him, he'd find himself instantly down, wriggling in mortal agony.

That was the power of faith.

It was the power that had enabled the Inquisitors, who were just non-magic humans, to hunt and destroy black wizards all over Old Earth in the Dark Ages.

"Oh, sorry," Julio said, checking himself. "I forgot how faith feels to you."

"It's fine," Alex said through gritted teeth. "I can deal with it."

"Ah," Lupen sighed and shook his golden mane. "No, Alex. I'm not asking you to forgive Professor Raewsky. I'm just asking you to forgive *yourself.*"

"You think I have something to forgive myself for, Mr. Lupen?"

"For the fact that you're alive." His clear blue eyes bathed Alex in compassion, though the latter would have preferred shit to his pity. "For the fact that you survived instead of someone else."

Alex spun the black ring around his finger. *Damn lights.*

"Whatever the priests may tell us, Mr. Lupen, life is not always a gift. I'm very aware that it's often a curse."

Julio smiled sadly.

Alex snorted.

"You look like you're going to treat me to some lemon drops."

"Only if you're planning on talking to a snake."

"I tried that. Didn't work. I messed the spell up and ended up speaking Farsi for a good ten days instead of talking to a snake. And I even had it backwards, always mixing up the syllables."

"Yes, Pavel told me about that. He was really proud of you. More than anyone or anything else in his life."

The office lapsed into silence again, this time for a much longer while.

"Not the briskest of conversations, yeah?" Julio flashed his usual smile, warm and sad.

"Something like that."

He'd always been surprised at how one of the world's most powerful dark wizards could make friends with one of its most powerful light wizards. *It's like two sides of the same coin. They're close, yes, tightly pressed against each another.*

But they're not supposed to meet. No way.

But still, Lupen and Raewsky *had* been friends. The best and closest of friends. They'd fought side by side in the Magic War, human and non-human as allies against the crazed hordes of magic beasts infesting Old Earth.

"I looked for you, Alexander. After the night the school burned down, I poured resources into finding you. But it didn't work. When I finally found out where you were, it was too late. Even I don't have the power to release a wizard serving three life sentences."

"...which brings us to a logical question."

Their eyes met. Blue and green. Light and dark.

Julio waved a hand, casting a golden aura that enveloped the office and screened out the rest of the world. Even Alex's lenses stopped working, let alone any cop sensors or other bugs that were in the room.

A Master. At level 62.

"The Guards visited me several months ago."

"I figured," Alex nodded, his guess confirmed. "It's a bit of a stretch to think you can get any goner off the street into First Magic just by inventing a good backstory for him."

"You really have lost weight, but I wouldn't call you a goner," Lupen said, attempting a joke that fell flat. Light wizards always had a poor sense of humor. "Yes, I had a rather lengthy talk with Major Chon Sook. And I ended up agreeing to help him."

"Why?"

Chapter 45

"Why?" More warm sadness. "Because you're someone who's close to me, Alex. Maybe even one of the closest still alive. And I certainly couldn't miss the opportunity to bring on board a wizard Professor Raewsky said would one day excel him."

Lupen's eyes sparked naughtily as he continued.

"Although, with twenty-six reports from Dean Lebenstein on my desk, I'm starting to second-guess that decision."

Silence again. This time, a forced one.

The rector stood and went over to the map. He passed by Central Boulevard, then left the city and stopped in its suburbs.

Almost exactly where Follen School had been. Maybe ten miles farther north.

Then he placed a hand on a golden emblem on the map, pulling a dossier out of a niche that opened.

Like any other old-school wizard, Lupen didn't trust anything digital. He only liked hard copies that couldn't be hacked by someone sitting on the other side of the globe.

"Read this." Lupen dropped the folder onto the desk.

The front cover was emblazoned in big letters: *RIZEN*.

"Bitch," Doom cursed. He knew already what he would find inside.

"We have a balance to maintain, Alex." Lupen sat back down at his desk and intertwined his fingers. "Follen School and Rizen School were an experiment...that only half-failed."

Doom opened the folder and started reading.

In a nutshell, it was all about another school, the one for light wizards (crammed with the best technology and a top teaching staff with monthly funding of several million credits). It was located near the dark wizard school headed by Raewsky.

Alex picked up the picture of the history teacher.

Miss Perriot. Just a bit younger...and pudgier.

Fitness has been good for her.

"We accepted two hundred students." Lupen apparently had trouble staying quiet. "But only five of them graduated."

Alex noticed pictures of those five all-too-familiar students.

The whole B-52 group. Small kids smiling (all but the karate boy) and waving at the camera.

"After Follen School was destroyed, we wanted to shut down Rizen, too, but…we couldn't just throw those five out onto the streets. So, we finished teaching them the full course and only then pulled the plug."

As Alex read the student dossiers, he felt the urge to smoke growing stronger. But he also remembered that Lupen was allergic to tobacco smoke, so lighting up would have been rude.

Alex had no desire to be disrespectful to someone who had a hand, even indirectly, in getting him out of prison.

"Why magic theory?" Turning one page after another, Alex discovered new sides of his students. Each of them had a unique gift.

Mara Glomebood: Direct command of any artifact that has a piece of her magic inside. An innate ability related to her dwarf blood.
Travis Chavert: Intuitive control over his magic.
Jing Wai: The only living shaman of the Wai Too line, the Snowy Mountain shamans.
Eleonora Wessex: Fire magic consumes less mana and delivers greater impact. Cause unknown.

And the last one.

Leo/Leonard Stone: Split personality. Leo Stone: No outstanding capabilities. Leonard Stone: VERY dangerous. Unstable. Maniac and sadist. Esper of unknown strength.

"Bitch," Alex said in a much calmer voice, more a pronouncement than a curse. "A split personality? How is that even possible?"

"Some mortals have the condition, too." Lupen poured some whiskey into a glass and offered it to Alex. The latter refused, barely holding back his vomit. "One personality can paint another Starry Night, while the other would mess up even the Black Square. And Stone…"

Lupen rolled up his right sleeve to demonstrate a burn covering half of his forearm.

"That happened when I accidentally scared Leo. He was trying a girl's dress on…eleven years old."

Alex nodded as though seeing and hearing things like that was old hat.

"Bitch," he said for the third time. "I get why Jing, Travis, and Leo are here. But Mara and Eleonora…they're from aristocratic families!"

"All of them were abandoned by their parents," Lupen said in a firm and apparently disapproving voice. "*All* of them, Alex. No exceptions.

They didn't just attend Rizen; they *lived* there. As one big family."

Alex glanced back down at the folder. It was several times thicker than his court case. *A lengthy read.*

"Can I take this?" he asked.

"Sure," Lupen replied with a shrug. "That's just a copy. When I hired you—and the decision was *mine*, whatever you may think—I was sure that even though you don't have official status, you do have the most extensive knowledge of black magic of all the living residents of Atlantis…who aren't members at the Abyss."

It wasn't a surprise that the rector knew about the Abyss in addition to the Guards. After all, Raewsky had been a VIP member.

"So," the Light Master went on, "I figured it was Fate bringing all of you together again. They're sort of your reflection. Younger—"

"…guinea pigs." It was Alex's turn to interrupt. "Follen School was first. Rizen followed. But one thing I'm not sure about: I wasn't able to find out whose experiment it was. I know for sure that Follen was created by the Shadow Court and the Assembly, but who created Rizen? And why? The Light—what do *you* all need places like that for?"

"That information is secret, Alex. Even from *me*."

"Great."

"That's all we have," the rector said, quoting one of Raewsky's favorite sayings.

"What are your plans for them, Mr. Lupen?"

"Plans? None, Alex. The Rizen project is closed. The kids are on their own. All I'm asking is for you to keep an eye on them for a while and help in any way you can. They really don't have anyone but you in the world to rely on. Believe me."

"Great," Alex said again. Without asking permission, he stood and walked toward the door.

Lupen's voice stopped him when he got there.

"Alex?"

He stopped and looked back.

The blue eyes were drilling holes in him.

A caring and sympathetic Light Master at level 62? Sure, sure. You don't climb that high by being naïve and well-intentioned. Those people drop like flies before ever getting close.

"How did you survive that night?"

Alex rolled the ring around his finger again without realizing it.

"Just good luck," he said.

"Yes, sure," the rector smiled. "Pavel used to say that you're as lucky as a little demon."

Doom left the office, ignoring the redheaded girl with the stunningly delicious booty as she invited him to join her for a cup of coffee. The heavy folder was hitting him on the belt as he walked.

Bitch.

Chapter 46

Sitting in the cafeteria, Alex skimmed through the personal dossiers of the Rizen students.

The number of free seats around him was surprising given that it was right in the middle of the seniors' lunch hour. When they saw Professor Dumsky drinking soda (that looked suspiciously like beer) through a straw and swearing heavily, the students all stayed as far away as possible.

In the less than a month Alex had been "teaching" at First Magic, he'd earned a reputation as the professor who hunted lazy students through their worst nightmares.

"What a mess!" Alex slammed the folder shut. *Why the abyss am I sitting here trying to shoehorn what I thought into reality when somewhere in this building is the person who can answer all my questions at once?*

"Hey, you!" Alex called over to a student who'd gotten separated from his pack.

The main rule of survival is to stay with the herd. You're easy prey when you're alone, and that's probably what the rest of the student body thought of their unfortunate compadre. Someone even gave him a sympathetic clap on the shoulder.

The tin tray loaded with a glass of milk, French fries, and two apples trembled so violently in the student's hands that Alex was afraid the poor kid was going to spill something on him.

That would have been a real tragedy—he couldn't afford another ArmaniMagico suit. At least, not in the near future.

"Y-y-yes, P-p-pr-r-rofes-s-sor-r D-d-d—"

"Where is Miss Perriot lecturing right now?"

"H-h-how sh-should I kn-n-now?"

Doom flashed his most suspicious and angry look.

The earthquake local to the student's tray jumped to a magnitude of 12 on a 10-point scale.

"Be-be-be-be-be…"

"Are you cosplaying a car horn? Just give me the hall number."

"B-53," the ashen student blurted out.

"Oh. Right next door."

He darted upstairs, folder in hand. On the way, he knocked a few girls over, tried to get one's phone number out of habit, flashed his famous tattoo at Lebenstein, and even seemed to invent a new spell.

Reaching the hall, Alex was about to grab hold of the door handle, but he jerked his hand away at the last moment and smirked.

"Not bad," he said, running his palm through the air over the handle.

His fingertips were tingling. Not that strongly, but still.

Miss Perriot was beloved by almost everyone at the university, with *almost* being the key word. The few exceptions to the rule were those who hated the whole esper race.

For most wizards, particularly those from old families, ESP-people were even worse than second-rate citizens.

They did not count as humans at all.

The curse had apparently been placed by a woman. It had to have been. Alex couldn't imagine a male wizard of any age cursing anyone with thrush of the vulva. *Gross.*

Doom ran his hand through the air over the handle. The spell took the form of a wriggling, agonizing misty worm a moment before evaporating.

"Who's the smartypants?" Doom drawled to himself. He didn't *really* teach dark magic to his students, which meant that someone was smart enough to craft something like that after just being presented with a single, extremely complicated seal.

But that wasn't Alex's main concern right then.

"...at roughly the same time, the current ranking of magic powers was adopted." Miss Perriot, wearing a strict business suit with the skirt ending below the knees and her hair in a tight bun, stood behind the lecture desk. She was facing a hall crammed with students.

The room was half-dark, all the windows curtained. The display board behind Miss Perriot's back flashed visuals and short documentaries.

Most students were tapping away with their fingers on the virtual keyboards of their tablets. Some used styluses instead, finding that more convenient, but *everyone* was taking notes.

And it wasn't because they had to, like for Doom's lectures. No, it was because they were actually interested.

"If anyone forgot this, though I doubt you did, you can write it down. You may need it for the exam. The current magic ranking approved by the Supreme Magic Council has five levels. The first level, from 0 to 250 points, is Apprentice. That's where the vast majority of living wizards stand. According to the most recent statistics, the Apprentice level makes up 80 percent of the population of Atlantis and Old Earth.

"The next level, from 251 to 1,000, is Practitioner. It makes up a much smaller percentage: between 14 and 16 percent, according to different sources. The third level is Mystic—from 1,001 to 3,000 points.

It's achieved by three to four percent of the population, though estimates again vary across sources.

"The fourth level is Adept, from 3,000 to 6,000 points. It's achieved by 0.25 to 0.5 percent of all wizards. And the fifth and final level is Master—6,000 to 13,000 points strong. As you know, the current interpretation is that each hundred points constitutes a separate sub-level.

"The strongest living wizard in the world is Tranquil Creek, a native North American. Although he identifies as a shaman rather than a wizard, that's still what he's acknowledged as. The latest measurement of his power showed 8,743 mana points, putting him at the 87th level of Master and atop the global wizard ranking. But you're highly unlikely to ever meet him. He prefers a life of solitude, avoiding all contact with the outside world."

A hand rose in the audience.

"Yes, Mr. Chipotle?"

Chipotle? Seriously?

Alex's stomach growled. He hadn't had a bite to eat in a long while, and that was such an appetizing last name.

"Miss Perriot?" The esper had no professorial title, so she was just addressed by her last name. "How do we know there isn't another wizard just as strong, or even stronger, than Tranquil Creek, maybe someone living in solitude somewhere else?"

Leia smiled and threw up her arms.

"We don't, Mr. Chipotle."

Alex wasn't sure if the conversation was making him want to laugh or find something to eat.

"None of this is an exact science—all the numbers I cited are approximate."

Another hand.

"Yes, Miss Lang?"

Is Superman coming, too? Or am I starting to hear things?

"What about the three Great Levels, Miss Perriot?"

The girl who stood up looked too grown-up to believe in children's stories—her breasts had to enter doors a good couple seconds before the rest of her. But she still asked the question.

"The levels of Grand Master, Arch Master, and Archmage are just myths and legends from the past, Miss Lang," the esper said in a mild, soothing smile backed by a firm voice. "Not a single historical document provides evidence that anyone with that kind of power ever lived."

"But what about Merlin? Morgana? Faust? Other—"

"Those are *legends*, Miss Lang. Nothing more. Actually, it's probable that the legendary Queens of the Fairy Courts, Titania and Mab, had powers like that, though no one ever met either of them. Just like no one has ever met Bagil, the dragon god of Ifrits. Or Gorgon, the progenitrix of Nags and Medusas. As for Merlin, Morgana, Baba Yaga, Koschei the Deathless, Baron Samedi, Sun Wukong, and Amaterasu, those stories are just mortals' attempts to explain what they don't understand."

"But their statues are by the university entrance!"

"We have paintings of angels, too, but that doesn't mean angels exist."

"Not that long ago, people thought the same thing about *unicorns*."

"Good reasoning, Miss Lang, but myths and legends were created by mortals and wizards. And those were slightly different."

"But how did they come to invent all those creatures?"

"Like I said, they were trying to explain things they couldn't understand. Let's take Baba Yaga and Koschei the Deathless. They're dark creatures from Slavic folklore, primitive attempts to explain the change between day and night. Also, the woods where the Slavic tribes used to live were far more dangerous at night than during the day.

"Aside from early animism and totemism, those tales were also influenced by the primitive idea of magic developed by human tribes before the fall of Atlantis and the world being split into two parts. Their myths tried to explain the division between light and dark magic. And now, let's end this lecture with a bang."

Miss Perriot chuckle immediately elicited laughs from her audience. *Damn. What a smart move.*

"Miss Lang, could you light a magic fire?"

The girl held out a hand. A small orange petal of flame flashed over her palm.

"The element of Fire qualifies as Light Magic. Can you explain why, Miss Lang?"

"Because it can either keep a person warm or hurt them," the girl said, reciting a memorized phrase. "While—"

"While…" Miss Perriot interrupted and turned to Alex. The whole audience turned with her. "Professor Dumsky. Could you be so kind as to summon *your* fire?"

Silently, Alex held out his palm. His fingertips flashed with small lilac flames.

"What can your fire do, Professor Dumsky?"

"Remember once and for all, Alex: they hate you, and they always will hate you. That's just something you have to deal with."

"But why, Robin? I've never hurt anyone."

"That doesn't matter—what matters is that you were born a black wizard. Black magic can do nothing but hurt. It can't save or protect; it just destroys and kills. What it brings is worse than death. It is the abyss."

"But I didn't choose that!"

"No one cares," Alex whispered, repeating Robin's words to himself before continuing out loud with a pirate's dashing smile. "It can burn Miss Lang, for instance."

"Let's not do that, Professor Dumsky." She looked at the students. "I hope you understand now. The Light can either hurt or take away pain. Heal. Save. Keep you warm. But black magic can only destroy, which is why it's called Dark. All right, that's all for today."

The students burst into applause and then started collecting their things.

Switching her display board off, Miss Perriot turned to Alex. She gave him an appraising once-over (and paused for a second when she saw the folder in his hand) before asking her question.

"Do they serve coffee at the Schooner?"

"Only instant."

"Well, I'm always up for a risk. Can we go get some?"

No. No. Leave. Now! a voice yelled in Alex's head.

But he used to be friends with Robin Loxley. He couldn't respond to an offer like that with anything other than: "Sure. I'd love to treat you."

Chapter 47

The Schooner was usually empty during the day except for the staff and the occasional detective stopping in for some stereotypical doughnuts. They were made quickly, they stayed warm and fresh for a long while, and they were the most reasonably priced in all of downtown.

"Oh, Alex! Hi!" Cherry flitted out from behind the counter when the small (and authentic) ship bell rang.

Cherry was the real (and legal) name of the red-haired, round-faced, and big-eyed girl with the slender body. Her slightly-above-average looks came with immense charisma and sex appeal that made her a magnet for guys. And those guys brought with them nighttime brawls and scuffles Doom had to sort out.

"Ah, Doom," a tall, skinny black guy with dreadlocks named Jay called with a wave. "You're early today."

"Oh, you brought a guest," Cherry said, smiling the part of a welcoming hostess. "What would you like?"

"A double latte and an éclair, please," Perriot replied as she sat down at the nearest table.

"Sure." Cherry rushed toward the bulky, grumbling, and sometimes clogging coffee machine. "How about you, Alex?"

"I'll do his." Almost elbowing Cherry away, Jay stepped over to the plain electric teapot and plugged it in. "Black tea with lemon, yeah?"

"Thanks," Alex said.

Perriot's choice of the table in the farthest corner was fine with Alex, so he walked around the upturned chairs on the genuine, authentic ship crew tables to sit across from her.

"What's wrong with that guy?" Leia was watching the pair behind the bar closely. "He practically hit the girl. Does he really hate her that much?"

"Quite the opposite."

"What do you mean?"

"The guy's name is Jay, and he's in love with the girl. But she friend-zoned him."

Perriot gestured vaguely.

"That's dumb."

"Not really," Alex drawled with a sly smile and fell silent.

When the pause drew out too far, Perriot rolled her eyes.

"Stop it, Professor Dumsky. Can't you just let a girl enjoy a bit of local gossip?"

"Sure, sure," Alex said, holding up his hands. "Cherry—that's her name—um…plays for the other team. Jay doesn't stand the slightest chance."

"Does he know that?"

"If he knew, he probably wouldn't be acting like a jerk."

Leia frowned.

"Why don't you tell him?"

"Because I'm a jerk," Alex replied, his sly smirk turning bloodthirsty.

To his surprise, Perriot laughed out loud instead of telling him off.

"Oh, Alex is a god of humor." Throwing sexy fluids around, Cherry flitted over to their table to set down a tray with their order. "Alex, are you in the kitchen or the main hall tonight?"

"Main hall. Why do you ask?"

"Well, some police officer is celebrating their birthday. So…"

"Don't worry, you femme fatale. I'll make sure none of the co—…the brave officers badgers you."

"Thank you." Cherry leaned forward, opening her low neckline, to peck Alex on his bristled cheek before flitting away to the kitchen.

She really was a young girl of about eighteen. Rather fickle (going out with a different girl almost every week), she was…*good*. (If it's appropriate for a black wizard to describe anyone as *good*.)

"So, you really do work here," Perriot said in astonishment. "I always thought that was just gossip. But why? I wouldn't think a bar hand would make more than a professor at First Magic University."

Alex's smile faded. *I can't forget.*

"Miss Perriot," he said in his coldest and most distant voice, "your coffee and éclair are here, and I have nothing but my tea and cognitive dissonance. So, please be so kind as to hold up your end of the deal to resolve the situation."

Perriot was taken aback by the abrupt transition from friendly small talk to business, but she got over it quickly.

"As you probably know from the rector, Professor Dumsky, your student group consists of the first and only graduates of Project Rizen, a boarding school for Light children with unique gifts. Honestly, I have no idea why *you* were appointed their supervisor."

She fell silent.

If Alex hadn't been a jerk, he would have kept quiet, too, but…

"It's my sterling qualifications," he replied with a venomous smirk.

The éclair in Leia's hand paused in midair.

"I spent six years of my life with those kids, *Professor*. That probably beats your qualifications."

"Still you're sitting there with your éclair, while the B-52 group is officially supervised by *me*."

Perriot returned her dessert to her plate, wiped her lips with a napkin, and was making a motion to transfer credits from her account to the Schooner's when Alex coughed.

"Breaking a deal with a black wizard is a *very* bad idea, Miss Perriot. And we *do* have a deal."

"Are you threatening me?"

"I'm prepared to accept your challenge to a duel whenever you like, Miss Perriot. But in the meantime, I'm just stating a fact. The deal is: coffee and éclair for Leo Stone's info."

"And the other students? Don't you need their info, too? They're also unusual wizards."

"Not unusual enough to leave a burn on a Light Master's arm."

"But maybe enough to leave one on a Dark Mystic's."

Alex's smile turned into a bloodthirsty grin, the shadows behind him beginning to move. Perriot edged backward and shuddered.

"Forgive me, Professor Dumsky." She pushed her cup of coffee away. "I forgot that I'm talking to a *black wizard*."

"It's okay, *esper*."

Leia's eyes flashed with evil fire, though she contained her anger. *That's a shame. Nothing ruins a relationship as well as being cursed so badly in a magic duel that you spend a month in the hospital.*

That move had never failed Doom before.

"As the rector told you already, he has a split personality, to put it in laymen's terms. The trigger that brings Leonard out is when he or one of his friends takes damage."

"Damage? Got it. And what can you tell me about Leonard as a person?"

"Have you seen the Silence of the Lambs?"

"Sure," Alex replied, a bit stung by the suspicion that he might not have.

"Take Hannibal, remove everything but his extreme cruelty and intelligence, and you have Leonard Stone." Alex sensed no fear in Leia's voice, only the kind of extreme concentration a trainer surrounded by tigers experiences. "His upper limit is unknown, and—"

"How's that possible?" Alex interrupted.

"It just is. His potential is different every time he comes out. Some doctors think the upper limit of his power is directly proportional to the perceived level of the threat."

"Wow," Alex drawled. "How did he come to have that?"

"His parents." Leia said the last word with outright hatred.

"They had the same kind of split personalities?"

"To some extent," Miss Perriot replied, her eyes on the bottom of her coffee cup. "When he was seven, Leo first tried a dress on. And they...beat him up. With a belt. An iron-studded one. When he was ten, they got a call from school to tell them he'd been spotted kissing a boy. And...he got *seventeen fractures*, Professor Dumsky. Over forty stitches."

"Was it his dad?"

"And his mom."

Doom contained his urge to swear. Robin had taught him not to use foul language with ladies present.

Although, to be fair, that had never stopped Alex before.

"And that happened in enlightened Myers City."

"Not-so-enlightened High Garden," Leia corrected. "In case you didn't know, it's a district in the city slums inhabited by...well, all sorts of scum. That's where Leo grew up. And Leonard with him."

"What happened to his parents?"

"You haven't guessed yet?" Perriot asked. "When they decided to give Leo some more of their special *discipline*, Leonard woke up and... Leo still thinks his parents died in a house fire."

That time a swear word did escape Alex's lips.

"The other kids' lives weren't much different, Professor. Jing's whole family was destroyed by ancient relic hunters. Travis has amnesia— no memory of anything that happened to him before the age of ten. For eight years now, he's been trying to find a trace of his parents. Elie...was born out of wedlock. Her mother died at the door of the hospital without getting any help, and her father took her in just to avoid tarnishing his reputation. And Mara...she's a half-blood. I think it's self-explanatory why she would jump at the first opportunity to move to Rizen."

Shit.

"So, what, Miss Perriot? You want me to feel bad for the kids? All I can say to that is that shit happens. To everyone. I asked you to tell me about Leonard so my conscience will be clear if I ever have to kill the bastard. I wasn't looking for all the ins and outs of the poor orphans."

Perriot jumped up.

The chair flew farther than it would have if the only kick it had been given was from mere inertia. Perriot's peach hair was twitching again.

"You really *are* a black wizard," she hissed.

"Absolutely." Alex held his mug of tea up to her as if it were a glass of wine. "In full regalia. I can show that regalia to you, by the way, but I'd have to strip naked for that."

"I wonder how you haven't been caged yet."

"Your Leo hasn't either," Doom replied with a shrug. "I'm no worse."

"Bastard!"

"You're not wrong."

Slapping the table, Perriot shouldered her bag and hurried off toward the door. When she got there, she turned with a hiss.

"Keep them away from the tournament, Professor. Or else..."

"Or else what?"

"Or else I'll kill you."

The small bell jingled as her peach hair vanished around the corner.

Cherry, radiant and smiling, sat down across from Alex.

"Do you really like her that much?"

"Oh, get lost."

***

"So, ladies and gentlemen, I think our first practice session could be described as anything but good."

The silent students watched their professor as he stood behind the desk in lecture hall B-52.

"Before we move on to the next one, I have a task for you. Remove your lenses and put them in this box. Over the next week, you'll be attending all classes without them."

"What?!"

"How can we...?"

"That's imposs—"

"I don't care," the professor interrupted, "if it's possible or not. If you're serious about winning the tournament, that's what you're going to do."

Chapter 48

Alex dropped the kickstand and habitually flicked his cigarette butt into the trashcan at the bus stop.

"Fop," Gribovsky said.

Alex hadn't heard from the Guards the whole week he'd spent messing around with the fosterlings of Follen School's light counterpart.

"I was hoping you kicked the bucket," Doom replied, his face as dark as a thundercloud.

Snorting, Gribovsky stepped away from the sports car he'd been leaning against. He walked past Alex, clapping him on the shoulder and mumbling sympathetically.

"Tough luck, pumpkin. Tough luck."

Rolling his eyes, Alex followed the lieutenant.

Farrokh had negotiated access with his contact, just as promised. It was time to get answers to a couple questions, as trivial as that might sound.

The week-long hassle with a bunch of wizards who were no different from mortals once they removed their lenses had been a real mess. Alex couldn't have imagined how much trouble he'd have training what appeared to be capable students.

The address Farrokh had given him was in the outskirts of the central district, somewhere in the middle between the giant skyscrapers of downtown and Amalgam Street.

It was a fairly fashionable spot with boutiques where the prices could have easily been mistaken for phone numbers.

16 7th Road was a small, four-story, and rather decrepit neo-gothic building with gargoyles and heavy bas-reliefs. It looked a bit out of place.

"Simon Shulman," Gribovsky recited, tossing colored candy drops into his mouth on the go. "Antique dealer and seasoned smuggler. Wanted by the police in at least nine Old Earth countries on suspicion of relic export fraud. A black wizard, for sure. No doubt about that."

After ascending the stone stairs, Alex and Gribovsky entered a spacious room somewhat resembling bald Bromwoord's shop. The only difference was that it skipped the cheap smuggling stuff in favor of *real* and heavily protected artifacts. They were secured under *adamantius*-splattered glass covers (a separate license was required for each) and enveloped in whirlwinds of serious magic shields. The amount of magic they contained had them glimmering.

There weren't that many items on exhibit in the hall. Everything else was presumably only available on order for regular and trusted customers.

The bulk of the goods, Doom guessed, was only sold to members of the Abyss in exchange for gold coins.

But even the few items displayed for everyone to see…

A small red notebook. Not the one used by Tom Riddle to write his secrets in, sure, but still containing an evil spirit. A conditionally permitted artifact priced at 248,000 credits. *Who would buy that? Only a crazy collector, I guess.*

The bell jingled over and over as it was slapped by the guardsman's merciless hand. Gribovsky had walked by the glass cases and shelves as if nothing there was worth his attention, and he soon confirmed that with a comment.

"Stop gaping, Alex. Nothing really special here."

"*Nothing?* But—"

"Pumpkin, if you behave, I'll get you a pass to visit the office's storage space. It has *tons* of shit like this."

Doom had no doubt that the Guards' bowels did indeed have tons of shit, but before he could say that aloud, a new character appeared on the stage. He appeared out of the dark corridor leading from inside the building in response to the doorbell.

And a colorful character he was.

Short, balding, with a crooked nose and a monocle on his shifty, greasy, and brown right eye, his left eye was poor-quality glass that presumably held sentimental value. Alex couldn't think of any other reason the owner of a shop like that one would walk around with it instead of buying a better one.

He was wearing a bespoke (Alex's practiced eye detected that immediately) three-piece suit, he had his thumbs in his pockets, and he looked around with the air of someone who can sell yesterday's trash to a landfill.

In a word, he was stereotypical, which was somewhat disappointing to Doom. The latter knew for sure he had Solomon's blood in him, too.

Some of it, at least.

"Good afternoon, Mr. Shulman."

"It *was* good, guardsman." The antique dealer's speech was completely devoid of any particular accent, which spoiled the picture. "But when you walked in, the shittiness meter jumped from a zero to a ten. And that's a five-point scale."

"I wouldn't say your business is that—"

"My business is fine," the balding Jew interrupted. "You're in no position to discuss my business with me anyway, young man. If you were, you wouldn't be working for secret offices or running errands."

Gribovsky held up his hands.

"Do you have what we're here for?"

"Shit, you mean? Ask your office for that. I just heard you say they have *tons*."

Despite the old dealer's rude tone and reply, Gribovsky just smiled and chuckled under his breath.

Alex looked at his hands. After the week he'd spent trying to teach kids who'd never practiced magic without their lenses how to do it unassisted by technology, he'd gotten somewhat better at sensing magic himself.

And right then his fingers were tingling.

It could have been the defensive magic around the artifacts. But on top of that, Alex distinctly smelled sulfur and wet leaves.

"Mr. Shulman." Gribovsky seemed to be enjoying their little duel. "Farrokh sent us, and you know that. So, let's stop beating around the bush. We need information about Poseid—"

"In this world, young man, even the shit you mentioned earlier has its price," the antique dealer interrupted, adjusting his monocle. "So, if you need something from me, please be so kind as to throw around some credits."

"How much is some?"

"Twenty-five thousand, and I'll sing you all the songs you want."

"*Twenty-five thousand?* That's absurd, you crazy old Jew!"

During the heated haggling that ensued, Simon and Gribovsky alike cited each other's genealogy, going all the way back to distant generations. Alex walked around the items on display.

Everything seemed absolutely normal. No cracks in the floor, not a speck of dust in the corners. All the spells in perfect condition. Each glass cover polished to a shine. Even a fire inspector stopping by to demand a bribe wouldn't have found anything to pick on.

Never before had Alex seen a business the Atlantis fire inspectors wouldn't have been able to find something wrong with.

The degree of perfection they were always looking for just didn't happen in real life.

No magic could have swept the place into such flawless condition.

...at least, not unless that flawless condition wasn't real.

"Shit," Alex hissed. "Not *that* again."

He pulled a handkerchief out of an inner pocket and, making sure neither of the two other men was looking at him, wrapped it around a cigarette. That done, he stepped over to the counter.

"Twelve thousand, Simon, and my immense gra—"

"Mr. Shulman?" Alex shouldered Gribovsky to the side and placed his little bundle on the counter. "Could you tell me what's inside this handkerchief?"

The single eye behind Shulman's monocle flashed slightly and started shifting, almost as if the antique dealer was trying to find a way out.

"How should I know that, boy? Who cares about your dumb handkerchief, anyway?"

"I'll ask you again, Mr. Shulman. What's in this handkerchief?"

The antique dealer ground his teeth, his right hand twitching convulsively.

Gribovsky reached for his gun.

"You came to ask about Poseidon's Ball, didn't you?"

"I heard a different name."

"Idiots! The real name is Poseidon's Ball. Poseidon used it to play—"

"Let me ask you for the third time, Mr. Shulman. *What's in this handkerchief?*" Alex pressed, throwing his will behind every syllable.

Shulman was twitching all over—it looked like he was going into an epileptic seizure. His monocle fell off and rolled across the floor.

"A cig—...cig—..."

"Shoot!" Alex screamed, using his will to throw up a shield-like black seal in front of him.

Without asking any questions, Gribovsky pulled the trigger.

Doom finally got to see an enchanted gun in action. When Gribovsky pulled the trigger, having yanked his gun out of its holster so fast that Alex saw nothing but a blur, dozens of overlapping magic seals flashed in front of the muzzle. A stream of red light burst out of the barrel to transform into a shiny Lancelot's Spear spell.

Just the heat it generated was strong enough to shake Alex's defensive spell. Made of pure light and fire, setting the air inside the shop ablaze, the spear pierced the antique dealers' chest, sending him flying off into the dark corridor to flare up there as a furious whirlwind of light and fire. He broke through the whole building and dissolved high in the sky.

[Spell detected: LANCELOT'S SPEAR of the Fire and Light School. Mana usage: 3,742.]

"Fucking shit," Alex cursed, standing up and finding himself amid the wreckage of the once-perfect shop. Broken floor planks. Smashed glass covers. Damaged artifacts and relics. Holes in the walls. Burn spots and acid traces. Flashes of spells dying away.

"That wasn't me," Gribovsky said instantly.

"Of course not," Doom replied with a nod. "Damn abyss. Old Shulman didn't go down without a fight."

"Wait, what? That was…an illusion? Then who was that? *Who* did I just shoot?"

Alex just pointed at the occasional fiery flashes popping out of the dark corridor.

"I wouldn't be so sure you shot him."

"*Who?* Who the fuck are you talking about?"

"A demon, Gribovsky. A very evil, very powerful…and now very displeased demon."

As though in confirmation, another fiery flash illuminated a figure in the darkness. It was a figure Doom would be seeing in his troubled dreams for a long time.

The twelve-foot creature roared, swept the remnants of the door away with its shoulders, and burst into what had been a flawless storefront.

Chapter 49

"What the devil is that?" Gribovsky, either insightfully or on gut instinct, refrained from sending another bullet hurtling at the monster. Instead, he jumped away, rolled across the floor, and hid behind the demolished statue of some ancient god.

That precaution saved the lives of both men.

Alex, falling instantly to his knees, slapped both hands on the floor. Spreading out around his fingers came flashing red sparks that merged to form a seal looking nothing like anything ever created by human wizards.

[ERROR. ERROR. Structure cannot be recognized. The authorized agencies have been informed.]

"Cancel that message!" Gribovsky bellowed in an unfamiliar voice. "Damn it, Alex. What the fuck are you doing?"

Doom bit his lip, saying nothing. Drops of blood fell onto the outer perimeter of the seal with a *roar*. The rumbling sound blew out the remnants of the double glazing still remaining in the windows, and lightning spanning all the visible colors gushed out of the seal to mix into a single, variegated mess.

It wasn't even demonology. It was…

"Demon magic," Alex hissed, feeling his strength leave him like sand from a broken hourglass. His other source (not the dark lilac, but the blazing crimson one) could only cast a few of those spells.

With the next drop of blood, the seal began to vibrate. The bolts of lightning entwined into a giant clawed paw that gripped the roaring monster a moment before its great sword came crashing down on Alex's head.

The monster looked almost human. Twelve feet tall and seven feet from shoulder to shoulder, it was covered in golden armor. Its goat legs ended in hooves, and paws flashed long claws. Only the muscular gray torso was bare for eyes to see and weapons to cleave.

The demon's right hand held a sword formed by two very broad blades, a void between them.

The creature's face couldn't be seen. In fact, Alex doubted it had one at all. Where the face should have been was a cast metal plate surrounded by hair that looked more like porcupine needles.

"So, it's true." Gribovsky involuntarily crossed himself. Alex gritted his teeth as bitter pain flashed through him suddenly. His seal shook, and the monster's sword edged lower. "You really can…"

"Lieutenant! It's a soldier demon from a second-hundred legion!"

Alex had his red source pour more force into the seal, and the clawed paw made of bloody lightning grew denser. The demon made a metal sound that was something between a growl and the clang of steel. "A dozen times as strong as that thing at the museum!"

"Why didn't you say so before?" Gribovsky asked as he aimed his gun.

"No!" Alex yelled. "It can absorb magic!"

"Damn." Spinning the gun around his finger, Gribovsky dropped it into his holster. "How long can you hold it?"

"Eight seconds, maybe."

"Four is all I need," the lieutenant replied with a nod. He got up from behind his cover and held out his left hand, which sported a broad leather wristband and a gleaming metal plate.

"Seal removal," he said in a commanding voice. "Authorized: Guard Warrior Julidor Gribovsky."

"Juli…shit…dor?"

"My parents were high when they named me," the red-haired warrior replied, shrugging.

The metal plate on his wristband flashed a silvery glow that enveloped his whole hand and stretched forward to form what Doom at first thought was a metal bar.

But when the glow vanished, it turned out to be a blade some six feet long and as wide as a man's palm. It had a bas-relief of a goat skull with spiraling horns stretching six inches to either side in place of a guard.

"Don't look so skeptical, pumpkin," Gribovsky said as he tossed another Skittle into his mouth and prepared to attack. "Our armorer is a big fan of Devil May Cry."

"A fan of what?"

"Ignoramus. Let our friend go."

Alex glanced over at the twelve-foot demonic "friend." Even absent the lieutenant's order, he wouldn't have been able to hold the creature back any longer without draining his second source completely.

As he took his hands off the floor, Doom simultaneously pushed off with both feet, sending his body flying. That was just enough for the monster's giant sword to sever the floorboards instead of his skull. A window down into the dark cellar appeared.

"Happen to have heard of the polka, pumpkin?" With that poor excuse for a battle cry, and brandishing his great steel weapon as if it were weightless, Gribovsky rushed in to attack. He hit the demon's genital area with his shoulder and…no, he didn't break his shoulder blade. His ribs stayed intact, too. The red-haired mortal with just six hundred mana points sent the giant, several-ton demon flying back ten feet.

Not happy with that result, Gribovsky pushed off the floor, soaring all the way up to the ceiling, and came down to land a powerful slashing blow on the reeling beast.

His two-handed sword, just a bit less monstrous than the demon's, cleaved through the air, leaving a smoky trace as it dug into the otherworldly creature's shoulder. Cutting through armor that could have withstood multiple direct artillery shell hits, it buried itself in the monster's hard muscle. The demon roared, plumes of greenish-black blood gushing through the air.

Tightening its free hand into a clawed fist, it drilled Gribovsky in the chest. A blow like that should have come out the other side; instead, it just sent the guardsman flying against the opposite wall. His back sent cracks spreading across the masonry. But Gribovsky landed catlike on his feet and rush back in for another attack, shouting as he ran.

The recovering demon wasn't about to wait where he was. Instead, almost mirroring his opponent's move, he also rushed forward. The double blade arced through the air so rapidly that Alex failed to spot where the move started or ended.

Gribovsky ducked beneath the swing. Almost touching the floor with his nose, he flew in an inch below the blades, wriggled like a snake, and thrust himself off the floor. He whirled around in the air.

He was like a whirligig with a deadly spike of a six-foot sword. *Made of* adamantius, Alex guessed based on the tingle in his fingertips. *Fucking dragon-blood-enchanted* adamantius. What else could explain the yellow fire flashing across the sword to both slice the giant demon into tiny bits and even *fry* it like an overdone steak served right from hell?

Landing on the floor, Gribovsky brushed the sweaty, sticky hair off his forehead, jabbed the sword into the floor next to where he was standing, and leaned on it happily.

The monster, or whatever remained of it, was smoking where it pooled, gradually spreading a mixture of slime and supernatural plasma. That was the end of all otherworldly creatures.

"Just like in Prague, that thing was too weak to get in a good workout." Gribovsky blew his nose on the creature's remains.

Doom shifted his gaze silently between the mortal, his sword, and the fallen demon.

Fucking Guards. I was so naïve to think they would employ Practitioners at the 6ᵗʰ level.

"By the way, pumpkin, thanks for your help. Did you get some rest while I Danted that demon?"

"Danted? You mean *dented*?"

Gribovsky cursed.

"Do you *really* not know who Dante from the Devil May Cry agency is?"

"I don't."

Gribovsky cursed again.

"And this guy works as a demon fighter for the Guards' dep—"

"I *don't* work for you," Alex interrupted. "And if that thing was so easy for you to kill, you probably won't have any trouble dealing with those, either."

"Those? What are you talking about?"

Alex just pointed at the dark corridor. Stepping out of it, slowly and sideways in a way that would have looked funny if it hadn't been so dangerous, were four monsters just like the dead one.

Gribovsky jerked out his sword and strode forward to shield Alex.

"Is the summoner that far away?" the lieutenant asked seriously.

"Probably not," Alex replied. Around his left hand, a chaotic glow appeared, the color hard to detect. "But by yourself, you—"

"Then go get the bastard." The redhead spat and spread the saliva around with the tip of his cowboy boot. "I'll deal with these kids."

"You sure?"

Gribovsky just jerked his head toward the door.

Alex wasn't about to argue.

"Hey, pumpkin?"

"Yeah?"

"Cut loose." Alex couldn't see Gribovsky flash a predatory smirk, but he could feel it. "You're not in a museum full of kids this time, so do your worst. The Guards will clean up after you."

It was Alex's turn to grin like a dashing pirate.

Chapter 50

Stepping outside and leaving the sounds of battle behind him, Alex stooped to wipe some of the thick, black slime off his shoe. He kneaded it with his fingers and blew on it.

Sparks flew from his lips, setting the substance on fire. It flared up instantly in a ball of green flame that vanished in dense smoke. The ball, which was resting on Doom's palm, bulged and bubbled until it turned into a scary-looking bird.

"Go find your master," Alex commanded.

The bird twitched, struggling to break free from the chains of Doom's will, but the latter was unwavering. No longer a novice in the black magic arts, he was even less so in the demonic ones.

As for what the lieutenant said…he decided to think about that later. He wasn't sure how the Guards came to know one of his main secrets.

Finally bending to Alex's will, the bird flew off along the empty avenue. The occasional car was the only thing out in the early evening—everyone else had heard the sounds coming from inside the antique shop and was staying as far away as possible.

Doom could hear the sirens, though. *The cavalry's coming.*

Running up to his bike, Alex jumped on the seat and rolled on the throttle as he pulled up the kickstand. The rearing chopper started right off the bat, rushing down the street.

The wind drew tears as it slapped his face, but Alex waved it aside—both literally and metaphorically. In front of his face, shielding him from wind and video surveillance alike, appeared a cloud of dark fog transparent only from the inside.

[ATTENTION! Prohibited spell used: DEAD MAN'S SHROUD of the Death and Darkness School. Mana consumption: N/A.]

If the Guards were on cleanup duty…

"Where *are* you?" Alex glanced around, trying to figure out where the bird was taking him. They raced away from the Central District and crossed the suspension bridge over Myers City's main river to arrive in the Financial District. It was where all tourist routes inevitably ended. Scraping the sky there were the tallest buildings, all owned by the Atlantis aristocracy.

It was the heart of the steel-and-glass jungle, not a single blade of real grass to be found outside the vast park at the district's edge.

Alex dashed over the street markings, ignoring the occasional horns and screeching brakes. The closer he got to where the rich families lived, the more expensive magic cars there were making those sounds.

"There we go." Wheeling his chopper around, Alex braked hard. He slid across the special road coating that looked nothing like plain asphalt as he watched the tall, shadow-cloaked figure pat the smoky bird clinging to it.

The figure's face was masked.

"Who are you?" Alex asked, firmly and loudly, not at all caring that they were in the middle of a busy eight-lane street watched by hundreds of eyes and dozens of surveillance cameras on every side. The cars flowed past like schools of fish. The neon light cast by billboards and club signs was bright enough to turn the night into a dusky kind of day.

Patting the bird one last time, the Mask closed his fingers around its slender neck to disperse the spell.

That wouldn't surprise a magic amateur, but Alex wasn't sure *he* could have dispersed a search spell that easily.

"Who are—"

Before Doom could finish, the Mask held out a palm. Dozens of red seals appeared in front of him like an impenetrable wall.

Just like the spells in the shop, they weren't from the demonology school. They were demon magic.

Just as pure as Alex's.

"That's imposs—... Who are you??"

Instead of answering, the seals flashed all the colors of Chaos, releasing a roaring maw with bared fangs. It belched black smoke and gray lightning bolts, covering four of the eight lanes.

The cars lucky enough to survive with just a brush flew in all directions like empty cans.

People screamed, running away and swarming like ants around a destroyed anthill. In just a moment, the city changed completely.

Soaring cars crashed through the boutique windows, restaurants, and clubs, even breaking office windows up to the eighth floor.

Anyone who found themselves directly in the spell's path was beyond helping. Neither flaring up nor turning into lumps of sliced metal, they just vanished, crumbling into fine dust. They had no time to scream or pray to their gods.

As he watched the approaching maw in what seemed like slow motion, Doom saw the monstrous jaws swallow a little toy kitten still clutched in a child's hand.

He took his hands off the handlebars and threw them forward.

Both of them.

Although he was capable of forming seals by pure will, he could put more magic in them within a much shorter time by using his hands.

Dozens of black and lilac seals flashed in front of him, forming a wall like the one the Mask had just cast.

The spell hurtling toward him was filled with pure demon magic. Neither First Magic University nor the Guards' practice ranges, not to mention anywhere else, could have prepared anyone for something like that.

And that was because everyone believed that no human or member of a sapient magic race could use demon magic.

No one but demons themselves were believed to be able to use it.

But there it was. And the fact that it was a spell made it similar to all the other spells out there.

Alex knew that better than anyone.

His thoughts galloped. *Add protection. Increase the temperature. Set the decay limit. Neutralize the elements. Condense. Twist. Break powers. Narrow shields.*

The spell formed right before his eyes, the overlapping black magic seals oozing strength and energy. The black strips entwined to form a long, thirty-foot spear in the shape of a ram's curved horn.

[ATTENTION! Unregistered modification of a prohibited spell used: BLACK GOAT'S HORN of the Death and Darkness School. Mana consumption: N/A.]

Just before the open maw reached Doom, it was hit by the black spear horn. A bolt of gray lightning flashed across its tip followed by the sound of a powerful explosion.

Alex covered his head with the flap of his jacket to protect himself from the road metal raining down. The pebbles (or whatever they really were) scattered like lead shot, preceding the ball of crimson-black fire formed by the two colliding spells.

Shattering windows and tearing through metal, the explosion transformed the well-groomed Financial District avenue into a cratered battlefield. People screamed and groaned all around. Alex spotted several elves trying to fit severed limbs back onto their bodies in shock. Someone was tapping away at their smartphone screen with bloody thumbs.

Amid the chaos, two figures held steady and unaffected. One was mounted on a chrome bike; the other was astride a lightning-riddled cloud.

Silently and emotionlessly, the Mask turned and flew off down the road on his cloud.

"Not so fast!" Alex shouted, pulling up his kickstand and throwing open the throttle to give chase. A long lash in his hand glared with red fire.

Creating the lash drained the last drops from Doom's second

magic source, but he couldn't let the Mask escape again.

He had to make sure.

He *had* to see the face hiding behind the mask.

Even if that meant demolishing the whole district.

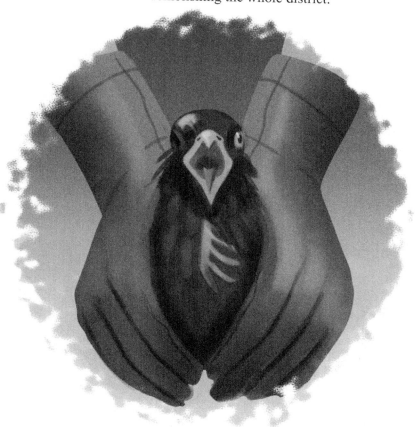

Chapter 51

Travis suddenly burst into the student dormitory where all the rest of the B-52 gang were. He cast a furious glare over the kitchen table his friends were seated at, sipping beer and playing board games.

"Are you nuts?" Travis yelled, rushing for the kitchen drawers in a hectic search for something he appeared to need urgently and desperately.

"He finally lost it," Elie said.

The rest watched Travis silently, forgetting the figures and counters on the map spread out over the table.

"...sitting there clueless," he grumbled. "Where the hell *is* it?"

"What are you looking for?" Jing asked flatly.

"The damn remote control!"

The friends exchanged silent glances as Mara, saying nothing, held it out to Travis. He was too busy with his search to notice, so she had to tap him on the back with the device.

"What now?!" the redhead bellowed, turning around so abruptly he almost knocked it out of her hand. But after seeing it, he grabbed it without a word of thanks and pressed a button.

The big screen on the opposite wall flashed on with what the group at first mistook for another big-budget movie trailer, but the news strip and the female reporter's familiar voice proved that guess wrong.

"We're reporting live from the heart of the Financial District." They couldn't see the reporter's face, and her voice was at times drowned out by the sound of the helicopter. "As you can see down there, the two wizards are continuing their chase right along the city streets. As far as we know, no security forces have admitted to employing them. The police and military alike are advising everyone to stay clear of the pair."

"What's going on—"

"Look!" Travis interrupted. "Just look!"

And there was a lot to look at. Right in the middle of the street, going the wrong way, a tall wizard in a gray trench coat and mask appeared to be using a flying device. But when the helicopter camera found a better angle, the device on the screen turned into a thundercloud riddled with lightning.

Hurtling after him on a chrome chopper sparkling with silver and black enamel came another man. His face at first sight appeared to be hidden beneath a mask as well, but the camera zoomed in to reveal that it was a presumably black magic spell.

A narrow tie fluttered behind the biker, his polished shoes

reflecting the city lights, and his expensive ArmaniMagico suit looking completely out of place.

"Oh my! That's—"

"The professor," Jing interrupted Mara, which was very out of character for him. "Professor Dumsky."

"What's he doing?" Elie half rose out of her chair. "What are they both doing?"

"I have no idea," Travis answered. "But he's... Just look at that! You don't even see stuff like that in fantasy movies."

The wizard in the real, physical mask, the thundercloud rider, waved a hand. The camera zoomed in so close the spectators could even see the gray leather gloves he was wearing.

Red seals flashed. Not fiery seals or those of the Blood Magic School, but something completely different. Even through the TV screen, they breathed something creepy, destructive, and otherworldly.

"I've never seen signs like those."

"Which magic school is that?"

"No idea."

From each seal burst a predatory, wriggling giant tentacle tipped with a scary claw and surrounded by a round fanged maw.

The four tentacle braids shot out in all directions around the wizard. Two of them uprooted lamp posts from the sidewalk to throw them like spears at the professor.

The flying posts melted as they flew, acid burns marking where they had been touched by the creepy spells. But the pursuing rider didn't turn to dodge the projectiles. He didn't even slow down as he maneuvered between the oncoming magic cars.

The long lash in his right hand glowed with the same otherworldly red light. He waved it over his head, and the lash, already no less than fifteen feet in length, stretched ahead to cover a distance three times that long.

Like the giant serpent painted by medieval artists, the wriggling lash flew over the cars to catch the lamp posts in the air, slashing them into the finest of melted steel ingots that fell to the ground in a fiery rain.

Without stopping, the lash stretched onward to the Mask, almost catching his cloak flaps before a red tentacle could dash over to intercept.

The two spells began fighting. Magic flashes reflected in the lens of the camera mounted on the reporters' helicopter. Someone was squealing into the microphone, but the students couldn't hear what they were saying.

If they'd begun to suspect that their professor's title as a black wizard wasn't just words, they still couldn't have begun to imagine that—

"Look! The guy in the mask has a car!"

The camera zoomed away, focusing on the red tentacle embracing a cheap SUV whose wheels spun helplessly in midair. Hanging down from the window of the soaring vehicle, the father let down a boy to be caught by his wife standing on the ground.

"Bastards," Travis hissed. "No one even thought to stop."

That time, not even Elie argued. None of the other cars slowed down even a little bit, everyone trying to get as far away as possible. And that was despite the fact that eighty percent of Myers City's residents had magic powers—four out of five cars were driven by full-fledged wizards.

"Oh no!" the reporter screamed. "He isn't going to make it! He's not!"

The father, already hanging twelve feet above the ground, was desperately reaching for another small hand stretching from the back of the car to meet his. Their fingers almost touched when the car jerked another twenty feet higher.

Shaken off, the man fell to the ground, right at the feet of his wife and a boy of eight. The shrieking woman would have dashed into the oncoming traffic after the SUV being dragged away by the tentacle if it weren't for her son holding her back.

The camera flashed to another boy, this one about five, almost falling out of the SUV.

The boy's hands clutched an action figure in a red cape and blue jumpsuit with a capital S on the chest.

Unfortunately, the real world had no superheroes.

Only supervillains.

With a wave of his hand, the Mask flung the SUV at his chaser.

The reporter screamed as the SUV flew over the street like a softball aimed right at the professor.

Mara and Elie covered their mouth with their hands. The guys, Leo included, clenched their fists.

It was clear that the professor's only option was to dodge; his spell was too busy fighting one of the tentacles. And the kid in the car…

At least he'd die quickly.

The pursuer took one hand off his handlebar and thrust it forward. Riding in a straight line at an absurd speed, he managed to maintain his balance with just his knees.

"Are you sure this isn't a movie?" Leo asked dubiously. No one replied—everyone's eyes were riveted to the professor. A few tar-black seals, oozing pure darkness, flashed in front of him, glowing with magic power that made the camera quiver. The flapping of thousands...*tens* of thousands of leather wings drowned out the sounds of the chase and traffic.

An enormous cloud of bats born of black mist rushed for the SUV, enveloped it in a dense shroud, and carried it out of the line of impact and over to the sidewalk. The passers-by, scattering at first, approached it warily to open the swinging door.

"The boy's fine! Thank god!" the reporter screamed.

"*God?*" Mara nervously drummed her fingers on the table. "The opposite, I would think."

"Look!" Travis jumped up, pointing at the screen. "How much mana does that spell have to be burning?"

"No idea," Jing replied, shaking his head. "More than we can imagine, anyway."

The avenue ended in a T-shaped crossroad at the foot of a 68-story skyscraper. The building was so wide it completely blocked the view of the next street.

But the Mask was not about to stop.

Without slowing down, he dashed for the skyscraper. Three of his four tentacles merged to dig into the road coating, carving a deep trench across the entire street.

Cars screeched to a halt and smashed into each other in an attempt to avoid the jagged outcroppings sprouting up right in front of their hoods.

The trench, about three feet deep and wide, became a natural obstacle between the Mask and his chaser.

"What is he doing?!"

Dispersing his red lash, the professor gripped the handlebars with both hands and hit the throttle.

The bike leaped forward, maneuvering between the hard-braking magic cars. When the trench was just a few feet away, a small seal formed in front of his face and shot a black ray out that hit a large pickup truck, popping the bed cover. Alex used it as a springboard to soar into the sky, fly over the trench, and land next to the skyscraper's underground parking entrance.

But the Mask was too far ahead.

Not only horizontally, but vertically, too.

His thundercloud was racing up the skyscraper's glassy surface just as easily as it had conquered the road.

"It's over," Travis sighed, sinking back into his chair.

"Not at all," Jing said softly.

He was proven right almost immediately.

Chapter 52

Alex looked up. Whoever the Mask was, he seemed to have a colossal mana reserve. Or, more probably, he was using an artifact to support his thundercloud. How else could he have overcome gravity and soared into the heavens so easily?

"You think you got away?"

Biting his lip, Doom wiped it with his thumb and ran it over the bike's gas tank. The bloody lines he left on the black enamel started to take the shape of a seal.

"I hope this wasn't just another one of your stories, Robin."

Alex had never tried the trick before, but, according to Loxley... Well, trusting Loxley was anything but a wise choice. The problem was that Doom was out of options.

Covering the bloody seal with hand, he called on the last drops of magic energy remaining in his second, miniature source.

"Ash'Mat'Nadok! To you I call. I, Black Wizard Alexander Dumsky. Blood of Solomon's blood. Blood of the blood of your tamer! Hear my call! Hear my blood!"

Alex could feel the source inside him quiver with the onslaught of force. A few feet away, a long fiery cut slashed open the very fabric of the world.

"By the keys of the Gate leading to the Beyond I call on you!"

A dry wind kicked up old newspapers and other scattered trash.

"By the seals of Solomon I bind you!"

The fiery slash quivered and started to widen. A creepy, abnormal neigh assaulted Doom's ears. Pouring in his last drops of magic, he uttered the final words in the ancient language spoken by wizards when most humans still lived in pits and caves.

"Bva l'evlm hzh any pvnh alyk, Ash'Mat'Nadok!"

Out of the slash, fiery tornados burst, producing the neighing sound that shook the windows bursting with heat and melted metal. Hooves clattered like the alarm bells of ruined churches, turning the sidewalk into flowing lava.

Taller than the bus stop. As black as the darkest abyss. With blazing yellow eyes and a mouth full of sharp, curved fangs. So muscular every sinew stood out. Mane and tail made of roaring, furious red flames, the same flames raging over the hooves and beneath the belly.

It was the demon Ash'Mat'Nadok.

Alex stared into its eyes and felt a blow slam against his soul. The urge came over him to kneel before the demon and, ripping his own heart out, present it as a gift to the powerful be—

"Obey my will, Ash'Mat'Nadok!" Doom held out his bloodied palm. "Obey my blood! Come hunt with me or go back to where I summoned you from!"

The demon horse reared and neighed.

The pressure was increasing.

Still, it was child's play compared to Baltael.

"You puny creature," Alex growled, "spat out by the abyss in the outskirts of reality. You are nothing but a servant to my will and my mind. You are nothing and nobody. A fleshless ghost born to Illusion. Obey me!"

Alex slapped the seal on his gas tank. The hell horse, still kicking fiery hooves in the air, suddenly transformed into a stream of fire flowing into Doom and pouring through his arm and hand into the seal and then inside the bike.

The Harley's wheels became fiery hooves, its handlebar the reins, its seat the croup, and its luggage rack the hellfire tail.

***

The students watched as silently as the female reporter. They couldn't make out the professor's words, though he was apparently shouting at the top of his voice.

The giant horse emerging from the fire became a strip of flame drawn into the bike. Then it returned, this time armored in chrome and black steel.

With a clatter of fiery hooves, Alex Doom resumed his chase astride the monster he'd summoned and apparently bound to his will. The hooves cut through the skyscraper's glass to carry the wizard higher and higher, a swarm of rainbow-colored sparks showering behind them.

"Can someone explain to me what artifacts those two are using?" the reporter screamed. "I'm a military reporter, and I've never seen anything like that!"

The silence at the students' table was oppressive.

Jing stared at the screen, something about his eyes showing that he knew a bit more than the others.

The Mask, racing along on his thundercloud, turned to face his pursuer for the first time. His serene demeanor unchanged, he threw out both hands to flash dozens of red seals. A variety of spells shot out, all producing the same uneasy feeling as the fiery horse the professor's bike had turned into.

Red lightning, spears, fireballs, clots of blackness, predatory birds, and other things harder to describe—all of it was hurled at the pursuer simultaneously. But the professor made no attempt to dodge or slow down. Instead, he thrust his hands into the fiery mane of the roaring horse and pulled them back out. Each of his palms held a blaze of red fire.

Like a major-league pitcher riding a horse galloping up the skyscraper's glassy wall, he knocked the Mask's spells down, intercepting them with balls of fire scooped from the horse's mane.

All of it looked as impossible as anything could be in a world where magic was made visible by hi-tech lenses.

"Turn! Now!" the reporter shouted, but it was too late.

One of the return spells smacked into a helicopter blade. For a while, the broadcast was interrupted by static.

The students jumped up, but before they could say anything, the shot flashed back to the studio, where the anchor, a headset pressed to her ear, spoke into the camera.

"Dear viewers, our special reporter Dina Clarke is all right. The helicopter is making an emergency landing at St. Patrick's Hospital…"

Alex followed with the corner of his eye the smoky trace of the news helicopter as it flew off. *Great. Fewer witnesses.*

The edge of the skyscraper was getting closer. Firing off another volley (*How many mana points does the bastard have? He's already used up an average Adept's reserve!*), the Mask disappeared up onto the rooftop.

This time Doom, jerking his possessed bike to the side, simply dodged the spell. The lump of blackness hit the window and, breaking through the glass, burst into the control room to instantly plunge the brightly lit skyscraper into complete darkness.

Alex leaped onto the rooftop astride his hell horse in search of the Mask…only to be met by a giant armored gorilla, an identical twin of the one he'd fought in the museum.

Behind the demon's back, the Mask was calmly dismounting his thundercloud. It had apparently been nothing but an illusion hiding the giant raven now hovering in the air by his side.

It was a cheap effect designed to keep the world from seeing the rather rare artifact he'd used for the flight.

An artifact only available for purchase at the Abyss.
Doom made a note to ask Farrokh a few more questions at their next meeting.

"We're not in a museum this time, you dick." Alex spat and lifted a palm overhead. He needed some more mana to feed his source.

A small silvery rune flashed on his black ring.

"Enjoy lightning, bastard?" Alex squinted. "Take that!"

A dark and glowing bolt of lightning so black that it was almost invisible in the night flashed out of the sky. Striking Alex's palm, it stretched into a long spear headed with a wolf's fanged maw and flew off to pierce the gorilla demon's chest.

[Prohibited spell used: ABYSS LIGHTNING of the Darkness School. Mana consumption: 1,682.]

How could Alex, having just 1,200 mana points, easily use a self-developed spell with a consumption that much higher? That's a whole other story.

Showering the skyscraper rooftop with black sparks, the spell buried itself in the demon. The gorilla took an awkward step forward and, before it could collapse to the gravel coating, vanished into smoke and stinking slime.

"That's not all." Alex brought his palms together. To the

uninitiated, it might have looked like a prayer, but he was actually preparing to use one of his strongest spells. He needed even more mana. *Far* more.

The glowing silvery rune on the ring was joined by another four.

Ten…twenty…thirty…fifty…a *hundred* seals flashed around Alex, all darker than the night and roaring with the force pouring into them. Screaming, Doom separated his palms, and everyone down at the foot of the skyscraper shuddered instinctively in fear.

The fear the prey feels just before it's hit with the predator's fangs and claws.

Howling echoed across the Financial District.

Alex on his fiery horse was surrounded by wolves looking like the one he'd used against Pyotr.

The Syndicate's emissary had only had to deal with one wolf, though, and now there were *hundreds*, all grinning with fanged jaws and scraping claws across the gravel. Each wolf had a glowing red pentagram on its face, not to mentioned powerful muscles that bulged beneath fur made of black fire.

[ERROR. ERROR. Structure cannot be recognized. The authorized agencies have been informed.]

I hope the lieutenant meant it when he said the Guards will take care of everything.

Using a prohibited or unregistered spell below 1,000 mana points was one thing. But a 4,000-point mix of black and demon magic was ano—

Clapping.

Alex watched the Mask applaud him.

Then he barked an order.

"Attack!"

The pack of hell wolves, sulfur saliva dripping, rushed at the enemy.

The Mask just waved his hand.

What happened next felt like a nightmare to Doom. A really scary nightmare.

The raven hovering around the wizard flapped its wings. Feathers fell off to turn into long, sharp swords that hailed down on the rooftop in a torrent of black-magic arrows.

The wolves vanished in flashes of dark fire, one after another. Only one of the hundred reached the Mask and attacked, and it was instantly dispersed by the raven's sharp claws.

Alex jumped off his horse a second before his chest would have been pierced by three of the feather swords. In disbelief, he watched the hell horse's shroud vanish, revealing his mangled steel friend slowly toppling over onto its right side.

"How is that even possible?!"

Alex had used his best invention ever. The strongest spell he had. But it...didn't even ruffle the flaps of the Mask's trench coat.

The mysterious wizard glanced down at Alex, who was sitting on the gravel, before turning away and stepping onto the back of his raven. It started to take off into the sky.

"Not so fast, you scum!" Alex shouted. Jumping up, he clutched at the Mask's ankle and pulled himself onto the artifact bird's back.

Chapter 53

Alex had learned the ins and outs of fist fights back at St. Frederick's Orphanage. He'd improved on that strong base in the Tkils gang and polished it in the wizard prison.

But, fucking shit, none of that prepared him to fight a wizard on the back of a giant raven flying a mile in the air above the rooftops of the city's tallest skyscrapers.

Dodging a direct blow to the head, Alex ducked and tried to grab his opponent by the knee. But the latter yanked it back out of reach and used his elbow to deliver an axe-like strike to Alex's spine.

Doom saw stars. His left arm went numb, but he ignored it.

He had to make sure.

There was no other choice.

Throwing his body forward, he buried the crown of his head in the Mask's belly, knocking his opponent down onto the raven's back.

The rooftops dashed past far below as Alex reached for the mask hiding the wizard's face. A knee hit his side, knocking the air out of him.

Pushing Doom off, the Mask kicked him so hard in the shoulder that he sent Alex flying off the bird's back. He would have fallen all the way down and splattered on the city streets if he hadn't grabbed hold of the bird's tail and swung himself around onto its back.

The two wizards continued landing physical blows like mere mortals.

Blocking a sweeping punch to his head, Alex tried to attack the enemy's groin with his knee. The move was instantly countered by a painful back-handed strike that turned into a sweeping chop to his Adam's apple.

Doom pressed his chin down to the throat. While he took the risk of losing consciousness to the blow, he avoided death, which was the priority. The Mask's relentless fingers weren't strong enough to break through the block and send him into an eternal sleep.

The longer the fight lasted, the more Doom realized that the Mask's style was awfully familiar.

Seizing an opportunity, Doom again reached for the iron mask hiding his opponent's face.

The Mask recoiled and, losing his balance, staggered back to restore it. Unfortunately, he did so by stepping on the raven's head.

Mistaking the move for a command, the bird dove steeply. Both wizards toppled off its back to hurtle downward next to it.

They continued to exchange blows as they fell.

A moment before the two crazy figures hit the roofs of some low, five-story buildings, the raven swooped beneath them. But they were falling too quickly for the bird to stop them.

Alex's back felt like it was being lashed.

They both landed hard.

First came the power lines; next came the washing lines. Doom was lucky enough to end his fall in a dumpster. The Mask was eventually picked up by his rapidly shrinking raven.

The two peered at each other silently.

The Mask stood next to a wall, his coat flapping in the wind. In the shimmering light cast by the streetlamps, his silvery armor had a Gothic look. His clenched fists emitted a red light, and red mist poured out of his eye slit.

And then there was Alex. Ragged, bloodied, and bruised, lying spread eagle in the dumpster.

The Mask turned away and walked slowly toward the road, the bloody bird hovering over his shoulder.

"Wa...it." Groaning, Doom literally fell out onto the ground. He didn't even have the strength to flash a thumbs-up, let alone give chase. "I'm...not...done...with you...yet. Just let me...have a smoke."

Your big mouth will be the death of you, Robin had always told him.

The Mask stopped.

Turned slowly and walking steadily, almost as if his shoulder wasn't bleeding and the two of them hadn't demolished half the city as they battered each other across the rooftops, he came over to Alex's prone figure.

He squatted down, so close Alex could smell the burned, wet leaves and sulfur on him. The smell of a demon.

"Got...you." With a shaking hand, Alex grabbed the runaway's boot.

The Mask just kicked his hand away. He flipped Doom onto his back, forcing a groan out of him.

The city slums. A heavy black sky. A dumpster nearby. What an ignominious en—

The Mask pulled the immortal pack of cigarettes out of Alex's inner pocket (or what remained of it). How had it survived the crazy chase? It was a mystery.

Tapping the filter, the wizard placed the cancer stick between Alex's lips. The matchbox was pulled out of his own coat. Shaking it, he swept a match along its side and lit Doom's cigarette. His movements were serene and rather slow despite the police sirens howling nearby—Gribovsky must have defeated the demons. He was out looking for his partner. But that didn't seem to bother the Mask.

He stood to watch the smoking Alex, as silent as before.

"I…will…get…you," Doom said through gritted teeth, holding the cigarette with his lips. "It's…personal…now."

Alex recalled hearing an explosion behind his back when he'd jumped onto the raven. The bike's engine had burst, punctured by a feather sword.

Another thread connecting Alex to his past was broken. When the last one was gone, what would he become?

Damn Baltael.

Alex felt sick. His vision was blurred, his head swimming, blood and mud streaming down his face. But still, it seemed like the Mask wanted to tell him something. He shivered slightly as he reached for his patterned mask. But finally, he just nodded, turned away, and vanished with his raven in a flash of green fire.

Alex was sure it wasn't an illusion. His eyes and mind weren't deceiving him—the wizard had actually entered the flames and disappeared.

What level was his opponent at?

If it was as high as Alex suspected, how was he still alive?

Lying on his back, he felt his consciousness escape into soft darkness. And the only thing he could do about that was mutter curses under his breath.

***

"Help us, Alex!"

"Help!"

"Save…"

Seeing the old wizard raise a dagger over him, the little boy prayed for the first time in his life.

"If there's anyone up there, please, please…" Hot tears ran down his face, though not out of fear for himself or even the pain caused by the words of the prayer. "…*please* help them! Dear lord, if you can hear me, please, please save them!"

The boy felt as if a red-hot steel sponge were being run over his body, squeezing the skin and flesh down to his bones before immersing those bones in scorching lava.

"Please, please, oh lord…if you can hear me…please help them! Protect them from Raewsky!"

Then everything froze.

Completely.

The dagger stopped half an inch before Alex's chest. The mad glow in the Professor's eyes faded. The drops of blood falling from the altars to the pentagram hung in the air.

"How dare you?" resounded a beautiful, melodious voice beneath the cellar ceiling.

The boy couldn't see the speaker, though he could feel the power emanating from the voice. Enough to stop what was going on.

"Please!" the boy screamed. "Please help them!"

He was on the verge of passing out from the most horrific pain he'd ever experienced, but he knew he couldn't faint at that moment. He had to stay strong for the sake of his family. His only family.

"You? You puny dark one dare beg my father for help?"

Alex heard a rustle of feathers and saw a shadow cast by a giant human-like figure with wings behind its back.

"Please." His tears were as bitter as the pain spreading across his whole body. "I've never hurt anyone. I never wanted to be a black wizard. I just happened to be born one…so why you—"

"Because you were born a puny dark spawn—exactly what you just said. Before your life is taken, I will punish you for your insolent words." The shadow held something out that looked like a big stick.

Alex's ears were hit by a loud whistling. He screamed from the pain in his chest as an overwhelming sensation seared into his flesh from his left shoulder to his right thigh.

The sense of the stranger's presence vanished. Looking down, Alex saw his reflection in a pool of his own blood, a large wound running across his whole torso.

Drained of his last strength, he collapsed to the floor. Blood squelched beneath him, throbbing out of his chest.

You lied to me, Miss Elisa. Alex could tell that something terrible was about to happen, something he had no power to stop. *You said that everything in my life would depend on my choices. But I didn't choose this! I didn't choose to be born a black wizard. And your god rejected me for that. Why? I haven't done anything evil.*

Scenes from his past flashed by, one replacing the other. He saw himself being ridiculed, stoned, locked in a closet, and starved.

Then he recalled coming to Follen, where Robin carried him on his shoulders. Where he played with the other kids. Where Anastasia taught him how to play piano.

Where the Professor talked to him in the evenings by the fireplace.
Where he was at home.

Now all of that was being taken away from him.

And the one who could have helped was just making it worse.

I don't need a god like that.

His despair gave place to fury.

I don't need that Light.

Broken hope gave place to rage.

Damn it all!

The gaping void inside the little boy was filled by fire. Cold, black fire. Bringing nothing but—

Everything depends on my choices, you say? Then I choose to become the strongest black wizard ever! One who will someday put out all your Light.

"You called me, child?"

Time remained frozen. Alex smelled burned wet leaves and sulfur.

"Who are you?"

"Who am I? I'm the one who tempted Paris into stealing Helen. The one who closed Hercules' eyes so he could kill his wife and children. The one who whispered the recipe of fiery death into the scholar's ear. I am the one who reversed the sign of the sun to make it my sign of death. And I am the one you called, child."

"What's your name?"

"Baltael, my child. Baltael is the name of your evil destiny."

"Will you help me, Baltael?"

"I'm helping you already, my child. Can't you feel it?"

Alex felt a red spark flash inside him, accompanied by Baltael's distant and inhuman laughter.

***

Alex opened his eyes.

Shimmering in his right hand was the black ring, its color a striking contrast to the snow-white hospital sheets.

On his chest, right over the heart, were the five glistening scars, each shaped like an upturned star.

The traces of Baltael's claws.

His sign.

Coming from the corridor were the sounds of a song. *Karliene's*

Become the Beast.

"Bitch," Doom breathed and leaned back on the pillows.

Chapter 54

"**I** couldn't agree more, Mr. Dumsky."

Feeling as doomed as a stereotypical horror movie character with a predatory monster behind his back, Alex turned toward the sound.

As he turned, Doom got a look at his one-bed hospital ward. It was palatial. Everything was stylish and modern, with a stretch ceiling, neon spots, loft-style walls made to look like metal, giant screens showing his vitals, the newest PlayStation, and a TV so large it could have doubled as a pool table.

Doom had spent nights with pretty girls in luxury hotel apartments that weren't that nice.

But he wasn't going to get to enjoy all the finery.

Seated in an armchair upholstered in green chintz (the only thing out of place in the apartment ward's ultra-modern and hi-tech style) by the French window spanning an entire wall was an all-too-familiar guardsman.

The fact that Doom failed to spot the major immediately wasn't surprising.

It was either Chon Sook's weird sense of humor or life itself playing a joke on him. (Life definitely had a sense of humor even if the major didn't.)

He was dressed in a green suit that was exactly the same color as the armchair, complete with a lighter-green shirt and an emerald bow tie.

In his hands the major held a women's needlework and knitting magazine. He was somewhere in the middle, so he'd apparently spent quite some time sitting there and waiting.

Yeah. Today's unlikely to get any worse than it already is.

"Not the most interesting read," he sighed, dropping the glossy volume into a drawer with two other magazines: women's lingerie and celebrity dirty laundry. "Still, the best the local library has to offer."

"Yes?"

"There was a middle-aged lady staying here right before you. Unfortunately, I can't introduce you unless you're up for a walk to St. Michael's Cemetery."

"She died?" Alex signed mournfully.

"Sadly, heart disease is sometimes lethal even with today's magic technology."

Alex hoped that wasn't intended as a threat. That hope grew particularly strong when he saw exactly how many small tubes were stuck in his right arm and how many sensors were suction-cupped to his chest and legs. There were another two connected to his temples.

They could fry me with electricity if they wanted. The perfect way to burn a witch in the enlightened 21st century. At least my bonfire will be a hospital bed good enough for a politician to die on.

"Relax, Alexander." Sticking out his little finger, Chon Sook drank some coffee from a china cup. It was so strong that the very smell made Doom a little dizzy. He'd never liked the drink, anyway—whiskey or chocolate were more his cup of tea. And sometimes literal tea. "We need you fully…operational. That's why the office for once was generous enough to shell out the credits for the city's best hospital."

"The best?" Alex arched his body to peer out the window. Yes. The hospital building was apparently right in the middle of Central Park, meaning he was at Dethrail, the Light Elves' healthcare center. A week of treatment cost as much as a two-bedroom apartment somewhere on Amalgam Street. "Bitch."

"You said that already, Mr. Dumsky. And swearing in a senior officer's presence is a bad idea."

That was when Alex remembered the major's cupboard-sized driver.

"Where's Duncan?"

"In the cafeteria." Chon Sook put the cup back on the tea trolley and picked up an éclair. "For whatever reason, he's not a fan of yours, so I'd rather have him appease his hunger with the local fast food than your blood."

"Is he a vampire?"

Alex wasn't surprised that Dethrail served fast food. For the money its patients paid, they could have been attended to by elite escorts instead of night nurses.

And ladies of their race of choice, too. With a degree in finance. Why finance? Because most inpatients were probably of the age where you enjoy discussing stock market trends more than sex.

But why only ladies? Because Alex was sexist.

"Sometimes I suspect he really is, but he keeps passing all the tests." The major allowed himself a slight smile before reassuming his usual kite-like expression to finish up the éclair and wipe his hands on a napkin. Intertwining his fingers, he shot Doom a smart, intent stare that bored right into his skull. "Mr. Dumsky, what can you tell me about our Mr. X?"

"The Mask?"

"Yes."

Alex thought for a few seconds. He had little to say, and he preferred to keep what he knew to himself.

"Nothing."

"Nothing?"

"Are we playing a game of ask-me-raccoon, Major?"

"Ask-me-raccoon? Why raccoon?" Chon Sook asked with a frown.

"So, we *are* playing," Alex sighed sadly.

"Do you really miss your prison games that badly, Mr. Dumsky?"

That time it was difficult not to pick up on the hint *and* threat.

Actually, there wasn't anything Alex missed about prison. And he had no desire to return in the near future.

"I have no idea what I can tell you about the Mask."

"No idea? That's an awfully feeble answer from someone who smashed up half the Financial District, inflicting damage estimated at sixty-nine million credits. And for the record, Mr. Dumsky, that number is going to fuck the Guards as well as you personally. Our budget is strained enough as it is."

"Some good news, at least," Doom breathed. The next moment he realized he'd said that out loud.

"Not really, Alexander. Not really. No performance bonuses for our whole department this quarter. And that's why Duncan is eating fast food right now even though he hates it."

"Bitch."

"I couldn't have picked a better word." The major's eyes flashed with a predatory and playful glimmer, something like the way cats look when they're playing with a mouse. "Thank Lieutenant Gribovsky for his slip of the tongue. If not for it, you'd owe the city a much bigger sum right now."

Alex closed his eyes and breathed a bit calmer. *They have me cornered. The Syndicate. The Guards. The Mask. The students. Miss Perriot with her fit booty and—*

Wait, what does the esper's booty have to do with anything?

"I really can't be any more specific about the Mask, Major. I can only say what you already know. He's a black wizard. He's strong enough to bend a demon from a second-hundred legion to his will. And finally, he—"

"...can use demon magic," the major finished. "Just like you."

Doom tensed up. He was already tense, but now his butt seemed to shrink to the size of an atom, sharp enough to tear through the silk sheet it was nested on.

"Inmates are fully examined before they're placed in their cell." As the major said that, Alex recalled the humiliating procedure of medical tubes and pumps being applied to his body any way the doctor's apparently perverted mind thought up. "In your case, the abnormality they identified went from dusty archive to dusty archive until it ended up in our department."

"Ah. Now I see why you got me out."

"It takes one to know one, Mr. Dumsky," the major replied. "We've been after the Mask for a long time. You're the ace up our sleeve. Your recent performance was bright enough to shut up all the skeptics, but I don't think the effect will be a lasting one. So, think again before you answer: *did you notice anything unusual about the Mask or what he did?*"

The major's eyes held Alex's for a while until the latter was forced to look away at the window.

The view really was amazing, and so much more pleasing to the eye than the blind stone walls of the underground jail.

"I really wish I had."

The major squinted, then stood with a clap of his hands. Stepping over to the door, he took a suit in a black case that sported the *VersaceMagus* logo off the coat rack, baring two more hangers with clothes hiding behind it. One had torn leather jeans, another a black hoodie and a biker jacket.

"What the...?"

"Suits like this aren't for liars," the major declared in an affected parental voice. "But I can chalk your failure to recognize the particular style of Professor Raewsky and Follen School up to your head injury. The other clothes are courtesy of Gribovsky. Return them to him later. Get better, Alexander."

A moment before leaving, the major turned.

"By the way, the first round of the tournament starts in two hours. I'd hurry over to First Magic if I were you. The trip is going to take much longer on foot now that you're without your bike. Anyway, Mr. Dumsky, we'll speak soon."

And Alex was left alone in the ward.

"Fuck..."

"A new word," came the reply from the other side of the door.

Chapter 55

Leaving the subway at University Square station (such an apropos name), Alex remembered exactly why he hated Myers City's underground transportation system so much. He never used it unless he absolutely had to.

For example, to escape cops with a stolen cat tucked into his belt, yelling and scratching. The pictures were probably still stored at the Abyss.

Any journey where he was liable to be shoved by a troll, have his toes stepped on by an orc, and get dressed down by an arrogant Light Elf was a test for his self-control. Like any black wizard, Alex was extremely sensitive to any intrusion into his personal space.

Shaking off the subway touch (literal and figurative alike), Doom rolled his eyes, stepping in a puddle to shatter his reflection.

The Guards.

The fact that they knew about Follen contrasted with the dossier Chon Sook had read him at their first meeting. So that had to have been info they'd obtained recently, digging in several directions at once. That did them credit as an organization.

But the Mask (and whoever was hiding beneath it) was Alex's prey and Alex's alone. He wasn't about to share his personal vendetta with anyone, even if that meant walking around in rags like the ones he was wearing for a while.

Pulling out his longstanding pack of cigarettes and slapping a cancer stick out, Doom caught it in the air with his teeth and inhaled deeply.

The cloud of smoke he blew out expanded gradually until it enveloped half the street. Some defensive artifacts worked in there, flashing magic over their owners. Car engines started, brakes screeched, and horns honked.

Some stronger wizards started to dispel the magic smoke. But the delay gave Alex enough time to elbow his way through the line of shocked and coughing people.

The first tour of the tournament (yes, an awkward and redundant way of putting it) was played on campus. Since the pick of the planet's next magic generation was participating in the competition, there were all kinds of visitors. All the checkpoints around campus had been opened, with eight more security guards hired to supplement Ban. But even nine gates and nine guards were apparently too few to handle such a plentiful—and extremely diverse—flow of visitors.

From citizens of Atlantis to Middle Easterners, everyone was there in their national dress. That even included guests from the lands of magic races. Alex spotted representatives of Schambal and Eldorado. VIP visitors were funneled through a separate entrance, and their well-coordinated response to his magic smoke...

"Professor...Dumsky..." Covering his mouth with a handkerchief as he coughed and wheezed, Ban rummaged around under the counter with his other hand to retrieve a gas mask and put it on. He was a really weak wizard. "You're just in time for the start."

"Great," Doom said with a salute. Given how Ban's voice sounded coming through the mask, he could have made a Luke-I-am-your-father joke, but...Star War jokes in the second half of the 21st century? Seriously?

"Please show your ID card, Professor Dumsky." No. It was getting really, really difficult for Alex to hold it in. Ban sounded exactly like Darth Vader in his prime.

Patting his jacket pockets, Doom realized he had none of his personal belongings except for his underwear, the cigarette pack, and the ring on his finger. Nothing else had made it to Dethrail.

Giving it a second thought, he didn't actually own anything else. But it didn't really matter. The elves totally deserved his escape through that wall, the literal wall he'd melted to make a way out. The bunnies would have made him fill out paperwork or something otherwise.

"Ban, my good man. It's me. Alex Doom."

"Your ID, Professor. Please," Ban said in a sad and weary voice. "That's the rule for today. You shouldn't have pulled that trick with the smoke."

Fire engine sirens grew louder as they approached.

"No one knows it was me," Doom said, pointing up at the sky.

"I saw you," Ban insisted.

"Then you can let me in, too."

"I saw the smoke, but I haven't seen your ID, Professor Dumsky."

Alex sighed and massaged the bridge of his nose. Did he say the day couldn't get any worse? It looked like he was wrong.

"The professor's with me," a familiar voice came from inside the dense smoke. Out into the campus fence lights stepped Miss Perriot, charming as ever in her high boots, red dress, and denim jacket.

What else did the day have in store for Alex?

She handed her ID card to Ban. He pressed a button. The artifacts supporting the defensive magic seal between the *adamantius* rods of the fence faded with a clanging sound, as did the seal itself.

"Let's go, Professor." The esper entered the campus first, peach mane waving. Alex followed. Her hair smelled pleasant and fruity.

"Thank you," he said.

"No problem," Perriot replied.

Their brief conversation was full of tension despite ending before it really began. Finding themselves on the neat but crowded campus footpaths, they headed for Magic Range One, which served as a miniature arena.

The actual arena was a giant sports complex on the distant outskirts of Myers City. It had been constructed long before to host the first Olympic Games in Atlantis.

Just as epically ambitious as any other construction project on the island, the Arena turned out to be the world's largest stadium, accommodating up to 300,000 people. It was to be used for the tournament's official opening and closing ceremonies as well as the Grand Finale. What was taking place then was just a qualifying round attended only by the biggest fans, the families of the contestants, VIPs, and other types commonly seen at similar events.

Alex inhaled.

"Do you remember our deal, Professor?"

"If that's your way of getting me to ask you out, Miss Perriot, it's not worth the effort. Even if you were the last living creature in the universe, I'd rather devour you than date you."

"If you ever ask me out, Professor, I'll call the police and have you arrested for trying to drive me crazy."

"Drive you crazy? That fast? Huh. I've always been good with women, but not *that* good. I must've unlocked a new lev—"

The esper stopped abruptly and wheeled around to face Alex. She was so close that Doom could...no, not feel her breath on his face. He wasn't that romantic.

Instead, he felt her breasts, so appetizing, almost touch his chest.

"If *anything* happens to them," she squinted, the ends of her peach hair stirring, "even a single bruise or scratch...I'll run you into the ground, Professor."

Doom gave a whistle and puffed out a cloud of smoke. Right into her face.

"You like dead bodies that much?"

The esper turned silently, the hem of her dress flapping at the abrupt move, and walked toward the range. The commotion in its overcrowded stands was clearly visible.

Doom looked down at the puddle at his feet...and recoiled at his reflection.

He looked really, really bad. He definitely needed a shave, a drink, and a fuck.

    Preferably in the reverse order.

Chapter 56

Walking beneath the archway toward the footpaths leading to the stands, Alex again appreciated the event's scale and...how down to earth it was. There were no designated VIP boxes or lengthy welcome speeches. It took Doom a while to find where the rector was.

Only a closer look at a distant sector that was guarded and less crowded than the rest showed Alex where to find Julio Lupen. Wearing another sweat suit, with a gold chain around his neck, he was having a casual conversation with...

Alex cursed, turning away abruptly and walking over to the umbrella-covered spots for the coaches. They were literal beach umbrellas over plastic benches lining the running track.

Under the gray, gloomy sky looming over Myers City, the umbrellas looked pretty out of place.

"Damn," Doom hissed.

He could still feel the stare of those black eyes with white pupils. The eyes of Maeve, Queen Mab's daughter. The Queen of the Winter Court seldom left her palace, unlike her daughter, who was a dark faerie ambassador. She represented their people at major events.

Alex had once tried to kill Maeve.

And bed her.

All in the same night.

It was complicated.

Anyway, being recognized by Maeve was the last thing he wanted right then. Even though the memory of her amazing body and satin skin made his pants tighter in the groin.

"Professor!"

Alex sighed and, using a very simple spell to make sure the faerie gave him nothing more than a passing glance, nodded to his students.

The blonde waving at him was the only one of the five contestants who looked great in the tournament uniform, an extremely clingy one-piece.

Seeing her in it, Doom started to wonder if Maeve's body was actually all that beautiful. Particularly when the heiress to one of the wealthiest clans around bent over slightly to retrieve a water bottle from the cooler.

Damn pants.

They're kids, Alex! Sure, you're a total jerk, but you're no pedophile.

Cooling himself down with those thoughts, Doom ducked under the umbrella (*could they have put it any lower?*), snatched the unopened bottle from Eleonora, and, saluting her, drained it in a single gulp.

The cold soda descended into a stomach that had been empty for several days, threatening to start the Second Magic War. Fortunately, his gut flora prevailed.

He tossed the bottle precisely at…

"Hey!"

…the head of a youngster from the rival Magic Engineering team. Then Alex snapped his fingers in front of Travis' face.

"Want to get cursed?"

"What do you…" The redhead with the dean's name didn't get it right away but, seeing the lilac flashes on Doom's fingertips, finally grasped the problem. "Oh, sure. Please sit down, Professor."

"I never say thank you," Alex replied, sprawling out on the hard plastic surface and lighting another cigarette. "I'm starving. What's the age limit here?"

All five, including Jackie Chan, stared at him with round eyes. Was it the clothes the major had given him? Doom wasn't actually sure that Versace case had contained a suit and not just some filling.

"W-w-why do you as-s-sk?" The stammering blonde took a step back, the ends of her hair sparking slightly.

Women and their hair. You can read a woman's life in her hair, practically like an open book. Just like you can read a man's life in his hands.

"I'm a *black wizard.*" Alex leaned back and crossed a heel over his knee, making himself as comfortable as he possibly could. It didn't matter that Mara and Jing, who were sitting on either side of him, had to shrink to fit into the remaining space. "It's almost five o'clock. Tea time for some, and for me time to gobble down some little kids. Are there any on the menu?"

After a moment's hesitation, the five students (who'd had several practice sessions with Alex and were somewhat used to his way of talking) gave some restrained, wary giggles. They sounded like they still weren't sure if he was joking or not.

"Eighteen plus," Jet Li replied briefly.

"Thank you, Ben Lam." Alex clapped him on the shoulder. "You've always looked like the smartest one to me. Well, if it's eighteen plus, then—"

"What's going on here?"

Alex looked up to see Lebenstein looming over him. That time, the short, plump man was wearing...a robe. A wizardry robe over his expensive business suit.

Hogwarts cosplay? Or a mental inpatient they're giving some free time?

"If your eyes are suddenly failing, Mr. Lebenstein, I don't mind filling you in—it's the first tour of the tournament. Ugh, that sounds really awkward."

The Theory and Magical Calculation Dean's superpower—the ability to change the color of his face—never ceased to amuse Alex. The transitions from light green to crimson...

"I'm perfectly aware of the event the university is currently hosting!" It was a shame the pleasantly deep, bass voice was such a poor match to his appearance. But no one is perfect. *Except for black wizards, of course.*

"That ask-me-raccoon game is popular again?"

"What?? What raccoon game?"

"Exactly." With a sad sigh, Doom shook his head dismally. "So, it *is* back."

Lebenstain scowled, puffing almost to the point of exploding...no, that was just spitting rain. Not drops of blood from the vein throbbing on the dean's temple.

"Stop clowning around, Dumsky!"

"*Professor* Dumsky," Alex corrected. "They're inseparable. Like Captain Jack Sparrow."

"What sparrow captain? First a raccoon, now a sparrow. Are you *coked up*?"

"Yuck, what ugly slang. No, I'm not *high*," Alex said with a dashing smile.

He heard giggles behind his back. They weren't wary that time, instead almost as obtrusive as the dean was, barely passed off as coughing.

Lebenstein apparently noticed them, too, as he straightened up and tried to calm down.

"Professor Dumsky, I'm fully aware of the tournament and its purpose. However much I am disgusted by the idea of the next generation seeing magic through the lens of violence rather than science or art, I'm still able to appreciate its benefits for liaisons between Atlantis and Old Earth as well as between humans and other races. But what I'm *not* able to appreciate is you, Professor, enrolling the B-52 group in the contest without my knowledge or approval. That contradicts both the spirit of our department and our principles of subordination. And what concerns me most is that I didn't even find that out from a written application. Instead, I had to be informed by Miss Perriot at the last minute. That's why I'm asking…no, I'm *demanding* an explanation. Now."

Lebenstein jerked his chin up, his eyes flashing arrogantly. *Not everyone can pull that off. Shorty has a gift.*

Then Alex looked at Leia, who was drilling through him with eyes that were practically yelling *gotcha*.

Damn. The esper had turned him in. Stabbed him in the back. *So low. So mean.* Alex was a fan. *Damn. Keep that up, and I'm going to fall in love.*

"Sir Dean. I'm…" Alex pretended to be struck through the heart. Wounded in the soul. Spat on and humiliated by Roman soldiers for trying to pull Christ down off the cross. In the depths of despair. "I did it…for the department…for us…"

Stunned at first, Lebenstein started listening to Alex with growing attention.

"When I joined our wonderful Department of Theory and Magical Calculation, superior in every sense and led by one of the world's brightest minds, a light of magic science…"

The dean straightened up and, adjusting his robe, puffed his chest out (his belly was still two lengths ahead). "…our department wasn't faring as well as it should be. We had to recruit new students from anywhere we could, even accepting kids who wouldn't have made it into *community college!* So, I decided to restore the department to its former glory and put its name on everyone's lips! The only problem was that I had to sacrifice my moral principles."

The dean signed mournfully and looked down at his feet.

"I appreciate your zeal, Professor Dumsky, and I share your pain. Still, I *can't* have B-52 become part of this barbaric entertainment, replicating gladiator fights for the amusement of mindless crowds."

Perriot exchanges glances with the students, looking almost as shocked as they were.

"But just imagine," Alex whispered persuasively. "If we win, the department will get a spotlight no money can buy. We'll attract brilliant students. Research grants. We'll be able to put display boards in each auditorium." (Lebenstein's eyes flashed with hope.) "There will be universal recognition for our department leader. For you, our brightest mind." (The dean looked like he was holding a press conference in his head.) "The Board of Governors will hear about you. They'll probably make you the next headmaster…"

"Yes…the Board of Governors…"

"Who knows?" Alex continued, his voice dropping lower and

lower. "Maybe after becoming headmaster, you'll be elected Minister of Magic…"

"Yes…Minister…" Lebenstein drawled, then froze with his mouth open before shaking his head. "No. Stop. What are you talking about? What Board of Governors? We don't have one of those. What headmaster? What Minister of Magic?"

"Wait, really?" Alex gasped, eyes wide. "We aren't in the middle of a Hogwarts cosplay? You have the robe and you're talking nonsense, so I thought—"

"This is the traditional garb of magic scholars!" Lebenstein interrupted with a squeal. "And *I'm* not the one talking nonsense! Pack your things *now*, take B-52 with you, and stay away until—"

The first signal for the draw rang out.

"Mara, go get the number," Alex ordered in a cold, steely voice. "You're the captain."

"But…"

"I have Rector Lupen's permission." Doom poured an icy, murderous glare over Lebenstein. The dean shivered, though he didn't look away. *He does have something in him.* "Dean, if you want to keep *my* group from participating, you have to get through *me*."

Doom then glanced past Lebenstein at the displeased Miss Perriot.

"That goes for *you*, too."

She just flashed her middle finger at him, striking his heart once more. *Ah, a real femme fatale.*

"By the way," Doom said with a broad smile as he turned back to the dean. "If we're going to watch this kitten parade together, what about pledging some money to a cat shelter?"

"What? What cat shelter?"

"The one I own. I love the fluffy rascals so much. But money has been tight recently, and…"

Alex spent the next fifteen minutes convincing the dean to donate. And he almost succeeded. But then the first tour began, and it was announced that B-52 would be facing the battle department group from American Magic University in the very first round.

Karma's a bitch.

I should have washed my hands at least. My nails taste really gross.

Chapter 57

Doom's nails didn't really make for a good meal, so he put his headset on and got down to coaching.

Everyone else on the B-52 team also wore an earpiece, albeit a smaller one. The youngsters were walking up to one of the many podiums where the duels were going to take place.

So many teams had entered the tournament that the committee was trying to weed out half of them on the very first day, employing a trivial but very efficient method: a fight-off.

The rules were simple: the first team to knock out two or more members of the other team won and lived to fight another day. *The bouncer team.*

It was violent but consistent with the new approach to magical education commonly adopted after the Magic Wars, a time when wizards had to confront whole hordes of monstrous creatures ravaging North Eurasia and North America. The brunt had been borne by the Scandinavians, Canadians, and Russians.

Before the wars, the department headed by Lebenstein had actually been the center of attention. But it had been eclipsed by the battle magic department. More and more wizards trained to become soldiers or magic creature hunters rather than researchers or scholars.

There was nothing special about the uniforms the contestants were wearing. Each team was dressed in jumpsuits, either blue or red, with strong defensive properties. Doom's little chicklets drew blue. After a jumpsuit took 1,000 mana points of damage or more, it turned white and the player wearing it was knocked out.

Quite a regular five-versus-five fu—

"Professor Dumsky," Lebenstein coughed, interrupting Alex. Sure, the dean had only interrupted his train of thought, but it was still an interruption. "I hope you understand that you're vouching with your life for—"

"We don't vouch with our lives where I come from." Alex turned away from the fat man to fix his eyes on the podium. "But don't worry. We'll fu—"

"Watch your language, Professor!" the dean squeaked. "There are children here."

"Sexually mature children. With voting rights. Hey, chicklets, roll out!"

Miss Perriot and Dean Lebenstein hiccupped simultaneously. Alex felt a twinge of anger that neither of them had apparently seen

Transformers. *Illiterates. Not much you can expect of them.*

"Jet Li," came Jing's calm voice over the headset.

"Barbie," Elie said with gritted teeth.

"Gimli," Mara whispered.

"Flashlight." Leo seemed to be polishing his nails out there. *What*
a—

"Weasel," the redhead said in a voice mimicking his blonde friend.

"At least you remember your nicknames. Well, we're lucky—this round looks easy. We'll walk over these guys like Jesus on water without getting our heels messy."

"Heels? But I didn't make a pedicure appointment—"

"Focus, Flashlight!" Doom barked. "Have you ever been on a job? All talk is strictly business. Not another word from you, lookout, unless it's a cop signal."

Dumsky was so into the game that he let a little of the street in. No man's fool, he'd bet ten grand on the chicklets' victory. Considering they came in at 1:3, the prospect of winning twenty stacks was too attractive to miss.

Overall, he got why they were so nervous.

Facing them were five gentlemen and…the feminist world wanted everyone to say *gentlewomen* but, as a sexist, Alex preferred *ladies.*

They all hailed from the holy land of cheap burgers and stunning movies like *The Shawshank Redemption,* shows Alex watched over and over again back in prison.

The five were apparently seniors. Two were big guys: a fair-haired and blue-eyed one who would have looked right at home in a Nazi uniform, and a seven-foot, fifteen-stone African-American who had apparently come straight from the football field, forgetting his weed, hoes, and bucket of fried chicken.

Not only did that sound racist, it actually was.

Doom was a black jerk (no mistake there).

And the three ladies. A sexy Latina with a prominent booty. A nerd, bespectacled and pug-nosed (Alex would only have fucked her with a bag over her head). And a mulatto who looked more dangerous than sexy.

"So," Alex said, covered his mike with a hand, "Nazi boy is a light wizard. Some 900 points. Give it to him with fire—odd as it sounds, light wizards are bad at resisting it. The other guy, football boy, is a voodoo master. Don't let him get your nails or hair. Latino stripper is a fire wizard. Barbie, take her hot and heavy, get all these guys horn—"

Miss Perriot coughed from behind me.

"Take her hard from the back and—"

Miss Perriot coughed again.

"I get it, Professor," blondie said in an icy voice that contrasted with her magic element.

"The next girl is a red nerd. Like our Weasel."

"There are lots of people with red hair," Travis protested.

"Of course," Alex nodded. "There are lots of idiots, too. Now for the most dangerous, the mulatto panther. She's…a literal panther."

"A shapeshifter?!" seven voices screamed at once—all five chicklets, the dean, and the esper, the latter two apparently listening the whole time. *Were they never told not to eavesdrop when they were little?*

"No, a summoner," Alex winced. "Jing, don't let her round you up. Keep it simple. Feel free to improvise, but go with our two-two-one tactic. Knock Nazi boy and stripper girl out first. The rest don't matter."

Alex was true to his habit of nicknaming everyone around him. Since his early years, it had been his favorite way of sizing up people and their most prominent parts.

Speaking of prominent parts, he didn't at all mean male geni—

"How do you know what their powers are?" Perriot interrupted.

What the hell? Some kind of hostile magic seemed to be turning the situation PG.

"Experience," Alex said honestly. "Please stop distracting me. I have five chicklets here who are about to get fu—"

"We can hear you!" the students shouted.

Alex rolled his eyes. There definitely *was* some wizardry keeping him from swearing.

The referee lifted a flare gun overhead and pulled the trigger. *No fucking doubt, it's about to go down.*

He'd done it!

Sadly, in his joy at being able to swear at last, he missed the beginning of the round. It was spectacular.

Standing shoulder to shoulder, Nazi boy and stripper girl drew a seal in the air (*Senior battle magic students drawing magic seals with their fingers! Why don't they use a stencil, too?*) that flashed with fire and light, so pure and clear it made Alex itch to hit the light thing as hard as he could.

Football boy, in the meantime, dropped a rag doll to his feet that instantly sprouted long, green, snake-like vines.

Panther kneeled, rolled her eyes, and put her hands on her podium to start summoning.

Their defense was handled by the red nerd, who spread her arms, singing into existence spells that flashed multi-colored shields around the five.

The Americans' well-coordinated effort was on point.

But Doom had his point, too. It was the trademark of the whiskey he'd kept in his old jacket, one that had died brave in his battle with the Mask.

The double sea the attacking couple made shot a fiery tornado that took the shape of a giant hand clutching a sword. It was formed by the finest rays of all-piercing light.

The magic sword cut through the shields Travis hastily put up without any problem whatsoever, smacking into Leo at the tip of the team's V formation.

Swept off his feet, the pink-haired guy flew across the whole podium and lost consciousness when he hit the ground, his jumpsuit turning white.

"Great!" Doom clapped, utterly surprising his fellow coaches, Miss Perriot, and Lebenstein, but not his chicklets. "The dead weight is gone. Now let's send those Yankees home! Barbie, fire!"

And Eleonora fired.

It was so hot that Alex was fucking stunned.

Chapter 58

Eleonora lifted her arms, her fair, nearly white hair, sparking with electricity. From between her hands, waves of orange light spread, swelling until they burst into roaring fire.

Magic lenses were completely disabled at the tournament for both contestants and coaches, so Doom had no idea how much mana her spell contained.

But he was happy enough that she'd created it without a single move of her hands.

That bought the team a couple seconds.

In magic duels between illiterates, the outcome is decided by speed.

Barbie deserved full credit for learning how to form her seal with pure mental effort in less than a month.

The roaring stream of fire had no distinct shape, just a pure elemental flow that spread like a flaming flower over the red nerd's shields. The Yankee girl doubled over, blood trickling from the corner of her mouth. There was no way she could have expected a blow on par with something the average Mystic could pull off—magic storage devices were prohibited at the tournament.

"Hulk! Smash!" Dumsky ordered.

Mara stooped and touched the ground the way she'd done in practice dozens of times. Fortunately, the podium was made of rock raised over the arena surface by earth magic. When the Glomebood half-blood stood, she was holding a rather heavy stone hammer in her hand. It glowed with dwarf runes and emitted a solid amount of magic energy. So solid, in fact, that Doom felt a slight tingling in his fingertips.

In a matter of seconds, Mara created a magic storage device and filled it with part of her reserve. It was just single use, but she didn't need anything more than that.

"That's a *storage!*" the Yankee coach standing beside Doom yelled. "Referee! Violation!"

But the referee didn't raise his flag.

Alex flashed a predatory smile.

The rules prohibited *bringing* storage devices onto the field, but not *creating* them on the spot. Chances were, no one present at Range One, including all the spectators, was able to do what Mara had just done.

Brandishing the hammer, she created a gray seal at her feet and two stone columns to toss it up into the air.

Football guy's snakes were already circling Jing, but the Asian knew his job. *And* he was the only one of the five who didn't wait for Alex's command to get to work.

The shaman tattoos on his legs glowed through the jumpsuit. The magic energy literally flowing from the adolescent's body formed big bubbles shaped like tiger paws, and that was when...Jet Li just vanished.

Despite all his experience, Alex lost track (though just for a moment) of the shaman's moves. That made sense—shamans weren't actually wizards.

Emerging a few feet behind the red nerd's back, Jing assumed an attacking stance, though he didn't strike.

He really did know his job.

Events from there unfolded so rapidly that Alex could hardly intervene with anything more than a brief command. And the fact that Travis responded to the summons in time was a testament to the job Rizen's teachers had done.

The seal that appeared in front of the panther was filled with signs and symbols unlike any of those used by the standard magic schools. The magic actually had much more in common with shamanism than with the classical schools.

A wingless manticore burst out of the seal with a deafening roar— a lion with a bat's head and a scorpion's tail. A D-rank magic creature according to the Hunter Guild's bestiary. It could have easily overcome a regular Practitioner or turned a student party like the tournament into a massacre. If the panther had lost control of the creature, the contestants on the podium would have felt like they'd been transported back into the heat of the Magic War.

The referee held out a hand that clutched a magic wand carved with runes, a battle magic storage.

But Travis was faster.

Faster than the referee.

Faster than Alex himself could remember which spell would destroy the creature.

Weasel held his palms together. When he spread them, a glowing glass needle seemed to hang in between, though it was actually made of compressed, crumpled space. It was better than any sword at cutting and piercing.

"Fucking Doctor Strange," Alex said with sincere admiration.

Space spells required absolutely perfect magic control. Doom had managed to create a very simple spell of that type only a month before he'd been jailed.

But the level of magic control Travis was showing right then, however much it pained Alex to admit it, was beyond his current ability.

He was somewhat excused by the fact that spells from the Space and Darkness schools were only unlocked at level 40 for Adepts and higher. That limited them to the cream of the Abyss Society.

Swinging widely, Travis flung the space needle spear, piercing the leaping manticor through. Its hard skin, which was capable of withstanding a shot from a sniper rifle, something that had been confirmed during the Magic War, and its anti-tank mine-proof skeleton both gave way.

"Now!" Alex barked into the mike.

By then, Mara had soared through the air, landing on top of the red nerd's shield to balance on a magic plateau she'd created. It rose like a bridge over the five Yankees.

She spun the hammer overhead and brought it crashing down on the shield dome where most of the other team's seals were concentrated.

Barbie's flaming flower was still raging at the front of the shield, meaning that it had just come under the full combined power of the magic storage wielded by the human-dwarf.

The red Yankee turned pale. Her shields glimmered, though they held.

But Alex and his chicklets didn't actually need to destroy the shields. Once the snake army darted toward Jing, he vanished again.

…only to reappear right behind red nerd's back. Before the Yankee could see that her shields had been penetrated, the edge of Jackie Chan's hand hit her neck. Her eyes rolled back, and she collapsed at the feet of Jing, who vanished once again—just in time to escape friendly fire.

The wave of gray magic energy coming from Mara's hammer crashed down on stripper girl and Nazi boy, leaving the couple huddling together in a tall stone cage placed directly in the path of the approaching a fiery column.

When the referee raised his flag, the only people left standing on the podium were the four B-52 members. The Yankees, literally swept off the stage, were on the ground, moaning, cut and bruised all over, and slightly burned.

"Take that!" Alex exclaimed as he jumped to his feet. "Like sitting ducks!"

"You're *too* emotional, Professor." Lebenstein, not much better at concealing his joy than the chicklets were (laughing, embracing each other, and jumping on the podium, with Barbie even shedding happy tears), stood and shot a sudden glance at Alex's jeans, rolled up so high they seemed too short for Doom when he stood. "Um…Professor? What's that on your ankle?"

Looking down, Alex sighed. *Gribovsky, you bitch.*

"Professor! Professor!" Barbie jumped over to Alex and took him by the arm. "Please come with us to the Schooner! We need to celebrate!"

Never before had Alex so appreciated an invitation to grab a drink.

"Only if you're paying," he replied with a smile.

"Professor Dumsky!" Lebenstein screamed, but it was too late.

The B-52 group left the range at its full strength of four chicklets, Leo levitating on a stretcher and muttering something about a pedicure, and one full-fledged black wizard.

Chapter 59

The Schooner was closed to visitors despite the fact that late evening was usually when it was at its busiest. Doom had convinced Diglan that the Guards would compensate him for all revenue lost by closing the bar for a private party of five B-52 students at an hour when the university sent the most visitors over.

The only employee waiting on the small party was Cherry. She spent the whole evening hitting on Eleonora, who apparently took her attention as mere friendliness.

Jay, the pimple overlord, skipped out on overtime to leave early—*for underground magic fighting*, as Doom strongly suspected. The boy's arms bore all-too-characteristic scars he desperately tried to hide. And his pimples looked like the consequence of a simple curse, persistent and not treated properly in time.

Of course, Alex wasn't going to share his suspicions with anyone.

The party had passed its drinking-and-dancing climax, with Alex the only one still on his feet. It took all of his willpower not to touch any of the alcoholic drinks the overjoyed Diglan had put out on the bar shelves.

Damn him. Over the moon from hearing that all his losses are going to be compensated double. How could anyone in their right mind believe utter nonsense like that? Particularly when it's coming from a black wizard.

Unsurprisingly, the bar owner had done twelve years for stealing a stolen Camaro right from…the police impound lot. *Bravery and stupidity all at the same time.*

The students and Cherry were all down and out. Literally. They were as good at having fun as the Tkils had been in their heyday, Alex had to admit. But far, far worse at drinking.

Travis was curled up in a ball under the bar counter, his face covered in highlighter doodles. He'd been the first to fall asleep.

Jing, who'd passed out right after the redhead, looked like he was about to deliver a speech on Confucian values. With his back straight, his arms crossed, and his eyes closed, he was leaning against the wall, his head right beneath the steering wheel and antlers. The other students had gotten some great pictures of him.

Leo's arms were around the wooden bear, leaving him asleep in a strange position somewhere between standing and lying on the animal.

Mara, Eleonora, and Cherry, the best drinkers, were intertwined like snakes on the far table. Doom covered them with one of the blankets the employees used to keep warm while doing overtime.

It wasn't that Alex had gone soft. The smell of the alcohol coming from them was too seductive, not to mention the smell of their fresh young bodies and the fact that some of their clothes were riding up and revealing parts that were too tempting a sight for a recent prisoner.

"At last." Doom wiped the sweat off his forehead, stood his mop up in the corner, and appraised his work.

The Schooner's floor was as shiny as a virgin's pocket mirror, having seen nothing more offensive in its whole life than lipstick a few shades too bright. All the plastic cups, pizza boxes, bottles, unfinished snacks, and other trash were heaped in a single giant pile ready to be cleaned up…

…by Cherry. It didn't matter that she was as yet unsuspecting of that, smiling blissfully in her sleep as she squeezed the blonde's prominent breasts.

Alex wasn't envious of her.

They. Are. Kids.

It didn't matter that they were just a bit more than three years younger than himself, nor that his bed had seen girls who were actually below the legal age despite looking much, much older before his arrest.

Those days were long gone.

Retrieving a cigarette from the same crumpled but immortal and eternal pack, Alex lit a cancer stick with his thumb and smoked away.

His train of thought was interrupted by the doorbell ringing.

"We're clo—"

There was no point finishing the phrase.

Pyotr looked just like he had at their first meeting, only his three-piece suit had been replaced by a two-piece number, his blue coat by a black one, and his dress shoes by brogues.

The only things that remained exactly the same about the Syndicate cleaner's appearance were his gloves and the army of tingles his arrival sent marching over Alex's fingertips. Each item of clothing the Adept had on was a top-class artifact.

Tossing the ashes into the sexist tray shaped like a port wench spreading her legs (in keeping with the Schooner's pirate theme), Alex furtively touched the ring on his finger.

"I hope you can make an exception for me, Mr. Dumsky," Pyotr said with the same thick Russian accent that made him sound so threatening despite his polite tone, correct phrasing, and amicable words.

"Sure, Pyotr." Smiling as welcomingly as a black wizard possibly could, Doom pointed at the chair next to his.

"May I?" Pyotr asked and, without waiting for a response, took his coat off and hung it on the rack.

It was the first time Alex was seeing the cleaner without his coat on. The collar of his dress shirt wasn't high enough to hide the thin stripe around the Adept's neck, apparently the top edge of the tattoos covering the muscular body of a seasoned fighter.

Stepping over to Alex's table, Pyotr pulled a chair out with a neat and gentlemanly move and sat down with his back as straight as a sword swallower's. He placed his interlocked fingers on the table, gloves still on.

"Mr. Dumsky." The Russian man's eyes flashed with malice that faded at once. "I'll admit that I'm happy with my job overall. Good pay. Good medical. Plenty of time off. Compared to what I used to make as a public servant in my home country, I'm a wealthy man now."

"I'm happy for you, Pyotr," Alex replied, inhaling again. "Welcome to Atlantis, the island where dreams come true."

"But my job has downsides, too," Pyotr continued, pretending not to hear. "For instance, I recently had to work overtime scouring High Garden for a guy who owes my employer money. I barely slept, and I had to spend time dealing with some rather unpleasant characters instead of relaxing at home sipping tea and reading Bulgakov."

Alex inhaled again. A few magic signs flashed on his ring. What chance did he stand against the Adept? He had a shot if the fight was a brief exchange of two or three spells. But if it lasted longer than that—and it was going to if the artifacts Pyotr had hanging on him like ornaments on a Christmas tree meant anything—things looked much worse.

"…and now, there I was, already resigned to missing out on my quarterly bonus, in the dead of the night, with my sleep mask on and the radio off…"

The radio? Seriously? People still use those things?

"…I get a call on my private line from the Myers City division head and have to hear all the unpleasant things he wants to tell me."

"Comes with the job, Pyotr." Alex knocked his ashes off again, keeping his eyes on Pyotr's hands and, more importantly, his eyes. Skilled wizards are always betrayed by their eyes rather than their hands. Only very young or undereducated wizards cast spells using their fingers. "Mine has some unpleasantries, too. Sometimes I have to throw out drunks, though the silver lining is that I find it to be good practice."

"Sure, Mr. Dumsky. Sure," Pyotr nodded. "Everything has a silver lining. When I was told you were spotted on channel one as a First Magic University professor, there was a positive side. I was able to find you. But I don't really like this new role of yours, so I had a couple rather…barbaric ideas on the ride over here. You'll have to forgive me for enjoying them as much as I did."

"Really? What sorts of ideas?"

"Well, Mr. Dumsky, if you insist… One was to stun you, take you to the port, and torture you there with electricity for a while until you told me why you haven't gotten in touch with the Syndicate for so long."

Alex made a helpless gesture.

"I don't have a phone. Plus, my debt is due by Christmas, and it isn't even Halloween yet."

"That's what stopped me from giving in to my baser instincts. Please take a look at this." Pyotr thrust his hand into his inner pocket. Alex tensed, the runes on his ring flaring up. A few small magic seals appeared where the Russian man couldn't see them.

"Easy, Mr. Dumsky," Pyotr said as he retrieved a small badge looking like the kind worn by anonymous support groups—alcoholics, gamblers, sex addicts…*violent psychos working as hitmen for organized crime.*

There was a number on the badge: *12.*

"Twelve years violence-free?" Doom asked with some hope in his voice.

"Twelve *weeks*, Mr. Dumsky. For twelve weeks I've stayed ahead of my inner beast." Pyotr dropped the badge back into his pocket.

Alex cursed filthily. To himself, of course. He had to keep playing the part.

"But there is, as you so eloquently put it, a silver lining to every cloud. And my employer found one in your mysterious yet…spectacular transformation."

Doom stopped smoking. Instead, he tensed back up as he asked his question.

"What do you mean?"

For the first time ever, he saw Pyotr smile.

"Oh, I think you know *exactly* what I'm talking about."

Alex turned around, puffed out a cloud of smoke, and looked over at his students, still fast asleep thanks to all the alcohol they'd had. And some light black-magic curses.

Yes. That would be better for everyone.

I get rid of the Syndicate debt. No harm comes to the chicklets in the finale. Miss Perriot stays away from me.

Definitely better.

Maybe…

"You're having second thoughts, Mr. Dumsky." Pyotr stood up, signaling an end to the conversation, and went to get his coat. "You'll get further instructions in a letter. And, please, for the sake of your own peace of mind and my badge, don't forget *what* you owe the Syndicate and *who* saved your life down there. I hope this is the last time we meet…Professor."

Pyotr walked out, leaving Alex alone with his memories.

***

It happened during Alex's second week at the underground prison's "extra" level. As a wizard at the 12th Mystic level, he actually shouldn't have been placed in the *living hell* that was the bottom floor of the prison. But some high-ranking officer was apparently dead set on burying Alex as deep as possible despite the fact that he was still a minor.

His first week was fairly peaceful. At least, if peaceful is the right word for sitting alone in a cement cell with no windows, so small that each of the walls is about as wide as the door. There was a tin toilet bowl barely fitting between the two walls, and a bed too narrow for anyone but a skinny kid to fit on was carved into the cement above it.

That was the living hell's quarantine zone where newcomers were locked for a week.

Quarantine was followed by *baptism*: the first visit to the communal shower.

Alex was standing right in the middle.

He was stark naked, armed with a sharpened toothbrush he'd stolen from a prison guard on the way there, and pressing his back against a wall. A dozen inmates stood facing him, short and tall, muscular and boney.

"Fresh meat." One man cracked his neck.

"Grade-A meat," another replied with a nod.

"Should've gone to the women's wing."

"Yeah. Just look at her ass."

"Motherfuckers," Alex said, spitting and gripping his weapon tightly. "Come on. Let's go, bitches. I'll poke holes in every last one of you."

The inmates laughed.

"Hear that, bro? The wench has teeth. She's going to poke us full of holes. Hasn't realized that *she's* the one that's going to get holed. No need for a line, I guess—she'll take two at once."

"Let's just take her teeth out first. She'll suck better that way."

Doom glanced over at the guard, whose back was turned to what was going on in the shower. He was pretending to hear nothing.

The surveillance cameras, judging by the faded lights, were off, too.

Damn cops.

But Doom wasn't going to let them have it easy. He would die to keep his anus as virgin as Mary!

Wincing from the burning pain, Doom prepared for his last fight.

Chapter 60

"Alex! Hey, Alex! Alex! Damn it."

Something wet slapped Alex on the back of his head. Wheeling around, he caught his opponent's arm, grabbed the first thing his groping hand found, and pressed it to his attacker's throat.

"Are you c-c-crazy?"

Alex blinked a few times before putting down the toothpick someone had forgotten on the bar counter.

He was holding Cherry. Her hair was bright orange, her lower lip was pierced, and her feet were sheathed in punk boots. *Why the drastic change?*

Suddenly, Alex remembered her saying something about that two weeks before. Or three? However much time had passed since the tournament's first tour. *Damn the redundancy.*

She'd met some high-school girl on Tinder who played in a post-magic-punk-heavy-apocalypse-rock garage band. Just the description of their genre made Alex feel old, almost like he was twenty-nine instead of his actual twenty-one.

"Sorry," Alex mumbled before turning toward the bar hall.

The Schooner was as crowded as it was every Friday evening. All sorts of people came by to drink, play pool or darts, flirt, and just have fun.

But what made that evening special was that Alex was trying his hand as a bouncer. Once a month, the Schooner turned into a shelter for lost souls wearing blue uniforms with silver stars on their chests.

The cops gathered there to celebrate birthdays and promotions. The Schooner was a convenient choice, located just two blocks away from the central police office. That evening, they were occupying half the bar, everyone congratulating a lean guy in his forties on his promotion to lieutenant and appointment to department head.

Sure, the people on the other side of the line, whose world was black and white, had *gray* souls. And Doom had to pull them apart every once in a while. Staying sober, he had no trouble with a couple drunken men whose reaction time lagged considerably behind their tempers.

Actually, that was his favorite part of the job. He loved it so much that he accepted it as decent compensation for all the inconveniences of being a bar hand at the Schooner and living in the attic.

"Hey, Alex?" Cherry waved the wet towel she'd brought down on the neck of her distracted colleague a couple of seconds before. "Are you high or what?"

"Nope," Doom sighed sadly. "Drinking is more my thing. Right now, I swear by the Abyss, I'd kill for a drink and—"

"...and a fuck," Cherry finished for him while pushing a glass of beer over the bar counter. It was caught by an officer at the far end. "I've heard that once or twice. How long has it been?"

Considering that the sky outside had been completely engulfed by heavy clouds, with a low mist creeping along the streets and passers-by shivering in their warm coats, Myers City's early spring wasn't giving place to a warmer season any time soon. The weather actually looked and smelled more like late autumn.

There were very few tourists around. Some brave souls would be arriving closer to Samhain (known to non-magic people as Halloween) to watch the regular dark parade along Merlin Avenue, the city's main street. It ran from the pompous Empire-style City Council building to Central Park (very similar to the one in the Big Apple).

Once, in his early years, Alex took part in the parade, riding on Robin's shoulders and waving a flag emblazoned with Baba Yaga's symbol.

Real ghosts flew by over his head.

October 31st is the day when the border between the realms of the living and dead becomes the thinnest. In the whole world. But it's only thin enough to pass through in Atlantis.

And that was why the whole island accepted martial law for the day. Not all of its inhabitants were in Myers City—many lived in small towns, on farms, and even in villages. Atlantis had lots of those.

If it weren't for the Dark Parade headed by the Shadow Council's ambassador...

Alex didn't want to think about that.

A ghost breakthrough into the real world would have caused too much trouble for light and dark wizards alike.

Thinking of ghosts as merely the imprints of dead people's souls was a mistake.

Truthfully, they *are* imprints. But not of the soul. They're the very last feeling the person experienced before death.

Not all feelings are calm or neutral. The stronger the emotion, the more powerful the ghost.

Knowing as much as he did about necromancy, Doom had an excellent idea of the damage ghosts like that could do. Especially if they were formed by vengeance.

It wasn't so bad if the vengeance was aimed at a single person or family. It was worse when the whole of humanity found itself in the crosshairs.

And that's just human ghosts. Things got really bad when it was a creature summoned by the dying emotions of an orc drug addict. Definitely not nearly as cute as the Stay Puft Marshmallow Man, who was eventually destroyed by just four nerds and a green poltergeist.

"*What the hell?*" Cherry snapped her fingers right in front of Alex's nose. "What's up with you today? Are you that nervous about the second tour?"

Oh, yes. The second tour. The day after tomorrow. At the Arena. The great stadium that had hosted performances by music legends like Lady Gel, Pop Floyd, Little Mephisto, and other groups and singers Alex had never heard of.

Thanks to Robin and Anastasia, he only listened to old-school rock from the 2000s and 2010s, sometimes even twentieth-century rock dinosaurs.

Sadly, rock in the modern world seemed to be dead. Or maybe twitching in its final throes of agony somewhere deep underground.

According to the official statistics, fewer people listened to rock than listened to symphony orchestras.

What a tragedy.

"…been like that the whole night!"

Alex shook his head and blinked twice. He'd thought he was standing in the hall watching the cops celebrating, but he realized he was actually in the Schooner's kitchen, its holy of holies. That was where Diglan worked his magic, both metaphorically and literally. No one but the one-legged pirate was usually allowed in. All the slicing, dicing, pouring, frying, boiling, and sprinkling devices worked on their own, leaving Diglan with nothing to do but taste the food when it was ready.

The Schooner's clientele came for the great dining as well as the drinks.

"Thank you for agreeing, Alex," the boss said with a grateful nod.

"No pro—… Hey, wait! *What* did I agree to?"

"You said you'd take Archibald, my son, to the theme park tomorrow. I can't do it myself—I'll be hosting some important visitors who want to talk…and pad their pockets. The inspectors."

"Archibald…" The name rang a bell for Alex. "The ten-year-old brat from your marriage?"

"He isn't a *brat*. He's my son." For the first time in his six weeks of employment, Alex saw Diglan's eyes flash with anger. "And I'm really happy his mother and that wimp of a stepfather are letting me see him this time without me taking them to court."

The story of Diglan and his ex-wife was an ugly, if standard one. They met in college. Neither had anything. He wanted a better life for her. She was fine with that.

But for what he wanted (and what he did to accomplish it), Diglan found himself in prison, where he lost a leg. The underground prison was far, far worse in the old days.

His first stint wasn't actually that long—just seven months. His wife (Rebecca or Becca, though Alex wasn't sure) never came to visit him. Once out, Diglan learned that she'd married his roommate two weeks after he'd been found guilty. Diglan's son, Archibald, was born a month later. It had taken Diglan almost eight years in court to see him for the first time.

Life in Myers City was hard on ex-cons. And even harder on wizard ex-cons.

Doom had learned all that about his employer when Diglan got drunk on Archie's birthday and told it to a gleaming gift box on his lap. That was yet another day when he was kept from seeing his son—Becca-Rebecca had taken him to visit her parents in Old Earth.

"What's in it for me?" Alex couldn't have cared less about Diglan's reasons, be they related to business or anything else. *Maybe he doesn't love the boy as much as he says, otherwise he'd make time for him.* The fact that Doom was in charge of a bunch of adolescents didn't make him the new Mother Teresa.

"A week off work."

"Um…" Doom mumbled at being offered a month of free rent in the Schooner's attic.

Why a month? Because…

"A month," Alex said.

"What?"

"A month."

"What do you mean?"

"I mean a month," Doom replied, rolling his eyes. The ask-me-raccoon game seemed to picking up steam in Myers City. "Thirty-one days off work. Well, I can make it thirty for you in exchange for some spending money. A hundred credits should work."

"So…you want a *month* off instead of a week? *And* a hundred credits on top of that?!"

"Exactly," Alex said with a calm nod. "Or you can get another babysitter. Not a highly-qualified Black Magic Professor at First Magic University, a full-fledged dark wizard, a fifth-rank necromancer, a fifth-rank blood magician, a fourth-rank malefic wizard, a third-rank sorcerer, and…well, just a nice guy. Me."

Diglan winced.

"Damn major."

"Oh, I'm with you there."

Cherry shifted her gaze between the two of them, then asked a question.

"What major?"

Damn raccoons.

Chapter 61

"Can I ride the roller coaster?"

Alex, looking as if he were carrying a cement cross toward Golgotha, waved a hand to transfer the remaining twenty credits to the boy.

"You can even stay there for the night," he mumbled.

"My dad wouldn't like that."

Alex was about to yell that his dad's heart could be devoured by hell's worms but contained himself. He needed a month off at the Schooner.

"Go, you pirate spawn."

"Thanks, Uncle Alex!" Archie quickly hugged Doom (who was still wondering how the boy had come to have an uncle with the same name) and dashed off toward the line for the roller coaster.

It didn't matter that the boy was ten and the roller coaster ride required adult supervision for kids younger than 16. The fast-developing youngster was just two heads shorter than Doom (not surprising, considering what a big man Diglan was) and easily mistaken for a very skinny young adult.

"I hope the voluntarily childless are allowed to cut in the line for heaven," Doom whispered to himself.

The theme park situated atop the causeway stretching along Amalgam Street Beach was packed that bright Saturday afternoon. (The same could not be said about the beach, empty but for a few surfers in wetsuits and even fewer freezing, goosebump-bespeckled Instagram models in bikinis.) In the crowd of noisy, yelling kids and their noisy, yelling moms, Doom felt like he was in Dante's hell. Although that version of hell had nothing in common with the real abyss, it still made him uneasy.

So uneasy that Alex kept his hands in the pockets of his (formerly Gribovsky's) shabby jeans. Slipping his hood over his head, he approached a small kiosk.

"Ice cream? Soda?" a pretty girl of about fifteen asked him. She was below the legal age, but Doom couldn't have cared less. It had been over four years since he'd last bedded a girl, and that felt totally crazy.

"One coffee," he said through gritted teeth. No time at all for the brown-eyed girl with very big... pupils. "Black. Strong. Dark roast. If you have virgin blood, throw some in there."

"We don't serve vampires." The girl, apparently a high-school student working there part-time after classes, instantly pulled back into the depths of the kiosk.

Alex didn't hear her at first. When it sank in, he cursed—it was early spring, and the sun hardly ever showed above the city. Vampires could use that kind of weather to walk among the living.

"There's not a cloud in the sky," he said, pointing up. "I'm not a vampire. And virgin blood…"

The girl's blush intensified, telling Alex that the cute young thing with the big…*pupils* had never been with a man.

Right, I'm not in High Garden. It's completely different here.

"I'm no bloodsucker." Alex showed her his left wrist, which was missing the magic seal the city government placed on all undead.

For three gold Abyss coins, you could have the seal completely removed. But that wasn't something anyone shared with outsiders.

"One black coffee." The schoolgirl, now pale and distant, placed the cup down. "A credit and a half."

"A credit and a half?!" Alex replied, all but collapsing in shock. "For *that* much money, I—"

"Hey, kid, let's go! You're holding up the line!"

"Yeah, hurry up. Take your coffee and move!"

Slowly, Doom turned to the fat man addressing him and noticed the mother of his (surprisingly lean) kid on his arm. Alex already had a couple ideas for how to curse the couple when—

"It's on me." the words came with a peach-and-daisy smell, and a wave of peach hair drifted past his eyes.

Shit.

"Come on, Professor." Taking the cup as the whole line watched, Miss Perriot walked toward a table canopied by a giant umbrella, pointless in the cool weather. Just as pointless as Alex refusing her.

The esper was dressed appropriately for the weather in jeans, sneakers, a warm coat, and a pink pullover. But even in her oversized clothes she looked stunning enough to make several guys stumble as they walked by. One even dropped his ice cream…

"Oh, sorry, dear. I guess I was daydreaming."

…right onto his girlfriend's shoe.

"Daydreaming? About what?"

"Um…that giant inflatable bear. You've got to have big lungs to blow that thing."

"They're *pumped*, not blown. Shit. My new shoes!"

Doom took his cup and glanced inside.

"I thought you didn't like coffee," Leia said, adjusting her peach hair. The color was far from the weirdest or creepiest body modification espers went for. Doom had once met an esper guy who had small tentacles in his eye sockets. *That* had been wild.

"I don't."

"Then why—"

Waiting for the moment when the fat couple with their skinny kid were walking by, Alex overturned his cup.

As though by magic (somewhat black magic), the drink didn't spill onto the table. Instead, the liquid dumped over the couple's heads, producing screaming and yelling.

"A bit of relief," Alex said as he exhaled and leaned back in his chair. "They were getting under my skin back in the ticket line."

Leia kept drinking her latte with a neutral facial expression as she watched the couple trying to wipe each other clean with paper napkins.

"That's kind of pet—"

She stopped short when she noticed that the stains weren't wiping off. As the couple worked, they just spread to take the shape of obscene words and symbols.

"Oh lo—" Leia stopped herself again. "Oh, excuse me."

"It's okay," Doom replied with a wave. He was in no mood for another argument with Leia.

"Is it really that painful?"

"Have you ever been burned with an iron?"

"Um… When I was little, I touched a boiling kettle by accident. My mom hated electric kettles, so she used a plain steel one to boil water for cezve over the stove."

"For cezve? I thought real coffee fiends boiled the water right in that thing."

"That was another of her quirks," Leia replied with a disarming smile.

Blowing on her coffee, she took a sip, holding the cup with both hands and both pinkies in the air. It was adorable.

"Ten times as much."

"As much as what? And…why look under the table?"

"Raccoon check."

"*What?*"

"Never mind," Alex replied. "Symbols of faith being held to my body hurt me ten times as much as a red-hot iron. Hearing words of faith is six times as painful."

Their eyes met. Alex could tell that Perriot understood—he knew how much red-hot irons hurt by experience.

That was his rite of passage into the Tkils gang. Alex had the scars to prove it, just like many other things in his life.

"Every time you hear them? Oh go—… Oh. Excuse me." Leia hastily cupped her mouth with a hand, but Alex just waved again.

"No, not every time." He slipped both hands into his jeans pockets and spread over the chair back like a spineless amoeba. "Only when they're coming from a *true* believer."

He glanced at the thin silver chain peeking out from beneath Leia's collar. She automatically touched the spot where the cross probably was, hidden by her clothes.

"What are you doing in the park?" she asked, apparently to change the subject.

Doom shrugged.

"I could ask you the same."

"I asked first," Leia smiled.

"Are you flirting with me?" Doom arched his right brow, and the esper's smile faded instantly.

"Just keeping up the small talk."

"Small talk?" Doom repeated. The damn raccoon seemed to have infected him too. "Well then. What am I doing here? Taking my boss' kid on a Saturday walk because his dad's occupied by the worm of bribery as it gnaws its way through the heart of our glorious city."

"The opposition manifesto. Word for word."

"I always liked those idiots. Let's bring down the government! Freedom of association and assembly! From each according to something, to each according to something else. Anarcho-Communists. That's what they really are."

Leia said nothing.

The majority of opposition members were espers.

"So," Alex said, holding up his hands, "I answered your question. Now, Miss Perriot, would you please be so kind as to answer mine? *Why have you been following me since I left the Schooner?*"

Chapter 62

urning grip, street

Tat the first intersection while enduring Archie's death Alex had spotted the BMWi, conspicuous among the traffic and apparently following him.

It turned out that Miss Perriot wasn't just an expert in invisible makeup; she also knew luxury magic sports cars. And she was a great driver.

On the ring road, he tried to shake her off his tail several times without giving away that he knew she was there, but he couldn't make it happen. And he was someone who'd spent his entire childhood and adolescence racing, either as a chaser or a chasee. The second role tended to be more common for him with the increased prevalence of the cops. Damn city mayor and his idea of hiring more blue uniforms.

"You knew?" Leia flashed surprise before hiding her eyes by looking down at her cup. "Sure, a black wizard from Old Earth must get a gut feeling when they're being watched. I heard you even revived the Inquisition over there."

The Inquisition. Another broad topic for discussion.

"Please don't change the subject, Miss Perriot. Yes, I saw you. Although both of us are nearly outlawed thanks to our innate gifts, I'm still not much into girls chasing me. I'd rather have it the other way around. And when I'm almost run down by a car that descended, however remotely, from the ones they assembled in Nazi concentration camps, my national pride takes a hit, as well."

"You hate BMW?"

"Honestly," Alex said with a frown, "I adore them. I used to drive one myself until I wrecked it. Since then, I've only had Aston Martins."

Leia smiled slightly. Every judge of city sports cars worth their salt knew that racing an Aston Martin was like…coming to a gun fight not even with a knife, but with a banana peel. All you can do is hope someone gets hurt slipping on it.

"I had no idea the black wizards on Old Earth were so well-off. Then—"

"*Stop* changing the subject," Alex interrupted. "Let's start again. *Why* were you following me?"

They had a brief staring contest. Alex knew the popular belief that you're not supposed to look a witch in the eyes. Or a black wizard for that matter. But Leia was neither a witch nor a female wizard. An esper is…kind of the bald man's accomplice from that X-logo movie. A magical mutant, to put it simply.

As for Alex, he'd only learned about his other magic source (apart from his black magic one) recently and didn't want to call on it unless absolutely needed. Every time he did, he disturbed the sharp, broken shards of memory that sat so deeply in his heart.

On the other hand, the pain they caused reminded Alex he still *had* a heart.

"I was leaving work—"

"On a Saturday?" Alex interrupted.

Leia squinted.

"Are you interrogating me?"

A young family walked by their table right then, the father and mother in their late twenties, the nice little girl wearing brightly colored sneakers and holding cotton candy. The expression of pure joy on her face disgusted Alex.

If he'd been an old-school wizard, he would have cursed her cotton candy to taste like swamp water.

Leia comparing him to an interrogating cop got to Alex.

"Forgive me," he said sincerely, apparently shocking and disarming her. "I didn't mean to."

"Um…" The esper was at a loss for words. "Never mind. What was I saying? Oh yes. As I was leaving work, I saw you with the boy. No, I didn't think you were a pedophile, and I didn't think you were going to sacrifice him, either. That's Archie, right? Diglan's son?"

Alex was about to ask a question but checked himself. Leia had been working at First Magic University for a while. It wasn't surprising that she would know about the Schooner and even the name and some personal information of the owner.

Archie sometimes, if seldomly visited his father at the Schooner. The ex-wife did everything she could to keep the boy away from Diglan.

"What happened next?"

"You don't have a phone."

"And?"

With a heavy sigh, Leia put her cup down on the table.

"It may be difficult for you to imagine or understand, but I just wanted to discuss some business with you."

That sounded simple. Really simple. Even *too* simple. And that was why it was unlikely to be a lie. It wasn't Doom's detective skills telling him that; it was just the practical wisdom he'd picked up in prison. *When you're in jail, you either learn to judge character or spiral down, messing with the wrong kinds.*

The same happens on the outside, actually. Just not as obviously.

"What business can't wait till Mond— Ah, yes. The tournament."

Leia nodded.

"The opening ceremony is held tomorrow, and the second tour, too. You know what's going to happen there, don't you?"

"The monster hunt," Alex replied.

Perriot sighed.

"I'm not surprised that you'd have inside info. Or at least it's *supposed* to be inside."

Not for people privileged to wear the Guards' collar bracelet. A few words whispered to Gribovsky had been enough for Alex to have him pull all the threads together and get the scoop on each tour. Of course, he'd shared that with his group.

"That could have been expected, anyway." Leia ran her finger along the brim of her cup. "Since the last Magic War, the number of urban monster attacks has been on the rise, in New and Old Earth alike."

It was true. The icy giants invading Vancouver and the river dragons infesting the Shinano Prefecture in Japan were just two of many recent incidents.

The world was growing more and more dangerous with each passing day. Many of the attacking monsters were resistant to non-magic firearms.

"So, you wanted to find out what the arrangements are for the second tour? Now you know."

"No, I didn't. Or rather, I wanted to know more than that. I wanted to ask if you're ready."

"Us? If you mean the B-52 kids, they are. I prepped them."

It was absolutely true, just not exactly the way Leia was sure to think. *Lie by telling the truth.* It was an art where black wizards were superior even to the fae who invented it.

"Great," Perriot replied, exhaling in obvious relief. "Please forgive me for flaring up at you back there at the Schooner. That's just...just me really caring about them. I've known them since they were kids. We're almost family. And this tournament is their only chance."

Mine, too, Alex thought without saying it aloud.

"Take Travis, for instance." Leia peered into her cup, probably seeing pictures from the past in the milk bubbles. "He hopes the finale broadcast and winner announcement will get him seen and found by his parents. The winners' pictures and names will be *everywhere*—on TV, on the radio, in the papers, all over the web. And he thinks... Well, you can probably empathize."

Alex could.

"Mara is a half-blood in a dwarf clan made up of Atlantis' best blacksmiths. Can you imagine how she feels there? She wants to prove she's worthy of her family name so they'll stop looking down on her father as a blood traitor. It's a bit naïve, but it's noble, too."

I'd call it stupid.

"Elie's situation is similar. Born out of wedlock. A Cinderella, just without the happy ending. And the prince."

"I heard she has a boyfriend."

"Daryl?" Leia smiled sadly and only with her eyes. "He never existed. She invented him. Upper-class boys and girl look down on Elie like—"

"Got it," Alex interrupted. He realized in a moment that surprised him that he didn't want hear the B-52 blonde called a slut or anything like that.

It was probably just that he was exhausted from walking with Archie.

"Jing wants to let the world know his shaman line continues. And tell them who killed all his kin—"

Leia stopped short once again. Alex said nothing.

He understood Jing's reasons, too.

Perhaps better than anyone else's. Probably better than anyone else.

Although he wished he didn't.

"And Leo…he just really loves his friends. They're all he has. His family. And Leonard feels the same way."

Alex almost shuddered at the mention of the weird wizard/esper's other personality. He wondered why Stone was still out there with his friends instead of being dissected in some top-secret government lab.

For the common good, obviously.

Isn't that what the Light Ones always do? Make some suffer for everyone else's benefit?

The Dark Ones were no better. But at least they never denied pursuing their personal benefit in the first place.

Doom had never hidden behind the common good.

Everything he did was for himself.

For his own sake.

Everything.

"That's some really valuable info," Doom said, nodding. "Totally worth cosplaying Mad Max in the city streets to tell me."

Leia looked up at him.

Her stare was evil.

"Every time," she started in a curt, harsh voice. "Every time I start to think you're not that bad, you—"

"Stop."

"Don't you—"

"*Shut up!*" Alex barked.

He didn't know what made her obey—raising his voice at her for the very first time, how rude he was, or something else. Regardless, she fell silent.

Doom closed his eyes and sniffed the air.

Bitch. Why here? Why now?

He smelled sulfur.

Chapter 63

He heard people shouting. The peaceful, festive atmosphere was gone in a moment.

Some electric generators exploded with characteristic crackling sounds. Columns of black smoke billowed up into the sky. Alex smelled burning plastic, paper, fabric, and, most unpleasantly, flesh. Everyone was running and screaming.

Alex saw the same nice little girl with the cotton candy kneeling and crying as she tried to wake her father, who was prostrate in front of her, covering her mother with his body.

Like hell she'll ever wake him up. Even Alex couldn't raise an undead from a man who'd been cut in half by an axe.

A shadow fell on the girl, cast by something eight feet tall. Hoofed legs covered in black, shabby hair. A mighty torso, bulging muscles brimming with the energy of Chaos beneath parchment-like skin. A bull's head with a black mane topped by goat horns.

A black battleax clutched in clawed paws.

A demon from a first-century legion. A puny creature unworthy of Alex's attention.

…if it had arrived in the world alone. But the chaos that had engulfed the theme park in a matter of seconds was wreaked by *dozens* of hellish creatures looking exactly like that one.

With a wild roar, creepier even than bestial, the demon lifted its axe over the little girl, though it never brought it down. Its torso was bound by a rope, its arms were twisted around its broken neck, and the soaring axe slashed the demon in two.

Alex turned to Leia. Pallid, she froze like a statue, hand outstretched and small trickles of blood coming from her nose and eyes.

A D-ranked esper killing a demon in a single move (albeit apparently expending all her strength to do it)? Alex wouldn't have believed it if he hadn't witnessed it.

The way he just had.

"Give me your phone," Alex barked.

Leia flung it onto the table and rushed for the girl. Picking the child up and glancing around, she dashed off in the direction opposite the largest group of demons.

About fifteen big, horned monsters were smashing everything in their path. Bloody pieces of flesh soared into the sky. Crimson rain washed down on the cobblestones. Shredded tents covered the dead bodies and their severed parts. Dozens and hundreds of men, women, and children perished at the paws of the marching fiends of hell.

A few demons separated from the rest and came over toward Alex, who was dialing a number over and over on the smartphone screen.

"O...u...r...s...," one of the demons said, sniffing at him. "O...r...n...o...t..."

Obviously, it spoke Demonic. But, as a pathetic first-century creature, it was a very bad speaker, sounding something like a chimpanzee trying to explain itself to a professor.

After taking a few more sniffs, the demon and its peers turned around and walked away.

Alex finally remembered the number he needed.

"Hi," he said into the phone.

"Doom? You scum!" came Gribovsky's panting voice. "Are you fucking crazy, calling me from—"

Whatever else he said was barely audible. To avoid getting distracted by the screaming and occasional spell flashes coming from the people who remembered they were *wizards* and not completely helpless, Alex covered his other ear with his hand.

"...state number! Destroy the phone!"

"Here, in the theme park—"

"We know!" Gribobsky bellowed. "We're on our way!"

Alex took another glance around. Just the demons he could see numbered over fifty, and there were probably more.

Damn.

He'd never heard of so many invading that layer of reality at the same time. It was supposed to be impossible.

It was almost as if the border between worlds and turned from a solid stone wall into a colander.

Samhain.

The approaching festival date made it possible.

"I hope you're bringing the army," Alex said into the phone before flinging it over his shoulder without hanging up. Right into the water.

"No!" someone screamed.

Doom turned toward the sound, but it was already too late.

Stupid, stupid girl.

Hiding in the kiosk shadow wasn't the best survival tactic. The demon's axe easily slashed through the wood and sparse steel, cutting the kiosk—and the schoolgirl with it—in half.

The upper half of her body flopped through the air, landed on the cobblestones, and slid right up to Alex's feet, leaving a trail of blood behind it.

Her glassy eyes were printed eternally with primal fear and utter bewilderment. She was supposed to be back in school on Monday. There was homework waiting for her at home. And her crush, her one love was dating another girl. How did death by demonic axe possibly fit into that picture?

Her emotions were still in the air, her soul gradually departing to the place no one ever came back from.

Ghosts are not souls.

"Forgive me," Alex whispered, squatting in front of her and running two fingers across the ground to collect her blood on his fingertips. He did his best not to touch her disemboweled entrails.

It was uncommon for black wizards to be clean and tidy. Alexander Dumsky was just such an exception.

Virgin blood had special power. It wasn't that sex makes people unclean. No, it's that a tiny, almost imperceptible particle of your partner's aura is added to your own, making your blood unusable for some magic rituals.

Alex ran his two blooded fingers over the dead girl's glassy eyes. It was pure blood that had only known parental warmth, eyes that had witnessed the last moment of death. And truth that was still in the air.

He tensed his fingers and stuck them into the dead body's eye socket, pulling a bloody eye out.

Black magic is never clean no matter how much some people wish it were.

Straightening up, Alex wrung his hands together and whispered the words of the ancient rite. Creating a magic seal by willpower in front of himself, he placed the dead eye right in the middle.

[ATTENTION! Prohibited spell used: DEAD MAIDEN'S GLARE of the Blood and Darkness School. Mana consumption: N/A. Code: 1A. Top Hazard. The authorized agencies have been informed in keeping with the Act...]

Alex stopped reading the lens message.

A breakthrough like the one he was facing could never have happened spontaneously. Not one on such a biblical scale.

To support the passage for the hordes of demons, the summoner had to be nearby. Somewhere very close to Alex. Cloaked in such a powerful illusion that Doom couldn't even *feel* its presence. A magic disguise of that level couldn't be penetrated by an ordinary spell.

Only a dark-magic ritual would do the trick.

And out of all the options the black magic wonder kid knew, the Dead Maiden's Glare was the best for the situation.

Given the fact that the ritual required a human sacrifice, you could be jailed up to twelve months just for studying it.

And practicing it…

But until the summoner was stopped, there was no point destroying the demons marching into the world by the scores and hundreds.

The Dark Ones don't do anything for the common good. Or do they?

Calling on his black magic source, Alex filled the spell with energy. A black-and-red seal flashed as magic streaming along its lines, soaking into the dead girl's eye hanging in midair. The eye swirled violently around its axis before stopping abruptly, staring up into the sky over the middle of the theme park. A whitish ray shot up into the air.

"There you are," Alex said with a bloodthirsty smile when the illusion broke down, revealing the black wizard standing on the giant raven's back. "This time I'll get you."

Chapter 64

Their glances met. Alex's green eyes crossed the glowing coal-red stare from the slits in the steel mask that concealed the demonologist's face.

The seal opening the gate into hell was floating in the sky, which was why Alex hadn't been able to detect it.

Demons came jumping out, one after another. The Mask kept his arms spread, the energy of Chaos streaming from them in long filaments. Demon magic.

That channel had to be broken.

A cigarette jumped into Alex's lips at the same moment as several magic seals flashed behind his back. The sparks from the burning tobacco came raining down toward the ground only to be intercepted by an invisible force and plunged into the seals.

Doom had never liked the spell he was about to use. It was too heavy. Too bulky, too cumbersome.

But it was also the farthest-reaching one he had, making it his only option right then. The Mask was a good mile away.

Just as the Bloody Lightning Rain was about to shoot off, the Mask suddenly nodded toward the side.

With an evil foreboding, Alex looked over in that direction.

Scraping the sky at the very edge of the mountain ridge (and of the park) was the monstrous Ferris wheel built to surpass even the London Eye. The white construction with its multi-colored capsules took half an hour to make a full rotation, and you could easily see the fields stretching far outside Myers City from the top.

But right then, the whole Ferris wheel was covered in clumps of climbing demons. And that wasn't the worst of it.

There was a different creature jumping across the capsules from roof to roof. Ten feet tall, hoofed and horned, it combined a human torso and arms with a bull's head. Its skin was brown, not the usual parchment color, and only visible in the gaps between its chainmail armor, shoulder and arm plates, and many hanging chains.

Fluttering behind the demon's back was a violet cloak and braided white hair. Its giant horns and both blades of its battleax were covered in glowing red runes.

A second-century legion demon.

The worst news of the day.

Actually, no, not the worst.

The monster moved purposeful, as though it was hunting someone. Someone sitting alone at the very top of the wheel.

Suddenly, the wheel jammed. The visitors' screams were heard through the fiberglass plastic shielding them from the wind.

And Archibald's scream was among them.

Alex turned toward the Mask. He couldn't see through the mask, but he was sure the bastard was smiling.

Damn.

If he didn't save the boy, he definitely wasn't getting his month off. Diglan wasn't going to be happy with his son getting devoured by some demon.

Black wizards do nothing for the common good. Just for themselves.

Doom reached for the phone Leia had left, but…

Bitch.

…he'd already tossed it in the water! *Well, let's hope Gribovsky and company are smart enough to take out a wanted terrorist hovering in the sky on a giant raven.*

"I've always wanted to try this."

Alex waved a hand, giving off a barely visible blade of black mist that took off the bolted metal top of the table where he and Leia had so recently been drinking coffee.

He inhaled deeply before flinging his cigarette under the table top and standing on it with both feet, exposing the contrast between his ArmaniMagico shoes and Gribovsky's casual outfit.

Sending the energy from both his sources into the smoldering cigarette, Alex simultaneously activated the levitation spell in his shoes.

A huge explosion hit his ears and tossed the tabletop with Doom, now almost weightless, up into the air. Instantly thirty feet in the air, he hurtled toward the Ferris wheel.

The shouts were muffled by the altitude and wind. Alex could still hear the music playing over the park loudspeakers. *Wow. Looks like their DJ has good taste.*

The song was Made for This by the old City Wolf.

"Bitch," Alex swore, remembering the lyrics. "I'm coming to fuck you!"

Several heartbeats later, it became painfully obvious that the tabletop wasn't even going to make it halfway there, so Doom activated another spell: the Air Walk. Its reach was just sixty feet but, combined with the active levitation, it enabled him to soar once more into the sky and fly some 150 feet before falling like a rag doll onto the roof of the cabin where Archibald was huddled up in the corner.

Unfortunately for Doom, the roof was slanted. Failing to grab hold of anything, he rolled head over heels, his momentum carrying him toward the edge. He slipped off, only to catch at the last moment a small handrail obviously used by window washers. Hitting the fiberglass with his whole body, he spread-eagled over it.

"Uncle Alex?" came a muffled voice from inside. Archibald must have been screaming at the top of his lungs for Doom to hear him.

"Hey, kid," Alex groaned. "The show's a killer, yeah?"

Winking at the shocked boy (to encourage himself more than Archie), Doom pulled himself back up onto the roof. He was greeted by the sight of the Capricorn leader towering one roof below.

From that close, the demon's grotesque body looked...even more grotesque.

Almost 1,000 feet above the ground, Alex stood facing a second-century legion demon, a monster almost as strong as the one Gribovsky had defeated in the late smuggler's shop.

"You...not...my...prey..." The demon's words were barely audible through all its growling and mooing. "Leave...my...hunt..."

Like it was nothing, Alex shook another cancer stick out of his eternal pack. He inhaled and brought his palms together.

"I need this kid *alive*," he said in an icy voice. "Bad news for you, goat."

Alex's sleeves flashed with lilac fire and melted away. The magic symbols tattooed on his forearms glowed bright, his palms gleaming with otherworldly energy. When he spread them, the threads of Chaos energy formed a spindle that instantly transformed into a five-foot, blood-red staff.

Alex twirling the staff overhead, straightened up, and thrust it into the roof by his side. Like a wizard from an old book of fairy tales.

A black wizard.

"Come on, you big cow. Let's see who's stronger."

The demon growled, pushed off the roof with hoofs that left it rocking like an autumn leaf, and took a crazy leap.

"Attacking a wizard with an axe? Are you *that* dumb?"

Alex slammed his demonic staff against the capsule roof.

[ERROR. ERROR. Structure cannot be recognized. The authorized agencies have been informed.]

Chapter 65

In a direct confrontation, outside the museum full of artifacts, unaccompanied by his Polish partner with his giant sword, and without an ace up his sleeve (like the single bullet the movie pirate kept over all his lonely years on the island), Doom didn't stand a chance against a second-century legion demon.

He was going to have to prevail through craft and trickery. When the giant cow leaped at him, brandishing the axe, Alex stayed where he was to dispel suspicion and lightly tapped the roof with his staff. The move caused neither an explosion of terrifying spells nor a stream of red demonic fire.

Instead, a harmless but very bright red light hit the demon's eyes. The infernal creature was taken aback, giving the seasoned black wizard enough time to gain an edge.

Holding out his left hand (and keeping the staff in his right), Alex said a few words, not to cast a spell but to refresh his memory. He'd last used the spell as a kid when he was playing with his friends at Follen School.

No seals came from his fingers (the spell was very low-level). Instead, trickles of green slime spread over the capsule. When the blinded demon landed on the slimy surface, it slipped right off the roof.

Alex peered over the edge to watch the demon land on one of the metal posts. The sharp end pierced its groin.

"That must hurt like the dickens," Alex said, wincing, before squatting and called on his other source, the one full of chaos and disturbance. "But unlikely to keep it for long."

The remnants of slime on his left palm vanished in a flash of red fire (with occasional flashes of colors beyond the rainbow inside). Doom ran his blazing hand over the metal roof. At his touch, the steel didn't just melt; it *disappeared*, instantly turning to gray ash carried away by the wind.

"Grab my hand!" Alex yelled, reaching into the gap.

"Are you crazy?!" the boy yelled back.

Alex didn't get it at first. Then, muttering a swear word, he extinguished the flames on his palm. He'd never learned the art of rescuing kids from fucking demons.

Archie deserved full credit for taking a firm grip of his hand once it was cleansed of demonic fire. His grip was so firm, in fact, that Alex gritted his teeth in pain.

The boy's mom had apparently never taught him how to clip his nails.

And she wasn't doing it for him.

Yanking Archie out onto the roof, Doom gave him a quick once-over.

"Five foot four inches," he whispered.

"*Five* inches," Archibald corrected proudly.

Who in their right mind would name their son Archibald? Names like that should come with a throne. A porcelain throne would have been perfect for Archie right then considering how pale he was. Still, he was putting a brave face on it.

"Did you have breakfast?"

"No. Why do you ask?" The boy was growing even paler. Although he couldn't see the climbing demon, he could feel the wheel rock under its weight.

"Magic relies on precise calculations, Archie." Alex turned thoughtful, dozens of formulae and calculation tables darting before his mind's eye.

"Uncle Alex!" Archibald leaped back, pointing at something behind Doom. Wasting no time turning around, Alex just trusted his ears. They reported a metal clang, then a loud screech. It had to have been the big cow sending its axe crashing through the capsule roof and almost getting up.

"Don't bother me, kid..." Alex smacked his staff against the roof again, spending another portion of strength from his demonic source and leaving around 200 points. He was down to about a quarter of his total capacity. Behind him, the searchlight flashed again, flooding the space around them with a bright red light.

"...when I'm inventing a new spell on the go," Doom finished. Wasting not a second more, he took a running start and, picking the screaming Archie up, leaped off the edge of the capsule edge. In the process, he also extinguished the glowing tattoos on his forearms, dispelled the red staff, and lifted a hand to send some energy from his black-magic source to the seal forming above him.

The sky and the ground stopped battling to see who would end up on top. The air stopped whistling past his ears. The only thing disturbing Doom's zen was Archibald's yelling.

His forced partner had at least one thing going for him: the volume he could command would have put a fire alarm to shame.

"We're falling!" the boy bellowed.

"Just flying downward," Doom said through gritted teeth.

As a black wizard, he hated lots of things. The fae. White bed sheets. Teddy bears. Demons with giant battleaxes jumping over enormous Ferris wheels like mountain goats in an attempt to get down to the ground faster than a levitating wizard.

But the thing he hated most was children screaming.

"What's with the Smurf head?" Archibald pointed up at the huge blue air balloon hovering over Doom's seal. "What if it doesn't work and we die?"

The great inflatable ball created by Doom's magic really did look like a Smurf, only with a black hat instead of the white one and a gaping maw with yellow fangs in place of the bright, shiny smile. Also, the eyes were more like a vampire's.

However, they were unlikely to die—there was still a second left in the levitation spell in Alex's shoes. Enough for them to survive.

"Kid, you're asking too much from an improvis—"

Doom felt a tingling sensation in his fingertips, though there was nothing he could do about it. His best option was to drop the oversized ten-year-old's dead weight and dodge the big cow's blow. But that would have meant saying goodbye to his month-long vacation and wasting all the effort he'd already put into saving the kid.

"Hold on!" Alex screamed, dismissing the spell. He unclenching his fingers to let the giant, black-magic Smurf air balloon fly away, getting smaller and smaller until it disappeared up into the sky.

The two of them, still some thirty feet above the ground, dropped like rocks. Alex gritted his teeth again, that time the anger coupled with pain.

The red wave washing off the big cow's axe blade cut his hand, albeit slightly. Clutching Archie to his chest, Doom's blood drizzled onto the boy.

Like any other black wizard, he tended to be pretty conscious of keeping his blood to himself.

Particularly when falling head-first right onto hard cobblestones.

Chapter 66

In the split-second before what would have been a lethal impact, Alex activated the last bit of levitation in his shoes. That cushioned the impact, keeping it from killing them if still leaving it awfully unpleasant.

Alex hit the cobblestones with his back, a zombically (if that's even a real word) pale Archibald clutched to his chest, and rolled with him to crash into a trader's cart abandoned by its owner.

Funny as it may seem, a small bucket of popcorn, someone's last order, was still on the counter. There was a bloody palm print splayed prominently on the side.

"Hide behind the cart!" Alex shouted, pointing behind his back.

Thank the abyss, Archie obeyed without arguing. He crawled beneath the cart to hide behind a large tank of fizzy water probably diluted with the plain stuff. Or maybe not, judging by the sky-high prices featured on the holographic sign.

"You won't be needing this." Doom reached for a woman's arm stretching out from beneath a smoldering tent enshrouding a bunch of human (and non-human) bodies. In one sharp movement, he ripped the sleeve off and, using his other hand and teeth, wrapped it around the wound left by the big cow's blow.

The flow of blood slowed but didn't stop. And there wasn't time for Alex to work any more magic.

"Why didn't anyone tell me this was the kind of entertainment they have here?" Alex sighed indignantly as he watched the giant demon leap off the Ferris wheel. It landed on its right knee, buckling the cobblestones to form a small crater. "Like some fucking movie superhero."

Whenever Alex was in grave danger, he chattered on and cracked his jokes. That helped him stay focused.

The demon straightened up, spread its upper paws, and uttered a powerful roar. So powerful, in fact, that a few smelly, sticky drops of saliva landed on Doom's face thirty feet away.

"Damn." Doom wiped his face with the edge of the sleeve he'd taken off the dead body.

The big cow, apparently unimpressed by the gesture, pushed off the cobblestones and raced ahead. The axe over its head glared with demonic fire capable of destroying any metal except for *adamantius*, even breaking down spell structures.

That fire was the reason unexperienced demonologists dropped like flies, confirming Darwin's theory. No wizard, even the most powerful, could directly attack a demon. Or an angel.

With no museum full of artifacts close at hand, all Alex could use was…a cemetery.

He ran his bloody palm over the ground, mixing his blood with the still-warm pools shed so recently. At the same moment, his mind seemed to subdivide into parts. Two. Four. Eight. Sixteen. And so on, until his field of vision was a kaleidoscope made up of over five hundred facets.

It was the strongest *raising* Alex had ever dared to attempt. The effort forced red trickles from his nose, eyes, and ears, but his mind held up under the pressure.

Gray seals formed by ash and death flashed in front of him, though they didn't hit the big onrushing cow. Instead, they spun like creepy sprockets as they sank into the blood.

When the demon lifted the axe over Doom, who was lying prostrate in his own and others' blood, it was literally swept away by the flow.

A flow of growling, bleeding, drooling, cut, slashed, ripped, limbless (or dropping their limbs as they went) zombies.

Like a school of piranhas, the scores of walking dead attacked the demon, burying it under the mass of bodies so recently still alive and full of hope. Hundreds more of them were climbing out of the ground.

Out of the corner of his eye, Alex spotted the same fat couple he'd doused in coffee, complete with their beloved son.

"The citizens of Myers City are always ready to lend a helping hand to those in need," Alex said, handing a dead arm to the fat zombie still stained with coffee.

It was the same arm he'd ripped the sleeve off of. And it looked like the arm was actually on its own—the lady it had previously belonged to was skipping on her only leg toward the demon, baring her teeth and oozing pus from where her other leg had been.

The fat zombie accepted the helping arm from Alex, waved it like a flag, and rushed into battle with a speed that belied its physique and undead nature.

[ATTENTION! Prohibited spell used: RAISING of the Blood, Darkness, and Death School. Mana consumption: N/A.]

"That one is prohibited, too?" Alex was surprised. When he'd left to spend four long years down at the resort, Raising was a spell that was permitted for wizards who hadn't had their magic source altered. *The black wizards who escaped vivisection at the hands of the glorious warriors of Light.*

"Bitches," Doom concluded in disappointment.

Sure, no one would have let him raise five hundred zombies at once, but...the city barely had a hundred wizards capable of that outside the Abyss' membership.

It wasn't even a questionn of their magic power. They just weren't skilled enough.

"Adelia would laugh her guts out." Doom, still down in the pool of blood, recalled the female necromancer who'd taught him the art after a couple rounds in bed. She'd have raised the whole park, feeding half the demons to the undead.

His gift was no match for hers.

While the demon fought off the undead, crushing them with the axe, ripping them apart with its bare paws, trampling them with its hooves, and just squeezing out every bit of fun it could, Alex caught his breath and crawled over to Archie.

"Hell of a day, huh?" he asked, poking the boy in the shoulder.

The kid was sobbing, clutching a stick with both hands. *Does he know that was just someone's cane?* Most likely, it had belonged to the old man latched onto the big cow's nostrils in an attempt to stop the demonic beast.

Alex sighed.

He felt like he had about 200 mana points left in his demonic source and half as much in his main black-magic one.

"I'll be honest, partner—things are about as shitty as they get." Doom sat down on the fizzy water tank. The tingling in his fingertips was growing stronger—there must have been more demons coming to the aid of their leader. "We're only going to get one last shot. So, let's think."

"Th-th-th-think-k-k-k?" the boy stammered.

Alex glanced over at Archibald. At least he hadn't pissed his pants. Although Doom at his age had already...well, it wasn't really the time for a trip down memory lane.

"As a good friend of mine named Robin used to say," Doom mumbled as he stood up, "*there's no such thing as too much soda.* Not when the soda is pressurized, boiling, and filled with black magic."

As he said that, Doom lifted both his hands. A red seal flashed over his left one, draining his demonic source, and a black seal appeared over his right palm to do the same to his other source.

With no idea whether he'd messed something up with the seals that time, Doom placed both hands on the fizzy water tank and applied the last of his physical and magic strength to hurl it in the direction of the already subsiding battle.

The undead were no match at all for the infuriated demon. In just a few moments, he'd shredded five hundred zombies (a record yet to be broken by any of the military branches).

The last few scores were still holding the big cow's attention when the soda tank slammed into its back and exploded immediately, not with cola but with a brown, sizzling mass that dissolved the demon's armor and infernal flesh like acid.

Bellowing in pain, the demon collapsed at the feet of the surviving zombies, who attacked it again, that time meeting far less resistance. The big cow fell silent a few moments later, showing no more signs of pseudo-life. Its flesh and armor spread across the ground as shapeless plasma—demon bodies didn't retain their normal look in this reality when bereft of their supporting magic power.

"I've got two pieces of news, partner." His hand trembling, Doom retrieved the second-to-last cigarette from his pack. It was time to restock. "The good one first: we smashed the big goat, though we made his kids really angry."

Surrounding Alex and Archibald were dozens of horned bastards eager to rip them to pieces.

"And now the *very* good news: the cavalry's here."

As soon as Alex said that, the red-haired Pole came slashing through the demon ranks with his physics-defying sword.

Hell's bells. Never in his entire life had Doom been so happy to see law enforcement.

Chapter 67

The operations staff was organized around the same long-suffering trader's cart not far from the metal tables of the terrace café where Alex had had his chat with Miss Perriot half an hour before.

Half an hour?!

Damn. It felt like it had happened at least a *year* before.

Doom wasn't ready for his life to become *that* eventful.

Little Archie, curling up beneath the plaid, was sleeping magically. Literally. Being a fae, Lieutenant O'Hara had the incredible ability to make human children sleep.

For many thousands of years, the fae of the Winter and Summer Courts alike had practiced stealing babies from their cradles, replacing them with vile changelings.

Major Chon Sook, crossing his legs and sticking out his little finger, drank from his flask as he watched people in unmarked radiation suits collect the dead bodies as well as the plasma left by the dissolving demons.

Gribovksy tapped the table nervously.

Lieutenant O'Hara took the seat furthest from Doom. A wise decision.

Sitting at the other tables were a dozen members of various races. There was even a huge, one-eyed orc dressed in a large business suit that was still very tight on his muscular body. He sat there honing his axe, a sight was so mundane and unnatural at the same time that it made Alex wonder if he'd gone crazy (him, not the orc).

"Mr. Dumsky." As usual, the major's voice was devoid of emotion. "The fact that you happened to be in the very museum where our masked friend decided to summon a demon is an *amazing coincidence*. But I don't even know what to call the fact that the same thing happened here."

"I already told you," Doom sighed, massaging the bridge of his nose beneath his glasses. Fortunately, the spells he'd put on them were strong enough to keep them on and undamaged even through the turmoil. "I was here with that little brat because Diglan asked me to bring him. And *you* were the one who got me working for the damn pirate!"

Despite his raised voice, Alex was as calm as one could be. Just a little...tired. With both his sources completely drained, he was going to have to spend whatever remained of that day and night in deep meditation if he wanted to restore at least half his mana reserves by the second tour of the tournament.

And Doom hated meditating.

"Lieutenant?" The major addressed O'Hara without turning to look at her.

"I confirmed it, sir." The fae, who'd already made all the workers in their yellow hazmat suits lick their lips in desire, folded up her phone and dropped it into her clutch bag. "Diglan is on his way."

"Have someone take his son to him."

"*I'll* do that," Alex jumped in, puffing a cloud of smoke. "My month-long vacation is at stake, and I have a feeling my feats will all have been wasted if the kid is handed over to Diglan without me."

"*Feats?!*" some smartass from the demon-fighting department squealed. "You were just saving your ass, you bastard! Your black magic permeated all the specters within a mile! All you did with it was disturb the peace of the dead, and—"

"…and kill the demon leader." Oddly enough, the smartass was interrupted by Gribovsky instead of Alex. "From what I can tell, Kyle, *your* department had nothing to do with detecting the Mask. If it hadn't been for the live streams from the bloggers walking in the park, we would have found out too late to do anything."

Doom didn't join the argument. Kyle had a silver chain around his neck, and that and what he said meant that there wasn't any point.

It would have been as useless as an African-American attempting to prove that he had the same rights as white people in the southern US of the 1900s.

"Let's change the subject, gentlemen." The major lifted a hand, stopping the bickering. "Mr. Johnson, do you have any ideas as to why the Mask selected this spot?"

Adjusting his glasses with his middle finger (probably a hint), Kyle paused before replying.

"We need more data. I'll be able to tell you more after the plasma remains of the demons are studied by experts, but so far my colleagues and I are leaning toward a planned terrorist attack."

"A terrorist attack," the major repeated, taking another gulp from his flask. Standing behind his back and drilling through Alex with his eyes was the bear-like Duncan. Alex ignored him. "The Mask's moves have looked like that in the past, though there was always another layer. And here…what's special about this area?"

"Could it be some kind of border?" Gribovsky suggested. "It marks the very edge of the city—there's nothing beyond it but the ocean."

That was absolutely true. The immense, placid body of water was exactly what Alex was feasting his eyes on right then.

As a ward at St. Federick's ward, he'd once seen a TV show about a private detective investigating a murder on a cruise ship. He'd been dreaming of taking a trip on a liner like that ever since.

Beautiful women. Casinos. Bars. Party drugs. Paid and free sex. What else could a black wizard need to be happy? But he hadn't been able to find six free months. Too many other things to do.

"Or maybe the Mask needed a large number of human sacrifices," O'Hara said. "According to the most recent data, how many were killed?"

Kyle slid his fingers over his tablet and adjusted his glasses again.

"2,372 killed. 639 injured. Mostly by the rush, not the demons. The closest hospitals and intensive care wards are all full already, so a state of emergency has been declared across the entire Amalgam Street District. Doctors are taking double shifts and—"

"…and thank you for the TMI, Kyle, as always," the fae interrupted. "Over 2,000 dead. That's a huge amount of death energy for the Mask to reap."

"Why don't we ask our *expert*?" Kyle asked mockingly.

Alex inhaled and, the gesture already becoming his trademark, blew a puff of smoke into the smartass' face. Kyle coughed but was apparently disliked by his colleagues even more than Dumsky—no one stood up for him.

You were right, Robin. No one likes a smartass.

"If the Mask had been reaping the death energy, I wouldn't have been able to raise any zombies," Alex said with the tone of an adult explaining general knowledge to small children. "So, that guess is wrong. Whatever he was up to, it had nothing to do with the magic of death."

"What ideas do *you* have, Mr. Dumsky?" the major asked.

"Just one."

"Care to share it with us?"

"This human child," Alex said, pointing at the sleeping Archie, "deserves to finally be taken to his father. And I deserve an attempt to get drunk that'll probably be interrupted yet again."

He doffed an imaginary hat (the actual one he'd stolen after leaving jail was at the Schooner) before continuing.

"And so, have a good day, gentlemen."

Saying that and pulling Archie up by the hand (the boy followed his lead obediently and without waking thanks to the damn fae spells), Alex headed for the barriers put up by the cops around the park.

The day was just starting, but it already felt bloody long.

Chapter 68

"**P**rofessor! Professor!" Elie waved.

With a flick of fingers, Doom sent his cigarette butt...into a Starbucks cup held by an unpleasant-looking security guard at the sports complex. He didn't notice and, without missing a step as he screened the male visitors, took a gulp from the cup.

He didn't even bat an eye.

Long lines of humans, orcs, trolls, elves, dwarves, and many other creatures dragged themselves through the archway magic detectors. Battle storages: prohibited. Firearms: prohibited. Artifacts rank B or higher: prohibited. It was easier to list what was *allowed*.

Even smoking and drinking while watching the event were prohibited.

Thanks to all that, the lines formed by representatives of all the sapient races moved rather slowly. Less than 24 hours had passed since the Mask had smashed up the theme park. Many people in Myers City were starting to take the threat seriously, their pockets holding weapons in addition to their phones.

The online market for magic grimoires was rumored to be up 42% over the previous 16 hours. The unheard-of spike in demand was mostly for battle and defensive spells.

The bald dwarf must be raking in the shekels.

Following some heavily perfumed and pompous magic aristocrat through the VIP archway, Alex found himself immediately sucked into the general commotion.

The second tour was called exactly that, though it actually followed the tournament's official opening ceremony.

"Oh lord," Mara gasped. Fortunately, the half-blood showing off her curves in the magic sports suit didn't believe in the human god, which spared Alex from the unpleasant sensations he'd otherwise have endured as a black wizard. "There are so many people here."

The participating teams, almost fifty of them, were seated in the first rows of the designated boxes.

The heart of the complex, the colossal Arena, was covered in a magic shield looking like an enormous white shroud that flapped in the cold October wind. It looked beautiful and impressive, Doom had to admit. Waves of white fabric rippling in the air. Each of them could have hidden a two-story house.

The giant sports complex flooded with the bright stadium lights was packed. The tickets had sold out ten minutes after they'd been made available for sale, which wasn't surprising given that it was the opening ceremony of the year's greatest and most anticipated sporting event.

The opening ceremony was attended by everyone who was anyone in the city. The magic aristocracy, including the Wessex and Glomebood families, took up seats in the central box along with all the other important Myers City figures. Doom thought he even recognized the very familiar face of an Arab wizard.

"Oh, you missed such an amazing show," Elie went on. "There were magic artists! They launched a water dragon and then flew into the air on colored bolts of lightning!"

"Then Ereni Malen sang," Leo added. "Her voice is incredible."

What it looked like Travis and even Jing were recalling was less the adored youth idol's voice and more her...appearance.

Ereni Malen was the pop princess, having ascended to the throne at sixteen and never subsequently leaving it.

Alex knew that because he was the same age as her. And he sort of knew her personally.

But that last bit of information wasn't one he was about to share with his students.

"And you missed so much more..."

"There was a fuse." Taking the coach seat, Doom put his earpiece in.

"A fuse? What fuse?"

Why are the Guards worrying about the Mask when they need to be stopping this damn raccoon infestation?

"A blown one. At the Schooner. Fixed it. Made me late. Did they give the speeches already?"

"Yeah. The city mayor—"

"Great," Alex cut in with a sigh of relief. "I've always hated listening to that idiot."

Mara was about to object when trumpets blared. Of course, they weren't live; it was just ear-splitting speakers hovering in midair. Alex wondered how they managed to avoid colliding with the numerous drones and flying cameras. Regardless, the sight was captivating.

The stands roared. Fireworks of all colors shot up into the sky. Overall, it wasn't much different from any other stadium event, only set apart by the fact that Myers City Arena was so immense. The whole thing oozed magic, too.

Literally.

Alex had a tingling sensation in his fingertips.

Courtesy of the committee, the team boxes had magic soundproofing that made the crazy roaring of the diverse crowd sound as though it was carrying from a distance.

The only annoying thing was the cameras flashing in Doom's peripheral vision.

Demons. From above, it probably looks like a second sun being lit in the city center.

"Did they have the drawing?" Alex asked, continuing his interrogation of the students.

"We're in the first four," Jing replied briefly and to the point. A smart guy.

It was a good thing they were in the first group. *Hell's bells.* Doom was unlikely to endure another half hour in that crowd, and that meant the game was likely to end fast enough for him to get some drinking in afterward.

But right then wasn't the time for daydreaming.

When the enormous white shroud tore off the arena to soar into the sky, the noise of the crowd even made it through the soundproofing spells.

Doom winced.

He'd never liked crowded spaces. A city dweller to the bone, he still preferred to have some solitude in among the concrete jungle, sticking to the darkest nooks rather than coming out into the light. (Pun intended.)

The crowd gradually fell silent, the sound of voices giving way to camera clicks and flashes merging into a single flow of white light.

The whole arena, the spot where the celebrities had just performed, had been transformed into a miniature world. The raised plateau in the middle had four zones, each roughly half the size of a regular football field.

One was overgrown by a tropical jungle, its other features indiscernible through the thick vegetation.

Another had snowy mountains, or rather their peaks, complete with heavy gray snow clouds above them and a blizzard lashing the few black chunks of rock peeking out from beneath the snow cover.

Right behind the mountains was a placid lake, looking so very peaceful. No doubt, there were some unpleasantries lurking in its depths.

The last quarter was a desert, a sandstorm swirling in the middle with flashes of red lightning coming from inside.

The whole picture didn't just startle the spectators and teams. Even Alex, for the first time in his life, was witnessing real magic at the Grand Master level.

The miracle had probably been wrought by one or two hundred Adepts flown in from all over the globe. Alternatively, it could have been built on some extremely rare and outrageously expensive artifacts.

Whatever the case, the beauty was totally worth the trip. Alex found the elaborate spells just as stunning as the four pieces of terrain.

He was in awe.

"Teams!" the loudspeakers thundered. "To the stage!"

"Well, you can't actually call that the *stage*," Alex said with a slight wince before holding up a hand and surprising his students. "A high five for your sensei, and then go kick some magic beast ass."

The first one to slap Doom's palm was Mara, the B-52 team captain. She was followed down the stairs by Elie, then by Travis and Leo. Last came Jing. For a while, he and Alex stared into each other's eyes. Then the descendant of the great shamans clapped the palm offered by his professor and hurried down the stairs after the rest.

"Good luck," Doom whispered as he watched the descending students through spread fingers that still bore the black dots of a very simple dark-magic curse. He'd known it would slip through the anti-doping spell checkpoint at the arena entrance.

Who in their right mind would check to see if a bunch of contestants had been cursed by their own coach?

***

"Jing! Move!"

"Professor! What should we do?"

"Leo, watch out!"

"Professor!"

"Elie, hurry! Elie? Elie?!"

"Mara, we can't—"

Four bodies, unconscious and shrouded in magic defense, were down on the sand. Towering over them was an ancient monster: Olgoi-Khorkhoi, the Mongolian death worm. Its maw looking like a screwdriver with teeth that squirted venomous acid.

Mara, armed with a sand hammer, tried to dodge, but her legs betrayed her and she collapsed to the sand, her scream drowned by the venom hissing on her protective jumpsuit. The magic defense flashed around the last B-52 team member. The challenge was over for them.

"The B-52 team completed the second tour!" a voice announced over the loudspeakers. "While the judges calculate their score, our stage workers will tame Olgoi-Khorkhoi."

Doom wouldn't have called it *taming*. The three Adepts stepping out onto the sand arena just used artifacts to drive the worm into a niche opening in the stadium wall. That sent a rather explicit message that the next team getting ready to fight in the desert would be facing a different monster.

"That's for the better," Alex whispered for some reason. It was as though he was convincing…himself.

He stood up, dropped the coach's earpiece on the armrest, dug his hands into his pockets, and walked off down the corridor leading to the accessory rooms. On the way, he thought he spotted a shock of peach hair in the stands. No time for her then, anyway.

Alex trudged deeper and deeper into the dark, reversing the journey made by all the spectators in their pursuit of the daylight over the stands, until he was in the maze of half-lit corridors. Some led to the bathrooms, others to cloakrooms, and a few more ended in small food courts where you could get a hot dog, a chocolate bar, or fizzy water.

He was so hungry he would have killed for a snack, which was why he stopped at one of the food courts.

"What'll it be?" a student employee with a bored expression on his face asked him.

"A cheeseburger," Alex replied, pointing at the icon on the holographic menu. "Make it a double. Extra cheese and bacon."

"Coming right up," the employee said with the same bored voice before turning toward a microwave. *Not all that impressive, but it'll do.*

"You're not health-conscious, Alex?" asked a voice from behind him. "Cholesterol kills faster than a bullet."

Doom turned around to see that his already lousy day had just gotten even worse. *Why couldn't they send Pyotr alone?*

The Syndicate's cleaner was there, too. Standing right behind one of the organization's heads.

Like the Hydra, the Syndicate had many heads. One of them was right there in front of Doom. A tall, beautiful woman dressed in black and red silks, her tanned, well-groomed skin glowed slightly, and her captivating green eyes were accentuated by perfect makeup.

Alex knew better than to fall for the charming, oh-so-feminine looks of the red-haired beauty. She had bigger balls than most men.

Her name was Brown, she was one of the Syndicate heads, and only someone bent on suicide would get in her way. That was all Alex knew about the woman. He'd only met her once before, when she'd visited her brother in prison. He was the one who'd saved Alex's life and indebted him to the Syndicate.

"Miss Brown," Doom said with a wry smile. "I can't really say I'm happy to see you."

Pyotr took a step forward but was stopped by a commanding gesture of her slender, graceful hand.

Oh Abyss. If she weren't a Syndicate head, she'd probably be in charge of a BDSM brothel.

"You held up your end of the deal, Mr. Dumsky," she said in a businesslike tone. "The Organization has no more charges against you. You're absolutely free."

She held out a hand. What was it like to shake a poisonous snake's hand? Alex was doing it for the second time.

"I have three seats reserved in the government box." She ran the tip of her thump over the back of his hand. "Care to join me there?"

Alex knew what female mantises do to males.

"Sorry, I have things to do."

"Well," she said with a flash of her green eyes. "I'm sure we'll be seeing each other, Alexander."

Releasing her grip on Alex's hand, she glided toward the stairs. Pyotr followed her like a silent shadow.

Doom swallowed and pressed his back against a wall. No demon scared him as much as that red-haired woman did. And he had enough gray matter inside his skull to be *scared* of her, not just crave her with his male parts.

As he closed his eyes, Alex suddenly heard a distinct and very familiar patter of heels. But when he turned, all he spotted was a brief flash of brown hair.

"Bitch," Alex cursed. "Why do dwarves have to recover *that* quickly?"

By the time the fast-food employee placed the boxed burger onto a tray, the visitor who'd ordered it was nowhere to be seen.

Chapter 69

"Have another?" Cherry asked, edging the glass of whiskey closer to Alex.

"No, thanks," he replied and continued playing. "What's today?"

"October 16th. What does that matter?"

Over the past fortnight, he'd barely left the Schooner except to give his lectures at First Magic. Very boring lectures. Not that they'd been the epitome of fun before, but now...

The B-52 group was boycotting their supervisor. They'd stopped attending his lectures and had even planned their everyday routes so as not to bump into him in the halls.

Dean Lebenstein was apparently too busy with his direct responsibilities to keep pestering Alex. Neither did he see any of Miss Perriot—she was obviously avoided him, too. Only the class schedule told him she was still teaching history.

As for the Guards, they were completely engrossed in brainstorming what the Mask was up to. He'd shown no signs of activity since the massacre at the park.

Given the fact that Alex had repaid his debt to the Syndicate by the fixing the tour and sending B-52 to the very bottom of the tournament table, there hadn't been any reason for Pyotr to visit again. And he hadn't.

That's how Alex came to be spending almost all his time at the Schooner despite being on vacation, tormenting the old piano in the farthest corner of the hall. He played it every evening, and Diglan was generous enough to offer him free drinks for his free concerts. That was probably his gratitude for saving his son's life.

"See that girl?" Cheery pointed at a female visitor in leather pants and leather vest over a white bra. She was sitting at the end of the bar closest to Alex. "She's had her eye on you all night."

"She has? Are you sure?"

"Absolutely," the irrepressible waitress replied with a wink. She'd gotten another drastic makeover, changing girlfriends more often than some people change their toothbrushes. "If you offer her a drink, she'll—"

"Thanks," Doom interrupted.

Closing the piano lid, he stood and walked over toward the groupie. When he got closer, she bent forward a bit, showing off her breasts, thin waist, and...all the other non-verbal communication she had to offer.

Alex walked right past her.

Leaving the astonished Cherry and disappointed groupie behind, he walked out into the street. The night was far from young in the wizard city. The tall buildings scraping the low, heavy skies glowed like columns of cold, neon light.

The occasional car dashed along the roads, probably carrying its passengers off on some important business...or maybe just going home. Or to Amalgam Street, with each of its nightclubs throwing a loud party at that hour.

A part of Alex wanted to go there. But instead, he headed off in exactly the opposite direction.

Smoking cheap, crumpled cigarettes, his hands thrust into his pockets, he wobbled through the maze of streets in his light leather jacket and jeans, torn sneakers, and stubble that was already turning into a real beard.

Alex loved the nighttime city.

It did away with all the masks. The enticing luxury of salons and boutiques was closed, all the glamor and sheen of dressed-up clowns worshipped by other clowns.

All the lies. All the blinders. Everything that was superficial and unimportant went to sleep at night or lurked in the places that still had light. That's why Myers City's streets at night were always far more vacant than in the daytime.

Truths are always outnumbered by the lies.

Alex wasn't surprised to find himself shortly roaming the familiar High Garden streets. He couldn't remember if he'd gotten there on foot or if he'd used public transportation. Whatever the case, he was walking the same streets he'd lived on as a kid. (If he ever was a kid.)

For some reason, one particular episode from his past came to mind.

***

The tall buildings blotting out the sky looked like gloomy, silent giants to the sixteen-year-old. They towered over the road as though guarding the passing cars from curious glances.

At times Alex smelled (apart from the vapor around sewer covers) the cheap entertainment in the air. He slowed down at the brothels to watch the often-homely women slathered in makeup laugh in the arms of drunken men.

Doom had hated that laughter ever since he was a kid. However merry and ringing it was, the eyes of the women who laughed like that were as cold and harsh as those of a worker on his second night shift.

Alex opened the throttle, his steel horse racing off in a direction he didn't know. The cigarette smoldering in his lips left wisps of smoke behind him. At times the young man took such abrupt turns that his knees almost touched the asphalt, clearing it by less than an inch.

The nights in High Garden were action-packed.

In one alley shrouded in vapor and mist, three gangsters were beating up a guy, a girl screaming next to them.

Two doors down, café visitors applauded another guy as he knelt in front of an embarrassed lady. Her hands trembled as she accepted a small red box containing a shiny ring.

In a passage next to the café, a dying homeless man sat on the ground, trying to get warm by embracing a flea-ridden dog. It was the only creature he loved, the only one that loved him.

Next to the road, a well-off family stood trying to catch a taxi. *What were they doing here? Maybe they mixed up metro stations and got off at the wrong one.*

The father had an arm out. The mother was dressed in furs, gold, and diamonds. The two sons in their suits looked more funny than formal. The younger boy had a balloon he wanted to give to the homeless man, but the mother clapped him on the back of the head. The boy froze, casting apologetic glances at the nearly dead man and his sad dog.

Alex wasn't sure which of the two (the homeless man or the family) stood a higher chance of living to see the dawn.

Sitting on a bench a block away, a couple was sharing what looked like a first kiss. A masked man was raping a gagged woman some four hundred feet from them.

Around the corner, some cops were arresting a petty crook for stealing a well-dressed lady's bag. The soft clatter of suppressed gunfire came from another block. *Italian mafia style. Maybe even the actual Italian mafia.*

High Garden didn't just have the Cosa Nostra. It was infested with the Chinese Triads, the Russian Bratva, the Japanese Yakuza, and lots of other criminal organizations that together made up the shadow world of Myers City.

But Alex still loved the place.

Unlike the central districts, it had…it had…

…absolutely everything. Blood dripping softly down shop stairs. Intoxicating lust at brothel entrances. Rivers of alcohol at cheap bars. Cigarette smoke engulfing billiard rooms. Flowering love on park benches and in cafes, raging passion in apartments and motels betrayed by doors creaking as quivering hands tried to turn keys in locks.

Glancing at his watch, Alex turned around again.

It was time to wrap up his farewell ride.

He passed by the alley, turning toward a biker bar. His steel friend would be safe there.

Alex stopped, turning the engine off and mulled it over, the ashes of his smoldering cigarette falling onto the mangled, cracked, bumpy asphalt.

Giving it some careful thought, Doom realized there was one thing the night was missing.

And that was why he immediately turned the engine back on and rode off without a backwards look.

He slowed down by the hotel at the road separating High Garden and Amalgam Street District. Concentrating, he created a set of keys with a wave of hand. He lurched, and his bike wobbled, but he stayed in the saddle, albeit nearly drained of magic.

Somebody else could probably have created a dozen sets without even getting a tingling sensation in their fingertips. But for black wizards, that sort of magic was exhausting.

Kicking the foot peg down, Alex handed the keys to the hotel valet and walked inside as calmly as if he owned the place. He knew it well, having spent thousands of credits a night there at his best times.

The doors kept spinning behind his back. The vast hall looked like a giant cave, shiny with sparkling velvets and golden paint. It was a five-star establishment, after all. Alex wondered how it came to be located so close to the city's criminal eyesore.

At 4 a.m., there was virtually no one around. Only seldomly did you see a sleepy guest turning their key in and plodding toward a waiting taxi, an equally sleepy bellhop right behind them with their suitcase.

Alex stood at the elevator. Then, groping around in his pocket for the eternal crumpled pack and finding it, he headed toward the lobby bar.

It was on the small side, accommodating no more than forty people at once. There were only seven there right then. Two men at a far table looking like mafia. A few other visitors. The bartender. A girl at the counter rocking a martini. Her sparkly red dress had already swept all the dust up off the floor. The polish on one of her nails was chipped, and her perfume couldn't drown out the smell of cheap cigarettes that contrasted sharply with her overall expensive looks and young face. She was apparently no older than Alex, probably below the legal age, but Doom couldn't have cared less. Her dark eyes stared straight through the wall of bottles. Her brown hair, once beautifully styled, was a mess.

The girl slid another cigarette out of the pack that sat next to her on the counter, probably forgotten by one of the guests. That was odd. The cheap pack in a luxurious hotel like the one they were in just served to spoil the overall picture. The lady flicked at the lighter courteously provided by the bartender, but it refused to produce even a semblance of a spark.

Coming over, Alex snapped his fingers to summon a lilac flame. "Thank you," she said.

Doom nodded and beckoned the bartender over with two fingers.

"Whiskey. The juice from a quarter of a lemon. Two ice cubes. Stir until they melt."

The bartender nodded. Soon Alex was sipping an expensive whiskey ruined by his Russian tea recipe—the two ounces cost him two hundred credits even. Exactly the amount he had left in his account.

The girl smoked away, paying no attention to anything else. Her makeup was smeared.

"Do you like me?" she snorted suddenly, swirling an olive around in her glass. "You keep looking at me."

Alex actually had been staring at the lady, and he wasn't at all embarrassed by her calling him out on it. Nothing about sex or relationships really bothered him.

"Yes. The tip of your nose is insanely beautiful. I've honestly never seen one like it."

The girl looked at him appraisingly, almost as if he were on sale in a shop window.

They sat like that for a while. Then she put a banknote on the counter and stood up. Walking to the entrance, she turned around.

"You coming?"

"Yes," Alex nodded. Leaving his unfinished glass behind, he followed the lady.

Silently, they waited at the elevator that for some reason lingered for a really long time at the twelfth floor.

Alex didn't know what the girl was thinking about, but it probably wasn't anything all that bright. He had absolutely nothing on his mind. That was something he was really good at that. According to the Professor *(may the worms of the Abyss shred him)*, that was the *only* thing he was good at.

When the door opened, Alex let the lady on first. She stood meekly, waiting for him to follow, then pressed the button. The door closed. The engine hummed, the cables stretched, and the elevator drifted upward.

"He proposed today," she said softly.

Alex didn't reply, busy examining the painting on the back wall and wondering why anyone would hang a painting in an elevator.

"I turned him down."

It was the sea. Doom loved the water, and the painting enchanted him. He'd dreamed of going on a cruise ever since he was young. It was his sex, drugs, and rock-n-roll.

"I just couldn't say yes."

Flashing before his mind's eye were scenes from a detective movie.

"He's just a poor doctoral student."

The movie was rich enough in sex scenes for Alex to do quite well his first time around. The Tkils gang had a *very* special rite of passage.

"I can't be with him! I have my first concert tomorrow! And he even…"

Alex turned to look at the girl. A tear ran down her cheek, streaking her black mascara as it did. No doubt she loved the guy.

"I—"

Before the wannabe singer could finish, Doom bent over to seal her lips with a kiss. His palm slid downward, plunging beneath her sparkly dress. The girl screamed and then groaned.

Alex didn't care what the dark-eyed beauty was telling him. The nighttime city had seen all sorts of things. It could handle that one just as well.

Like anyone ever cared.

The door opened.

***

Doom knocked off the ashes. Sitting on a bench next to the wrought-iron fence, he listened to the crows cawing over the dumpsters.

Five years had passed since that night.

He wondered if the dark-eyed girl had found happiness as one of the day's most popular singers. He knew for sure *he* hadn't as one of the day's most knowledgeable black wizards.

"How many years, Alexander?"

"Five, holy father," Alex replied. "Five since I last visited her."

A tall, sturdily built man with plenty of gray hair sat down on the bench next to him. He was wearing a black cassock, a white square making up the tall collar around his throat.

"I'm happy to see you, Alexander."

"Me too, Father Vinsens."

It was probably a weird sight: a black wizard smoking on a bench next to a Catholic priest, an old church towering behind them.

The only church in High Garden.

But the nighttime city had seen all sorts of things. It could handle that one just as well.

Like anyone ever cared.

Chapter 70

The old church was the only place in all of High Garden where everyone's life was safe. A zone of universal truce. Anyone who broke the truce incurred the wrath of the entire district, from the pettiest drug-addicted crooks to the big gangs and mafias all the way to the Syndicate, the crown of the criminal world. (No one knew for sure where the Syndicate was headquartered. Some said Ireland. Others claimed it was the UAE. Still others insisted on Brazil. Whatever the case, it was top secret.)

The credit for the old church attaining that status belonged entirely to Father Vinsens.

A tall man with strong shoulders and the neck of a bull, his face bore two scars that formed a cross over the bridge of his nose. The pupil of his left eye was deformed by one of them running right through it. If it hadn't been for magic, Immortal Vinnie (the nickname he'd earned during gang wars) would have been half-blind.

Why immortal?

Because like fuck you'll ever kill him.

As a kid, Alex didn't have heroes from books. He had Immortal Vinnie, the man who'd been tortured by orcs. Who'd wrestled a mountain ogre. Who'd been shot with twelve bullets from an assault rifle. Who'd stopped a sniper bullet with his belly. Who had more broken bones than Jackie Chan.

Vinnie had survived all of it. But when he got tired of pushing his luck, he retired and built a church in the middle of the district. He became a priest, leaving his ungodly past behind him and kind of trying to set the local gangsters and other scum on the straight and narrow.

He wasn't much of a success at that.

But, since almost all the major gangsters knew Vinnie (and had worked with him in the past), most of them either liked or deeply respected him. The priest became the district's mascot, the church untouchable.

Once, a stray drug addict got into the church looking for money for a fix. Vinnie—Father Vinsens—was the kind of guy who'd give what little he had without any resistance. But the drug addict wanted more and got so angry he hit Vinsens over the head with a candlestick.

The priest wasn't even knocked off his feet. He just stood there in the church doorway and watched the addict run off with the stolen stuff.

The next morning, several very expensive black cars with gas engines stopped by the church. All the stolen items were returned to the priest. Two dozen hunks from the Shanti gang, which had the honor (no overstatement there) of catching the crook, also painted the church fence, fixed the gate, cleaned all the ancient gravestones in the graveyard, and installed several benches.

Over the next week, the gangs all pledged money to the church. Father Vinsens used everything he got to feed all the homeless and needy he could find for a month.

Alex was one of those people. After Follen's fall (sounds like a pun), he was living under the bridge, and the only food he had was a bowl of peanut soup he got at Father Vinsen's church. Paid for by gang money.

That was what later prompted him to join the Tkils, but that's a different story.

The waxing moon glowed overhead. It was going to be full on Samhain/Halloween, making the ancient holiday even more powerful, the border between the realms of the living and the dead even thinner.

"Do you have some?" the priest asked with a gleam in his eye.

"Always," Alex replied with a nod.

"Spare me one?" the priest almost begged.

Avoiding touching the church fence (it would have burned like napalm) with his back, Doom retrieved the crumpled cigarette pack from his jacket pocket. He used it, old and taped together, as the case he always had with him.

The only person besides Doom himself who could touch it without getting grossly cursed was Father Vinsens.

Alex would have long since been feeding the worms or fish if it hadn't been for the priest.

With work-weary, calloused, and knotted fingers that never would have been mistaken for a regular churchman's, the former gangster retrieved a cigarette from the pack. But all he did was close his eyes and wave it slowly back and forth under his nose, breathing in the tobacco aroma. With a dreamy smack of his lips, he handed the cigarette back to Alex.

"Almost ten years, wonder kid," Vinsens said somewhat tragically, "since I gave those things up. If it weren't for little indulgences here and there, I'd have started again a long time ago."

"Still get the craving?"

Father Vinsens wrung his hands together and turned toward the nearest intersection. It was messy, with battered streets and mangled sidewalks. A crooked, unsteady streetlamp blinked on and off. Dark, then light, then dark again.

"*Everyone* craves what comes easy," the priest replied. Even a fool would have realized he wasn't just talking about smoking. "What doesn't take the effort of trying to do the right thing."

Alex looked over at the streetlamp, too. The first and second floors of the building facing the church were occupied by the police station, the third and fourth by High Garden's best brothel.

It went without saying that the officers of the law working there were the wealthiest in the whole city.

Which law did they serve?

Alex suspected that it was the law of the concrete jungle.

"I wish someone could tell me what's right and what's wrong." Alex retrieved a cigarette, too, lighting it with the lilac fire on his thumb and taking a pull.

Father Vinsens sniffed at the air dreamily.

"I thought you'd smoke less after jail."

"Are kidding me? There's absolutely nothing to do down there but play poker for tobacco or smoke it. Well, that and reading."

"I remember you smoking a pack a day before jail. How much do you smoke now?"

Turning thoughtful, Alex estimated how much he spent on cigarettes and reached a sad conclusion.

"About two and a half."

The priest shook his head in disappointment.

"And that's when most quit, the rest moving over to those electronic things."

"Electronic stuff instead of real tobacco? That's like giving up sex for masturbation." Alex winced and knocked the ashes off into the trashcan by his side.

"Agreed. But hey, wonder kid, I have a feeling you're *alone* contributing every tenth credit to the tobacco companies' revenues."

Alex smiled. Father Vinsens smiled back at him. They sat like that for a while.

"What will it be this time?" the priest asked at last.

Doom ran a palm in front of his lenses to summon the payment system interface and transfer 29 credits to the priest's account.

"Roses, daisies, and lilies. She liked that combination."

"For that amount, the bouquet will be—"

"…five times as big as usual," Alex nodded. "I've missed several anniversaries."

Father Vinsens nodded in reply.

"You need help, boy," he said suddenly, more a statement than a question.

Immortal Vinnie was, again, the only man in the world who could address Alex as *boy* without earning himself a mortal enemy for the brief and painful rest of his life.

"I just need a drink and a fu—"

"Don't quote Robin to me, wonder kid," the priest interrupted. "You know he got all that stuff from *me*."

Doom inhaled again. The streetlamp kept blinking on the periphery of his vision, a sign the brothel was closed that night.

The cops must be keeping the hookers for themselves.

"You grew up, Alex. Got tall. Skinny, though that's probably all the state-served foods. But that's all on the outside. Deep down, you're still the little boy who wasn't stopped by not being able to enter this building." The priest pointed behind him. "He wanted to go in, and that's what he did. He risked his life just because he wanted to. He wanted to throw himself against everything. Absolutely *everything*. Because that was *easier* for him. You haven't changed at all, boy. Still doing what's easier, not what's right."

Alex snorted.

"I'm a black wizard. We always do what's easier. That's written in our destiny."

"Written? By who? *Who* can prescribe what a man can do, leaving him no choice? Can you tell me their name, boy?"

Mirroring the other man's gesture, Alex pointed behind him at the church steeple with its massive shiny brass cross looming against the overcast sky.

"Oh, wonder kid," the priest said with a sigh. "I don't think *he* ever prescribed anything to anyone. We're all completely free to choose how we live our lives. Trying to make the world a bit better than what we found it or—"

"Die trying to stop the damn fairies," Alex interrupted, "when no one asked you to do that."

Vinsens' eyes gleamed. Not with anger, but with deep sorrow.

She'd been fourteen.

Her parents died in a house fire. In the dead of night, no one had hurried to answer a call from one of the most dangerous neighborhoods in High Garden.

The whole family perished with the exception of the little girl, who miraculously survived the inferno. The cops who showed up the next morning found her covered in cinder and ashes. The ashes of her family.

They washed her clean, gave her some water, and brought her there. Not to the church, although it had already been around for quite a while.

To the blinking lamp.

She was only fourteen, but the cops didn't care. If it hadn't been for Father Vinsens stepping in, then…then…

Alex clenched his fists.

If it hadn't been for the priest, Miss Elisa would never have come to St. Frederick's Orphanage, finding her home at the church.

She was buried right there next to the ashes of her family.

In the holy ground.

Where Alex couldn't visit her grave to tell her how he was doing.

Where he couldn't…couldn't beg her forgiveness. For not helping her back then. For running away like a coward. Betraying the only one who had always been there for him. Who had always been kind to him despite everything he was, and had never been scared of him.

That's why he handed two letters to Father Vinsens.

"Please read these to her," he said. Then he stood up, tossed his cigarette butt into the trashcan, and walked off down the street.

"I really miss her too, boy," called the voice from behind him. "I'd rather not miss *you* the same way."

Alex turned the next corner and walked on until he reached a phone booth, probably the only surviving one not only in High Garden, but in all of Myers City.

The box inside smelled like ammonia and cheap alcohol. In cold or rainy weather, homeless people used it as their drinking spot or toilet. Sometimes both at the same time.

Transferring a few cents to the city account, Doom picked up the phone. A few signal tones, and…

"Gribovsky."

"It's Alex."

"Oh, pumpkin, how did you get my state number? Is there something I don't know about you?"

"I'm in the street."

"In the street? Are you kidding me? This city still has phone booths?!"

"We need to talk."

"Oh. You're not exactly my type, pumpkin. Don't get me wrong— I couldn't care less if you're male or female, but I never date people from wo—"

"Set up a meeting or whatever you want call it. With the smartasses, the whore, the Asian, and the Asian's hoodlum."

"The *whore* is what you call O'Hara? And why call the group in, anyway? We just brainsto—"

"I know when and where the Mask is going to strike next."

The clowning tone vanished from Gribovsky's voice.

"I'll pick you up in an hour at the Schooner," he said in a deadly serious, metallic voice. "Don't be late."

Alex hung up, thrust his hands into his pockets, and plodded off toward the bus stop.

He hated buses. But he hated the cold even more.

Chapter 71

"We should've *camped* here." Tossing a red Skittle into his mouth, Gribovsky winced. "I bloody hate the red ones."

"Then why eat them?"

The Polish man faded suddenly. He literally faded, something that was anything but easy to accomplish with his red cheeks and hair.

He clutched the pack in hand and rustled it around for a while. Alex had gotten to know his partner's habits, and that was something he always did when he was feeling nervous or had something unpleasant on his mind.

"Because if it weren't the red ones, it would be something else," he said without his usual sarcasm. In a long black leather trench coat, high military boots, and a Dead Clock T-shirt, not to mention his cut face, he fit in perfectly. "Not Skittles. And I like Skittles, not something else."

Snorting, Doom lit up. Only the one cigarette remained in his pack. He hadn't availed himself of the opportunity to replenish when he got back to the city, and he was facing the consequences of that misstep.

"I didn't think you had that in you."

"Had what?" Gribovsky asked, pulling himself away from his brooding.

"A philosophical side."

"Who doesn't get the urge to say something smart when they know they might be dead in a couple hours?" Gribovsky crossed himself, but...he wasn't a true believer. At least not as true as Miss Elisa, Leia Perriot, Immortal Vinnie, or their kind. "Damn you, pumpkin. Small wonder you ended up such a gloomy character growing up around here."

"You should see it in the summer," Doom replied with a smirk.

"In the summer? Is that when you hang the entrails of dead bodies, bathe in the blood of virgins, and dance with the walking dead?"

"No, that's New Year."

They exchanged glances and laughed. Standing on a hill and resting their backs against Gribovsky's tiny sports car, they peered down at the small valley among the creepy, leafless woods. In the middle were the ruins of an ancient mansion, once beautiful in its own way.

Follen School. The place where Doom had spent his best years.

Where he'd learned the meaning of family.

"Does it hurt?" Gribovsky asked.

It was difficult not to get what he meant.

"You're asking me that now after *two weeks*?" Doom asked with a brow arched. "After bringing me here on my vacation, after us spending two weeks sitting on each other's heads in that motel and working our guts out in this damn valley? I thought things were better with the Guards' finances."

"They are, of course," Gribovsky nodded as he tossed a green Skittle into his mouth. "But the demon-fighting department is a hole that gets a trickle from the budget river. It's like we're pissed on with money by some pumpkin who takes a leak once a month at best."

Alex snorted. That actually was funny.

"What are you doing there if it's a hole of a department?" Doom asked.

"I was transferred when…hey, wait." The Polish man threw his hands up. "Is this when we open up to each other since we're facing a deadly threat? I tell you about the fuck-up that got me dumped into the Guards' worst hole, and you tell me how you got caged?"

"Sort of. Yeah, I guess."

Gribovsky squinted.

"You know, when the people in the old movies start talking about that stuff, one of them is about to die."

"Totally," Alex nodded. "You found me out—I was going to get you to open up so some demon would knock you off right where you stand."

"Ha, sorry, pumpkin. You're not getting rid of Lieutenant Gribovsky like that. By the way, are you *sure* the Mask is going to come here at the start of Samhain?"

"Positive," Alex replied with another nod as he rolled his eyes. "Almost thirteen years ago, a baron demon from a fourth-century legion was summoned here and—"

"Easy, easy, I don't know much about aristocracy."

"Basically, an ultra-mega-super-duper demon was pulled here by its hair, one strong enough to reduce the whole city to mincemeat."

"That was perfect." The guardsman flashed a thumbs-up. "I get it now."

"As I already told the major and his smartasses, this is the border between the realms of the living and the dead, heaven and hell."

"Heaven doesn't actually exist," Gribovsky shot back.

No. He was *not* a true believer.

"Whatever," Doom replied with a dismissive wave. "This is where that border is maximally penetrable. During Samhain, it'll be as open as a sieve, perfect for summoning even a count demon from a fifth-century legion who's strong enough to turn the whole of Atlantis into another Abyss."

"That's *really* strong."

"It is."

Gribovsky tapped his teeth on another piece of candy.

"Well," he waved carelessly. "That's a good enough reason for us to suffer through two weeks making a trap up here."

Just then, the walkie-talkie under the lieutenant's trench coat squawked.

"Nest to Red," came the voice. "Nest to Red. Do you copy? Over."

"Red to Nest," Gribovksy replied, pressing a button. His voice turned solid metal again. "Loud and clear. Over."

"Red, how are things? Over."

"Red to Nest. It's stable. We see the entrance point. The target is not yet in sight. Everything's ready. Over."

"Nest to Red. Stay ready. Awaiting the major's order. Keep a low profile. Over."

"Red to Nest. Got it. We'll be ready. Over and out."

Taking his finger off the button, Gribovsky clipped the walkie-talkie back onto his belt.

"That's total crap, Lieutenant. Sounds like two crazy dudes on the phone."

"It does," the guardsman sighed. "But that's the procedure. Everything we say is heard by forty other posts, not to mention the emergency response team."

Alex glanced back at the ruins by the foot of the hill. There, surrounding what was left of Follen School, the cradle of black wizards, no less than a hundred guardsmen stood in wait. The mansion and the valley around it were shielded off with a bevy of spells and charms.

Doom had helped set up many of them. That was why the Guards got him a break from lecturing and brought him there along with the Pole. Every morning, they had to drive about fifty miles to the mansion from the nearest motel.

But driving wasn't crawling.

On that infamous night thirteen years before, Alex had made the same journey on foot, trudging, crawling, and otherwise dragging his body through the dead forest to the nearest highway.

"Look! The parade is starting," Gribovsky said, holding up his phone so Alex could see Myers City's Central Boulevard on the screen. The parade was marching right down it. Thousands of people in costume. Large floats with people on them dancing and singing, with others on the heads and other body parts of giant monster figures.

The whole thing looked a lot like the Carnival in Rio de Janeiro, just with a major Halloween theme (the amount of skin on display was roughly comparable).

The parade was fenced off from the sidewalk by barriers and lines of cops shielding the spectators from the marchers with their backs.

Giant hot air balloons shaped like monster heads had been launched into the sky. Then came the airships—long out of everyday use in Myers City, they were only flown on special occasions.

"I've always wanted to see it," Gribovsky said sadly. "Looks like I'm going to miss it this year as well. What a shame. The march is supposed to reach the Arena right when the tournament finale starts. It's going to be an amazing show."

"How far is the city?"

"About three hours if you ignore traffic rules. What does that matter? I wouldn't mind leaving my post for the occasion, but we'd still be at least an hour late."

"Three hours," Alex said thoughtfully. "That'll have to do. Two and a half till the next check."

Gribovsky slowly shifted his gaze to Doom. The Polish guardsman was no idiot, and he knew what Alex was up to…it just too late.

Alex's hand flashed a blazing seal and touched the lieutenant's forehead. Going limp at once, the latter's body fell into Doom's arms.

"Fatty," Alex groaned, easing the lieutenant to the ground. Gribovsky was still conscious; Doom wasn't as good at casting magic sleep as the fae. "Sorry, partner. I'm a black wizard, so you're probably going to have some nightmares."

Alex straightened up and, using a few moves and a couple magic seals, picked the sports car's lock. Climbing in the driver's seat, he lowered the window.

"When you wake up, call the major and tell him to find the seal center. He should know what that means."

Ignoring Gribovsky's furious glare, Alex pressed the magic engine ignition button. When the magic crystal charge flashed full on the dashboard and the exhaust pipe belched the electronic sound of non-existent fumes, Doom planted his foot on the gas pedal and, twisting the wheel violently, raced off down the country road.

He had to cover a distance that normally took three hours to drive in no more than two.

"Music on," Alex commanded. "Last Standing Rock-n-Rolla radio station."

A couple moments later, the electronics-packed car found the wavelength he was looking for.

"...and now..." Doom was pleasantly surprised to hear the voice of the same DJ who'd worked the station many years before. "...I give you Bad by Royale Deluxe."

"Always the perfect hit," Doom said with a smile.

The car dashed toward the highway, leaving behind the trap Doom had set.

Not for the Mask.

The trap he'd baited for the Guards.

Chapter 72

O'Hara had seen her boss, Major Chon Sook, in a variety of moods. But she'd never seen him angry and...scared at the same time.

Scaring an elite battle wizard specializing in lightning strikes was virtually impossible.

Whoever had done it was in big trouble.

"I heard you, Lieutenant. Get everyone together and wait for orders from me." The major hung up and locked his fingers.

O'Hara was itching to say that using a black wizard had been a bad idea from the start, but she bit her tongue in time.

That would have been pushing it too far.

"Find the seal center," the major drawled, deep in thought. "O'Hara, give me a city map."

Without asking why, the Fae stood. Her high heels clattered as she walked to the filing cabinet and pulled out a paper map. Chon Sook hardly ever used tablets or anything else digital.

The major spread the map on the table and leaned over it with a thoughtful air.

"The seal center," he said again. "Maybe...? No. Or... Where we first encountered the Mask?"

O'Hara instantly pointed at the second port berth. It was a curious correlation: the Mask's first attack had happened right above the Guards' base.

"And second?"

O'Hara pointed at a different spot. The major highlighted it.

"Mark all the rest." He handed the highlighter to his subordinate, who marked five more locations. There were a total of seven.

"Seven...seven..."

"...apexes!" O'Hara and the major exclaimed together. Using a ruler, they connected the highlighted dots and drew a circle through them. The seal they came up with centered around...

"Goodness." The major dropped into his armchair. Grabbing his smartphone, he dialed Gribovsky. "Lieutenant, get everyone to the Arena. Now!"

Pressing a red button, the major dialed another number.

"Major Chon Sook. Authorization code: alpha, bravo, seventeen, jango, forty-five, whiskey, twenty-one. Requesting backup at the Arena, Myers City. Threat code: red. Respond immediately. I repeat, requesting…"

He continued speaking, but O'Hara was no longer listening. She was busy leafing through the paper folder of case materials they'd opened before they'd even known it would lead to a series of demon summons.

"Major," O'Hara whispered, pointing at the date of the very first case record. "Look."

Setting his smartphone down on the table, Chon Sook leaned over the folder.

It was a day of discoveries when it came to the head of the demon-fighting department.

For the first time ever, O'Hara heard the major use that kind of foul language.

***

Elie was on the ground with a broken arm and a wounded leg. Jing stood over her, reeling and barely conscious. There were magic glowing tiger paws flashing and fading around his legs.

Leo-Leonard was inside a magically generated black box held shut with heavy, smoking chains. Even his power wasn't enough to get out of the creepy artifact.

Mara was applying pressure to Travis' slashed artery with both hands, but his face was growing paler with each passing second.

Still, even in their condition, they looked better than the rest of the teams. Everyone else who had reached the finale, a magic battle royale, was dead, the torn pieces of their bodies scattered around the ravaged magic forest the stadium arena had been transformed into. It was gradually shedding the illusion of magic verdure, its true appearance beginning to peek through.

The stands were becoming visible, too. Clouds of dust and stone dust billowed into the sky. Sparks showered down from the smashed stadium lights. A few fires flared up.

People were screaming. Some were trying to pull loved ones out of the rubble. Others, in a state of complete shock, were silent in their seats, their empty eyes staring straight ahead like living glass.

Just a short time before, they'd been having fun, enthusiastically cheering on their favorite teams. That had been before the terrorist the media had dubbed the Mask had disguised himself as one of the contestants and turned the place into a hell on earth.

Lilac fire devoured the stands. The ground shuddered as it was pummeled by giant pieces of cement. The screams were so loud they drowned out the sounds of helicopters and the sirens of police cars and fire engines rushing for the Arena.

"My life didn't prepare me for this," Travis said, trying to crack a gurgling joke. He was humorous even on the verge of death.

"Stop." Tears were running down Mara's cheeks.

"Did…we…wound…him?"

Mara turned to look at the Mask. A torn black cloak fluttered behind him, his gauntleted hands clutching a battle magic storage shaped as a grimoire, and his face hidden by a heavy mask with narrow eye slits.

He walked unhurriedly across the soft grass as it wilted and shriveled beneath his boots, turning into smooth sand. The Mask seemed to drain the life strength from everything around him. He literally oozed black magic.

"It's…the professor…for sure," Travis said as his eyes closed.

"Trav!" Mara screamed. "Trav, wake up!"

But the redhead was silent.

Wailing, Mara turned toward the dark figure.

"Professor, we trusted you! Even after you sold us out in the second tour, we still trusted you. How *could* you? How could you do this?"

The Mask (Alexander Dumsky in disguise, something the B-52 group had suspected all along—they'd actually asked him to be their coach so they could expose him as a terrorist) took another step forward.

Mara peered through the slits, but she couldn't see the arrogant, green eyes on the other side.

How could she have been so wrong?

Even when *everyone* was saying what he'd pulled in the financial district was just a distraction, Mara had still trusted him. Because…because…

A yellow circle flashed in front of the Mask. Clutching Travis against her chest, Mara squeezed her eyes shut.

Her heart took a beat. Then another. And yet another.

But nothing happened.

Mara finally opened her eyes to see…not really a bird, but something similarly winged and flying.

A sports car, two giant raven wings flapping in place of its doors, crashed into the belly of the Mask, who'd just turned toward it. That was all he had time to do. No magic burst from his seal, which was already dissolving.

Falling out of the car, to Mara's and Jing's total astonishment, came Professor Alexander Dumsky.

He was bruised all over, an eyebrow gashed, a shoulder dislocated, and his clothes torn. Collapsing onto the sand with a dirty swear, he hit it with his shoulder to crunch it back into place.

"…bitch!" the black wizard finished his foul expression. Standing up, he trudged past the Mask toward his students.

"Professor! You—"

"Thank me later, padawans," the professor interrupted Mara. Stopping, he pulled her hand away from Travis's neck to empty a small vial right into the wound.

Nothing happened for a moment. Then all the blood lost by Travis' body swirled up into the air and whooshed into the wound, which instantly closed. All that was left was a thin scar.

Chavert, gasping as if he'd just been rescued from drowning, sat up to gawk at the professor with round eyes.

"You…"

"Aqua Viva," Mara whispered with admiration, interrupting her confused friend. "But how did you…?"

"I always keep some for myself," the professor interrupted in turn before swearing again. "I must've been a lousy coach for the five of you if you can't bring down one little leech."

The professor straightened up, glancing over at the still-living Mask and then back at the students.

"Leech?" Mara asked in bewilderment.

"I'm going to teleport you outside the Arena," he said in a composed, even distant voice. "Once you get there, look around for a tall, red-haired guy, very angry, and tell him to shoot their super-duper-gun here if I'm not done in ten minutes."

"*What?*"

"But I hope I can pull it off. And give you imbeciles a hellish practice session so you stop looking like a flock of whiny puppies. It's going to last all six years you study at First Magic."

"A pack," Jing corrected. "It's a pack of puppies."

"I don't give a fuck, Jet Li." The professor flashed his middle finger tattooed with Doom. "Well, whatever. Let's go."

He spread his arms. Between them, an imposing black seal flashed as black ravens darted out of it.

"But, Professor! The Mask is—"

"Just a distraction," the professor replied. Flying in circles around him were hundreds of graveyard birds. "Now he—"

But before he could finish, the earth shuddered again, that time not because the arena stands were collapsing. It was the boiling force of the giant magic seal all the open ground beneath their feet was gradually turning into.

The lines and borders of the monster were rivers of blood. The living crimson flowed from beneath the rubble, threading away from the dead bodies to fall into the bottomless magic chasm, adding more and more color.

The professor made a brief gesture. A hundred ravens surrounded his students, digging their claws and beaks painfully into their bodies and lifting them into the air.

"What about *you*, Professor?" Mara shouted at his rapidly receding figure.

"Just another day at the office," he called back, his reply reaching the girl's ears a moment before an impenetrable magic dome slammed shut right in front of her nose, walling off the whole Arena. The professor, the Mask, and the giant bloody seal were all that was left inside.

Chapter 73

Alex, oblivious of the fact that he was walking through the revived blood flowing into the chasm formed by the magic lines of the giant seal, came over to the Mask, who'd been hammered into the sand. Stooping over the still breathing (if one can say that about a leech) body, he lifted the mask.

Thick black hair scattered over the white sand. Blue eyes flared brighter than the stadium lights. Only the face looked gray, burned, and dead, like a creased paper bag.

Alex ran his palm over the seal painted on the forehead, dissolving it like watery ink and restoring light to the eyes. It wasn't for long, however. The mind trapped in the undead body was about to be lost forever.

"You grew up so handsome, Sasha." A cold, shivering, dead hand touched Alex's cheek.

But, Loki knew, Doom hadn't felt so *warm* in a long time.

"You didn't change at all, Anastasia," he whispered.

She tried to smile at him, but her dead skin and muscle wouldn't comply.

Although Alex was looking down at a creepy leech, a creation of Supreme Necromancy, it was still…it was still Anastasia. The girl who had made him tea. Who had taught him how to play the piano. Who had always been there for him.

He loved her. Not as a son loves a mother. As a man loves a woman. He'd never told her that.

She was Robin's girlfriend and twice as old as him. She would never have seen him as anything but a little boy.

But still, he loved her.

"Liar." Anastasia's voice turned more and more machine-like as the magic of death left her body. "Did you learn…the third act?"

"Yes, Anastasia," Doom replied with a nod. "I did."

"Good. Very good." She closed her eyes. When they opened again, they were totally black.

Her dead throat produced a scream that resembling a banshee howl. A clawed zombie hand reached for Alex's neck, but before it could rip his Adam's apple out, his palm, enveloped in lilac fire, touched the burned undead face. The whole body flashed with black-magic fire and crumbled to ash.

"I'm going to keep my word, Anastasia."

All that remained beneath the smashed car was the old, torn cloak, the steel gauntlets, the mask, and...

The grimoire had vanished.

It was that very storage that Anastasia, resurrected as a leech, had filled with the energy of death. O'Hara, with her guess about *reaping*, had been very close. She'd just jumped to conclusions.

A few thousand deaths weren't enough for real *black* magic. That took *tens* of thousands. Alex knew that. But he'd been asked a different question, and there's no reason to say things you don't have to.

Clap. Then again: *clap, clap.* And once more: *clap, clap, clap.*

Alex straightened up to see who was hiding in the folds of light.

"Bravo, Alexander."

Stepping out of the light was Julio Lupen, rector of First Magic University. A light wizard at level 62nd with an incredible mana reserve of 6,298 points.

The architect of the terror that had held sway over Myers City for the previous few years.

"Oh, don't be so surprised," Julio said with a dismissive wave. He was wearing his usual sweat suit, the usual chain around his neck. "You're not the only one who learned the art of lying by speaking the truth from Goddess Danu's people."

His vow.

He hadn't *wanted* things to be what they were. He'd *made* them that way.

"Raewsky, that old man... He never wanted to look just a bit father ahead. I *told* him. Tried to persuade the stubborn Russian to help me. But he only wanted a better life for black wizards—the devil could take the rest. And that's after what the two of us saw during the Magic War. After we recaptured his home city from the Icy Giants! After we buried my dau—" Julio shook his golden mane. "That evening, Alexander, I came to him with my final offer. But he turned it down. What else could I do? Sit and wait for humanity to become so fat and weak they'd be devoured by the monsters? Or..."

Lupen stopped short again. In his hands was a crimson-glowing grimoire festooned with stripes the color of the rainbow.

Demon magic.

Julio looked up at the sky on the other side of the impenetrable dome.

"Poseidon's Shield," he said. "That's the *real* name of the artifact. And it wasn't there to hide Atlantis from the rest of the world. No, it was made to help humans defend against the ones we now call our *elder brothers*. The fae, elves, orcs, trolls, ogres, dwarves, and other ungodly creatures."

Alex winced slightly. Lupen *believed*.

"Raewsky, it won't be long before they turn against us. Before the United Races Organization becomes just a mocking echo of the past, a past where humans were so stupid as to wrap their arms around those freaks of nature."

Alex didn't know if the Guards' weapon could penetrate the defense created by the artifact. He didn't even know if it was true that the Guards had launched a magic weapon of mass destruction into space. One theory held that magic was just a particular kind of magnetic field produced by Earth—the farther from the planet, the more of it dispersed and was lost, with not a single drop reaching as far as the Moon.

"It's time for everyone to wake up," Julio went on. "It's time to open humanity's eyes! The monsters are no longer at the gate. They live *among* us. Dress like us. Talk like us. And we do nothing! We let them live in god's world!"

Another mention of the name lashed Alex's chest like a fiery whip.

"Do you have any idea how much sales of battle grimoires have gone up over the past year? More people are studying battle magic. More volunteers are showing up to join the magic military than they can accept. The Monster Hunter Guild is growing every day. And it's all thanks to *me*."

Alex said nothing.

The sand beneath his feet was white as snow. Doom had always loved snow. It made even the blackest things pure.

"But that's not enough!" Lupen said, his voice raising. "Not enough! Today I'm going to show the world how weak man has become. When the ashes settle and millions of people are done mourning their nearest and dearest, their rage will awaken. From it, like from the finest metal, they'll forge their weapons of war. The war that's coming, Raewsky!"

Alex wasn't sure if Julio was talking to him or his late friend. Not that he really cared.

"Sooner or later, it's coming! The world can't belong to us *and* them. There can only be one. And I don't want it to be the ungodly monsters! Earth was created for man. It's our home! And it's time to wash it clean of the filth that infests it."

The weather forecasters had promised rain. Alex couldn't tell if it was coming through the shield.

"I want you to see it! It's our game of chess, and now it's time to make a sacrifice. A big one, yes. A bloody one. But I've thought it through. When I let the duke demon into the world, I'll be in complete control." Lupen pointed at the grimoire he had in hands. "Six years. Six long years I've been preparing for this day. And you're not going to—"

Lupen stopped short. It was like he'd stumbled in the middle of his speech, stopping to stare at Alex. With very different eyes.

"Don't you get tired of talking?" Doom asked, keeping his hands in his jeans pockets. "Loki and the serpent. Do you supervillains all use the same guide? Or have you just seen too many Marvel movies? Actually, no. Judging by how gloomy your whole shtick is, it was probably DC."

"You—"

"I," Alex interrupted, "couldn't give a shit about anything you just said. I don't care if everyone in this world goes crazy and kills each other. All I care about is getting *you*."

"Six years ago," Lupen whispered, "I sent Anastasia to the port. But the Guards' base turned out to be right there. Supreme leeches retain some shards of memory, so she escaped through—"

"Through High Garden," Alex interrupted again. "Right where I was drinking my tea on a bright summer day."

"In a week, there was news that a black wizard had gotten away from the cops."

"You don't serve the main course right away," Doom said with a nod. "The appetizers come first."

"That was when you first got spotted—"

"By everyone. But first and foremost by the Syndicate."

"It was their attention you needed. It was—"

"Theirs, too. Who needs just another nobody from the Abyss Society? Even a skilled and seasoned nobody. No. I needed a special sort of reputation. As an exile, I was my own man. No past connections. *Usable.* Just take away my source of income, and you're left with an obedient puppet. But that's still not enough. You need an incentive. And what kind of incentive do you offer a criminal? Another criminal, the one a step higher. How could an organization like the Guards be unaware of the Syndicate? Or the other way around?

"So, with just a simple bar brawl, so well-staged it set my teeth on edge, you get me and throw me into prison. Like your Plan B in case Plan A doesn't work. Or just an ace up your sleeve for the long game. And the game *gets* long. The Guards realize they're not going to get the Mask themselves. They need someone who doesn't just have human magic, but also has… Wait a second, is the ace actually a joker? Examining him reveals a demonic source. What a stroke of luck! Let's get him out now and control him using this…"

Alex pointed at the unclasped runic bracelet hanging from his index finger. The one O'Hara had slapped on him two months before.

That brawl was well-staged mostly due to how well Alex had acted. He'd played his part much better than the two racists attacking the young witch in the bar. The witch was apparently a decoy, and both gangsters had fought like they'd learned hand-to-hand combat at police school.

"...this and my debt to the Syndicate. Enough to keep your main ace where it needs to be."

Lupen blinked a few times and laughed.

Alex's belief in the existence of the supervillain guide grew stronger. He'd just delivered his own speech for no apparent reason. Was it his vanity? Just like any black wizard, he had plenty of it.

Or maybe he just wanted someone to know he was actually the hunter, and not the prey.

Hey, Alex, Robin had laughed. *If you want to fit in, be like me. A careless daredevil. No one will think you're anything else.*

Robin *(may the serpent meet him)* had been right on the damn money.

"I *told* Chon Sook his dossier didn't match up with the wonder kid I met at Follen," Lupen replied, still lauging.

"I was raised on the best movies, man." Alex flashed his middle finger again. "Stanislavski's stuff was my bedtime stories."

When the light wizard stopped laughing, the Arena lapsed into complete silence.

"Over all the years I spent trying to figure out who was behind the Mask, I came across lots of other threads." Sighing, Alex clenched a fist. "*Lots*. At first, I thought all of them led to you...though I didn't yet know who you were. Well, whatever. Now it's your turn, Julio Lupen. Tell me *everything* you know about Follen, Rizen, and their founders."

The rector smiled. The magic seals around him glared with dazzling light, seals filled with the power of a level 62 Master.

"You may be a wonder kid, boy, but you're still just an ant—"

"Don't patronize me!" Alex screamed in terror. He'd gotten so used to imitating Robin that breaking character was practically impossible. "Don't make me recite that Chinese saying about the ants and the elephants. Do you remember asking me how I survived what happened at Follen? I didn't lie to you, but I didn't tell you the whole truth. *I* wasn't the one who killed that demon. It was Professor Raewsky."

He rolled the ring around his finger, making all that was white black, turning light into darkness. And the center of that ever-lasting night was Alex Doom.

Chapter 74

"I'm helping you already, my child. Can't you feel it?"

Alex felt a red spark flash inside him to the tune of Baltael's inhuman laughter coming from far away.

The little boy was down in the pool of his own blood amid the creepy pentagram. His friends were all dying around him. He could feel the magic of death increase in each of them as their lives were sacrificed to the great pentagram.

But everything was going to be all right.

The one who called himself Baltael would help them.

Yes, the price was dear.

He had to pay *his soul.*

Alex *knew* that. He knew it just as well as he knew how to breathe or walk, the knowledge poured into him with the demon's power and...

In this life, there's only one thing you truly own. He suddenly saw Miss Elisa in front of him. *It's the only thing in the world that is completely in your hands, entirely up to you.*

What's that?

Your decisions, you little devil. They're the only thing that always comes from you.

Miss Elisa. She'd been wrong.

If God created you like that, he did it for a reason.

Yes. Created to reject later and...

Through his pain and tears, Alex suddenly made out the figure of Professor Raewsky. If he hadn't been a black wizard, he wouldn't have recognized the se—

No! the boy yelled in his head.

The demon Baltael was shoved backward.

"What?"

"You can't," the boy said, panting. "That's my will. My soul. I didn't give you permission. And I'm not giving it to anyone. Go away, puny creature of the Fallen One. Go, Baltael. I'm not giving my soul away. It's *mine.* And only I decide what to do with it."

The care and friendliness instantly disappeared from the demon's voice.

"You miserable bag of bones and flesh." A scary figure formed in the shadows, complete with claws, horns, and fangs. It was absolutely different from the normal, well-dressed man Alex had just seen there. "I'll rip your heart out."

A clawed paw reached out of the shadows toward the boy, but…

The demon screamed in pain as its claws crashed into the golden veil blocking its way.

"A bag of bones and flesh I may be, but I'm not as puny a creature as you. You can't break the law. You can't do anything to me until I give up my will to you. I'm free. And you're just a slave to your substance."

"You vile offspring of Adam and Eve!" the demon roared. "I was crushing empires long before you were bo—"

"Begone!" the boy shouted again. "I'm telling you, demon! Go back to where you came from! Because I'm the blood of Solomon's blood. By the keys of the Gate leading to the Beyond, I bind you!"

Clanging chains wrapped themselves around the demon.

"By the seals of Solomon, I lock you in!"

Shadows condensed around the demon, pulling it deeper and deeper into the dark.

"I cast you out, demon, not in his name, but by *my* will!"

The demon bellowed. The words of the black exorcism were dispatching him back to hell. Alex hadn't known if it would work; he just *believed*. However weird that may sound.

"Baltael is my name!" the demon growled. Its burned paw edged through the golden veil, just a tiny bit, but enough for the five claws to reach Alex's chest. The boy screamed in pain as the five scars in the shape of overturned stars printed on his body.

"Baltael is the name of your evil destiny! When the time comes, I'll be right there by your side."

The demon vanished. But Alex knew he now bore Baltael's marks forever. The particles of the demon's power were in him, an indelible trace marking him as prey easily found at any time.

But there was something more urgent to deal with.

Fighting through the pain, Doom reached for his own blood. He took a scoop and threw it at the professor, who had almost brought his dagger down.

The blood spread over Raewsky's face and covered the seal on his forehead, one someone else was using to control his mind. They were only screened off for a moment, perhaps too brief for any other wizard to shed the strings yanking him around like a puppet.

But not for Professor Raewsky.

"What's go—" He dropped the dagger and stumbled.

"Too late," Alex sighed.

The seal beneath him and the altars around him flashed with power.

Shaking his head, Raewsky suddenly moved his hand over Alex, wrapping him in a black cocoon.

"We'll figure this out, boy," he whispered as he turned the ring around his finger.

When a creepy demon's head came up from the seal, all the white around them turned to black. Light became darkness. Professor Raewsky, having become the heart of the ever-lasting night, began his fight with the Supreme Demon.

***

Alex regained his senses among the ruins. Something was burning. Crackling. Smoking. He was in pain.

"Anastasia?" he cried. "Robin?"

Nobody replied.

He crawled forward through the soot and smoke until he bumped into a supine body. Anastasia's body.

She was clenching an arm stretching from beneath the rubble. Robin's arm.

"No," the boy whispered. "No, no, no, please. Not again... not again..."

He shook the girl by the shoulder, but her eyes wouldn't open. Her cold flesh burned his hands.

"*No!*" Hot tears fell onto her pale skin, but their warmth couldn't bring back what had been lost. "Please..."

"Alex."

The boy looked back. There was Professor Raewsky, reclining on the stones, covered in wounds. He handed his black ring to Alex. "Take..."

"Professor?"

"...and run." Raewsky's arm went limp. His chest forced out one last breath. The ring rolled, jingling across the debris to come to a stop right at the boy's feet.

Alex picked it up and combed Anastasia's hair with a shivering hand.

"I'll find out what happened," he whispered, swallowing hot tears. "I promise you. And when I do, you'll hear *their* death screams wherever you are."

Before getting to his feet, he picked up a crumpled pack of cigarettes.

Robin had been a heavy smoker.

Limping, the little boy made his way out of the burning ruins of the mansion that had been his home.

***

Shadows crept up behind Alex, embracing him tighter until they became a cloak that wrapped itself around him. The darkness in his hands condensed, taking the shape of a long, misty staff. Death enveloped his face to form a ghostly helmet. His jacket dissolved, baring a chest that gradually sank into his ribcage, the life-draining veins of darkness gnawing at it.

The ring provided magic power.

In exchange for life energy.

His cloak of darkness was clasped by a thumping black heart.

[Item: Leech King's Heart artifact
Item rank: S
Mana reserve: 5732/6800
Physical resistance: 0%

Magic resistance (general): 0%
Magic resistance (particular): 0%
Extra powers: Life exchange
Maximal usage time on healthy body: 99 seconds
Remaining number of activations: 0/6]

It wasn't a battle storage. No, just a conventional artifact. (As conventional as a Leech King's heart confined inside a ring could be.)

That was Alex's last bullet, the one he'd held onto all those years.

He struck his staff, and a wall of darkness erected itself behind him.

Chapter 75

"**A** Master-level artifact?" Lupen squinted. "Interesting. If I remember correctly, Raewsky found it in some icy desert. But if you think an artifact will make you strong enough to challenge me, you're an *imbecile*, not a wonder kid."

The light wizard touched the chain hanging around his neck. White, unnaturally pure light flashed, cloaking him just like darkness cloaked Alex.

The youthful, vigorous rector aged rapidly, his golden hair growing gray, then turning white. His sweat suit fluttered before transforming into a white cloak over blue robes. In his hand appeared a red-glowing staff crowned by a golden whirlwind of pure, virgin light.

In the middle of the ravaged Arena beneath Poseidon's Shield, over the blazing seal opening right into hell, and facing the darkness-cloaked black wizard trying to stop the rite stood the light wizard dressed in white who had started it all, staff in his right hand and grimoire in his left.

"Raewsky was a blind fool. That's why he died." Even Lupen's voice was elderly. Rasping. Croaking. "You grew up to be just like him, Alexander Dumsk—"

"My name's Alex Doom." The very darkness seemed to interrupt him in a soft, rustling voice that crept into the soul. "Black magic professor by day, and by night…the damn terror that flaps. Dzhan'Kaz'Moharkai!"

Doom lifted his staff and slammed it into the ground.

The wall of darkness behind him started to come apart. Like a smashed glassy surface, it rained myriads of shards down onto the sand glowing with the power of the bloody seal. Each of the quivering shards expanded, drawing into the shadows cast by the fires burning in the ruins. Growing larger and larger until from their depth came skeletons glaring with blue fire. They were wearing armor crushed by swords and axes, with helmets marked by giant claws. An entire army stood behind Alex.

[ATTEN…]

"Damn," Doom swore, sliding a palm across his eyes to remove his lenses. He wasn't going to be needing them in that battle.

He was going to deal with the bastard the old-fashioned way.

The way they did it at Follen School.

The undead host yelled and pointed their weapons at Lupen. Flows of death magic from their blades joined to form a single pale dead curtain.

"*Eluria Caxc Comentes!*" Lupen moved his staff in front of him.

The ball of light on top shone brightly, fine threads filtering off it like trickles from a cracked tank of water. They grew and stretched, turning into a haze of yellow light.

Out of that haze stepped a fifteen-foot woman, her hair a glistening white cloud. Her body was a frozen golden flame patterned with light so pure it would have shamed a saint.

She lifted her hands, hurling forward a column of fire as tall as a five-story house and as broad as a city block. It engulfed the death magic flow and with it even Alex and his skeleton army.

The flames raged like a tempest coming to reap its harvest of terror. The heat was so intense it melted the cement and concrete remaining from the arena and instantly reduced the bodies of the dead spectators to ash. The sand turned to glass.

That was the power of Light Magic. The magic that absorbed the power of all the elements...

...except for one.

Caw! Raven wings flapped deafeningly.

A graveyard bird of prey soared over the roaring stream of fire, devouring all in its path. The cloak of darkness behind Alex's back unfurled and lifted him up to the very edge of the impenetrable dome created by Poseidon's Shield.

He brandished his staff and said a few words. Doing magic at that level meant adding a verbal component to the seal—human minds weren't capable of controlling power like that without anchoring it to a particular set of words.

The staff in Alex's hands grew in size until it hurtled off as a spear as large as a lamp post. It harpooned the light maiden's chest.

She clutched the spear shaft with her fiery hands. Flames rushed from them to devour the Darkness, but with each passing moment, there was more smoke and less fire. Finally, a solid lava crust spread over the maiden's body. An explosion ripped through the air.

The explosion was so powerful it shook the dome. The broken fragments of the seemingly eternal Arena that hadn't yet been devoured by fire were crushed to dust by the shock wave. The blast sent Alex flying across to the opposite end of the battlefield. But even from there, he saw the swirling ball of darkness absorb the power of the brightest light.

Before he could hope the explosion affected Lupen (at least a bit), he saw a glowing white horse.

It was as if someone had reached into the sky and collected gleaming starlight like water in a jug, sculpting it into a silvery horse. But they didn't stop there.

Next, they pulled bolts of lightning from the sky. They were used to forge a sword held by a snow-born rider who drove away the darkness with a single strike of heavenly fire.

It was a sign that any darkness could be pierced through with a beam of new hope.

Rearing back on his starry horse, the rider galloped toward Alex.

Breathing heavily, Doom got down on one knee and placed his hand on the sand. He sensed death in it. Heard the screams of dying people. Their blood called to him. Their death and despair lured him with sweet power.

But Doom refused it.

He went deeper.

He touched what the dead were unwilling to give away. Their past. Their brightest hopes. Their fears. Everything that made them who they were.

He took that.

He ripped it out with fangs and claws. Using the power of the artifact, he reached into each of the thousands of souls and tore a piece from them. It was all too possible that in so doing he was creating a whole host of restless souls condemned to an eternity of torture.

That was real black magic.

One of its blackest spells.

"I heard the voice of the fourth living creature say, 'Come!'" Doom said, though his voice sounded strange. Otherworldly. His words were Death coming to a feast. He spoke a language so ancient no one living had ever heard it before. "I looked, and there before me was a pale horse. Its rider was named Death, and Hades was following close behind him. They were given power over a fourth of the earth to kill by sword, famine, and plague, and by the wild beasts of the earth."

A hellish neigh screamed over the Arena, resounding even outside the dome. Inside it, the Abyss opened before the white rider on his starry horse.

Waves of red glow filled half the space, pounding the walls of starlight and lightning bolts. From that red mist made up of the souls ripped apart by Doom and sacrificed to his spell came another rider.

His horse was pure rage. A rage that knows no foe or friend, only a lust for blood. In his bony hands, he held a scythe that reaped guilty and innocent alike. The robe covering his wet red bones seemed formed by blazing blood.

The two riders clashed in the middle of the arena, and another explosion hit the ancient god's shield. Alex felt the familiar touch of burning steel across his chest.

Flying some thirty feet away, he would have broken every bone in his body if it hadn't been for the dark shrouds forming his staff and cloak. Standing up, he watched with open glee as Lupen clutched at his bleeding side.

The light wizard was stronger, but Alex...Alex had Darkness. The power of destruction. The power of death. The magic that could only destroy. And it was matchless.

Thrusting his dark staff into the ground, Doom growled and dug both hands into the staff's dark matter.

"By the keys of the Gate," he said, starting to read off the ancient rite, "I open the Beyond!"

The tattoos on his arms flashed.

"What are you doing, you fool?!" Lupen yelled, but it was too late.

"By the seals of Solomon, I set you free! Hear my blood! Hear my call! The dog eating the moon! The death of gods!"

Alex ripped his hands off of the staff as it turned into a giant whirlwind of darkness. The space was cleaved by a creepy howl. Emanating from the Arena where the two Masters were fighting, waves of energy spread to push back the helicopters and scatter the barriers formed by the military, police, fire fighters, and ambulance teams.

From the darkness came a fanged maw resembling both a wolf's and a bird's. Every fang was as long as a spear, emitting bright green light. The light of rot and decay.

Now it was Lupen's turn to drive his staff into the ground, then remove his chain and place it on top. The silver cross flashed with bright fire.

The wolf bellowed in pain. Alex collapsed to his knees, red blisters spreading across his chest.

"Even when I walk in the valley of darkness, I will fear no evil," Lupen sang. Out of his cross came a long, plain sword that looked like it had been forged by a blacksmith's apprentice. "...for you are with me."

Following the sword, the hand holding it emerged from the silvery flames. Alex collapsed to the sand, feeling like he was burning from the inside.

"You set a table before me in the presence of my adversaries." Lupen held out his palms. The flows of light darting from them soaked into the cross.

The plain-looking sword sliced the giant wolf in two.

Doom's cheeks tore as he screamed. He choked on his own blood and pain. His dark cloak tried to shield him from the feathers of white fire raining down from the sky, the shards of the broken sword sending the death of gods back to the Beyond.

But Darkness failed.

The black heart clasp on Alex's chest slowed its beat. His long shadow cloak was reduced to scraps.

The purpose of black magic was destruction, and it was unsurpassed. But even the greatest wave can be shattered by a breakwater. And that breakwater was the magic of light.

Everything went quiet. Alex was crumpled on the sand, his emaciated body no longer covered by the cloak, no mask on his face. Only his bony hands still clutched the staff twisted from darkness.

Lupen towered over him in his robes, grimoire in hand.

"You will witness my ordeal for humanity," he said before turning to the seal. He dropped the grimoire, which soared over the arena. It opened, its leaves turned, and it spread flashing, chaotically glowing waves.

The demon summons circle was as large as several football fields. It was powered by thousands of deaths and Loki-knows-what else.

It was difficult to imagine exactly *who* the light wizard was going to let into the world.

"Not...so...fast," Alex said, coughing on his own blood.

Black wizards have no honor.

They have no qualms about stabbing people in the back.

There's even a kind of perverse pleasure they take from it.

Doom held out his staff. Before Lupen could look back, the air started to swirl over the staff tip made from pure darkness, pulling inside a tiny black dot.

The dot shot out a dark ray. Buzzing like a wasp hive, it pierced Lupen's light cloak and chest before hitting Poseidon's Shield. It crackled, enduring the blow, but a moment later the small black ray went out.

"You missed." Lupen lurched but kept his balance, holding onto his staff. "You should've aimed for my head."

Behind his back, a red arm forty stories tall burst from the seal, reaching the dome and scratching at it with black claws.

Alex gave a wry smirk.

"It's Tor who missed," he spat. "Not me."

Saying that, withered and emaciated to the bone, he gathered his last strength to dash toward the enemy, driving his shoulder into Lupen's chest. They both fell head over heels into the seal.

***

"Did he say exactly that?" the major asked Gribovsky, behind whom was a girl looking suspiciously like one of the Glomebood family's daughters.

"He did," the lieutenant nodded. "He planned it from the very start."

The major drummed his fingers on the table. Silence fell over the improvised command post. The window of the hotel room temporarily occupied by the Guards offered an excellent view of the Arena dome and what was going on around it. A magic duel was apparently being fought inside, the power being brought to bear so great that it resounded outside Poseidon's...whatever the damn artifact's real name was.

"Kyle!" Chon Sook turned to the smartass sitting at his cased laptop. "Enter my confirmation code."

"Sir!" the smartass replied, jumping up. "We can't take the shield out with a single shot, and we won't have time to reload. We need—"

Duncan's giant shadow fell over him.

"The major gave you an order," his towering figure thundered. "Do it."

Swearing, Kyle sank back behind his desk.

"We're all going to die just because of one amateur upstart."

But he typed in the confirmation code and pressed Enter. In a few moments, people in every corner of Atlantis could see the heavy black clouds pierced by a bright blue ray that hit the very center of Myers City.

***

Alex, locked around Lupen, fell into the seal. He knew that, even with the artifact he had, he didn't stand a chance of beating a level 62 Master.

But he didn't need to.

He just needed to weaken the dome a bit. He didn't have the strength to do it alone...

...so he borrowed some from the rector.

Over there, above their heads, the ray from the ultra-mega-super-duper gun was already piercing the clouds.

"Smart move," the rector whispered. "But this is just one small battle, wonder kid. And I'm only a pawn on the board. You can't stop *them*."

"Them?"

"I can't do necromancy, boy."

Then the whole world was enveloped in a shroud of pure magic. The two of them were hit by compressed magic energy—liquid mana. A more destructive weapon even than nukes.

Alex smiled.

There, in the light, he saw Miss Elisa watching him with the same warmth she always gave him.

His life was his alone.

And so was his death.

Real black wizards take no orders, be they from god or the devil.

His only regret was leaving no one to look after the cat shelter.

...and failing to keep his promise.

***

Dying isn't scary at all.

It really isn't.

Alex knew that for sure.

His necromancy lessons weren't all about carnal pleasures. She'd taught him many other things, and one of them was...

What?

Alex opened his eyes.

He gasped for air, feeling his body all over. It seemed absolutely normal, his limbs in place, no cuts on his skin. Just his old scars (left by demons, angels, and a dozen other encounters) burning terribly. The rest of his body was freezing cold.

Falling from the sky was black snow...or so it seemed to him at first.

In truth, it was the collapsing dome, for some reason changing color.

The first drops of rain splashed against his face.

The weather forecasters were right, surprisingly enough.

By some happy miracle, groping in the back pocket of what remained of his pants (they looked more like the Hulk's shorts), Alex found his pack of cigarettes.

He lit one.

Sirens howled; people ran toward him. He was even pretty sure he could make out the major's shouts and Gribovsky's swearing.

His partner sure was foul-mouthed.

The storm was leaving the city, leaving behind the smell and freshness of rain.

How did you survive? That would probably be the first question they'd ask him.

And, hell's bells, Alex wished he knew the answer. He'd have given quite a bit for it. But right then, he was happy that Lupen was down and dead by his side, and there was no demonic Bigfoot smashing its way through his beloved city.

You shouldn't try to destroy something a black wizard loves. You really shouldn't.

The wizards running out onto the arena waved their hands, dispelling the few ruins that were still standing. The military arrived in their armored vehicles. Sirens howled as fire trucks and ambulances rushed up.

Alex lay in the fake snow, smoking and watching the rain.

Except for the fact that he'd torn his pants, it had been just another day at the office.

Epilogue

Three months later

Sitting at the oval table in the office were several humans and non-humans. A tired Korean man spoke on the old-fashioned landline, his carved staff resting against the table.

"Colonel Chon Sook here," he said and instantly straightened up. Everyone at the table realized something was wrong. As far as they could remember, their department head had never showed that kind of respect for anyone. "Yes, sir. I see. Excuse me? The faerie embassy bombed? Just a moment ago? We don't... How do *you* know? Told by the queen? Excuse me? Didn't just tell...?"

The major...no, the *colonel* pulled the receiver away from his ear a bit, letting anyone who wanted to enjoy the shouting coming from it.

"Yes, sir. We're starting immediately. Yes, sure. Our very best."

The colonel replaced the receiver back with caution. After sitting in silence for a while, he retrieved a bottle of brandy and a glass. He glanced down at the bottle, then at the glass, then at the bottle again, before uncorking it and taking a pull without touching the glass. Wincing slightly, he called over.

"Captain Gribovsky."

"Yes, sir?" the redhead replied, standing to attention.

"That call was from the United Races. Some two minutes ago, the faerie embassy was bombed." As the colonel spoke, the sound of running feet, raised voices, and calls outside the door grew louder.

"Why do *we* have to deal with that?"

"Because, Captain, their surveillance cameras took a few very interesting shots. There were humans controlling demons."

Everyone in the office exchanged glances.

"So, the investigation is *yours*. And, please, none of your usual I-work-alone stuff."

"I wasn't going to say that, sir."

The silence grew even...quieter? Lone wolf Gribovsky was prepared to work with a partner? The world must have gone mad.

"Explain."

Straightening up, the redhead replied.

"Sir, I'm asking your permission to partner with our independent consultant, Black Magic Professor at First Magic University, full-fledged dark wizard, fifth-rank necromancer, fifth-rank blood magician, fourth-rank malefic wizard, third-rank sorcerer, and...well, just a nice guy. Alex Doom."

"His name is Alexander Dumsky," the colonel corrected with a heavy sigh.

"And unlike any of you lot," Gribovsky continued, looking around the room, "he's always dressed well enough for me to not to be ashamed when I'm seen with him in public."
***

"Thank you, O'Hara." Sitting in his office alone with his assistant and right-hand woman, the colonel gratefully accepted a cup of coffee from her.

"Are you afraid they won't be able to solve the case?"

"Alex and Gribovsky?" The colonel smiled and looked out the window. "Oh, I don't doubt they *will* solve it."

O'Hara looked at the maj...the colonel before finally daring to ask the question she'd had on her mind for the previous three months.

"Colonel, sir, you *knew* it then, five years ago, that Dumsky fell into our trap on purpose, didn't you? You knew he was after the Mask and everyone behind him...behind her. You knew he wanted to use us...and you used him? A perverted kind of mutually beneficial collaboration."

The colonel took a gulp of coffee, peering silently out the magic window.

Realizing she wasn't going to get an answer to her question (which actually was a kind of answer), O'Hara asked another.

"What are you worried about then?"

"A new bill from the city to cover their damages. Alexander might've already forgotten how much he still owes."

O'Hara couldn't help but chuckle. *Outsmart the major? The black wizard lost the second that idea came into his head.*

The second he showed up, offering himself as an independent consultant and even negotiating some terms. But the truth was the Guards had him by the balls.

He still owed the city about a million credits.

"If you find it that funny, Lieutenant Colonel Thaney O'Hara, then your job is to keep an eye on those two and report back to me."

The fae pulled herself to attention.

"Sir. Yes, sir."
***

Alex woke up reluctantly to the sound of the smartphone vibrating on the table. *Loki got me to buy that hellish thing.*

Carefully lifting the woman's arm off his neck, he picked it up and went over to the opposite side of the room. A whole three steps.

Alex was still living in his tiny apartment over the Schooner. Diglan let him stay without paying rent. Perhaps it was the fact that Doom had saved his son's life; maybe it was that his piano playing in the evenings attracted more visitors.

Whatever the case, Alex liked how close the apartment was to the university, not to mention the free drinks he could get whenever he wanted at the Schooner. Sometimes he was lucky enough to bounce a drunken cop out.

That was actually his favorite part.

"Yes?"

"Doom, pumpkin?"

"Fuck off, Gribovsky."

Alex was about to hang up when he heard the voice continue.

"Hey, wait. It's a consulting job."

Alex sighed and massaged his temples.

"What? What job? Hey, I have a terrible hangover. Break ends tomorrow, which means I'll be back to lecturing the—"

"Meet me in the fae quarter. Now."

"Why?"

"The usual: kick some ass, save the world, find out who bombed their embassy."

"And the pay?"

"The maj—...colonel promised double."

"The fae, you said?"

"Yeah. The fae."

"I hate those bloody fairies."

Alex hung up. Casting a lustful glance at the beauty asleep in his bed, he left her a note and dressed quickly, putting on old, threadbare pants, a washed-out shirt, and a vest. A shabby leather trench coat rounded out the ensemble.

Running down the stairs, he ruffled the yawning Cherry's hair and smiled at Diglan in parting. The latter was standing over his laptop calculating cash flows.

The city was just waking up, the sky in the east colored by a red dawn.

Retrieving the crumpled pack of cigarettes from the pocket of his Dolce pants, Alex smoked and mounted his brand-new steel horse. His professor's salary was pretty high, but...the entire sum went toward repaying his debt to the city.

So, how did he come to have a Dolce suit and a gasoline chopper?

That's a really fascinating story.

"Here we go," the DJ's familiar voice said over his headphones. "These Streets by my favorite City Wolf."

With a growl, the bike dashed off down the road.

To be continued...

Printed in Great Britain
by Amazon

73374763R10220